EVERYONE WORTH KNOWING

Lauren Weisberger is the author of *The Devil Wears Prada*, which spent more than a year on the *New York Times* hardcover and paperback bestseller lists. The film version starring Meryl Streep and Anne Hathaway won a Golden Globe Award and grossed over $300 million worldwide. Her third novel, *Chasing Harry Winston,* is out now in paperback. She lives in New York City with her husband.

Visit www.AuthorTracker.co.uk for exclusive information on Lauren Weisberger.

D1085875

everyone
worth
knowing

lauren weisberger

HARPER

HarperCollins*Publishers*
77–85 Fulham Palace Road,
Hammersmith, London W6 8JB

www.harpercollins.co.uk

First published in Great Britain by
HarperCollins*Publishers* 2005

Lyrics to 'Baby You're A Rich Man' by John Lennon & Paul
McCartney reproduced with kind permission by SonyATV Music
Publishing / Northern Songs.

A catalogue record for this book
is available from the British Library

ISBN 978-0-00-783182-1

Set in Sabon

Printed and bound in Great Britain by
Clays Ltd, St Ives plc

To my grandparents:
This should help them remember which grandchild I am.

1

How does it feel to be one of the beautiful people?
– From 'Baby, You're a Rich Man' (1967)
by John Lennon and Paul McCartney

Though I'd caught only the briefest glimpse from the corner of my eye, I knew immediately that the brown creature darting across my warped hardwood floors was a water bug – the largest, meatiest insect I'd ever seen. The superbug had narrowly avoided skimming across my *bare feet* before it disappeared under the bookcase. Trembling, I forced myself to practice the chakra breathing I'd learned during an involuntary week at an ashram with my parents. My heart rate slowed slightly after a few concentrated breaths of *re* on the inhale and *lax* on the exhale, and within a few minutes I was functional enough to take some necessary precautions. First I rescued Millington (who was also cowering in terror) from her hiding place under the couch. Then, in quick succession, I zipped on a pair of knee-high leather boots to cover my exposed legs, opened the door to the hallway to encourage the bug's departure, and began spraying the extra-strong black-market vermin poison on every available surface in my minuscule one-bedroom. I gripped the trigger as though it were an assault weapon and was still spraying when the phone rang nearly ten minutes later.

The caller ID flashed with Penelope's number. I almost screened her before I realized that she was one of only two potential refuges. Should the water bug manage to live through the fumigation and cruise through my living room again, I'd need to crash with her or Uncle Will. Unsure where Will was tonight, I decided it'd be wise to keep the lines of communication intact. I answered.

'Pen, I'm under attack by the largest roach in Manhattan. What do I do?' I asked the second I picked up the phone.

'Bette, I have NEWS!' she boomed back, clearly indifferent to my panic.

'News more important than my infestation?'

'Avery just proposed!' Penelope shrieked. 'We're engaged!'

Goddammit. Those two simple words – *we're engaged* – could make one person so happy and another so miserable. Autopilot quickly kicked in, reminding me that it would be inappropriate

– to say the least – if I were to verbalize what I really thought. *He's a loser, P. He's a spoiled, stoner little kid in the body of a big boy. He knows you're out of his league and is putting a ring on your finger before you realize it as well. Worse, by marrying him you will be merely biding your time until he replaces you with a younger, hotter version of yourself ten years down the line, leaving you to pick up the pieces. Don't do it! Don't do it! Don't do it!*

'Ohmigod!' I shrieked right back. 'Congratulations! I'm so happy for you!'

'Oh, Bette, I knew you would be. I can barely even speak, it's just all happening so fast!'

So fast? He's the only guy you've dated since you were nineteen. It's not like this wasn't expected – it's been eight years. I just hope he doesn't catch herpes at his bachelor party in Vegas.

'Tell me everything. When? How? Ring?' I rattled off questions, playing the best friend role fairly believably, I thought, all things considered.

'Well, I can't talk too long because we're at the St Regis right now. Remember how he insisted on picking me up for work today?' Before waiting for my answer, she raced breathlessly ahead. 'He had a car waiting outside and told me it was just because he couldn't get a cab, and said that we were expected for dinner at his parents' house in ten minutes. Of course, I was a little annoyed that he hadn't even asked if I wanted to go to dinner there – he'd said he'd made reservations at Per Se, and you know how tough it is to get in there – and we were having pre-drinks in the library when in walked both our parents. Before I knew what was happening, he was down on one knee!'

'In front of all your parents? He did the public proposal?' I knew I sounded horrified, but I couldn't help it.

'Bette, it was hardly public. It was our *parents,* and he said the sweetest things in the world. I mean, we never would've met if it weren't for them, so I can see his point. And get this – he gave me two rings!'

'Two rings?'

'Two rings. A seven-carat flawless round in platinum that was his great-great-grandmother's for the real ring, and then a very pretty three-carat ascher-cut with baguettes that's much more wearable.'

'Wearable?'

'It's not as though you can roam the streets of New York in a seven-carat rock, you know. I thought it was really smart.'

'Two rings?'

'Bette, you're incoherent. We went from there to Per Se, where my father even managed to turn off his cell phone for the duration of dinner and make a reasonably nice toast, and then we went for a carriage ride in Central Park, and now we're at a suite in the St Regis. I just had to call and tell you!'

Where, oh where, had my friend gone? Penelope, who'd never even shopped for engagement rings because she thought they all looked the same, who had told me three months earlier when a mutual college friend had gotten engaged in the back of a horse-drawn carriage that it was the tackiest thing on earth, had just morphed into a very close approximation of a Stepford Wife. Was I just bitter? Of course I was bitter. The closest I'd come to getting engaged was reading the wedding announcements in *The New York Times*, aka the Single Girls' Sports Page, every Sunday at brunch. But that was beside the point.

'I'm so glad you did! And I can't wait to hear every last detail, but you've got an engagement to consummate. Get off the phone with me and go make your fiancé happy. How weird does that sound? "Fiancé."'

'Oh, Avery's on a call from work. I keep telling him to hang up' – she announced this loudly for his benefit – 'but he just keeps talking and talking. How has your night been?'

'Ah, another stellar Friday. Let's see. Millington and I took a walk over to the river, and some homeless guy gave her a biscuit along the way, so she was really happy, and then I came home, and hopefully killed what must be the largest insect in the tristate area. I ordered Vietnamese, but I threw it out when I remembered reading that some Vietnamese place near me was shut down for cooking dog, and so now I'm about to dine on reheated rice and beans and a packet of stale Twizzlers. Oh, Christ, I sound like a Lean Cuisine commercial, don't I?'

She just laughed, clearly having no words of comfort at that particular moment. The other line clicked, indicating that she had another call.

'Oh, it's Michael. I have to tell him. Do you care if I three-way him in?' she asked.

'Sure. I'd love to hear you tell him.' Michael would undoubtedly commiserate with me over the entire situation once Penelope hung up since he hated Avery even more than I did.

There was a click, which was followed by a brief silence and then another click. 'Everyone there?' Penelope squealed. This was not a girl who normally squealed. 'Michael? Bette? You guys both on?'

Michael was a colleague of mine and Penelope's at UBS, but since he'd made VP (one of the youngest ever) we'd seen much less of him. Though Michael had a serious girlfriend, it took

Penelope's engagement to really drive the point home: we were growing up.

'Hi, girls,' Michael said, sounding exhausted.

'Michael, guess what? I'm engaged!'

There was the tiniest beat of hesitation. I knew that, like me, Michael wasn't surprised, but he would be trying hard to formulate a believably enthusiastic response.

'Pen, that's fantastic news!' he all but shouted into the phone. His volume did much to compensate for the lack of any genuine joy in his voice, and I made a mental note to remember that for next time.

'I know!' she sang back. 'I knew you and Bette would be so happy for me. It just happened a few hours ago, and I'm so excited!'

'Well, we'll obviously have to celebrate,' he said loudly. 'Black Door, just the three of us, multiple shots of something strong and cheap.'

'Definitely,' I added, happy for something to say. 'A celebration is most definitely in order.'

'Okay, honey!' Penelope called into the distance, our drinking plans understandably of little interest. 'Guys, Avery's off the phone and is pulling on the cord. Avery, stop! I've got to run, but I'll call you both later. Bette, see you at work tomorrow. Love you both!'

There was a click and then Michael said, 'You still there?'

'Sure am. Do you want to call me or should I call you?' We'd all learned early on that you couldn't trust that the third line had disconnected and therefore always took the precaution of starting a new call before talking shit about the person who'd hung up first.

I heard a high-pitched voice in the background and he said, 'Dammit, I just got paged. I can't talk now. Can we talk tomorrow?'

'Sure. Say hi to Megu for me, okay? And Michael? Please don't go and get engaged anytime soon. I don't think I can handle you, too.'

He laughed. 'You don't have to worry about that, I promise. I'll talk to you tomorrow. And Bette? Chin up. He might be one of the worst guys either of us has ever met, but she seems happy, and that's all you can ask for, you know?'

We hung up and I stared at the phone for a few minutes before twisting my body out the window in a futile attempt to see a few inches of comforting river landscape; the apartment wasn't much, but it was, thankfully, all mine. I hadn't shared it in the nearly two years since Cameron had moved out, and even though it was so long and narrow that I could stretch my legs out and almost touch the opposite wall and even though it was located in Murray Hill and even though the floorboards were warping slightly and the water bugs had taken over, I had reign over my own private palace. The building was a cement monstrosity on Thirty-fourth and First, a multi-winged behemoth that housed such illustrious tenants as one teenage member of a dismantled boy band, one professional squash player, one B-list porn star and her stable of visitors, one average Joe, one former childhood actress who hadn't worked in two decades, and hundreds upon hundreds of recent college graduates who couldn't quite handle the idea of leaving the dorm or the fraternity house for good. It had sweeping East River views, as long as one's definition of 'sweeping views' includes a construction crane, a couple of Dumpsters, a brick wall from the building next door, and a patch of river approximately three inches wide that is only visible through unfathomable acts of contortion. All of this glory was mine for the equivalent monthly cost of a four-bedroom, two-and-a-half-bath single-family home upstate.

While still twisted on the couch, I reviewed my reaction to the news. I thought I'd sounded sincere enough, if not downright ecstatic, but Penelope knew ecstatic wasn't in my nature. I'd managed to ask about the rings – plural – and to state that I was very happy for her. Of course, I hadn't mustered up anything truly heartfelt or meaningful, but she was probably too giddy to notice. Overall: a solid B-plus performance.

My breathing had normalized enough to smoke another cigarette, which made me feel slightly better. The fact that the water bug hadn't resurfaced yet helped, too. I tried to assure myself that my unhappiness stemmed from my genuine concern that Penelope was marrying a truly terrible guy and not from some deep-rooted envy that she now had a fiancé when I didn't have so much as a second date. I couldn't. It had been two years since Cameron had moved out, and though I'd cycled through the requisite stages of recovery (job obsession, retail obsession, and food obsession) and had gone on the usual round of blind dates, drinks-only dates, and the rarer full-dinner dates, only two guys had made third-date status. And none had made fourth. I told myself repeatedly that there wasn't anything wrong with me – and regularly made Penelope confirm this – but I was seriously beginning to doubt the validity of that statement.

I lit a second cigarette off the first and ignored Millington's disapproving doggy stare. The self-loathing was beginning to settle upon my shoulders like a familiar, warm blanket. What kind of evil person couldn't express genuine, sincere happiness on one of the happiest days of her best friend's life? How conniving and insecure does one have to be to pray that the whole thing turns out to be a giant misunderstanding? How did I get to be so wretched'?

I picked up the phone and called Uncle Will, looking for some sort of validation. Will, aside from being one of the brightest and bitchiest people on the planet, was my perpetual cheerleader. He answered the phone with the slightest gin-and-tonic slur and I proceeded to give him the short, less-painful version of Penelope's ultimate betrayal.

'It sounds as though you feel guilty because Penelope is very excited and you're not as happy for her as you should be.'

'Yeah, that's right.'

'Well, darling, it could be far worse. At least it's not some variation on the theme where Penelope's misery is providing you with happiness and fulfillment, right?'

'Huh?'

'*Schadenfreude*. You're not emotionally or otherwise benefiting from her unhappiness, right?'

'She's not unhappy. She's euphoric. I'm the unhappy one.'

'Well, there you have it! See, you're not so terrible. And you, my dear, are not marrying that spoiled little brat whose only God-given talents appear to be spending his parents' money and inhaling large quantities of marijuana. Am I mistaken?'

'No, of course not. It just feels like everything's changing. Penelope's my life, and now she's getting married. I knew it would happen eventually, but I just didn't think eventually would be so soon.'

'Marriage is for the bourgeoisie. You know that, Bette.'

This triggered a series of mental images of Sunday brunches through the years: Will, Simon, the Essex, me, and the Sunday Styles section. We'd dissect the weddings for the duration of brunch, never failing to collapse into evil giggles as we creatively read between the lines.

Will continued. 'Why on earth are you eager to enter into a lifelong relationship, the only purpose of which is to strangle every iota of individuality out of you? I mean, look at me. Sixty-six years old, never married, and I'm perfectly happy.'

'You're gay, Will. And not only that, but you wear a gold band on the ring finger of your left hand.'

'So what's your point? You think I'd actually *marry* Simon, even if I could? Those same-sex, San Francisco city hall weddings aren't exactly my scene. Not on your life.'

'You've been living with him since before I was born. You do realize that you are, essentially, married.'

6

'Negative, darling. Either one of us is free to leave at any point, without any messy legal or emotional ramifications. And that's why it works. But enough of that; I'm not telling you anything you don't already know. Tell me about the ring.' I filled him in on the details he really cared about while munching the remaining Twizzlers, and didn't even realize I had fallen asleep on the couch until close to 3 A.M., when Millington woofed her desire to sleep in a real bed. I dragged us both to my room and buried my head under the pillow, reminding myself over and over that this was not a disaster. Not a disaster. Not a disaster.

2

Just my luck that Penelope's engagement party fell on a Thursday night – the night of my standing dinner date with Uncle Will and Simon. Neither appointment could be denied. I stood in front of my ugly, postwar, high-rise Murray Hill apartment building, desperately trying to escape to my uncle's huge duplex on Central Park West. It wasn't rush hour, Christmas, shift change, or torrentially pouring, but a cab was nowhere to be found. I had been whistling, screaming, and jumping skywards like a lunatic for twenty minutes to no avail, when a lone cab finally pulled up to the curb. The cabbie's response when I requested to go uptown was 'Too much traffic!' before he screeched off and disappeared. When a second driver actually picked me up, I ended up tipping him 50 percent out of relief and gratitude.

'Hey, Bettina, you look unhappy. Is everything okay?' I'd insisted that people call me Bette, and most did. Only my parents and George, Uncle Will's doorman (who was so old and cute he could get away with anything), still insisted on using my full name.

'Just the usual cab hassle, George.' I sighed, giving him a peck on the cheek. 'How's your day been?'

'Oh, just dandy as always,' he replied without a hint of sarcasm. 'Saw the sun for a few minutes this morning and have been happy ever since.' Nauseating.

'Bette!' I heard Simon call from the lobby's discreetly hidden mailroom. 'Is that you I hear, Bette?'

He emerged from the mailroom in tennis whites, a racket-shaped bag slung over his broad shoulders, and picked me up in a bear hug as no straight man ever had. It was sacrilege to skip a weekly dinner, which in addition to being a good time also provided by far the most male attention I received (not counting brunch).

Will and Simon had developed lots of rituals in the almost thirty years they'd spent together. They vacationed in only three places: St Barth's in late January (although lately Will had been complaining that it was 'too French'), Palm Springs in mid-March, and an occasional spontaneous weekend in Key West. They drank gin and tonics only out of Baccarat glasses, spent every Monday night from seven until eleven at Elaine's, and hosted an annual holiday party where each would wear a cashmere turtleneck. Will was almost six-three, with close-cropped silver hair, and he preferred sweaters with suede elbow patches; Simon was barely five-nine, with a wiry, athletic build that he swathed entirely in linen, irrespective of the season. 'Gay men,' he'd say, 'have carte blanche to flout fashion convention. We've earned the right.' Even now, moments off the tennis court, he'd managed to don some sort of white linen hoodie.

'Gorgeous girl, how are you? Come, come, Will is sure to be wondering where we both are, and I just know that the new girl has prepared something fantastic for us to eat.' Always the perfect gentleman, he took my exploding tote bag from my shoulder, held the elevator door open, and pressed PH.

'How was tennis?' I asked, wondering why this sixty-year-old man had a better body than every guy I knew.

'Oh, you know how it is, a bunch of old guys running around the court, tracking down balls they shouldn't even try for and pretending they've got strokes like Roddick. A little pathetic, but always amusing.'

The door to their apartment was slightly ajar and I could hear Will talking to the TV in the study, as usual. In the old days, Will had scooped Liza Minnelli's relapse and RFK's affairs and Patty Hearst's leap from socialite to cult member. It was the 'amorality' of the Dems that finally pushed him toward politics instead of all things glamorous. He called it the Clinton Clinch. Now, a few short decades later, Will was a news junkie with political affiliations that ran slightly to the right of Attila the Hun's. He was almost certainly the only gay right-wing entertainment-and-society columnist living on the Upper West Side of Manhattan who refused to comment on either entertainment or society. There were two televisions in his study, the larger of which he kept tuned to Fox News. 'Finally,' he was fond of saying, 'a network that speaks to *my* people.'

8

And always Simon's retort: 'Riiight. That huge audience of right-wing gay entertainment-and-society columnists living on the Upper West Side of Manhattan?'

The smaller set constantly rotated between CNN, CNN Headline News, C-SPAN, and MSNBC, perpetrators of what Will referred to as 'The Liberal Conspiracy.' A handwritten sign sat atop the second TV. It read: KNOW YOUR ENEMY.

On CNN, Aaron Brown was interviewing Frank Rich about the media coverage surrounding the last election. 'Aaron Brown is a lily-livered milquetoast pantywaist!' Will snarled as he put down his crystal tumbler and hurled one of his Belgian shoes at the TV.

'Hi, Will,' I said, helping myself to a handful of the chocolate-covered raisins he always kept in an Orrefors bowl on his desk.

'Of all the people qualified to discuss politics in this country, to offer some insight or an intelligent opinion on how media coverage did or did not affect these elections, and these idiots have to interview someone from *The New York Times?* The whole place is more bleeding than a rare steak, and I need to sit here and listen to their opinion on this?'

'Well, not really, Will. You could turn it off, you know.' I suppressed a smile as his eyes stayed riveted ahead. I silently debated with myself how long it would take for him to refer to *The New York Times* as *Izvestia,* or to bring up the Jayson Blair debacle as further proof that the paper's trash at best and a conspiracy against honest, hardworking Americans at worst.

'What, and miss Mr Aaron Brown's blatantly opinionated coverage of Mr Frank Rich's blatantly opinionated coverage of whatever the hell they're talking about? Seriously, Bette, let us not forget that this is the very same paper whose reporters simply create stories when deadline looms.' He took a swig and jabbed at the remote to silence both televisions simultaneously. Only fifteen seconds tonight – a record.

'Enough for now,' he said, hugging me and giving me a quick peck on the cheek. 'You look great, honey, as always, but would it kill you to wear a dress once in a while?'

He'd not so deftly moved to discussing his second-favorite topic, my life. Uncle Will was nine years older than my mom and both swore they'd been born to the very same set of parents, but it seemed impossible to comprehend. My mother was horrified I'd taken a corporate job that required me to wear something other than caftans and espadrilles, and my uncle thought the travesty was the suit as uniform instead of some killer Valentino gown or a fabulous pair of strappy Louboutins.

'Will, it's just what they do at investment banks, you know?'

'So I've gathered. I just didn't think you'd end up in banking.' That again.

'Your people, like, love capitalism, don't they?' I teased. 'The Republicans, I mean – not so much the gays.'

He raised his bushy gray eyebrows and peered at me from across the couch. 'Cute. Very cute. It's nothing against banking, darling, I think you know that. It's a fine, respectable career – I'd rather see you doing that than any of those hippie-dippy-save-the-world jobs your parents would recommend – but you just seem so young to lock yourself into something so boring. You should be out there meeting people, going to parties, enjoying being young and single in New York, not tied down to a desk in a bank. What do you *want* to do?'

As many times as he'd asked me this, I'd never come around to a great – or even decent – answer. It was certainly a fair question. In high school I'd always thought I'd join the Peace Corps. My parents had taught me that that was the natural step following a college degree. But then I went to Emory and met Penelope. She liked that I couldn't name every private school in Manhattan and knew nothing about Martha's Vineyard, and I, of course, loved that she could and did. We were inseparable by Christmas break, and by the end of freshman year, I had discarded my favorite Dead T-shirts. Jerry was long dead, anyway. And it was fun going to basketball games and keg parties and joining the coed touch-football league with a whole group of people who didn't regularly dread their hair, or recycle their bathwater, or wear patchouli oil. I didn't stand out as the eccentric girl who always smelled a little bit off and knew way too much about the redwoods. I wore the same jeans and T-shirts as everyone else (without even checking to see if they originated in a sweatshop) and ate the same burgers and drank the same beer, and it felt fantastic. For four years I had a group of similar-minded friends and the occasional boyfriend, none of whom were Peace Corps–bound. So when all the big companies showed up on campus waving giant salaries and signing bonuses and offering to fly candidates to New York for interviews, I did it. Nearly every one of my friends from school took a similar job, because when you get right down to it, how else is a twenty-two-year-old going to be able to pay rent in Manhattan? What was incredible about the whole thing was how quickly five years had gone by. Five years had just vanished into a black hole of training programs and quarterly reports and year-end bonuses, leaving barely enough time for me to consider that I loathed what I did all day long. It didn't help matters that I was actually good at it – it somehow seemed to signify that I was doing the right thing. Will knew it was wrong, though, could obviously sense it, but so far I'd been too complacent to make the leap into something else.

'What do I want to do? How on earth can I answer something like that?' I asked.

'How can you not? If you don't get out soon, you're going to wake up one day when you're forty and a managing director and jump off a bridge. There's nothing wrong with banking, darling, it's just not for you. You should be around *people*. You should laugh a little. You should *write*. And you should be wearing much better clothes.'

I didn't tell him I was considering looking for work at a nonprofit. He'd start ranting about how his campaign to unbrainwash me from my parents had failed, and he'd sit dejectedly at the table for the rest of the evening. I'd tried it once, just merely mentioned that I was thinking of interviewing at Planned Parenthood, and he'd informed me that while that was a most noble idea, it would lead me straight back down the path to rejoining, in his words, the World of the Great Unshowered. So we proceeded to cover the usual topics. First came my nonexistent love life ('Darling, you're simply too young and too pretty for your job to be your only lover'), followed by a bit of ranting about Will's latest column ('Is it my fault that Manhattan has become so uneducated that people no longer wish to hear the truth about their elected officials?'). We cycled back to my high school days of political activism ('The Incense Era is blessedly over'), and then once again returned to everyone's all-time favorite topic, the abject state of my wardrobe ('Ill-fitting, masculine trousers do not a date outfit make').

Just as he was beginning a small soliloquy on the far-reaching benefits of owning a Chanel suit, the maid knocked on the study door to inform us that dinner was on the table. We collected our drinks and made our way to the formal dining room.

'Productive day?' Simon asked Will, kissing him on the cheek in greeting. He had showered and changed into a pair of Hefesque linen pajamas and was holding a glass of champagne.

'Of course not,' Will responded, setting aside his dirty martini and pouring two more glasses of champagne. He handed one to me. 'Deadline's not until midnight; why would I do a damn thing until ten o'clock tonight? What are we celebrating?'

I dug into my Gorgonzola salad, grateful to be eating something that hadn't originated in a street cart, and took a gulp of champagne. If I could have somehow finagled eating there every night without appearing to be the biggest loser on earth, I would've done it in a second. But even I had enough dignity to know that

11

being available for the same people – even if they were your uncle and his partner – more than once a week for dinner and once for brunch was truly pathetic.

'What, we need to be celebrating something to drink a little champagne?' Simon asked, helping himself to a few pieces of the sliced steak their housekeeper had made for the main course. 'Just thought it would be a nice change. Bette, what are your plans for the rest of the evening?'

'Penelope's engagement party. I'm going to have to head there soon, actually. The mothers put the whole thing together before either Avery or Penelope could veto it. At least it's at some club in Chelsea, though, rather than somewhere on the Upper East Side – I think that was their one concession to their children actually enjoying themselves.'

'What's the name of the club?' Will asked, although there was little chance he knew anything about it if it wasn't dark, wood-paneled, and filled with cigar smoke.

'She mentioned it, but I can't remember. Begins with a B, I think. Here,' I said, pulling a torn slip of paper from my bag. 'It's on Twenty-seventh between Tenth and Eleventh. It's called – '

'Bungalow 8,' they replied in unison.

'How did you both know that?'

'Honey, it's mentioned so often in Page Six that you'd think Richard Johnson owned the damn place,' Will said.

'I read somewhere that it was originally modeled after the bungalows at the Beverly Hills Hotel, and that the service is just as good. It's just a nightclub, but this article described a concierge who will cater to any whim, from ordering in a special kind of rare sushi to arranging for helicopters. There are places that are hot for a few months and then vanish, but everyone agrees that Bungalow 8 has staying power,' Simon said.

'I guess sitting at the Black Door on my nights out isn't really helping my social life,' I said and pushed my plate away. 'Do you guys mind if I bail early tonight? Penelope wanted me there before the hordes of Avery's friends and her family arrive.'

'Run, Bette, run. Stop only to reapply your lipstick and then run! And it wouldn't hurt a damn if you found yourself a dashing young gentleman to date,' Simon declared, as though there would be roomfuls of gorgeous, eligible guys who were just waiting for me to walk into their lives.

'Or even better, a dashing young bastard to play with for one evening.' Will winked, only half-kidding.

'You guys are the best,' I said, kissing each one's cheek before gathering my bag and cardigan. 'You have no compunction whoring out your only niece, do you?'

'Absolutely none,' Will announced while Simon shook his head gravely. 'Go be a good tart and have some fun, for Christ's sake, will you?'

There was a crowd – three deep and a block long – when the cab pulled up in front of the club, and if it hadn't been Penelope's party, I would've had the cabbie keep driving. Instead, I plastered on a smile and strolled to the front of the forty-person line, where a giant guy wearing a Secret Service earpiece stood, holding a clipboard.

'Hi, my name is Bette and I'm with Penelope's party,' I said, surveying the line and not recognizing a single face.

He gazed at me blankly. 'Great, nice to meet you, Penelope. If you could just wait in line like everyone else, we'll get you inside as quickly as possible.'

'No, this is Penelope's party, and I'm her friend. She asked me to be here early, so it'd really be better if I could go in right now.'

'Uh-huh, that's great. Listen, just step aside and—' He placed a hand over his earpiece and appeared to listen intently, nodding his head a few times and studying the line that now looped around the corner.

'Okay, everyone,' he announced, his voice causing immediate silence among the barely dressed would-be partiers. 'We're already at capacity right now, as determined by the FDNY. We'll only be letting people in as others leave, so either get comfortable or come back later.'

Groans all around. *Well, this simply isn't going to work,* I thought. *He must not understand the situation.*

'Excuse me? Sir?' He peered at me once again, now visibly annoyed. 'You've obviously got a lot of people waiting to go in, but it's my friend's engagement party, and she really needs me there. If you only knew her mother, then you'd understand how imperative it is that I get inside.'

'Mmm. Interesting. Look, I don't care if your friend Penelope's marrying Prince William. There's no way I can let anyone else in right now. We'd be in violation of the fire code, and you certainly don't want that.' He backed off a bit. 'Just hang out in line and we'll get you in as soon as possible, okay?' I think he was aiming for soothing, but it only served to incense me more. He looked vaguely familiar, although I wasn't sure why. His faded green T-shirt was tight enough to show that he was quite capable of keeping people out if he so desired, but the slightly baggy, faded jeans that hung low on his hips suggested he didn't take himself too seriously. Just as I was conceding that he had the best hair I'd ever seen on a guy – longish, dark, thick, and annoyingly shiny – he shrugged on a gray corduroy jacket and managed to look even cuter still.

Definitely a model. I restrained myself from announcing something super-snotty about what a power trip this must be for someone who most likely hadn't made it past seventh grade, and skulked to the back of the line. As repeated attempts to call both Penelope's and Avery's cell phones went straight to voice mail, and the front-door goon was only allowing in an average of two people every ten minutes, I stood there for the better part of an hour. I was fantasizing about the many ways I could humiliate or otherwise harm the bouncer when Michael and his girlfriend slinked outside and lit cigarettes a few feet from the door.

'Michael!' I shrieked, aware of how absolutely pathetic I sounded, but not really caring. 'Michael, Megu, over here!'

They both looked over the hordes of people and spotted me, which probably wasn't hard considering I was screaming and waving with zero dignity. They waved me over, and I practically ran to them.

'I need to get inside already. I've been standing outside this goddamn hellhole forever, and that guy won't let me in. Penelope's going to kill me!'

'Hey, Bette, great to see you, too,' Michael said, leaning over to kiss my cheek.

'Sorry,' I said, hugging first him and then his girlfriend, Megu, the sweet Japanese med student with whom he now shared an apartment. 'How are you guys? How on earth did you both get out for this?'

'It happens like once every six months.' Megu smiled, taking hold of Michael's hand and tucking it behind her back. 'The schedule just falls into alignment for one twelve-hour period when I'm not on call and he's not at work.'

'And you came here? What, are you crazy? Megu, you're a really good sport. Michael, do you realize what a girl you have here?'

'Sure do,' he said, gazing at her adoringly. 'She knows Penelope would kill me, too, if we didn't make an appearance, but I think we're out. I've got to be at work in, oh, let's see, four hours now, and Megu was hoping to sleep for a full six-hour block of time for the first time in a few weeks, so we're going to bail. It looks like people are headed inside now.'

I turned to see a massive exchange of gorgeous people: one crowd surged outside, apparently on their way to a 'real' party in TriBeCa, and another seeped in through the door when the bouncer lifted the velvet rope.

'I thought you said I was next on the list,' I said flatly to the bouncer.

'Feel free to visit Princess Penelope,' he told me, sweeping expansively with one arm and adjusting his earpiece to hear what I'm sure was crucial information with the other.

'See, there you go,' Michael said, pulling Megu out into the street with him. 'Call me this week and let's grab a drink. Bring Penelope – I didn't get a chance to even talk to her tonight, and it's been forever since we all caught up. Tell her I said good-bye.' And they were gone, undoubtedly thrilled they'd managed to escape.

I turned around and saw that there were only a few people loitering on the sidewalk, talking on cell phones, apparently indifferent to whether they went inside. Just like that, the crowd had evaporated, and I was finally being granted entry.

'Gee, thanks. You were extraordinarily helpful,' I said to the bouncer, brushing past his massive frame and walking through the velvet rope he held open. I yanked open the giant glass door and stepped into a dark foyer, where Avery was talking very closely to a very pretty girl with very big breasts.

'Hi, Bette, where have you been all night?' he said, immediately moving toward me and offering to take my coat. In the same second Penelope bounded over, looking flushed and then relieved. She was wearing a short black cocktail dress topped with a sequined shrug and extraordinarily high-heeled silver sandals, and I knew immediately that her mother had dressed her.

'Bette!' she hissed, grabbing my arm and leading me away from Avery, who immediately resumed his intense conversation with the girl. 'What took you so long? I've been suffering alone all night.'

I raised my eyebrows and looked around. 'Alone? There must be two hundred people here. All these years, and I didn't know you had two hundred friends. This is quite the party!'

'Yeah, really impressive, right? Exactly five of the people in this room are here to see *me*: my mother, my brother, one of the girls from the real-estate department, my father's secretary, and now you. Megu and Michael left, right?' I nodded. 'The rest are Avery's, of course. And my mother's friends. Where have you been?' She took a gulp of her drink and passed the glass to me with slightly shaking hands, as though it were a pipe and not a champagne flute.

'Honey, I've been here for over an hour, as promised. Had a bit of trouble at the door.'

'You didn't!' She looked horrified.

'I did. Very cute bouncer, but a total creep.'

'Oh, Bette, I'm so sorry! Why didn't you call me?'

'I did, a few dozen times, but I guess you couldn't hear your

15

phone. Listen, don't worry about it. Tonight's your night, so try and, well, uh, enjoy it?'

'Let's get you a drink,' she said, pulling a cosmopolitan from a circling waiter's tray. 'Do you believe this party?'

'It's crazy. How long has your mother been planning this?'

'She read in Page Six weeks ago that Gisele and Leo were seen "canoodling" here, so I guess she called and booked it right after that. She keeps telling me that these are the kinds of places I should be patronizing because of their "exclusive clientele." I didn't tell her that the one time Avery dragged me here the clientele was basically having sex on the dance floor.'

'It probably would've only encouraged her more.'

'True.' A model-tall woman wedged herself between us and began air-kissing Penelope in a manner so insincere I actually cringed, gulped my cosmo, and sneaked away. I got pulled into some inane conversation with a few people from the bank who'd just arrived and who looked a little shell-shocked to be away from their computers, and I chatted as briefly as possible with Penelope's mother, who immediately referenced both the Chanel suit and the heels she was wearing and then pulled Penelope by the arm to another cache of people. I surveyed the designer-clad crowd and tried not to shrink in my outfit, which had been purchased online from a combination of J. Crew and Banana Republic at three in the morning a few months ago. Will had been particularly insistent lately that I needed 'going out' clothes, but the catalog orders were not what he had in mind. I got the feeling that any of these people could – and would – feel perfectly comfortable roaming around naked. Even better than the clothes (which were perfect) was the confidence, and that came from somewhere else entirely. Two hours and three cosmos later, certifiably tipsy, I was considering going home. Instead, I grabbed another drink and ducked outside.

The line to get in had cleared up entirely; only the bouncer who'd held me in club purgatory for so long remained. I was preparing my snide remarks should he address me in any way whatsoever, but he just grinned and returned his attention to the paperback he was reading, which looked like a matchbook in his massive hands. Shame he was so cute – but jerks always are.

'So, what was it about me that you didn't like?' I couldn't help myself. Five years in the city and I'd tried to avoid places with doormen or velvet ropes unless absolutely necessary; I'd inherited at least a bit of my parents' egalitarian self-righteousness – or intense insecurity, depending on how you looked at it.

'Pardon?'

16

'I mean, when you wouldn't let me in before, even though it's my best friend's engagement party.'

He shook his head and half-smiled to himself. 'Look, it's nothing personal. They hand me a list and tell me to follow it and do crowd control. If you're not on the list or you show up when a hundred other people do, I have to keep you outside for a little while. There's really nothing more to it.'

'Sure.' I'd all but missed my best friend's big night because of his door policy. I teetered a bit and then hissed, 'Nothing personal. Right.'

'You think I need *your* attitude tonight? I've got plenty of people who are far more expert at giving me a really fucking hard time, so why don't we just stop talking and I'll put you in a cab?'

Perhaps it was the fourth cosmo – liquid courage – but I wasn't in the mood to deal with his condescending attitude, so I turned on my too-chunky heels and yanked the door open. 'I hardly need *your* charity. Thanks for nothing,' I snapped and marched back inside the club as soberly as I could manage.

I hugged Penelope, air-kissed Avery, and then beelined to the door before anyone else could initiate any more small talk. I saw a girl crouched in a corner, sobbing quietly but with a pleased awareness that others were watching, and sidestepped a strikingly stylish foreign couple who were making out furiously, and with much hip grinding. I then made a big show of ignoring the meathead bouncer who, incidentally, was reading from a tattered paperback version of *Lady Chatterley's Lover* (sex fiend!) and threw my arm in the air to hail a cab. Only the street was completely empty, and a cold drizzle had just begun, practically guaranteeing that a taxi was nowhere in my immediate future.

'Hey, you need some help?' he asked after opening the velvet rope to admit three squealing, tottering girls. 'This is a tough street for cabs when it rains.'

'No thanks, I'm just fine.'

'Suit yourself.'

Minutes were starting to feel like hours, and the warm summer sprinkles had rapidly become a cold, persistent rain. What, exactly, was I proving here? The bouncer had pressed himself against the door to get some protection from the overhang and was still reading calmly, as though unaware of the hurricane that now whipped around us. I continued to stare at him until he looked up, grinned, and said, 'Yeah, you seem to be doing just fine on your own. You're definitely teaching me a lesson by not taking one of these huge umbrellas and walking a couple blocks over to Eighth, where you'll have no trouble getting a cab at all. Great call on your part.'

'You have umbrellas?' I asked before I could stop myself. The water had soaked entirely through my shirt and I could feel my blanket-thick hair sticking to my neck in wet, cold clumps.

'Sure do. Keep 'em right here for situations just like this. But I'm sure you wouldn't be interested in taking one of them, right?'

'Right. I'm just fine.' To think I'd almost begun warming up to him. Just then a livery cab drove by, and I had the brilliant idea to call UBS's car service for a ride home.

'Hi, this is Bette Robinson with account number six-three-three-eight. I need a car to pick me up at—'

'All booked!' barked back an angry-sounding female dispatcher.

'No, I don't think you understand. I have an account with your company and—'

Click.

I stood there soaking wet, anger boiling inside me.

'No cars, huh? Tough,' he said, clucking sympathetically without looking up from the book. I'd managed to skim *Lady Chatterley's Lover* when I was twelve and had already gleaned as much about sex as possible from the combination of *Forever, Wifey* and *What's Happening to My Body? Book for Girls,* but I didn't remember anything about it. Perhaps that had to do with a poor memory, or maybe it was the fact that sex hadn't even been a part of my consciousness for the last two years. Or maybe it was that the plots of my beloved romance novels crowded my thoughts at all times. Whatever it was, I couldn't even recall something snide to say about it, never mind clever. 'No cars.' I sighed. 'Just not my night.'

He took a few steps out in the rain and handed me a long executive's umbrella, already unfurled, with the club's logo emblazoned on both sides. 'Take it. Walk to Eighth, and if you still can't get a cab, talk to the doorman at Serena, Twenty-third between Seventh and Eighth. Tell him I sent you, and he'll work it out.'

I considered walking right past him and getting on the subway, but the idea of riding around in a train car at one in the morning was hardly appealing. 'Thanks,' I mumbled, refusing to meet what would surely be his gloating eyes. I took the umbrella and started walking east, feeling him watch me from behind.

Five minutes later, I was tucked in the backseat of a big yellow taxi, wet but finally warm.

I gave the driver my address and slumped back, exhausted. At this hour, cabs were good for two things and two things only: making out with someone on your way home from a good night out or catching up with multiple people in three-minute-or-less cell-phone conversations. Since neither was an option, I rested

18

my wet hair on the patch of filthy vinyl where so many greasy, unwashed, oiled, lice-ridden, and generally unkempt heads had rested before mine, closed my eyes, and anticipated the sniffling, hysterical welcome I would soon receive from Millington. Who needed a man – or even a newly engaged best friend – when you had a dog?

3

The week following Penelope's engagement party was nearly unbearable. It was my fault, of course: there are many ways to piss off your parents and rebel against your entire upbringing without enslaving yourself in the process, but I was clearly too stupid to find them. So instead I sat inside my shower-sized cubicle at UBS Warburg – as I had every day for the past fifty-six months – and death-gripped the phone, which was currently discolored by a layer of Maybelline Fresh Look foundation (in Tawny Blush) and a few splotches of L'Oreal Wet Shine lip gloss (in Rhinestone Pink). I wiped it off as best I could while pressing the receiver to my ear and rubbed my grubby fingers clean underneath the desk chair. I was being berated by a 'minimum,' someone who only invests the million-dollar minimum with my division and is therefore excruciatingly demanding and detail-oriented in a way that forty-million-dollar clients never are.

'Mrs Kaufman, I truly understand your concern over the market's slight decline, but let me assure you that we have everything under control. I realize your nephew the interior decorator thinks your portfolio is top-heavy with corporate bonds, but I assure you our traders are excellent, and always looking out for your best interests. I don't know if a thirty-two percent annual gain is realistic in this economic environment, but I'll have Aaron give you a call as soon as he gets back to his desk. Yes. Of course. Yes. Yes, I will absolutely have him call you the moment he returns from the meeting. Yes. Certainly. Of course. Yes. Naturally. Yes. A pleasure hearing from you, as always. All right, then. Bye-bye.' I waited until I heard the click on her end and then slammed down the phone.

Nearly five years and I'd yet to utter the word *no,* as apparently you need to have at least seventy-two months' experience before being qualified to go there. I went to send Aaron a quick email begging him to return Mrs Kaufman's call so she would finally stop stalking me and was surprised to see that he was back at his desk, busily blast-emailing us his daily inspirational bullshit.

> Good morning, folks. Let's remember to show our clients our high energy levels! Our relationships with these good folks comprise our whole business – they appreciate our patience and consideration as much as our results-oriented portfolio handling. I'm pleased to announce a new weekly group meeting, one that I hope will allow us all to brain-storm ways we may better serve our clients. It will be held each Friday at 7 a.m. and will provide us with an oppor-tunity to think outside the box. Breakfast is on me, folks, so bring yourselves and your thinking caps and remember, 'Great discoveries and improvements invariably involve the cooperation of many minds.' – Alexander Graham Bell.

I stared at the email so long my eyes began to glaze over. Were his insistence on using the word *folks* and his constant references to 'thinking outside the box' more or less annoying than his inclu-sion of the phrase *thinking caps*? Did he craft and send these emails just to add to the all-pervasive misery and hopelessness of my days? I pondered this for a few moments, desperate to think about anything other than the seven A.M. meeting announcement. I managed to move beyond it long enough to field another frantic call, this time from Mrs Kaufman's nephew, that lasted a record fifty-seven minutes, ninety percent of which he spent accusing me of things that were entirely beyond my control while I said nothing or, occasionally, just to switch things up, agreed with him that I was, in fact, as dumb and useless as he claimed.

I hung up and resumed staring listlessly at the email. I wasn't exactly sure how Mr Bell's quote applied to my life or why I should care, but I did know if I planned to escape for lunch, now was my only chance. I'd abided by the no-leaving-for-lunch policy my first few years at UBS Warburg and dutifully ordered in each day, but lately Penelope and I had brazenly begun sneaking out for ten, twelve minutes a day to retrieve our own takeout and cram in as much whining and gossip as possible. An IM popped up on my screen.

> **P.Lo:** Ready? Let's do falafel. Meet at the 52nd Street cart in five?

I punched in the letter Y, hit Send, and draped my suit jacket over the back of my chair to indicate my presence. One of the managers glanced at me when I picked up my purse, so I filled my mug with steaming coffee as additional proof that I hadn't left the premises and placed it in the middle of my desk. I mumbled something about the bathroom to my fellow cubicle dwellers, who were too busy transferring their own facial grime to their telephones to even notice, and walked confidently toward the hallway. Penelope worked in the real-estate division two floors above me and was already in the elevator, but like two well-trained CIA operatives, we didn't so much as glance at each other. She let me exit first and circle the lobby for a minute while she ducked outside and casually strolled past the fountain. I followed as best I could in my ugly, uncomfortable heels, the humidity hitting my face like a wall. We didn't speak until we'd blended into the line of midtown office drones who stood both quietly and restlessly, wanting to savor their few precious minutes of daily freedom but instinctively getting pissy and frustrated at having to wait for anything.

'What are you having?' Penelope asked, her eyes scanning the three different carts of sizzling and highly aromatic ethnic food that men in varying costumes and facial hair were steaming, slicing, sautéing, skewering, frying, and heaving toward the hungry suits.

'It's all some sort of meat on a stick or dough-filled something,' I said tonelessly, surveying the smoky meats. 'Does it matter?'

'Someone's in a great mood today.'

'Oh, I'm sorry, I forgot, I should be thrilled that five years of slave labor have turned out so well. I mean, look at us, how glamorous is this?' I waved my arms expansively in front of us. 'It's sad enough we don't get to go out to lunch at some point in the middle of a sixteen-hour workday, but it's fucking *pathetic* that we aren't even permitted to pick out our food ourselves.'

'This is nothing new, Bette. I don't know why you're getting so stressed about it now.'

'Just a particularly lousy day. If it's possible to distinguish one from the next.'

'Why? Anything happen?'

I wanted to say 'Two rings?' but restrained myself as an overweight woman wearing a skirt suit worse than mine and a pair of white leather Reeboks over her tights spilled hot sauce down the front of her embroidered, ruffled blouse. I saw myself in ten years and nearly lurched forward with queasiness.

'Of course nothing happened, that's the whole point!' I all but screamed. Two blond guys who looked fresh off the Princeton eating club path turned and looked at me curiously. I thought about composing myself for a minute since, well, they were both really cute, but I soon remembered that these obscenely hot lacrosse players were not only way too young, but most likely also had obscenely gorgeous girlfriends eight years my junior.

'Seriously, Bette, I don't know what you're looking for. I mean, it's a job, right? It's still work. It doesn't matter what you do, it's never going to be like sitting at the country club all day long, you know? Sure, it sucks to spend every waking minute at work. And I don't exactly adore finance, either – I never fantasized about working at a bank – but it's just not *that* bad.'

Penelope's parents had tried to push her toward a position at *Vogue* or Sotheby's as the final finishing school in the pursuit of her Mrs degree, but when she'd insisted on joining the rest of us in corporate America, they'd acquiesced – it was certainly possible to find a husband while working in finance, as long as she kept her priorities straight, didn't display any overt ambition, and quit immediately after the wedding. Truth be told, though, while she whined and complained about the job, I think she actually liked it.

She handed over a ten-dollar bill to cover both of our 'kebab' plates, and my eyes were drawn to her hand like a magnet. Even I had to admit the ring was gorgeous. I said as much, for the tenth time, and she beamed. It was hard to be upset about the engagement when she was so obviously giddy. Avery had even stepped it up since the proposal and had managed to impersonate a real, caring fiancé, which of course had made her even happier. He'd met her after work so they could go home together, and had even brought her breakfast in bed. More important, he had refrained from clubbing, his favorite pastime, for a full three weeks now, the only exception being last week's soiree in their honor. Penelope didn't mind that Avery wanted to spend as much time as humanly possible wedged in between banquettes – or dancing on them – but she wanted no part of it. On the nights he was out with friends from his consulting firm, Penelope and I would sit at the Black Door, dive-bar extraordinaire, with Michael (when he was available), drinking beer and wondering why anyone would want to be anywhere else. But someone must've clued Avery in that while it's acceptable to leave your girlfriend home six nights a week, ditching your fiancée is different, so he'd made a concerted effort to cut back. I knew it would never last.

We retraced our steps to the building and sneaked back into the office with only a single dirty look from the rule-abiding UBS shoe-shine guy (who, incidentally, was also forbidden to leave during lunch in case a pair of wing tips desperately needed a spit-shine between one and two P.M.). Penelope followed me back to my cubicle and planted herself on the chair that was theoretically for guests and clients, although I'd yet to host either.

'So, we set a date,' she said breathlessly, digging into the fragrant plate she balanced on her lap.

'Oh, yeah? When?'

'Exactly one year from next week. August tenth, on Martha's Vineyard, which seems appropriate since that's where it all began. We've been engaged for a few weeks, and already our mothers are going berserk. I seriously don't know how I'm going to put up with them.'

Avery's and Penelope's families had been vacationing together since the two were toddlers. There were scads of photos of the whole lot of them sporting grosgrain flip-flops and cheap-chic L.L. Bean monogrammed totes in Martha's Vineyard during the summer and Stubbs and Wootton slippers during ski vacations in the Adirondacks each year. She'd gone to Nightingale and he'd been at Collegiate and both of them had spent a good chunk of their respective childhoods being paraded around by their socialite mothers to various benefits and parties and weekend polo matches. Avery embraced it, threw himself on every junior committee of every foundation that asked, went out six nights a week with his parents' unlimited line of credit, and was one of those New York–born-and-bred kids who knew everyone, everywhere. Much to her parents' chagrin, Penelope had no interest whatsoever. She repeatedly rejected the whole circuit, preferring to spend all her time with a group of misfit artist types on scholarship, the kind of kids who gave Penelope's mother night sweats. Avery and Penelope had never really been close – and certainly not remotely romantic – until Avery had graduated high school a year before her and headed to Emory. According to Penelope, who'd always harbored an intense secret crush on Avery, he'd been one of the most popular kids in school, the charming, athletic soccer player who got adequate grades and was hot enough to get away with being really, really arrogant. From what I could tell, she'd always blended into the background, like all exotically pretty girls do at an age when only blond hair and big boobs count, spending a lot of time getting good grades and trying desperately not to get noticed. And it worked, at least until Avery came back for summer break after his freshman year in college, looked across the hot tub at their families' shared house in the Vineyard, and saw everything about Penelope that was long and graceful and gorgeous – her doe-like limbs and her stick-straight black hair and the eyelashes that framed her enormously wide brown eyes.

So she did what every good girl knows is completely wrong

– for the reputation, the self-esteem, and the strategy of making him call the next day – and slept with him then and there, mere minutes after he leaned over to kiss her for the very first time. ('I just couldn't help it,' she'd said a million times while retelling the story. 'I couldn't believe that Avery Wainwright was interested in me!') But unlike all the other girls I knew who'd had sex within hours of meeting some guy and never heard from him again, Penelope and Avery proceeded to attach themselves to each other, and their engagement was little more than a much approved and applauded formality.

'Are they being worse than usual?'

She sighed and rolled her eyes. ' 'Worse than usual.' An interesting phrase. I would've thought it was impossible, but yes, my mother has managed to become even more unbearable lately. Our last knock-down brawl was over whether or not you could rightfully call something a wedding dress if it wasn't designed by Vera Wang or Carolina Herrera. I said yes. She obviously disagreed. Vehemently.'

'Who won?'

'I caved on that because, really, I don't care who makes the dress as long as I like it. I figure I have to pick my battles very, very carefully, and the one I will not be compromising on is the wedding announcement.'

'Define "wedding announcement."'

'Don't make me.' She grinned and took a swig of Dr Pepper. 'Say it.'

'Please, Bette, this sucks enough. Don't make me say it.'

'C'mon, Pen. Own up. Go on, it'll get easier after the first time. Just say it.' I nudged her chair with my foot and leaned in to relish the information.

She covered her perfect, pale forehead with her long, thin hands and shook her head. *New York Times.*'

'I knew it! Will and I will be gentle, I promise. She's not kidding around, is she?'

'Of course she's not!' Penelope wailed. 'And naturally, Avery's mother's dying for it also.'

'Oh, Pen, it's perfect! You guys make such a cute couple, and now everyone else can see it, too!' I cackled.

'You should hear them, Bette, it's hideous. Both of them are already fantasizing about all those fancy private schools they can list between them. Do you know I overheard my mother on the phone the other day with the Weddings editor, saying that she'd like to include all the siblings' schools as well? The woman told her that they won't even discuss it until six weeks before, but that hasn't discouraged anyone: Avery's mom already made an appointment for the photo shoot and has all sorts of ideas about how we can pose so that our eyebrows are level, which is one of the published suggestions. The wedding is still a year away!'

'Yes, but these things require lots of advance planning and research.'

'That's what they said!' she cried.

'What about eloping?' But before she could answer, Aaron made a big show of knocking on my cubicle wall and waving his arms to imitate regret at breaking up our 'little powwow,' as he irritatingly called our lunches.

'Don't mean to break up your little powwow, folks,' he said, as both Penelope and I silently mouthed the words along with him. 'Bette, may I have a word with you?'

'No worries, I was just leaving,' Penelope breathed, obviously grateful for the chance to flee without talking to Aaron. 'Bette, we'll talk more later.' And before I could say anything, she was gone.

'Saaaaaaaay, Bette?'

'Yes, Aaron?' He sounded so much like Lumbergh from *Office Space* that it would have been funny had I not been on the receiving end of his 'suggestions.'

'Weeeeell, I was just wondering if you had a chance to read today's quote of the day?' He gave a loud, phlegmy cough and raised his eyebrows at me.

'Of course, Aaron, I have it right here. "Individual commitment to a group effort – that is what makes a team work, a company work, a society work, a civilization work." Yeah, I have to say, that one really spoke to me.'

'It did?' He looked pleased. 'That was yesterday's, but I'm glad it had such impact.'

'Sure. It was really appropriate. I learn a lot from all of them. Why? Is something wrong?' I asked in my most ingratiatingly concerned tone.

'Nothing's wrong, *per se,* it's just that I couldn't find you for nearly ten minutes before, and while that doesn't sound like much, I'm sure to Mrs Kaufman – who was waiting on an update – it feels like an eternity.'

'An eternity?'

'I just don't think that when you're away from your desk for such long periods of time that you can adequately be providing our clients, like Mrs Kaufman, with the kind of attention we pride ourselves on here at UBS. Just a little something to think about for next time, okay?'

'I'm really sorry. I was just picking up lunch.'

'I know that, Bette. But I don't have to remind you that company policy says employees shouldn't be taking time out to pick it up. I have a whole drawer full of delivery menus if you'd care to look at them.'

I remained silent.

'Oh, and Bette? I'm sure Penelope's supervisor needs her just as much as I need you, so let's try to keep those powwows to a minimum, okay?' He flashed me the most patronizing smile imaginable, revealing thirty-seven years' worth of splotchy, stained teeth, and I thought I'd vomit if he didn't stop immediately. Ever since watching *Girls Just Want to Have Fun* for the first time when I was twelve, I've never been able to get Lynne Stone's rumination out of my mind. She's escorting Janey home after Janey skips choir practice to rehearse with Jeff (and of course gets caught by the evil, rotating-closet-owning bitch, Natalie), and she says, 'Whenever I'm in a room with a guy, no matter who it is – a date, my dentist, anybody – I think, "If we were the last two people on earth, would I puke if he kissed me?"' Well, thanks to Lynne, I can't help wondering it, either; the unfortunate outcome, though, is that I envisioned myself kissing Aaron and felt ill.

'Okay? How does that sound?' He shifted nervously from foot to foot and I wondered how this anxious, socially inept man had managed to climb at least three levels above me in the corporate hierarchy. I'd watched clients physically recoil when he went to shake their hands, and yet he glided up the ladder like it was lubricated in the very oil he used to slick back his few remaining strands of hair.

All I wanted was for him to disappear, but I made a crucial miscalculation. Rather than just agreeing and going back to my lunch, I said, 'Are you unhappy with my performance, Aaron? I try really hard, but you always seem displeased.'

'I wouldn't say I'm *unhappy* with your performance, Bette. I think you're doing, well, um, just fine around here. But we all seek to self-improve now, don't we? As Winston Churchill once said—'

'Just fine? That's like describing someone as "interesting" or saying a date was "nice." I work eighty-hour weeks, Aaron. I give my entire life to UBS.' It was useless to try to highlight my dedication in an hours-worked formula since Aaron beat me by at least fifteen hours every single week, but it was true: I worked damn hard when I wasn't shopping online, talking to Will on the phone, or sneaking out to meet Penelope for lunch.

'Bette, don't be so sensitive. With a little more willingness to learn and perhaps a bit more attention paid to your clients, I think you've got the potential to get promoted. Just keep the powwows to a minimum and really throw your heart into your work and the results will be immeasurable.'

I watched the spittle form on his thin lips as he mouthed his favorite phrase, and something inside me snapped. There was no angel on one shoulder or devil on the other, no mental list of pros and cons or quick scans of potential consequences, ramifications, or backup plans. No solid thoughts of any sort whatsoever – just an all-pervasive sense of calm and determination, coupled with a deep understanding that I simply could not tolerate one additional second of the present situation.

'All right, Aaron. No more powwows for me – ever. I quit.'

He looked confused for a minute before he realized I was completely serious. 'You what?'

'Please consider this my two weeks' notice,' I said with a confidence that was beginning to waver slightly.

Appearing to consider this for a minute, he wiped his sweaty brow and furrowed it a few times. 'That won't be necessary,' he said quietly.

It was my turn to be confused. 'I appreciate it, Aaron, but I really do have to leave.'

'I meant that the two weeks won't be necessary. We shouldn't have much trouble finding someone, Bette. There are loads of qualified people out there who actually want to work here, if you can imagine that. Please discuss the details of your departure with HR and have your things packed by the end of the day. And good luck with whatever you'll be doing next.' He forced a tight smile and walked away, seeming self-assured for the first time in the five years I'd worked for him.

Thoughts swirled in my head, coming too fast and from too many directions for me to actually process them. Aaron had balls – who knew! I'd just quit my job. Quit it. With no forethought or planning. Must tell Penelope. Penelope engaged. How would I get all my stuff home? Could I still charge a car to the company? Could I collect unemployment? Would I still come to midtown just for the kebabs? Should I burn all my skirt suits in a ceremonial living-room bonfire? Millington will be so happy to hit the dog run in the middle of the day! Middle of the day. I would get to watch *The Price Is Right* all the time if I wanted. Why hadn't I thought of this before?

I stared at the screen a while longer, until the gravity of what had just happened settled in, and then I headed straight to the rest-room to freak out in the relative privacy of a stall. There was laid-back and there was plain fucking stupid, and this was quickly beginning to resemble the latter. I breathed a few times and tried uttering – coolly and casually – my new mantra, but *whatever* came out sounding like a choked cry as I wondered what the hell I'd done.

4

'Christ, Bette, it's not like you maimed someone. You quit your job. Congratulations! Welcome to the wonderful world of adult irresponsibility. Things don't always go according to plan, you know?' Simon was trying his best to soothe me while we waited for Will to get home because he couldn't tell that I was already completely relaxed.

The last time I'd felt this zen, I thought, might have been the ashram retreat. 'It's just kind of eerie, not having any idea what to do next.' It was that same involuntary calm-cum-paralysis.

Though I knew I should be more panicked, the last month had actually been pretty great. I'd intended to tell everyone about quitting, but when it came time to actually make the calls, I was overtaken by an all-consuming combination of ennui, laziness, and inertia. It's not like I couldn't tell people I quit – it was just a matter of dialing and announcing – but the effort of explaining my reasons for leaving (none) and discussing my game plan (nonexistent) seemed utterly overwhelming each time I picked up the phone. So instead, in what I'm sure was some sort of psychologically distressed/avoidance/denial state, I slept until one every day, spent most of the afternoon alternately watching TV and walking Millington, shopped for things I didn't need in an obvious effort to fill the voids in my life, and made a conscious decision to start smoking again in earnest so I'd have something to do once *Conan* was over. It sounds comprehensively depressing, but it had been my best month in recent memory and might have gone on indefinitely had Will not called my work number and spoken to my replacement.

Interestingly, I had lost ten pounds without trying. I hadn't exercised at all save for the treks to hunt and gather my food, but I felt better than ever, or certainly better than I had working sixteen-hour days. I'd been thin all through college but had packed on the pounds quite efficiently as soon as I'd started work, having no time to exercise, choosing instead to down a particularly disgusting daily diet of kebabs, doughnuts, vending-machine candy bars, and coffee so sugar-heavy my teeth felt permanently coated.

My parents and friends had politely ignored my weight gain, but I knew I looked terrible. Annually I'd declare my New Year's resolution of more dedicated gym-going; it usually lasted a solid four days before I'd kick my alarm clock and claim the extra hour for sleep. Only Will repeatedly reminded me that I looked like hell. 'But, darling, don't you remember how scouts would stop you on the street and ask you to model? That's not happening anymore, is it?' Or 'Bette, honey, you had that no-makeup, fresh-faced, all-natural girl thing working so well a few years ago – why don't you spend a little time trying to revisit that?' I heard him and knew he was right – when the button on the single pair of Sevens I owned nestled so far into my fleshy stomach that it was sometimes difficult to locate, it was hard to deny the extra poundage. That unemployment made me thinner was telling. My skin was clearer, my eyes brighter, and for the first time in five years the weight had melted off my hips and thighs but stayed squarely put in my chest – surely a sign from God that I wasn't supposed to work. But of course I wasn't supposed to enjoy being shiftless and lazy, so I was trying to demonstrate the appropriate combination of chagrin, regret, and distress. Simon was buying it.

'I think a cocktail is exactly what's in order right now. What can I make you to drink, Bette?'

Little did he know that I'd taken to drinking alone. Not in that desperate, solitary, 'I must drink to deal, and if I happen to have no company, well then, so be it' sort of way, but in the liberated 'I'm an adult and if I'd like a glass of wine or a sip of champagne or four shots of vodka straight up' way, well then, why the hell not? I pretended to consider his offer before saying, 'How about a martini?'

Uncle Will swooped in at that moment and, as he usually did, charged the air with an energy that was immediate and intense. 'Ab fab!' he announced, stealing the phrase from his sneaked sessions of BBC-watching, which he relentlessly denied. 'Simon, make our little banker-no-longer an extra-dry martini with Grey Goose and three olives. I'll have my usual. Darling! I'm so proud of you!'

'Really?' He hadn't sounded too thrilled when he'd left me a message earlier that day, ordering me to be at the apartment that night for drinks. ('Bette, darling, your little game is up. I just spoke to the terrified little mouse who now claims to occupy your cubicle, which makes me wonder what, exactly, you're doing at this moment. Highlights, I'm hoping? Perhaps you've taken a lover. I'll expect you tonight at six on the dot so you may provide us with all the gory details. Plan on accompanying us to a little dinner party afterward at Elaine's.' *Click*.)

'Darling, of course I am! You finally left that dreadful bank.

29

You are an absolutely intoxicating creature, so fascinating, so fabulous, and I think that dreary job of yours was suppressing it all.' He placed his huge, well-manicured hands around my middle and almost shrieked. 'What is it I see? A waist? By God, Simon, the girl's got her figure back. Christ, you look like you've spent the last few weeks getting lipoed in all the right places. Welcome back, darling!' He raised one of the martinis that Simon had made for all of us (Will was no longer permitted to make the drinks because of his notoriously heavy-handed pouring) and simultaneously removed the charcoal wool hat he'd been wearing since before I was born.

Simon smiled and raised his glass as well, clinking ours lightly so as not to splash any of the precious liquid. I, of course, wasn't so careful and slightly soaked my jeans in the boozy mixture. I would've licked it off the denim directly had I been alone. Ahem.

'There,' Will announced. 'It's official. So what will be next? Writing for a magazine? A stint in fashion, perhaps? I hear *Vogue* is hiring right now.'

'Oh, come on.' I sighed, resenting being made to think about it at all. '*Vogue*? You think I'm in any way equipped or qualified to work for that editor in chief – what's her name?'

Simon chimed in here. 'Anna Wintour. And no on both counts.'

'No? Well, what about *Bazaar,* then?' Will asked.

'Will . . .' I looked down at my scuffed, ugly flats and back at him again. I might have graduated from Birkenstocks and pigtail braids, but I was still fully entrenched in the post-college Ann Taylor work wardrobe.

'Oh, stop your whining, darling. You'll find something. Remember, you're always welcome to join me, you know. If you get truly desperate, that is.' Will had been mentioning this as delicately as possible since I was in high school, the offhand comment about how much fun it would be to work together, or how I had natural talent as a researcher and a writer. My parents had saved every essay I'd ever written and sent copies to Will, who had sent me a huge flower arrangement my sophomore year when I'd declared myself an English major. The card had read TO THE FUTURE COLUMNIST OF THE FAMILY. He mentioned often how he'd love to show me the ropes because he thought it'd be something I could really get into. And I didn't doubt that part. It was only that recently his columns had become more like conservative rants and less like the society-and-entertainment commentary readers had been slavishly devoted to for years. He was a master at this very specific genre, never bothering to cover outright gossip but also never taking himself too seriously. At least until recently, when he'd written a thousand words on why the United Nations was the devil incarnate (A summary: 'Why, in this age of super-technology, do all those diplomats in New York City need to physically be here, taking up all the best parking places and the best tables at restaurants, adding to the non-English-speaking environment in the city? Why can't they just email their votes from their respective countries? Why should we have to deal with gridlock and security nightmares when no one listens to them anyway? And if they absolutely refuse to work electronically from their home countries, why don't we move the whole production to Lincoln, Nebraska, and see if they're all still dying to come here to better the world?') Part of me would love to learn his business, but it just seemed too easy. Hey, what luck! Your uncle is a famous, highly syndicated columnist, and you just happen to work for him. He had a small staff of researchers and assistants who I knew would resent the hell out of me if I stepped in and started writing right away. I was also worried about ruining a good thing: since Will was my only family nearby, a dear friend, and soon to be my entire social life now that Penelope was getting married, it didn't seem like the best idea to work together all day.

'According to my ex-boss, I haven't yet mastered the ideals put forth in a single quote of the day. I'm not sure that's someone you'd want working for you.'

'Puh-lease! You'd be better than those kids in my office who pretend to be fact-checking while they're updating their nerve.com profiles with seductive pictures and grotesquely unoriginal come-ons.' He snorted. 'I applaud a complete and utter lack of work ethic, you know. How else could I write such trash every day?' He finished his drink with an appreciative swallow and pushed himself off the leather divan. 'Just something to consider, is all. Now, let's go. We've got a dinner party to oversee.'

I sighed. 'Okay, but I can't stay the entire time. I've got book club tonight.'

'Really, darling? That sounds like it borders on social. What are you reading?'

I thought quickly and blurted out the first socially acceptable title that came to mind. '*Moby-Dick*.'

Simon turned and stared at me. 'You're reading *Moby-Dick*? Are you *serious*?'

'Of course she's not.' Will laughed. 'She's reading *Passion and Pain in Pennsylvania*, or something to that effect. Can't quite kick the habit, can you, darling?'

'You don't understand, Will.' I turned to face Simon. 'No matter how many times I've explained it to him, he refuses to understand.'

'Understand what, exactly? How my lovely and highly intelligent

English-major niece not only reads but obsesses over romance novels? You're right, darling, I can't understand.'

I stared at my feet, feigning unfathomable shame. 'The Very Bad Boy is brand new . . . and highly anticipated. I'm hardly alone – it's one of the most preordered books on Amazon and had a mailing delay of three weeks after publication!'

Will looked at Simon, shaking his head in disbelief. 'Darling, I just don't understand *why*. Why?'

Why? Why? How could I ever answer that question? It was something I'd asked myself a million times. It had started innocently enough, with the discovery of an abandoned copy of *Hot and Heavy* in the back pocket of a plane seat during a flight from Poughkeepsie to Washington, D.C. I was thirteen and old enough to sense that I should hide it from my parents, which I did. The damn thing was so good that I claimed a sore throat when we got to the hotel and begged out of the NARAL march they were both attending so I could finish reading it. I learned to recognize romance novels instantly, ferreting out the right library shelves in seconds, slipping them off the wire turn-carts at the bookstore and quickly handing over my meager allowance in the pharmacy section of the drugstore while my mother paid for her purchases up front. I went through two or three a week, vaguely aware that they were contraband and therefore keeping them hidden in the little crawl space of my closet. I read them only after lights-out and always remembered to restash them before falling asleep.

When I first discovered romances, I was embarrassed by the obvious suggestions of sex on the cover, and of course by the graphic depictions inside. Like any teenager, I didn't want my parents to know that I knew anything about the subject, and sneaked my reads only when they surely wouldn't see. But by the time I was about seventeen, maybe a junior or senior in high school, I'd come out of the closet. I'd accompanied my dad to a local bookstore to pick up a special order he'd placed, and when it came time for him to pay, I slid a copy of *Her Royal Bodyguard* onto the counter, casually murmuring, 'I didn't bring my wallet. Can you buy this now and I'll pay you back when we get home?'

He'd picked it up and held it between two fingers as though it were roadkill. The expression on his face indicated he found it about as appetizing. A moment later, he laughed. 'Bettina, come now. Put this awful thing back wherever you found it and select something worthwhile. I promised your mother we'd be home in twenty minutes – we don't have time to play around anymore.'

I persisted and he bought the book, if only to leave the store as soon as possible. When he mentioned my purchase at the dinner table that night, he sounded confused. 'You don't actually *read* those things, do you?' he asked, his face scrunched up as though he was trying to understand.

'Yes,' I said simply, my voice not revealing the embarrassment I felt.

My mother dropped her fork and it clattered on the plate. 'You do not.' It sounded like she hoped it would be true if she stated it forcefully enough. 'You can't possibly.'

'Oh, but I do,' I sang in a halfhearted attempt to lighten the mood. 'And so do fifty million other people, Mom. They're relaxing *and* interesting. I mean, there's agony, ecstasy, and a happy ending – who could ask for more?' I knew all the facts and figures, and there was no denying they were impressive. The two thousand romances published each year create a $1.5 billion industry. Two-fifths of American women buy at least one romance a year. More than one-third of all popular fiction sold each year are romances. A Shakespearean scholar (and Columbia professor) had recently admitted she'd authored dozens of romances. Why should I be ashamed?

What I didn't tell my parents then – or explain to Will or Simon now – was how much I loved romances. Escape was part of it, of course, but life wasn't so miserable that I had to revert to a fantasy world. It was inspirational to read about two gorgeous people who overcame all obstacles to be together, who loved each other so much that they always found a way to make it work. The sex scenes were a bonus, but more than that, the books always ended happily, offering such optimism that I couldn't keep myself from starting another immediately. They were predictable, dependable, entertaining, and most of all, they depicted love affairs that I could not deny – no matter how much feminism or political correctness or women's empowerment my parents could throw at me – I desperately wanted more than anything in the world. I was conditioned to compare every single date in my life to The Ideal. I couldn't help it. I wanted the fairy tale. Which, needless to say, does not describe Cameron, or most New York liaisons between men and women. But I wouldn't stop hoping – not yet.

Was I about to explain this to Simon? Clearly not. Which is why I laughed and made some self-deprecating remark like 'I just can't handle the real stuff' whenever someone asked why I read the books.

'Oh, whatever.' I laughed lightly, not making eye contact with Will or Simon. 'It's a silly little thing I got into as a kid and haven't quite given up yet.'

Will found this understatement particularly hysterical. 'Silly little thing? Bette, darling, you belong to a book club whose sole mission is to examine and more deeply appreciate your selected genre?' he howled.

This much was true. Until the book group, no one in my life had understood. Not my parents, my uncle, my friends in high school or college. Penelope merely shook her head every time she spotted one in my apartment (which, by the way, wasn't hard, considering I had over four hundred of them stashed in boxes, closets, under-bed bins, and occasionally – when the cover wasn't too embarrassing – on shelves). I knew the facts said that whole armies of women read them, but it was only two years ago that I'd met Courtney at a midtown Barnes & Noble. I'd just left work and was reaching for a romance from the circular wire rack when I heard a girl's voice behind me.

'You're not alone, you know,' it said.

I'd turned around to see a pretty girl about my age with a heart-shaped face and naturally pink lips. She looked like a china doll with ringlets reminiscent of Nelly's from *Little House on the Prairie*, and her other features were so delicate they looked like they might crack at any moment.

'Excuse me? Are you talking to me?' I asked, quickly covering my copy of *Every Woman's Fantasy* with an oversized English-Greek dictionary that resided nearby.

She nodded and moved in closer to whisper, 'I'm just saying, you don't have to be embarrassed any longer. There are others.'

'Who said I'm embarrassed?' I asked.

She peered down at my now-shielded book and raised an eyebrow. 'Look, my name's Courtney and I'm hooked on them, too. I've got a college degree and a real job and I'm not afraid to admit that I love these goddamn books. There's a whole group of us, you know. We meet once or twice a month to talk about them, have a few drinks, convince each other that it's okay to do what we do. It's part book club and part therapy session.' She rooted through her Tod's shoulder bag and found a crumpled receipt. She uncapped a Montblanc pen with her teeth and scrawled an address in SoHo and an email address.

'Our next meeting is this Monday night. Come. I've included my email address if you have any questions, but there's not much to know. We're reading this' – she discreetly flashed a copy of *Who Wants to Marry a Heartthrob?* – 'and we'd love to have you.'

Perhaps it's a sign of true addiction that I actually showed up at a stranger's apartment a week later. I soon learned that Courtney had been right. Each of the other girls was smart and cool and interesting in her own way, and each loved romances. Except for one set of twin sisters, none of the women were friends or colleagues from the outside; all had stumbled upon the group in much the same way I had. I was surprised and somewhat delighted to see that I was the only one who was out about my habit: not one of the other girls had yet revealed to husbands or girlfriends or parents the real content of their book club. In the two years since I'd joined, only one had admitted her reading preferences to her boyfriend. The ridicule she endured from him was life-changing; she eventually broke up with him after realizing that no man who truly loved her (like a hero in a romance novel, it was implied) could ever mock her so mercilessly for something she enjoyed. We'd seen each other through new jobs and weddings and even one lawsuit, yet if we'd run into one another on the street or at a party, there'd be nothing more than a curt hello and a knowing look. After missing last week's meeting, I'd been looking forward to tonight's session all week, and I was not about to let Will ruin it for me.

Simon, Will, and I piled immediately into a car, but when we pulled up to the restaurant at Eighty-eighth and Second, we were clearly not the first to arrive.

'Brace yourselves!' Simon managed to hiss just before Elaine waddled over.

'You're late!' she barked, pointing to the back room, where a few people had gathered. 'Go deal with your people, I'll bring you back your drinks.'

I followed them to the back room of the casual but legendary restaurant and looked around. Books covered every square patch of wall space and competed only with framed and autographed photographs of what seemed like every author who'd published in the twentieth century. The woody and familiar ambience might just feel like a regular neighborhood joint had I not been able to recognize the handful of people who'd already clustered around the table set for twenty: Alan Dershowitz, Tina Brown, Tucker Carlson, Dominick Dunne, and Barbara Walters. A waitress handed me a premixed dirty martini and I began slurping at it immediately, downing the last drop just as the table filled completely with an eclectic group culled primarily from the media and politics.

Will was offering a toast for Charlie Rose, whose new book we were all gathered to celebrate, when the only other woman under forty leaned over and said, 'How'd you get roped into this one?'

'Niece of Will, given no choice.'

She laughed softly and placed her hand on my lap, which made me very nervous until I realized she was trying to discreetly shake my hand. 'I'm Kelly. I put together this little dinner party for your uncle, so I guess I'm sort of obligated to be here, too.'

'Nice to meet you,' I whispered back. 'I'm Bette. I was just sitting at their apartment earlier and somehow ended up here. It seems like a very nice dinner, though.'

'Honestly? Not really my scene, either, but I think it works for your uncle's purpose. Good group of people, everyone who RSVP'd actually showed – which never happens – and Elaine held up everything on her end, as usual. All in all, I'm pretty happy with the outcome. Now if we can just keep them all from getting too drunk, I'll say the evening was perfection.'

The group quickly polished off the first round of cocktails and was now tucking in to the salads that had appeared before them. 'When you say you "put this on," what does that mean, exactly?' I asked more out of an effort to just say something rather than any genuine interest, but Kelly didn't seem to notice.

'I own a PR company,' she said, sipping a glass of white wine. 'We represent all sorts of clients – restaurants, hotels, boutiques, record labels, movie studios, individual celebrities – and we do what we can to increase their profile through media placements, product launches, stuff like that.'

'And tonight? Who do you represent here? Will? I didn't know he had a PR person.'

'No, tonight I was hired by Charlie's publisher to put together a dinner of media elites, those journalists who are recognizable in their own right. The publisher has internal PR people, of course, but they don't always have the connections to put on something this specialized. That's where I come in.'

'Got it. So how do you know all these people?'

She just laughed. 'I have an office full of people whose job it is to know *everyone* worth knowing. Thirty-five thousand names, actually, and we can get in touch with any one of them at any time. It's what we do. Speaking of which, what do you do?'

Thankfully, before I could piece together some appropriate white lie, Elaine discreetly beckoned for Kelly from the doorway, and she scooted out of her chair and strolled to the front room. I turned my attention to Simon, who was seated on my left, before noticing that a photographer was subtly snapping photos without a flash from a crouching position in the corner.

I remembered the first media dinner Will had dragged me to, when I was fourteen and visiting from Poughkeepsie. We'd been at Elaine's that night, too, also for a book party, and I'd asked Simon, 'Is it weird that there's someone taking pictures of us eating dinner?'

He'd chuckled. 'Of course not, dear, that's precisely why we're all here. If there's no photo in the party pages, did the party really happen? You can't *pay* to get the kind of press he and his book will receive from tonight. That photographer is from *New York* magazine, if I remember correctly, and as soon as he leaves, another one will slip right in. At least, everyone hopes so.'

Will had begun teaching me that night how to talk to people. The key was to remember that no one cares what you do or think, so sit down and immediately begin asking questions to the person on your right. Ask anything, feign some sort of interest, and follow up any awkward silences with more questions about them. After years of instruction and practice I could manage a conversation with just about anyone, but I didn't enjoy it that night any more than I had as a teenager, so I said my good-byes and ducked out after the salad course.

The book club meeting was at Alex's apartment in the East Village. I jumped on the 6 train and scrolled through my iPod playlist until settling on 'In My Dreams' by REO Speedwagon. When I got off the train at Astor Place a very petite woman who resembled a school librarian literally body-checked me. I apologized for my role in the incident (being there) with a sincere 'Excuse me,' at which point she whipped around with the most contorted, demon-like face and screamed, 'EXCUSE ME? MAYBE THAT WOULDN'T HAVE HAPPENED IF YOU WALKED ON THE RIGHT SIDE OF THE SIDEWALK!' and then walked away muttering profanities. Obviously she could use a few hours with *The Very Bad Boy,* I thought.

When I had walked the long six avenues east, I rang the bell at Alex's building on Avenue C and began the dreadful climb. She claimed her studio was a sixth-floor walk-up, but considering a Chinese laundry occupied the ground floor and the numbers didn't begin for one full flight up, it was technically seven floors off the ground. She was your stereotypical East Village artiste, with head-to-toe black clothes, ever-changing hair color, and a small facial piercing that appeared to rotate regularly from lip to nose to brow. An East Village artiste with a passionate dedication to romantic fiction for women. She obviously had the most to lose if any of her peers found out – a sort of artistic street cred, if you will – and so we all agreed to tell her neighbors, if asked, that we were there for a Sex Addicts Anonymous meeting. 'You're more comfortable telling them you're a sex addict than a romance reader?' I'd asked when she'd given us the instructions. 'Clearly!' she'd answered without a moment's hesitation. 'Addiction is cool. All creative people are addicted to something.' And so we did as she wished.

She looked more punk than usual in a pair of rocker-chic leather pants and a classic faded CBGB T-shirt. She handed me a rum and Coke and I sat on her bed and watched her apply another six or so coats of mascara while we waited for the others. Janie and Jill were the first to arrive. They were fraternal twins in their early thirties; Jill was still in school, getting some sort of advanced degree in architecture, and Janie worked for an advertising agency. They'd fallen in love with Harlequins as little girls, when they would sneak-read their mom's copies under the covers at night. Following closely behind them was Courtney, my original link to the group and an associate editor at *Teen People* who not only read every romance novel ever written but who just so happened to enjoy *writing* them as well; and finally, Vika, a half-Swedish, half-French import with an adorable accent and a coveted job as a kindergarten teacher at an Upper East Side private school. We were clearly a motley crew.

'Anyone have any news before we dive in?' Jill asked as the rest of us slurped down our drinks as swiftly as the syrupy-sweet liquid would allow. She always took charge and tried to keep us on track, an utterly useless gesture considering our meetings more closely resembled group therapy than any sort of literary exploration.

'I quit my job,' I announced merrily, holding up my red plastic Solo cup.

'Cheers!' they all called while clinking cups.

'It's about time you left that nightmare,' Janie said.

Vika agreed. 'Yes, yes, your boss will not be missed, of this I am sure?' she asked in her sweet but odd accent.

'No, that's for sure, I won't be missing Aaron.'

Courtney poured her second drink in ten minutes and said, 'Yeah, but what are we going to do for a quote of the day now? Can someone forward them to you?'

At the second meeting I'd attended, I'd begun sharing the joy and wisdom of Aaron's inspirational quotes with the entire group. After introductory remarks, I'd read the best one from the previous few weeks and we'd all crack up. Lately, the girls had begun coming prepared with their own anti-quotes, nasty or sarcastic or mean-spirited little epigrams that I might take back to the office and share with Aaron, if I were so inclined.

'Which reminds me,' I announced grandly, pulling a printout from my bag, 'I received this one a mere three days before I left, and it's one of my all-time favorites. It says, "Teamwork: Simply stated, it is less me and more we." That, my friends, is insightful.'

'Wow.' Janie sighed. 'Thanks for sharing. I'm definitely going to try to figure out how to have less me and more we in my life.'

'Me, too,' said Alex. 'That goes nicely with a little quote I recently stumbled upon. It's from our friend Gore Vidal. "Whenever a friend succeeds, a little something in me dies."'

We all laughed until Janie interrupted with a rather shocking announcement. 'Speaking of bosses . . . I, uh, I had an incident with mine.'

'An incident?' Jill asked. 'You didn't tell me anything!'

'Well, it just happened last night. You were asleep when I got home, and I'm only seeing you for the first time now.'

'I'd like you to explain the "incident," please,' Vika said with raised eyebrows.

'We, uh, sort of hooked up,' she said with a coy smile.

'What?' Jill was shrieking at this point, staring at her sister with a combination of horror and delight. 'What happened?'

'Well, he asked if I wanted to grab dinner after we pitched a new potential client. We went for sushi and then drinks. . . .'

'And then?' I prompted.

'And then more drinks, and then the next thing I know, I'm naked on his couch.'

'Oh, my God.' Jill began to rock back and forth.

Janie looked at her. 'Why are you so upset? It's not such a big deal.'

'Well, I just don't think it's going to do great things for your career,' she replied.

'Well then, you obviously don't know how talented I can be in some areas, do you?' Janie smiled wickedly.

'Did you sleep with him?' Alex asked. 'Please say yes. That would really make my whole night. Investment banker Bette up and quits her job with no backup plan and you screw your boss? I'd feel like I was finally starting to have some influence around here.'

'Well, I don't know if I'd say we actually had sex,' Janie said.

'What the hell is that supposed to mean?' Alex asked. 'You either did or you didn't.'

'Well, if he weren't my boss, I probably wouldn't have even counted it. Just in and out a few times – nothing major.'

'That's more than I've done in two years,' I said.

'*Interesting*. What I'm wondering is just how many other guys fall into the not-major-enough-to-count category. Janie? Wanna fill us in?' Courtney asked. Alex returned from her fridge-and-hot-plate kitchen with a tray of shot glasses, each filled to the brim.

'Why even bother to talk about *The Very Bad Boy* when we have our own very bad girl right here?' she said and passed the glasses around the room.

We were off and running.

5

Another three weeks slipped by in much the same manner as my first month of unemployment, made only slightly less pleasurable by the daily phone calls from Will and my parents, who claimed to just be 'checking in.' Here's how it usually went:

Mom: Hi, honey. Any new leads today?
Me: Hi, Mom. I'm pounding the pavement. There's a lot that sounds promising, but I haven't picked the perfect thing yet. How are you and Dad?
Mom: We're fine, dear, just worried about you. You remember Mrs Adelman, right? Her daughter is the head of fund-raising for Earth Watch and she said you're welcome to call her, that they could always use more dedicated, qualified people.
Me: Mmm, that's great. I'll look into that. [Channel flip to ABC as *Oprah* begins.] I better get moving. I have some more cover letters to write.
Mom: Cover letters? Oh, of course. I don't want to keep you. Good luck, honey. I know you'll find something soon.

Aside from those seven painful minutes every day when I insisted I was fine, the job search was fine, and I was sure I'd find something soon, everything actually was terrific. Bob Barker, Millington, an apartment full of trashy paperbacks, and four bags of Red Hots a day kept me company as I languidly surfed online job sites, making the occasional printout and the even more occasional application. I sure didn't feel depressed, but it was kind of hard to judge, especially since I rarely left my building and thought of little besides how to maintain my current lifestyle without ever getting another job. You hear people all the time making statements like 'I was only out of work for a week and I went crazy! I mean, I'm just the kind of person who needs to be productive, needs to make a contribution, you know?' Nope, I didn't know. My cash flow was in jeopardy, of course, but I figured something would turn up eventually, or I'd throw myself at the mercy of Will and Simon. It would be silly to waste time worrying when I could be learning genuinely valuable life lessons from Dr Phil.

Collecting the mail killed a solid ten minutes each day. Although

I knew that the mail came at two each afternoon, I usually wasn't motivated to fetch it until late evening, when I would grab the armful of bills and catalogs and bolt for the elevator. Thirteenth floor. Unlucky thirteen. When I'd hesitated before seeing the apartment for the first time, the broker had sneered, saying something like, 'What, do you believe in astrology, too? You can't seriously be concerned about something so ridiculous . . . not when it's got central air-conditioning at this price!' And since it seemed to be a distinctly New York phenomenon to be abused by the people you paid to perform a service, I'd immediately stammered out an apology and signed on the dotted line.

Today, luckily, my mailbox contained the latest issue of *In Touch*, which would occupy at least another hour. After retrieving it, I unlocked the door, scanned the floor for potential water bugs, and braced for the usual hysterics from Millington. She always seemed convinced that this was the day I would abandon her forever and met my homecoming with a frenzy of wheezing, snorting, sniffing, jumping, sneezing, and submissive peeing so frantic that I wondered if she might one day die from the excitement of it all.

Remembering the half-dozen training manuals that the breeder had thrown in 'just in case,' I made a big show of ignoring her, casually setting down my bag and tossing my coat and calmly making my way over to the couch, where she immediately leapt into my lap and stretched herself upward to begin the ritual licking of my face. Her little wet tongue worked its way from my forehead to underneath my chin, incorporating an unsuccessful attempt at getting inside my mouth, before the kissing stopped and the sneezing began. The first one sprayed across my neck, but she managed to collapse before the real groove got going and she sneezed a giant wet spot onto the front of my skirt.

'Good girl,' I muttered supportively, feeling slightly guilty that I was holding her in midair at arm's length while her entire body shook, but a *Newlyweds* rerun was starting and the sneezing could last for ten minutes. I'd just recently reached the point where I could look at Millington and not think of my ex-boyfriend Cameron, which was definitive and welcome progress.

Penelope had introduced Cameron and me at some barbecue Avery had thrown when we were both two years out of school. I'm not sure if it was the shiny brown hair or the way his butt looked in his Brooks Brothers khakis, but I was smitten enough not to notice his tendency toward vicious name-dropping or the vile way he picked his teeth after each meal. For a while, at least,

I fell madly in love with him. He spoke lovingly of bonds and trades, his prep-school lacrosse days, and weekend jaunts to the Hamptons and Palm Beach. He was like a sociological experiment – a not-so-rare but alien creature – and I just couldn't get enough of him. Of course, it was doomed from the start – his family was a permanent fixture in the Social Register; my parents had once been on the FBI's dangerous agitators list due to protest activities. But when paired with my job in banking, his aggressive preppiness went far in showing my parents that I wasn't dedicating my life to Greenpeace. We moved in together a year after meeting, when both our rents went up at the exact same time. We'd been living together for exactly six months when we realized that we had absolutely nothing in common beyond the apartment, our jobs in finance, and friends like Avery and Penelope. So we did what any doomed-for-failure couple would do and immediately went shopping for something that could bring us closer together, or at least give us something to talk about other than whose turn it was to plead with the landlord for a new toilet seat. We opted for a four-pound Yorkie, priced at $800 per pound, as Cameron calculated for me more than once. I threatened to kill him if he announced one more time that he had, in fact, ordered entrées at Peter Luger bigger than this dog, and repeatedly reminded him that it had all been his idea. Oh, sure, there was the small issue of my being allergic to anything with fur, alive or stuffed, animal or outerwear, but he'd thought that one through, too.

'Cameron, you've seen me around dogs before. I don't know why you'd want to subject me – or yourself – to that again.' I was thinking of the first time I'd met his family for a winter weekend in the Adirondacks. They'd rounded out the picture-perfect WASP gathering – real fire in the fireplace! no remote control! no store-bought logs! – with tartan-plaid J. Crew pajamas, free-standing decorative wooden mallards, enough alcohol to warrant a liquor license, and two loping, oversized golden retriever puppies. I sneezed and watered and hacked to such an extent that his permanently tipsy mother ('Oh, dear, another glass of sherry should clear that right up!') began making passive-aggressive 'jokes' about being contagious and his openly drunk father actually set down his gin and tonic long enough to offer me a ride to the ER.

'Bette, don't worry about a thing. I've looked into all of that, and I've found us the perfect dog.' He looked smug and satisfied, and I mentally counted the days until the lease was up. One hundred seventy. I occasionally tried to recall what had attracted us in the first place, what had existed before the icy détente that had become the hallmark of our relationship, but nothing really specific emerged. He had always been a little dim, something that all the private schools had managed to mask but not repair. He was undeniably cute in that clean-cut, Abercrombie-catalog-boy way, and he did know how to pump out the charm when he needed something, but mostly I remember it just being easy: we had the same friends, the same fondness for chain-smoking and complaining, and a nearly identical pair of salmon-colored pants. Could a good romance have been modeled after my relationship with Cameron? Well, no, I don't suppose so. But his unspectacular, watered-down version of companionship in those weird, early postcollege years felt perfectly adequate.

'I don't doubt it's a very special dog, Cameron,' I said slowly, as though I were speaking to a third-grader. 'The problem is that I'm. Allergic. To All. Dogs. You understand that sentence, don't you?' I smiled sweetly.

He grinned, undeterred by the best bitchy, condescending tone I could muster. Impressive. He really was serious about this. 'I've made some calls, done some research, and I've found us – drum roll, please! – a hypoallergenic dog. Can you say "hypoallergenic"? C'mon, B, repeat after me, "hypo—"'

'You found us a hypoallergenic *dog*? What, do they breed them to be that way? The last thing I need in my life is some genetic mutation of an animal that will most likely send me straight to the hospital. No way.'

'Bette, don't you see? It's perfect. The breeder promised that since Yorkies have real hair, not fur, it's impossible to be allergic to them. Even for you. I made an appointment for us to pick one out on Saturday – they're in Darien, right near my office, and they promised to reserve at least one boy and one girl so we could have our pick.'

'I have to work,' I said listlessly, already vaguely aware that adding responsibility to this particular relationship was only going to sabotage it faster. Perhaps we should have just ended it then, but December's such a tough time to find apartments, and the place really was a decent size, and well, dogs are cute and distracting . . . so I agreed. 'All right, Saturday it is. I'll go to the office Sunday instead, and we can go pick out our hypoallergenic dog.'

He bear-hugged me and told me all about his plans to rent a car and maybe visit a few nearby antiques stores (this coming from the boy who'd argued tirelessly to retain his beanbag chair when we'd combined our stuff) and I wondered if maybe, just maybe, this little genetic mutation of a dog was the answer to all our problems.

43

Wrong.

So very, very wrong.

Well, that's misleading. The dog certainly didn't fix anything (surprise, surprise), but Cameron was right about something: Millington turned out to be hypoallergenic after all. I could hold her, snuggle her, rub her furry little mustache right against my face without so much as a hint of an itch. The problem was that the dog herself was allergic to everything. *Everything.* Somehow, her tiny little puppy sneezes seemed endearing when she was tucked among her littermates in the breeder's kitchen. It was adorable . . . the only little-girl puppy had caught a little cold, and we were there to nurse her back to vibrant puppy health. Only the cold didn't go away, and little Millington didn't stop sneezing. After three weeks of round-the-clock care and nursing – Cameron chipped in, I'll give him credit there – our little ball of joy wasn't improving, even with the nearly $3,000 we'd spent on vet consultations, antibiotics, special food, and two late-night emergency-room visits when the wheezing and choking got particularly terrifying. We were missing work, screaming at each other, and bleeding money in the process – my banking and his hedge-fund salaries were barely enough to cover the dog's expenses. Final doggy diagnosis: 'Highly reactive to most household allergens including, but not limited to, dust, dirt, pollen, cleaning fluids, detergent, dyes, perfumes, and other animal hair.'

The irony was not lost on me. I, the most allergic person on earth, somehow now owned a dog that was allergic to absolutely everything. It would've probably been funny if Cameron, Millington, or I had slept more than four consecutive hours in three weeks, but we hadn't, and it wasn't. *What would most people do in this situation?* I remember asking myself as I lay awake on the first night of the fourth sleepless week. A sane couple in a functional relationship would simply shuttle the dog right back to the breeder and take a long vacation somewhere warm and laugh about what would surely become a fond memory and funny future party story. So what did I do? I hired an industrial cleaning service to remove every piece of hair, every particle of dirt, every smudge from every surface so the dog could breathe, and I asked Cameron to leave once and for all, which he did. Penelope told me eight months later – with what I thought was a little more excitement than the event required – that he'd gotten engaged to his new girlfriend while wearing a kilt on a golf course in Scotland, and that they were moving to Florida, where her family owned a small island. That clinched it: everything worked out exactly as it was meant to. Two years later, the dog had learned to tolerate the smell of

Wisk, Cameron toasted fatherhood in the family tradition with a stiff gin and tonic, and I had someone so excited to see me each night that she peed upon my arrival home. Everyone's a winner.

Millington finally stopped sneezing and settled into a narcoleptic nap beside me, her little body pushed against the side of my leg, rising and falling with her rhythmic breathing, in tune to the TV that I constantly kept on for background noise. After *Newlyweds*, I stumbled across a *Queer Eye* marathon. Carson picked through some straight guy's closet with a pair of salad tongs, describing items as 'So Gap '87,' and I realized they'd probably be just as horrified to check out my closet – as a girl, I was probably expected to do a little better than the off-the-rack Ann Taylor suits, one measly pair of Sevens, and the cotton tank tops that constituted my 'going out' clothes.

The phone rang a little after eleven P.M. I held it and stared, patiently waiting for the caller ID to register my caller. Uncle Will: to screen or not to screen? He always called at odd hours on his deadline nights, but I was too exhausted from my day of nothingness to deal with him. I stared at it a moment longer, too lazy to make any real decision, but the machine had already answered.

'Oh, Bette, pick up the goddamn phone,' Will said into the machine. 'I find this caller-revealing feature highly offensive. At least have the savoir faire to brush me off once we're mid-conversation – anyone can look at a little computer screen and decide not to answer; the impressive accomplishment is extricating yourself from the real-time situation of actually speaking with the person.' He sighed. I laughed.

'Sorry, sorry, I was in the shower,' I lied.

'Sure you were, darling. In the shower at eleven P.M., just getting ready to go out for the night, huh?' he teased.

'Would that be so hard to believe? I have gone out before, you know. Penelope's party? Bungalow 8? The only person in the Western Hemisphere who didn't know where it was? Any of this ringing a bell for you?' I took another bite of my Slim Jim, a snack I'd been inhaling since I'd discovered how much they horrified my parents.

'Bette, that was so long ago I barely remember it,' he pointed out thoughtfully. 'Look, darling, I didn't call to give you a hard time again, although I fail to see any reason why an attractive girl your age should be sitting home alone at eleven on a Thursday night, chewing imitation meat sticks and talking to a five-pound dog, but that's neither here nor there. I just had the most brilliant idea of all. Do you have a minute?'

We both snorted. I clearly had nothing but. 'You've got it all wrong. I'm talking to a four-pound dog.'

'Bette, listen to me. I don't know why I didn't think of this earlier, I'm positively idiotic for not seeing the potential, but tell me, darling, what did you think about Kelly?'

'Who's Kelly?'

'The woman you sat next to at Charlie's dinner at Elaine's. So, what do you think?'

'I don't know, she seemed really nice. Why?'

'Why? Darling, you are positively brain-dead these days. What do you think about *working* for Kelly?'

'Huh? Who's working for Kelly? I'm so confused.'

He sighed. 'Let's take this slowly. Being that you are currently out of a job and seem to be enjoying that fact a little too much, I was thinking that perhaps you would like to work for Kelly.'

'Planning parties?'

'Darling, she does a lot more than just plan parties. She chitchats with club owners and trades on gossip she has about other people's clients to the columnists so they'll write good things about her own clients and sends gifts to celebrities to convince them to attend her events so the press will as well – all the while looking very pretty when she goes out every night. Yes, the more I think about it, the more I'd like to see you in event-planning. How does that sound?'

'I don't know,' I said. 'I was thinking it might be good to do something, uh, you know, something sort of . . .'

'Meaningful?' he offered, pronouncing the word the same way one might say 'murderous.'

'Well, yeah. I mean, not like that, not like the parents,' I mumbled. 'But I do have a meeting at the Meals on Wheels head-quarters tomorrow. Just a change of pace, you know?'

He was quiet for a moment and I knew he was weighing his words carefully. 'Darling, that sounds lovely, of course. It's always sweet to make the world a better place. However, I would be remiss if I didn't remind you that rerouting your career path in that direction puts you at risk of falling back into your Patchouli Rut. You remember what that was like, don't you, darling?'

I sighed. 'I know, I know. It just seemed like it might be interesting.'

'Well, I can't necessarily say that planning parties would be as interesting as helping the needy, but it would be a hell of a lot more fun. And that, darling, is not a crime. Kelly's company is new, but easily one of the best – boutique-y, very impressive client list, and a great place to meet all sorts of wildly shallow and self-involved people and get the hell out of that hole in which you've recently sequestered yourself. Are you interested?'

'I don't know. Can I think about it?'

'Of course you may, darling. I'll give you twenty-four hours to debate all the pros and cons of accepting a job where you can party for a living. I expect you'll make the right decision.' He clicked down the receiver before I could say another word.

I went to sleep late that night and spent the entire next day procrastinating. I played with the puppies at the pet shop on the corner, made a pit stop at Dylan's Candy Bar, and alphabetized the paperbacks visible in my apartment. Admittedly, I was curious what the job would entail. There was a part of it that seemed really appealing, the chance to meet some new people and not sit at a desk all day long. Years of banking had taught me to be very good with details, and decades of Will-prompted socializing had ensured I could pretty much talk to anyone about anything – and actually seem interested, even if I was crying with boredom inside. I always felt a little awkward, a bit out of place, but I could keep my mouth moving at all costs, which went a long way toward making people think I had some social skills. And of course, the mere thought of printing more résumés and pleading for interviews sounded significantly more dreadful than organizing parties. All of this, combined with the fact that my checking account had just dipped below the minimum required amount, made PR sound like a dream.

I called Will.

'Okay. I'll write to Kelly and ask for some more information about what it entails. Can you just give me her email address?'

Will snorted. 'Her what?' He refused to buy so much as an answering machine, so a computer was definitely out of the question. He typed all his columns on a clanking typewriter and had one of his assistants key it into Microsoft Word. When it came time for him to edit, he'd stand over her shoulder, press his finger to the computer screen, and command her to delete, add, and expand the text as he watched.

'The special computer address where I can write her an electronic letter,' I said slowly.

'You're adorable, you really are. Bette, don't be ridiculous. Why would you need that? I'll have her call you to set a starting date.'

'Don't you think we're getting a little ahead of ourselves, Will? It might be better if I sent her a résumé first, and then if she likes it, we can take it from there. That's how it usually works, you know.'

'Yes, I've heard that,' he said, sounding more and more disinterested. 'Time wasting at its best. You'd be perfect for the job because you've honed those banking skills – detail-oriented, anal-retentive, deadline-adherent. And I know she's a great girl because she used to be my assistant. I'll just give her a little call and let her know how lucky she'd be to have you. Not a thing to worry about, my dear.'

'I didn't know she was your assistant!' I said, mentally trying to calculate Kelly's age.

'Indeed. I had her straight out of college. Hired her as a favor to her father. Best thing I ever did – she was bright and motivated and got me organized, and I, in turn, trained her from scratch. She went on to work at *People* and then switched to PR. She'll welcome you aboard. Trust me.'

'Okay,' I said with not a little hesitation. 'If you think so.'

'I know so, darling. Consider it done. I'll have her call you to discuss the details, but I anticipate no problems whatsoever. As long as you edit that wardrobe of yours to eliminate all skirt suits – and anything that looks like a skirt suit – I think everything will be just fine.'

6

Kelly herself was waiting in the building's lobby and embraced me like a long-lost friend when I arrived for my first day as instructed, at exactly nine A.M.

'Bette, honey, we're so happy to have you with us!' she breathed, casting a quick glance over my outfit. A fleeting, wide-eyed look – not quite panic, closer to distress – passed over her face before she fixed on a broad smile and led me by the hand to the elevator.

I'd had the good sense to avoid a full suit, but it wasn't until I'd caught a quick glimpse of everyone else's attire that I realized I still hadn't calculated correctly. Apparently my notion of business casual (cuffed charcoal gray pants, baby blue Oxford shirt, and understated low heels) differed slightly from that of the rest of the staff at Kelly & Company. The office was a sprawling downtown space with floor-to-ceiling windows that afforded views all the way down to Wall Street and west to New Jersey, giving it a decidedly loft-like feel. Around a large circular table sat a half-dozen people; each and every one, without exception, possessed unnervingly good looks and wore all black. The most malnourished-looking of the girls called out to Kelly, 'Page Six for comment on prenup trend, line two,' and Kelly motioned for me to take a seat before reaching up and adjusting what looked like a very tiny earpiece. A second later she was greeting someone on the other line with giggles and compliments while pacing the length of the southern-facing windows. I sat next to the super-skinny girl and turned to introduce myself but found myself staring at her hand, one finger of which pointed upward in a clear sign that I should wait. It was then that I noticed that each person around the table was chatting enthusiastically at the exact same time, although it didn't appear that they were talking to each other. It took me another moment to see that they all had tiny wireless phones tucked into their ears. I didn't know then that in a few short weeks I would feel completely naked – exposed! – without that phone constantly attached to the side of my face . . . right then it just looked weird. The girl nodded gravely a few times and glanced in my direction, muttering something indecipherable. I politely looked away and waited for someone to notice me.

'Hello? Hello? What did you say your name was?' I heard her ask as I surveyed the rest of the group. It was a surprisingly even split between guys and girls, their primary commonality being the level of almost-disturbing attractiveness among them. I was beginning to stare when I felt a tap on my back.

'Hey,' the skinny one said. 'What's your name?'

'Me?' I dumbly asked, convinced she was still on the phone. She laughed. Not nicely. 'Who else's name do you think I don't know here? I'm Elisa.' The hand she held out was ice-cold and very, very thin. I watched a diamond right-hand ring swing around her emaciated middle finger in little loops before I remembered to respond.

'Oh, hi. I'm Bette. Bette Robinson. It's my first day.'

'Yeah, I heard. Well, welcome aboard. Kelly's not likely to get off that call anytime soon, so why don't I introduce you around?' She worked her wavy reddish-blond hair into a messy topknot and secured it from underneath with a claw clip. A few strands in front fell out and she tucked them behind her ear. She felt to make sure that the hair was sprouting just so from the clip in that cool, casual way I always tried to achieve but could never manage, and then she stuck a pair of oversized black plastic sunglasses on her head to hold everything together. I could see from the silver G's that they were Gucci. She was effortlessly chic, and I had the feeling I could simply watch her forever.

Elisa walked to the far end of the table and flicked the light switch three times in quick succession. Immediately I heard a chorus of voices announcing to their headsets that a very important person was calling for them on the other line, and could they call back in just a few moments? Almost simultaneously, six manicured hands reached toward six ears and removed six earpieces, and within seconds, Elisa had commanded the complete attention of the entire room without saying a word.

'Hey, everyone, this is Bette Robinson. She'll be working primarily with Leo and me, so try not to give her a hard time, okay?'

Nods all around.

'Hi,' I said, my voice sounding squeaky.

'That's Skye,' Elisa started, pointing at an edgy-looking girl in dark indigo jeans, a tight, long-sleeved black T-shirt, a two-inch-thick leather belt with a massive jeweled buckle, and the most fabulous pair of broken-in cowboy boots I'd ever seen. She was pretty enough to pull off her ultra-boyish short haircut, which only complemented her curvy, feminine figure. Again, I just wanted to sit and stare, but I managed to say hello, and Skye returned my greeting with an enigmatic smile. 'Skye's working on the Kooba bag account right now,' Elisa said before turning her pointing finger on the next person. 'That's Leo, the other senior person besides me. And now you,' she added in a tone I couldn't quite identify.

'Hi, honey, nice to meet you,' Leo said, standing up from his chair to kiss me on the cheek. 'Always glad to have another pretty face in the office.' He turned to Elisa and said, 'Sorry, sweets, but I've got to run and meet the Diesel jeans guy for a late breakfast. Tell Kelly for me?' She nodded as he slung a messenger bag across his chest and bolted toward the door.

'Davide, say hello to Bette,' Elisa instructed the only guy left at the table. Davide's dark eyes peered out broodingly from under heavy eyelashes and a thick lock of dark hair. He ran his fingers through the front part and stared at me. After a few more awkward moments he said 'Allo' in what immediately sounded like a questionable accent.

'Hi, Davide,' I said. 'Where is that great accent from?'

'He is originally from Italy, of course,' Elisa answered quickly on his behalf. 'Can't you tell?'

I decided then and there that there was something going on between Elisa and Davide – there was a vibe between them that just screamed 'dating,' and I congratulated myself on being perceptive enough to figure it out. But before I finished marveling at my own cleverness, Elisa fell into Davide's lap, wrapped her arms around his neck like a little girl would with her daddy, and then kissed him full on the mouth in a most undaughterlike manner.

'Seriously, Elisa, spare us the office PDA, will you, please?' Skye whined, her eyes rolled back quite far in her head. 'It's bad enough we all have to envision you guys having sex on your own time – don't make it a reality for us, okay?'

Elisa just sighed and stood up, but not before Davide managed to grab her left breast and squeeze. I tried to imagine two coworkers at UBS sharing the same interaction in the conference room and nearly laughed out loud.

'So, yeah,' she continued as though the mini in-office grope session hadn't occurred. 'Skye, Leo, and Davide are the senior people. Those three over there' – she pointed to three pretty young girls, two blonds and a brunette, who sat hunched over PowerBook laptops – 'they're the List Girls. Responsible for making sure we have all the information for everyone we'd ever want or need to attend an event. You know how someone once said that there are only a few people worth knowing in the world? Well, they know them.'

'Mmm, I see,' I mumbled, although I had no idea what she was saying. 'Totally.'

Three hours later I felt like I'd worked there three months. I observed a staff meeting where everyone lounged casually around the loft drinking bottles of Diet Coke and Fiji water and talking about the party they were throwing for Candace Bushnell's new book. Skye ran through a checklist as various people updated her on the venue, invitation status, menu, sponsors, photographer placement, and press access. When she was finished, Kelly hushed the room and had one of the List Girls read the most recently updated RSVP list as if it were the word of God. Each name elicited a nod, a sigh, a smile, a mutter, a head shake, or an eye-roll, although I recognized only a handful of them. Nicole Richie. Karenna Gore Schiff. Natalie Portman. Gisele Bundchen. Kate and Andy Spade. Bret Easton Ellis. Rande Gerber. The entire cast and crew of *Sex and the City*. Nod, sigh, smile, mutter, shake, roll. It went on for nearly three hours, and by the time they'd finished debating the merits and pitfalls of every single individual – what each might add to the party and, therefore, the coverage or, worse, what they might take away – I was more exhausted than I would have been had I just hung up on Mrs Kaufman. By two o'clock, when Elisa asked if I wanted to grab a coffee with her, I couldn't say yes fast enough.

We each smoked a cigarette on the walk over and I was struck by the sudden and overwhelming desire to be sharing a plate of falafel on the bench outside UBS with Penelope. Elisa was providing some sort of running commentary on office politics, who really ran the show (her), and who really wanted to (everyone else). I called upon my valuable can-talk-to-anyone-about-anything skill and kept asking her questions while tuning out her answers entirely. It wasn't until we were settled into a corner table with our coffees – Elisa's was skim, decaf, and dark – that I actually heard something she said.

'Oh. My. God. Will you fucking *look at that*?' she hissed.

I followed her gaze to a tall, lanky woman who was wearing

a very unremarkable pair of jeans and a basic black blazer. She had sort of drab, brownish hair and a fairly mediocre body, and everything about her seemed to say 'average in every way.' Elisa's excitement seemed to indicate the woman was a celebrity, but she didn't look the least bit familiar to me.

'Who is it?' I asked, leaning in conspiratorially. I didn't really care, but thought I should.

'Not "who," "what"!' she practically scream-whispered. She hadn't yet moved her eyes from the woman.

'What?' I asked, still clueless.

'What do you mean, "what"? Are you *kidding*? Do you not see it? Do you need glasses?' I thought she was mocking me, but she reached into her oversized tote bag and pulled out a pair of wire-rims. 'Here, put these on and *check that out.*'

I continued to stare, clueless, until Elisa leaned in closer and said, 'Look. At. Her. Bag. Just try and tell me it's not the most gorgeous thing you've ever seen.'

My eyes went to the large leather bag the woman had nesting in the crook of her elbow while she ordered her coffee. When it came time to pay, she rested it on the counter, rooted through it, and pulled out her wallet before returning the bag to her arm. Elisa groaned audibly. It looked like any other bag to me, just bigger.

'Ohmigod, I can barely stand it, it's so amazing. It's the crocodile Birkin. Rarest of them all.'

'A what?' I asked. I briefly considered pretending to know what she was talking about, but it felt like too much effort at that point in the day.

She peered at me, examining my face as though she'd just remembered that I was there. 'You really don't know, do you?'

I shook my head.

She took a deep breath, sipped her coffee for strength, and placed her hand on my forearm as if to say, *Now listen closely because I'm telling you the only piece of information you'll ever need to know.* 'You've heard of Hermès, right?'

I nodded and saw a wave of relief wash over her face. 'Sure. My uncle wears their ties all the time.'

'Yes, well, much more important than their ties are their bags. The first huge hit was the Kelly bag, named for Grace Kelly when she began carrying it. But the really big one – about a thousand times more prestigious – is the Birkin.'

She looked at me expectantly and I murmured, 'Mmm, it looks lovely. Very nice bag.'

Elisa sighed. 'It sure is. That one's probably in the twenty-grand range. It's so worth it.'

I inhaled so quickly that I swallowed wrong and actually choked. 'It's how much? You're joking. That's impossible! It's a *purse*.'

'It's not a *purse*, Bette, it's a way of life. I would pay that in a heartbeat if I could just get my hands on one.'

'I can't imagine people are lining up to spend that much on a bag,' I pointed out. Which, in my defense, sounded eminently logical at that moment. I couldn't have known just how stupid I sounded, but luckily Elisa was prepared to inform me.

'Christ, Bette, you really have no clue, do you? I didn't think there was anyone left on the planet who wasn't at least on the *list* for a Birkin. Put yourself on immediately and maybe – just maybe – you'll get one in time to give your daughter one someday.'

'My daughter? Twenty thousand dollars for a bag? You're kidding.'

At this point Elisa collapsed in frustration and put her head down on the table. 'No, no, no,' she moaned, as though in great pain. 'You just don't get it. It's not just a *bag*. It's a lifestyle. It's a statement. It summarizes who you are as a person. It's a *reason for living*.'

I laughed at her melodrama. She bolted upright in her seat again and began talking at a rapid-fire pace.

'I had a friend who fell into a horrible depression after her favorite grandmother died and her boyfriend of three years broke up with her. She couldn't eat, couldn't sleep, couldn't drag herself out of bed. She got fired because she never showed up for work. Huge bags under her eyes. Refused to see anyone. Never answered her phone. When I finally showed up at her apartment after months of this, she confided that she was considering suicide.'

'How awful,' I murmured, still racing to keep up with the rapid subject change.

'Yeah, it was awful. But you know what got her through? I'd stopped at the Hermès store on the way over to her apartment, asked for an update . . . just in case. And you know what? I was able to tell her when I got there that she was only eighteen months away from her Birkin. Do you believe it? Eighteen months!'

'What did she say?' I asked.

'What do you think she said? She was ecstatic! The last time she'd checked it was going to be five years, but they'd trained a whole new crew of craftsmen and her name was due up in a year and a half. She got in the shower that very moment and agreed to go to lunch with me. That was six months ago. Since then she got her job back and has another boyfriend. Don't you see? That Birkin gave her a reason to live! You simply cannot kill yourself when you're that close . . . it's just not an option.'

It was my turn to examine her to see if she was joking. She was not. In fact, Elisa looked positively radiant from her retelling of the story, as though it had inspired her to live her own life to the fullest. I thanked her for educating me in the ways of the Birkin and wondered what, exactly, I had gotten myself into. This was a far cry from investment banking, and I clearly had a lot to learn.

7

It was seven-thirty in the evening on day four of my working at Kelly & Company as a party planner. The newsstand near my apartment had only a single copy of the New York *Daily News* with Will's column by the time I headed home after work. I'd been reading 'Will of the People' nearly every week since the time I'd learned the alphabet, but for some reason I'd never managed to subscribe to any of the papers that ran it. Of course, I had never broached the subject of the column's gradual shift to a soapbox for Will's crotchety rants about every social 'tragedy' that had befallen his beloved city, but it was becoming increasingly more difficult to keep my mouth shut.

'Bette! Great column today, if I do say so myself!' my doorman, Seamus, howled boozily as he pulled open the door to my building and waved a copy of the paper. 'That uncle of yours hits the nail on the head every time!'

'Is it good? I haven't read it yet,' I said absently, walking and talking quickly, the way people do when they're trying desperately to avoid a conversation.

'Good? It's fantastic! Now there's a man who gets it! Anyone who can poke a little fun at Hillary Clinton is a friend of mine! I thought I was the only person in this whole city who voted for George W., but your uncle assures me I'm not.'

'Mmm. I suppose that's true.' I headed toward the elevator, but he was still going.

'Any chance he'll be coming 'round to visit you anytime soon? Would just love to tell him in person how much—'

'I'll definitely let you know,' I called as the elevator doors finally shut him out. I shook my head, remembering my uncle's one visit to my building and the way Seamus had fallen all over himself when he recognized Will's name. It was upsetting, to say the least, that Seamus personified my uncle's target demographic.

Millington nearly collapsed in paroxysms of joy when I opened the door, even more excited than usual now that I'd returned to working all day. Poor Millington. *No walk for you tonight,* I thought as I gave her a perfunctory scratch on the head and settled down to read Will's latest rants. She scampered off to use her Wee-Wee Pad, realizing immediately that she wasn't leaving the apartment today, either, and then jumped onto my chest to read with me.

Just as I was settling in with my folder of takeout menus, my cell phone vibrated across my coffee table like a wind-up toy. I debated whether or not to answer it. The cell phone was company-issued and, much like my new colleagues, didn't ever seem to rest. I'd been out the last three nights, attending events the company had put on, following Kelly as she did everything from consulting with clients to firing slow bartenders, hosting VIPs, and arranging for press passes. The hours were even more grueling than at the bank – a whole day of office work followed by a full night out – but the office buzzed with young, pretty people, and if one has to spend fifteen hours a day at work, I thought I might prefer DJs or champagne cocktails to diversified portfolios.

TXT MESSAGE! appeared on my color screen. Text message? I'd never before received a message or sent one. After a moment's hesitation, I looked at the screen and hit Read.

din 2nite @ 9? cip dwntn on w.broad. c u there.

What was that? Some sort of cryptic dinner invitation, for sure, but where and with whom? The only clue to its origin was a 917 number I didn't recognize. I dialed it and a breathless girl answered immediately.

'Hey, Bette! What's up? You in for tonight?' the voice said, crushing my hope that the person had simply dialed the wrong number.

'Uh, hi. Um, who is this?'

'Bette! It's Elisa. We've only worked together twenty-four/seven for the past week! We're all going out tonight to celebrate being done with the Candace party. It'll be the usual crew. See you at nine?'

I'd planned to meet Penelope at the Black Door since I'd barely seen her during my unemployment hibernation, but I didn't see how I could turn down my first social invitation from my new colleagues.

'Uh, yeah, sure, that sounds great. What was the name of that restaurant again?'

'Cipriani Downtown?' she asked, sounding a bit incredulous that I wasn't able to deduce as much from her earlier shorthand. 'You've *been*, right?'

'Of course. I love it there. Do you mind if I bring a friend? I had plans already and—'

'Fab! See you both in a couple hours!' she screeched and hung up.

I snapped my phone shut and did what every New Yorker does instinctively upon hearing the name of a restaurant: I checked *Zagat*. Twenty-one for food, twenty for decor, and a still respectable eighteen for service. And it wasn't a one-word name like Koi or Butter or Lotus, which might seem innocuous but almost always guaranteed an exceptionally horrid time. So far, everything looked promising.

'To see or be seen is never the question' at this SoHo Northern Italian where watching Eurobabes 'air kissing' and 'pretending to eat their salads' is more to the point than the surprisingly good 'creative' fare; natives may 'feel like foreigners in their own country,' but the high ratings speak for themselves.

Ah, so it was going to be another Eurobabe night. Whatever that meant. And more to the point, what was I supposed to wear? Elisa and crew seemed to rotate between black pants, black skirts, and black dresses at work, so it was probably safe to stick with the formula. I dialed Penelope at the bank.

'Hey, it's me. What's up?'

'Ugh. You are so unbelievably lucky that you left this wretched sweatshop. Is Kelly looking to hire anyone else?'

'Yeah, I wish. But listen – what do you think about meeting everyone tonight?'

'Everyone?'

'Well, not everyone, just my immediate work group. I know we had plans, but since we always go to the Black Door, I thought it might be fun to go to dinner with them. Are you up for it?'

'Sure,' she said, sounding too tired to move. 'Avery's going out with a bunch of friends from high school tonight and I was just so not interested. Dinner sounds fun. Where is it?'

'Cipriani Downtown. Have you been?'

'No, but my mother talks about it obsessively. She's been dying for me to become a regular.'

'Should I be upset that your mother and my uncle seem to know every cool place in the city, and we're completely clueless?'

'Welcome to my life.' She sighed. 'Avery's the same way – he knows everyone and everything. I just can't be bothered. The effort required for mere maintenance is too exhausting. But tonight will be fun. I'd like to meet people who plan parties for a living. And the food's supposed to be great.'

'Well, I'm not sure that's a huge selling point with this crowd. I've spent forty hours with Elisa this week and haven't seen her eat a thing. She seems to subsist solely on cigarettes and Diet Coke.'

'Hot-girl diet, huh? Good for her. You've got to admire that level of commitment.' Penelope sighed again. 'I'm headed home in a few. Want to share a cab downtown?'

'Perfect. I'll pick you up at the corner of Fourteenth and Fifth a little before nine. I'll call when I get in the cab,' I said.

'Sounds good. I'll wait outside. Bye.'

I headed for my closet. After some discards and retries, I settled on a pair of tight black pants and a plain black tank top. I extracted some decently high heels, bought during a shopping trip in SoHo, and took the time to blow out the exceedingly thick black hair I inherited from my mother – the kind that everyone thinks they want until they realize it barely fits in a ponytail and instantly adds thirty minutes to any preparation time. I even attempted some makeup, which got put to use so infrequently that the mascara wand was all clumpy and a few of the lipsticks were stuck inside their tubes. *No matter!* I thought, singing along to Mike & the Mechanics' 'The Living Years' as I worked on my face . . . this was even kind of fun. I had to admit, the end results were worth the extra effort: my love handles no longer bulged over the waistline of my pants, my boobs had retained their chubby-girl fullness even though the rest of me had shrunk, and the mascara I'd haphazardly brushed across my lashes had accidentally smeared to perfection, giving my somewhat bland gray eyes a sexy, smoldering look.

Penelope was waiting outside at exactly ten to nine, and we were deposited at our requested address right on time. There were a ton of restaurants on West Broadway, and everyone seemed to be clustered at outdoor tables looking exceedingly well-scrubbed and unnervingly happy. We had a little trouble finding the place because the restaurant management had neglected to post a sign. Perhaps it's an issue of practicality; since the shelf life of most New York hot spots is under six months, it actually leaves one less thing to remove when they close. Luckily, I remembered the street number from *Zagat* and we scoped it out from the far corner. Groups of scantily but expensively clad women congregated around the bar as older men kept their drinks filled, but I didn't see Elisa or anyone else from the office.

'Bette! Over here!' Elisa called, a champagne glass in one hand and a cigarette in the other. She was planted in the middle of Cipriani's outdoor tables, leaning seductively against one of the Italians' chairs, her branch-like limbs looking as though they might snap at any moment. 'Everyone else is inside. So glad you could come!'

'Jesus Christ, she's skinny,' Penelope muttered under her breath as we walked toward the tables.

'Hi,' I said and leaned in to kiss Elisa hello. I turned to introduce her to Penelope but noticed that Elisa was still waiting there, her face thrust forward and filled, eyes closed. She had expected the traditional Euro double kiss, and I'd given up halfway through. I'd recently read a convincing piece in *Cosmo* decrying the double kiss as a stupid affectation and decided to make a stand: there would be no more double kisses for me. I left her hanging but said, 'Thanks for inviting me. I absolutely love it here!'

She recovered quickly. 'Ohmigod, me, too. They have the best salads of anywhere. Hi, I'm Elisa,' she said, offering a hand to Penelope.

'I'm so sorry, that was so rude of me.' I flushed, realizing I must have sounded ridiculous to Penelope. 'Penelope, this is Elisa. She's been showing me around all week long. And, Elisa, this is Penelope, my best friend.'

'Wow, fab ring,' Elisa said, grabbing Penelope's left hand instead of her right and softly fingering the massive stone. 'That carat-glare is, like, blinding!' Penelope was, in fact, sporting her 'wearable' three-carat rock, and I wondered what Elisa would think of her second ring.

'Thanks,' Penelope said, clearly pleased. 'I just got engaged last—' But before she could finish, Davide grabbed Elisa from behind and wrapped his arms around her tiny waist, careful not to hug too hard and break her. He leaned in and whispered something in her ear and she threw her head back with laughter.

'Davide, honey, behave! You know Bette. Davide, this is Bette's friend, Penelope.'

We all air-kissed on both cheeks (my no double-kiss rule hadn't lasted twenty seconds), but Davide didn't manage to remove his eyes from Elisa for a single second. 'Our table. It is ready,' he announced gruffly in Italian-accented English, patting Elisa's bony ass and leaning his pretty face toward her neck again. 'Come in when you are *finito*.' Something about Davide's accent still didn't sound quite right. It seemed to meander from French to Italian and back to French again.

'I'm finished,' she sang merrily, tossing her cigarette underneath a table. 'Let's go in, okay?'

We had a table for six tucked in the back corner. Elisa immediately informed me that marginally cool people obsess about getting a table in the front of the restaurant, but the truly cool request tables in the back. Skye, Davide, and Leo comprised the rest of the group that had worked on the Candace Bushnell book party the night before, and I was relieved to see that Elisa and Davide were the only couple. They were all sipping drinks and arguing about something, looking relaxed in the way that only the truly confident ever can. And naturally, no one was wearing black. Skye and Elisa were wearing almost identical short dresses, one in a bright coral color with gorgeous silver heels and the other in a perfect aquamarine with matching metallic sandals that tied halfway up her calves. No matter that it was mid-October and relatively cold at night. Even the guys looked like they'd been prepped at Armani before dinner. Davide was still wearing his charcoal gray suit from work. Although it was significantly snugger than most American men would wear, it looked fabulous on his tall, built frame. Leo was the perfect combination of hip and casual in a pair of distressed Paper Denim jeans, a tight vintage T-shirt that said VIETNAM: WE WERE WINNING WHEN I LEFT, and the new orange Pumas for guys. I went to claim the last remaining seat next to Leo, but he hoisted himself effortlessly to his feet without so much as a break in his sentence, kissed both my cheeks, and pulled the chair out for me, and then one for Penelope, who was obviously trying as hard as I was to act like this was a usual night out for us. When we'd settled in, Leo handed us menus and motioned for the waiter to take our drink orders, although he still hadn't so much as paused in the conversation.

I racked my brain trying to think of some remotely cool drink, but after years of only drinking with my uncle, it was impossible. Absolut was popular these days, wasn't it?

'Um, I'll have an Absolut and grapefruit juice, please,' I mumbled when the waiter looked to me first.

'Really?' Elisa asked, looking at me, wide-eyed. 'I don't even think they serve Absolut here. Why don't we get a few bottles of wine for the table to start?'

'Oh, sure. That would be great.' Strike one.

'Don't feel too bad – I was going to order a beer,' Penelope leaned over and whispered. I laughed like it was the most amusing thing I'd ever heard.

Davide spoke to the waiter in fourth-grade Italian, supplementing with hand gestures and at one point kissing his fingertips as though the mere thought of his order was too delicious to resist. Elisa and Skye just gazed at him in adoration. He switched to his faux-accented English for the rest of us monolingual idiots. 'I have ordered three bottles of this Chianti to start, if this is acceptable. In the meantime, everyone prefer sparkling or flat?'

Elisa turned to me and announced, 'Davide is from Sicily.'

'Oh, really? How interesting,' I said. 'Are his parents still there?'

'No, no, he's been here since he was four, but he still has such affection for his birthplace.'

Votes were tallied for the bottled water preference – I wisely resisted saying that I'd be fine with plain old tap water – and Davide ordered three of each. By my calculations, we'd already spent just under $300 and hadn't so much as ordered an appetizer yet.

'Great call on the wine, Davide,' Skye announced while punching her manicured nails into her cell phone's keypad. Texting, I guessed. 'I can vouch for it personally. We've summered in Tuscany for years and it's the only one I'll touch.' She turned her full attention to her phone, which was ringing, and tucked it back into her bag after looking with distaste at the caller ID display.

I busied myself examining the menu, wondering if every employee of Kelly & Company was in possession of an enormous trust fund. I couldn't very well contribute much about the subtleties of Chianti. My parents' idea of 'summering' was driving from Poughkeepsie to Cayuga Lake in Ithaca, where they'd hold a vegan barbecue on the porch with locals and drink their licorice tea. Nothing like blowing your first week's pay on a single meal you didn't want to have in the first place.

'So how tough was last night?' Davide asked. 'I mean, what are the chances that not a single A-list celebrity showed up?'

'Some of the *Sex and the City* cast were there,' Leo pointed out thoughtfully.

'Um, excuse me, I don't think Chris Noth and John Corbett count as A-list!' Skye said. 'Did you see Sarah Jessica Parker? No! Besides, SATC' – she used the abbreviation here – 'is *so* over. The whole thing was a nightmare.'

The group had been commissioned by Warner Books to throw the book party for Candace Bushnell's newest novel, and apparently it had been a zoo. Since I hadn't worked on it from the beginning, I'd attended another event that night, a dinner welcoming the CEO of one of Kelly & Company's new accounts.

Leo sighed. 'I know, you're right, of course. It was just so, so . . . B and T!'

'Yes, it was, wasn't it? I mean, who were all those girls on the outside patio? They were positively *attacking* the champagne – you'd think they'd never seen it before. And those two guys with the Staten Island accents who actually got in a fight? Hideous,' Skye added.

'Yeah, Penelope, you didn't miss anything,' Elisa reassured her, even though Penelope clearly had no idea what anyone was discussing. 'That's the beauty of book parties, though. The publishers are usually so out of the loop, they have no clue whether it actually drew a good crowd or not.'

Davide delicately sipped his wine and nodded. 'At least we won't have to endure another "Why the List Makes the Party" speech from Kelly. I honestly don't think I could listen to it again.'

I'd been hearing about 'The List' since Monday, but Kelly hadn't yet taken any time to introduce me to the 'most comprehensive database of everyone worth knowing.' She'd set aside the next day, a Friday, to demonstrate for me the glory that is The List. I was still waiting for the other shoe to drop, not quite able to accept that Kelly really was the insanely upbeat woman she appeared to be, but so far she'd maintained her relentless optimism on full throttle. And even though I don't think Will had given her much of a choice in hiring me, she seemed genuinely happy to have me there. I'd invested four full days in studying her intently, desperate to discover some hideous flaw or irritation, and I still hadn't managed to uncover a single negative aspect of her personality. Could it be possible that she really was all-around adorable, sweet, and successful? The most serious offense I'd found so far was her tendency toward chipper emails with numerous emoticons. But she hadn't once used the word *powwow* or placed any sweaty hands anywhere inside my workspace, so I was more than content to let it slide.

My phone rang just as everyone began arguing about whether or not Kelly had already had her eyes done at the ripe old age of thirty-four, and although I scrambled to silence it, I realized that this crowd not only didn't mind if I answered it, they expected as much.

'Bette, hey, how are you?'

It was Michael, and he sounded slightly confused.

'Michael, honey, how are you?' Honey? I'd let it slip without even realizing it. The table looked on curiously, none more so than Penelope. 'Honey?' I saw her mouth at me questioningly.

'Honey?' Michael laughed on the other end. 'What, are you drunk? I got released early! Tell me where you are and I'll come meet you.'

I laughed ingratiatingly, totally unable to picture Michael, who was a dead ringer for Jon Cryer, punning in his sweetly dorky way as Davide waxed on about the villa they'd just rented in

Sardinia for next August. 'I'm at dinner with a few colleagues, but we'll be finished here in an hour or so. Can I call you when I get home?'

'Sure,' he said, sounding even more confused. 'Call me on my land line, though, because my cell's out of battery.'

'Talk to you then.' I clicked the phone shut.

'Was that *our* Michael?' Penelope asked, clearly curious.

'Who was thaaaaaaaat?' Elisa asked, leaning hungrily across the table. 'Love interest? Hot manager from the bank? Unresolved feelings that can finally be acknowledged because you no longer work together? Do tell!'

And even though the thought of having sex with Michael was less appealing than sleeping with my own uncle and Michael was madly in love with his sweet and adorable girlfriend and Penelope knew full well that Michael and I had absolutely nothing between us, I went with it. 'Um, something like that,' I said, deliberately looking down while the table's attention focused on me for the first time all evening. 'We're, uh, just figuring things out now.'

'Ooh,' Elisa squealed. 'I just knew it! Make sure Kelly adds him to The List so he can bring all his gorgeous banker friends to the events! What fun. Let's have a toast! To Bette and her new boyfriend!'

'Well, he's not exactly my—'

'To Bette!' everyone chorused, raising wineglasses and clinking. Penelope raised her glass but stared straight ahead. They all sipped. I gulped and nudged Penelope. Blessedly, everything started to get a little fuzzy around dessert.

'So I spoke to Amy and she said we're good for Bungalow tonight,' Leo announced, brushing his flawlessly highlighted hair away from his eyes. So far I'd heard them discuss the best places in the city to get a facial, the really stylish new men's flip-flops at John Varvatos, and how annoying it was when their favorite Pilates instructor started class ten minutes late. And only Leo was gay.

'Bungalow? Is that Bungalow 8?' I asked, my usual filter having been relaxed by the free-flowing wine.

Conversation slammed to a halt and four perfectly groomed and/or made-up faces swiveled toward me. It was finally Skye who summoned the strength to withstand the burden of my question.

'Yes,' she said quietly, refusing to make eye contact, clearly humiliated *for* me. 'Amy Sacco owns Bungalow 8 and Lot 61 and is a *very* good friend of Kelly's. We're all on the list for tonight, which is the best party of the week.'

Everyone nodded.

'I'm game for whatever,' Davide said, playing with Elisa's hair. 'As long as it's guaranteed we'll have a table. Can't deal otherwise – not tonight.'

'Obviously,' Elisa agreed.

When the check came it was already well after midnight, and even though Penelope was chatting amicably with Leo, I could tell she was dying to get home. But Bungalow sounded like fun, so I shot her a few significant looks and left for the bathroom, where I waited for her to meet me.

'What a nice night,' she said neutrally.

'Yeah, they're cool, aren't they? Something different.'

'Definitely. Hey, I hope you don't mind if I cut out early,' she said, sounding more than a little distant.

'Is everything okay? What's wrong?'

'No, nothing at all. It's just kind of late and I'm not sure I'm up for, uh, for a club. Avery and I agreed to meet at home tonight, so I'd better get going. Whatever, dinner was great. I think I'm just tired, but you go and have a good time, okay?'

'Are you sure? I could just as easily share a cab home and go to sleep. I'm not sure I'm up for it, either,' I offered, but she saved me the trouble.

'Don't be ridiculous. Go and have fun for both of us.'

We walked back to the group and took our seats again, where what I hoped would be a final bottle of wine was making its way around the table. When the waiter presented the check with a flourish to no one in particular, I inhaled sharply. A quick mental calculation told me that I would owe somewhere in the neighborhood of $250. But apparently splitting the bill wasn't an option because Davide reached for the little leather folder and nonchalantly announced, 'I've got this one.'

No one blinked or even attempted to argue with him.

He slipped a jet-black credit card into the folder and handed it to the waiter. There it was, the mythical American Express Black Card, available by invitation only to those who charged a minimum of $150,000 a year. I had only just learned about it myself. It was mentioned in a blind item, as in, 'Who needs a Black Card when she has a daddy with bottomless bank accounts?' in reference to an anonymous socialite's daughter. No one else appeared the least bit interested.

'We ready?' Elisa asked, smoothing her dress over her adorable little hips. 'We'll need two cabs. Leo and Skye, why don't you grab the first one? Davide, Bette, Penelope, and I will meet you there. If you get there first, I'd prefer the table closest to the bar on the left, okay?'

'Oh, listen, I think I'm going to head home,' Penelope said.

'Dinner was great, but I've got to be at work early tomorrow. It was so nice meeting all of you.'

'Penelope! You absolutely cannot go home. The night is just beginning! Come on, it's going to be a great party,' Elisa shrieked.

Penelope smiled. 'I'd love to, really I would, but I just can't tonight.' She grabbed her coat, gave me a quick hug good-bye, and waved to the rest of the table. 'Davide, thank you for dinner. It was so nice meeting all of you,' she said, and before I could tell her that I'd call her later, she was gone.

We all stumbled into our preassigned cabs while I managed to nod and make *hmm* sounds at the appropriate times. It wasn't until we were actually standing outside the velvet rope at Bungalow 8 that I realized I was slightly drunk from dinner and, having almost no experience whatsoever with remotely cool nightspots, was in a perfect position to do or say something really, really humiliating.

'Elisa, I think I better head out,' I said feebly. 'I'm not feeling great, and I need to be up early tomorrow for—'

She emitted a high-pitched shriek and her sunken face came alive. 'Bette! You've got to be joking! You're practically a Bungalow *virgin* and we're already here. Going out is part of your job now, just remember that!'

I was semi-aware that the thirty or so people in line – mostly guys – were staring at us, but Elisa didn't seem to care. Davide was doing some sort of clap-high-five-knuckle-bumping greeting with one of the bouncers, and I found that I was incapable of anything but the path of least resistance.

'Sure,' I muttered weakly. 'Sounds great.'

'Sammy, we're on Amy's list tonight,' Elisa announced confidently to Davide's bouncer. He was about six-three, two hundred twenty pounds, and happened to be the exact same guy who'd been working the door the night of Penelope's party. He didn't appear to be particularly amused by the chaos at the door, but as soon as Elisa unwrapped herself from him, he said, 'Of course, Elisa. How many of you are there? Come on in. I'll have the manager get you a good table.'

'Great, honey, thanks so much.' She pecked him on the cheek and grabbed my elbow, leaning in close to whisper in my ear: 'These guys think they're special, but no one would ever even talk to them if they weren't working the door here.'

I nodded, hoping he didn't hear us, even if he did deserve it. I glanced up and saw him peering back at me.

'Hey,' Sammy said, nodding at me in recognition.

'Hey,' I replied cleverly, managing to refrain from pointing out that he didn't appear to have a problem letting me in tonight. 'Thanks for that umbrella.'

But he didn't hear me; he'd already turned away to rehook the red velvet rope and announce to the remaining hordes that their time had not yet arrived. He said something into his walkie-talkie and pulled open the door. We cruised past the coat check and were immediately enveloped in a cloud of smoke.

'How do you know him?' Elisa asked as Davide greeted everyone within a twenty-foot radius.

'Who?'

'The door loser.'

'Who?'

'The idiot working the door,' she said, exhaling what appeared to be more than a lungful of smoke.

'You seemed to like him enough,' I said, remembering how warmly she'd embraced him.

'What else am I supposed to do? It's all part of the deal. Such a waste of a face. Do you know him?'

'No. He was pretty hostile to me at Penelope's engagement party a few weeks ago. Made me wait outside forever. I know I've seen him somewhere before, but I can't place him.'

'Hmm,' she murmured, sounding less interested with every passing second. 'Let's get a drink.'

For one of the hottest clubs in the country, it still didn't look all that major. The whole place was one rectangular room, with a bar at the far end and about eight tables with banquette seats along each side. People were dancing down the middle of the room while others congregated at the bar, and only the high all-glass ceiling and rows of palm trees made me feel that we were somewhere a touch exotic.

'Hey, guys, over here,' called Leo, who was tucked into a couch in the far left corner, just as Elisa had requested. A hidden DJ was blasting 50 Cent, and I noticed that Skye had already settled onto some guy's lap and was grinding rhythmically to the music. There was a sort of minibar set up on their table with scattered bottles of Veuve Clicquot, Ketel One, and Tanqueray. Carafes of orange, grapefruit, and cranberry juice were provided for mixers, as well as a couple bottles of tonic and sparkling water. Penelope had mentioned the prohibitive cost of her party, so I knew that we were paying many hundreds of dollars a bottle.

'What can I make you to drink?' Leo asked, coming up behind me.

I wasn't risking another uncool drink order, so I just asked for a glass of champagne.

'Coming right up,' he said. 'C'mon, let's dance. Skye, you coming?'

Leo stood, but in the last six minutes Skye had progressed to a full-fledged make-out with the random guy she was straddling. We didn't wait for an answer.

The crowd was almost uniformly beautiful. Everyone fell into a ten-year age range, from mid-twenties to mid-thirties, and they'd all obviously been there before. The women were tall and thin and completely comfortable baring wide expanses of thighs and ample décolletage in a decidedly untacky way. The men danced at their sides, moving their hands over hips and backs and shoulders, never perspiring, never letting a girl's drink run low. It was nothing like the one rebellious teenage night I'd spent awkwardly camped out in a corner, terrified of the writhing masses at Limelight.

By the time I'd finished scanning the scene, Leo had already selected a beautiful dark-haired guy. The two of them danced with a model-hot straight couple, all four of them moving perfectly in tune against each other's bodies. Occasionally they'd reposition themselves so the 'girls' would be facing one another, grinding.

I went to the bathroom, and before I could see who owned them I felt a pair of arms wrap themselves around me. I caught a glimpse of waist-length wavy hair, a sort of mousy light brown color, and I smelled the scent of smoke and mouthwash in equal parts.

'Bette, Bette, I can't believe how long it's been!' the girl shrieked into my shoulder. Her chin was squished against my breasts in a way that was fairly uncomfortable considering her identity was still in question. She hugged me for a few more seconds, and when she pulled away, I could not have been more surprised.

Abby Abrams.

'Abby? Is that you? Wow, it's been a really long time,' I said carefully, trying not to show just how unhappy I was to see her. I had nothing but terrible memories of her from college and had somehow managed to forget she existed once we'd all moved to the city. Until now, it had been a big enough place to spend a half-decade without a single run-in. My luck had clearly expired. The five years since college graduation had made her look harder, older than her age. She'd obviously had a nose job and an extra-heavy serving of collagen in the lip area, but most noticeable were her breasts. Her now super-sized chest seemed to occupy her entire four-eleven frame.

'I go by Abigail now, actually,' she immediately corrected. 'So crazy, isn't it? Of course, I'd heard you work at Kelly, so I knew I'd run into you here sooner or later.'

'Huh? What do you mean? How long have you been living in the city?'

She stared at me, slightly horrified, and pulled me by the wrist onto a couch. I tried to shake loose, but she maintained her death grip and leaned in much too close. 'Are you, like, serious? Have you not heard? I'm at the *vortex* of the media world!'

I had to use my left hand to cover my mouth while pretending to cough so she wouldn't see me laughing uncontrollably. Since our days at Emory, Abby had loved declaring how she was 'at the vortex' of something or other – sorority rush or the men's basketball team or the college newspaper. No one really knew what it meant – it was the wrong usage, actually – but for some reason she'd latched onto the phrase and refused to let go. We'd lived on the same floor our freshman year. I'd noticed right away that she seemed to have an uncanny knack for sensing people's insecurities. She was always grilling me on what boy I liked, only to 'coincidentally' be seen throwing herself on whoever I named within twelve hours of my admission. I'd overheard her once in the dorm bathroom grilling an Asian girl for tips on how to get that 'sexy, slant-eyed look' using an eye pencil. She'd once 'borrowed' one of her classmates' history papers and turned it in as her own, only admitting to the 'mix-up' once the professor threatened to fail both of them. Penelope and I met Abby around the same time, in freshman writing seminar, and we immediately agreed that Abby was to be avoided. She'd been creepy from the beginning, the kind of girl who would make subtle but mean comments about your hair or boyfriend or outfit and then feign horror and regret when you inevitably took offense. We ditched her often and regularly, and she never seemed to get it. Instead, she'd purposefully make contact in order to put us down. Not surprisingly, she'd never had any real girlfriends, but she kept herself quite busy working her way through nearly every fraternity house and athletic team at Emory.

' "Vortex of the media world," huh? No, I didn't know that. Where are you these days?' I asked in the most bored tone I could muster. I vowed not to let her get under my skin.

'Well, let's see. I started at *Elle* and then made the jump to *Slate* – so much smarter, you know? Had a brief stint at *Vanity Fair,* but the office politics were so intense. Now I'm freelancing – my byline's everywhere!'

I thought about that for a moment and couldn't remember seeing her name . . . anywhere.

'And you, missy, how's the new job?' she screeched.

'Um, yeah, it's been about a week, I guess, and it's pretty cool so far. I'm not sure if it's at the *vortex* of the public-relations world, but I like it.'

She sensed no sarcasm whatsoever, or she ignored it. 'It's such a hot firm; they're repping all the best clients these days. Ohmigod, I absolutely love your shirt – it's the absolute best call ever if you're looking to hide a little tummy, you know? I wear mine all the time!'

I involuntarily sucked in my gut.

Before I could point out something nasty, like how five pounds on her frame would look like twenty, she said, 'Hey, so tell me, have you spoken to Cameron recently? That was your boyfriend's name, right? I heard something about him leaving you for a model, but of course I didn't believe it.'

So much for not sinking to her level.

'Cameron? I didn't think you knew him. Then again, he is a guy who's breathing and living in New York City, so . . .'

'Oh, Bette, it's really so great to see you,' she said, ignoring my comment. 'Let me take you to lunch, okay? We have so much to catch up on. I've been meaning to call you forever, but you just vanished since college! Who do you hang out with? Still that quiet girl? She was so sweet. What was her name?'

'Oh, you mean Penelope? She's gorgeous and engaged and, yes, I still see her. I'll be sure to tell her you said hello.'

'Yes, yes, definitely do that. So, I'll call you at work next week and we'll go somewhere fab for lunch, 'kay? Congratulations on finally leaving that dreadful bank and joining the real world. . . . I can't wait to introduce you to everyone. There are just, like, so many people you need to meet!'

I was preparing what would surely be an even wittier response when Elisa materialized beside us. I never thought I'd be so happy to see her.

'Elisa, this is Abby,' I said, waving my arm at her listlessly.

'It's Abigail, actually,' Abby interjected.

'Right, uh-huh. And, Abby' – I looked at her pointedly and continued— 'this is my coworker Elisa.'

'Hey, we've met before, haven't we?' Elisa mumbled, her front teeth clamped around a cigarette as she dug in her bag for a lighter.

'Totally,' Abby said. She plucked a matchbook off the nearest table and gallantly lit Elisa's cigarette. 'Do you have another ciggie for me?'

They made the exchange and began chattering about some new gossip roundup called New York Scoop. I'd heard it discussed in the office. Apparently, even though it had been published for years, nobody had cared about it until the arrival of a saucy new column written by someone using the unclever pseudonym Ellie Insider. It was published twice a week in both the online and print versions, although Ellie's column – unlike similar Page Six columns by Cindy Adams or Liz Smith – did not have an accompanying photo of the writer. Now Abby was insisting that it was the hottest thing to hit media circles in years, but Elisa was saying that, according to her sources, only select groups from the fashion and entertainment world were reading it obsessively – although she predicted others would soon catch on. This conversation topic remained interesting for a solid minute and a half, before I had the blessed realization that I could simply excuse myself and leave.

It wasn't until then that I realized I was standing alone in a swarm of gorgeous people who all just happened to have amazing rhythm, and I couldn't move. Dancing had never been my thing. I'd somehow managed to shuffle my way through a few painful slow songs at high-school dances (always trying desperately to avoid the eight-minute rendition of 'Stairway to Heaven') and hop drunkenly along to the jukeboxes at our college dive bars, but this was truly intimidating. Before I could even manage to sway, I was overwhelmed with the same sixth-grade fears. It happened in a fraction of a second, but the feeling that everyone was staring at my baby fat and braces came rushing back. I needed to leave, or at the very least get back to the table and avoid the hell of dancing, but just as I made up my mind to escape, I felt a hand on the small of my back.

'Hi there,' said a tall guy with a British accent and a tan so perfect it could have only come from the great indoors. 'Dance?'

I had to consciously keep from turning around to see if he might be talking to someone else, and before I could even worry about my smoky breath or my shirt, which was damp with perspiration, he had pulled me toward him and started moving. Dancing? We were dancing! I hadn't been this close to someone since the last time a pervert on the subway had pressed up against me on the morning commute. *Re-lax, have fun, re-lax, have fun,* I chanted silently, hoping to remain calm and cool. But I didn't need to do much self-convincing at all; my brain checked out as my body snuggled closer to the golden-skinned god who was offering me another glass of champagne. I sipped that one and then downed the next, and before I knew what was happening, I was perched on his lap, laughing with the table about some scandal or another while the gorgeous stranger played with my hair and lit my cigarettes.

I'd entirely forgotten I was inappropriately dressed in black, that I'd just been insulted by the pint-sized bitch who used to torment me in school, and that I possessed nothing resembling rhythm. I remember watching, slightly reaction-impaired, as one of the Englishman's friends came over and asked who might be the new, charming creature on his lap. I didn't even realize they were talking about me until he hugged me from behind and said, 'She's my discovery – brill, isn't she?' And I, the charming creature, the *brill* discovery, giggled delightedly, grabbed his face between both my hands, and kissed him squarely on the mouth. Which is, thankfully, the very last thing I remember at all.

8

The sound of an angry male voice jolted me awake. I wondered briefly if there was actually someone standing above the bed, driving a shovel into my head. The throbbing was so steady it was almost comforting, until I realized that I was not, in fact, in my own bed. Nor was last night's all-black-all-wrong outfit in sight; instead, I was wearing a pair of unnervingly tight gray Calvin Klein boxer briefs and a giant white T-shirt that read SPORTS CLUB LA. *Don't panic,* I instructed myself, trying to make out the words of the faraway male voice. Think. Where were you and what were you doing last night? Considering that I was not in the general habit of blacking out and waking up in strange places, I congratulated myself on a good start. *Let's see. Elisa called, dinner at Cipriani's, cab to Bungalow 8, everyone at a table, dancing with . . . some tan British guy. Shit. The last thing I remember is dancing with a nameless man in a club and now I'm in a bed – albeit a huge, comfortable one with extremely soft sheets – I don't recognize.*

'How many times do I have to tell you? You simply cannot wash Pratesi sheets in hot water!' The male voice was shouting now. I jumped out of bed and checked for escape routes, but a quick glance out the window told me we were at least twenty floors off the ground.

'Yes, sir, I am sorry, sir,' said a whimpering female voice with a Spanish accent.

'I'm keen to believe that, Manuela, I really am. I'm a reasonable bloke, but this just cannot continue. I'm afraid I have to dismiss you.'

'But, sir, if I can just—'

'I'm sorry, Manuela, but my decision is final. I'll pay you your wages for the rest of the week, but that will be all.' I heard some rustling and muffled crying, and then there was nothing but silence until a door slammed shut a few minutes later.

My stomach sent me the signal that it wasn't going to tolerate its hangover much longer, and I glanced around frantically to locate the bathroom. I was rooting around for my clothes, debating whether it was better for him to see me half-clothed or throwing up since there clearly wasn't time to remedy both issues, when he walked in.

'Hello,' he said, barely glancing in my direction. 'Are you feeling all right? You were fairly pissed last night.'

His appearance distracted me to such an extent that I actually forgot I was about to be sick. He looked even tanner than I remembered, which was only highlighted by a skintight white T-shirt, flowy white pants, and some of the straightest, brightest teeth I've ever seen in a British mouth. He was like Enrique in *The Tycoon's Virgin Bride*, his looks utterly begging to be on a dust jacket.

'Uh, yeah, I guess I was. This, uh, has never really happened to me before. I'm afraid I don't even remember your name.'

He seemed to remember that I was an actual person and not a bed adornment, and sat down next to me on the pillow.

'I'm Philip. Philip Weston. And don't worry about it – I only brought you back here because I couldn't get two taxis and didn't want to maneuver to the East Side. Nothing happened. I'm not some rapist. I'm an attorney, actually,' he said with not a little pride in a thick, upper-crust English accent.

'Oh, well, thanks so much. I really didn't think I drank that much, but I don't remember anything after dancing with you.'

'Yes, well, it happens. Stressful fucking morning so far, don't you think? I loathe having my post-yoga calm shattered by rubbish like this.'

'Yeah.' *He* didn't just wake up in a stranger's bed, but I wasn't feeling great about my arguing position.

'My housekeeper was washing my Pratesi sheets in scalding-hot water. I mean, what bloody good are they if you have to double-check every move they make? Can you imagine what a disaster it would've been if I hadn't spotted it?'

Gay. He was definitely gay. He wasn't Enrique, but Enrique's fey friend Emilio. This was a tremendous relief.

'What would have happened, exactly?' I washed my own sheets in hot water and dried them on high because it seemed like the best way to make them softer faster. But then again, I'd bought them at Macy's and admittedly didn't spend all that much time thinking about it.

'What would have happened? Are you *serious*?' He strode across the room and spritzed some Helmut Lang cologne on his neck. 'She would've burned out the thread count, that's what! Those sheets cost twenty-eight hundred pounds for a king set, and she would have destroyed them!' He put the bottle down and began patting what I hoped was aftershave but was more likely moisturizer into his golden skin. I did a quick calculation: four thousand dollars.

'Oh. I guess I didn't understand. I, uh, I didn't know sheets could be that expensive. But I'm sure if I paid that much for them, I'd be concerned, too.'

'Yes, well, I'm sorry you had to endure all that.' He pulled the T-shirt over his head to reveal a completely bare, perfectly sculpted chest. It was almost a shame he was gay, considering just how good-looking he was. He closed the bathroom door briefly and turned the shower on, and then a few minutes later he emerged wearing only a towel. Pulling a dress shirt and suit from the oak-paneled walk-in closet, he handed me my clothes in a neatly folded pile and discreetly left the room while I stripped.

'Will you be all right getting home?' Philip called from what sounded like a million miles away. 'I must be off to work. Early meeting.'

Work. Jesus Christ, I'd completely and entirely forgotten that I was currently employed, but a quick check of the bedside clock reassured me that it was only a little after seven. He'd already been to yoga and back, and we couldn't have possibly gotten home before three in the morning. I had a brief but intense flashback to the one and only time I'd gone to yoga. I'd been fumbling through my first class for thirty minutes when the teacher had announced thirty seconds into our current pose – the half-moon pose, to be precise – that it was equivalent to eight hours of sleep. I'd accidentally snorted and she'd asked me if there was a problem. Luckily I'd been able to restrain myself from asking what was really on my mind: namely, why had no one before enlightened us to the miracle of the half-moon pose? Why, for all these centuries, have humans wasted a third of their lifetimes sleeping when they could've just bent at the waist for one half of one minute? Instead, I mumbled something about it being a 'really cool concept' and sneaked out when she wasn't looking.

Philip's hallway was longer than the entire length of my apartment, and I had to follow the sound of his voice to find the right room. Colorful abstracts hung on the walls and the dark-stained wood floors – real wood, not New York parquet – highlighted the stark, metal-frame furniture. The entire place looked like a Ligne Roset floor sample, as though it had been plucked directly from the showroom and put back together in this guy's apartment. I counted a total of three full bathrooms, two bedrooms, a living room, and a study (complete with floor-to-ceiling built-in bookcases, two Mac G4 computers, and a wine rack) before I found him leaning against his granite countertop, feeding blood oranges into a high-tech juicer. I didn't even own a can opener.

'You do yoga? I don't know any guys who do yoga.' *Any straight guys, that is,* I thought to myself.

'Of course. It's smashing strength training, and I love how it clears your mind as well. Very American, I suppose, but worthwhile nonetheless. You should try it with me.' And before I knew what was happening, he lifted me up on the counter, pushed my knees apart so he could come closer, and began kissing my neck.

Instinctively, I jumped off the counter, which resulted only in my pushing even farther into him.

'I thought, well, um, aren't you . . .'

Two clear green eyes stared back at me, waiting.

'It's just that, uh, considering last night and the whole, you know, Pratesi thing and the yoga class . . .'

Still waiting. No help here.

'Aren't you gay?' I held my breath, hoping he wasn't still in the closet or, worse, out but self-hating.

'Gay?'

'Yeah, as in, liking guys.'

'Are you serious?'

'Well, I don't know, it just seemed—'

'Gay? You think I'm a homosexual?'

I felt like I was roaming around on the set of some sort of reality TV show where everyone was in on the secret but me. Clues, so many clues, but no real information. I was trying to piece it all together as quickly as possible, but nothing was quite working out.

'Well, of course, I don't know you at all. It's just that, well, you dress so nicely and seem to care a lot about your apartment and, uh, you have Helmut Lang cologne. My friend Michael wouldn't even know who Helmut Lang is . . .'

He flashed those shiny teeth once more and tousled my hair like one would a toddler's. 'Perhaps you're just spending time with the wrong blokes? I assure you, I'm very, very straight. I've just learned to appreciate the finer things. Come now, there's time to give you a lift home if we hurry.' He shrugged on a cashmere sweater and grabbed his keys.

We didn't say anything at all in the elevator ride to the lobby, but darling Philip did manage to pin me against the wall and nibble on my lips, which somehow felt utterly disgusting and heart-stoppingly amazing all at once.

'Mmm, you're delicious. Come here, let me taste you one last time.' But before he could once again use my face as his own personal Chupa pop, the doors swept open and two uniformed doormen turned to witness our arrival.

'Bugger off,' Philip announced, walking ahead of me and raising his hand up, palm forward, to the grinning men. 'I don't want to hear it today.'

They snickered, obviously accustomed to the routine of Philip escorting strange women out of his apartment, and silently pulled open the door. It wasn't until we stepped outside that I had any idea where we were: Christopher and Greenwich, all the way west, about a block from the river. The famous Archives building.

'Where do you live?' he asked, pulling a silver helmet out from underneath the seat of a Vespa, which was resting under a mono-grammed tarp three feet from the building's entrance.

'Murray Hill. Is that okay?'

He laughed, not nicely. 'I don't know, you tell me. *I* sure wouldn't clamor to live in Murray Hill, but hey, whatever turns you on.'

'I meant,' I said tightly, no longer even attempting to keep up with his psycho-style mood swings, 'is it okay for you to drop me off? I can certainly take a cab.'

'Whatever you want, love. No worries for me. My office is midtown east, so you're right on the way.' He occupied himself by fishing his keys from his pants pocket and securing his Hermès bag to the back of the bike. Scooter. 'Let's just get a move on, okay? People are needing me right now.' He swung his legs over the bike and deigned to look my way. 'So?'

I was momentarily speechless, until he actually snapped his fingers. 'C'mon, sweetheart, decision time here. Ride or not? It's not so difficult. You sure didn't seem this indecisive last night. . . .'

I've always harbored the classic girl fantasy of having a real reason to slap some jerk across the face, and the opportunity had just presented itself in Technicolor. But I was dumbfounded by the finger snapping and the suggestion that something actually *had* happened last night, so I just turned my back and began walking down the block.

He called out, sounding almost worried, 'You don't have to

be so sensitive, love. I was just kidding around. Absolutely nothing went down last night. Not you, not me. . . .' I heard him chuckle at his own cleverness, but I just kept walking.

'Fine. Be that way. I don't have time for the drama right now, but I'll track you down. Seriously, it's not often a woman can resist my charms, so consider me duly intrigued. Leave your number with my doorman and I'll give you a call.' The Vespa's engine caught and he sped away, and although I'd just been insulted and abandoned, I still felt like I'd somehow won . . . if he was telling the truth, of course, and I actually hadn't slept with him in a wasted stupor.

The victory lasted all of forty minutes, during which time I jumped in a cab, raced home, took a washcloth-bath in the bathroom sink, and applied copious amounts of deodorant to my underarms, baby powder to my scalp, and scented moisturizer everywhere else. I raced around the apartment looking for clean clothes and wondered how I would ever manage to be a good mother when I couldn't even remember to care for my own dog. Millington was sulking in the corner under the coffee table, punishing me for abandoning her the previous evening. She'd also peed on my pillow for good measure, but there wasn't time to clean it up. I managed to wedge between the throngs of commuters and arrive at the office at exactly one minute after nine. I was fantasizing about devouring the only known hangover cure, a large street coffee and bacon, egg, and cheese on a buttered roll, when Elisa motioned me over. She'd saved a space near the sunniest window and appeared to be quite eager to talk to me.

The office was a giant rectangle, surrounded on all sides by sleek leather couches and sitting areas. There weren't technically individual desks, just two giant, half-moon-shaped tables that formed a circle with two small breaks where the half-moons didn't quite meet, allowing access to the shared faxes and printers in the middle. We each had our own laptop that we could either lock in the closet or take home at night, and workspace was doled out on a first-come-first-served basis every morning. We all scrambled to sit in the two or three spots around the circle where Kelly couldn't see your computer screen from her office, and Elisa had managed to snag a few feet of prime space. I dropped my laptop on the table and very carefully removed the coffee from its paper bag, taking care not to spill a single golden drop. Elisa was practically panting.

'Oh, Bette, sit the hell down already. Tell me everything, I can barely stand it.'

'Tell you what? I had a great time last night. Thanks for inviting me.'

'Shut up!' she was squealing, which appeared to be her only method of communication. 'How was . . .' Pause. Deep breath. 'Philippe?'

'Philippe? Don't you mean Philip? He sure didn't seem French to me.'

'Oh, God, you are truly missing the point. He's absolutely fabulous, don't you think?'

'Actually, I thought he was kind of a jerk,' I said, which was partially true. This also made him tremendously intriguing, of course, but it didn't seem necessary to admit that.

Elisa inhaled sharply and fixed her gaze on my face. 'What did you say?' she whispered.

'I said, I thought—'

'I heard you.' She was nearly growling now. 'I just can't imagine why you'd say something like that. You sure looked like you were having fun when you were all over him on the dance floor. He's pretty good, huh? Who said practice doesn't make perfect?'

She very well could've still been talking about dancing, but something in her expression, now dreamy and slightly far-off, indicated otherwise.

'Elisa, what do you mean?'

'Oh, Bette, come on! This is Philip Weston we're talking about here.'

'And that should mean something to me?'

'Ohmigod, Bette, this is *so* humiliating for you. Are you serious? You have no idea who he is?' She began ticking things off on her fingers, one by one. 'Graduate of Eton and Oxford, with a law degree from Yale? Youngest lawyer *ever* to be named partner at Simpson Thacher? Grandfather is a duke; father owns the majority of land between London and Manchester, with additional large chunks in Edinburgh? Trust fund large enough to rival the country's national debt? Ex-boyfriend of Gwyneth, current boy toy of multiple Victoria's Secret models, and crowned "Nightlife Adonis" by none other than *Vanity Fair*. Any of this ringing any bells?' She was almost panting at this point.

'Not really,' I said, trying to synthesize everything she'd said while the sound of blood rushed through my ears. A duke? *Gwyneth??*

'It's so ironic,' she mumbled to herself. 'Every girl on the planet makes it her lifelong goal to have sex with Philip Weston and you go and do it without even knowing who he is? It's almost too much.'

'Have sex with him? What?' *If by 'having sex' you mean 'listening as he fires the maid for gross neglect of $4,000 sheets,' then yes, we had a mind-blowing night.*

'Bette! Give up the "I'm so innocent" routine. We all saw you last night!'

At that exact moment, it was impossible to comprehend anything other than the fact that the same man who used to have sex with Gwyneth Paltrow had not only seen me naked, but had also witnessed period underwear, unshaved legs, and a viciously overgrown bikini line.

'Nothing happened,' I muttered, wondering how quickly I could pack my bags, change my name, and move to Bhutan.

'Riiiiight.' She smiled lasciviously.

'No, really. Granted, I woke up at his place, and granted, I was wearing his clothes, but absolutely nothing happened.'

She looked dumbfounded and disappointed. 'How is that even possible? He's much too gorgeous to resist.'

'Did *you* sleep with him, Elisa?' I asked teasingly.

She looked as though she'd been slapped. 'No!'

'I'm sorry, I didn't mean to suggest . . . I was just kidding, I didn't think you had—'

'Way to rub it in, is all. I've only been lusting after him forever now, but he barely even glances in my direction. I see him out all the time, of course, and he, like, totally knows who I am, so maybe it's just a matter of time. . . .' Her voice once again took on a dreamy quality.

I coughed and she snapped back to attention. I was just about to be flattered by the fact that Philip had taken me home last night when he could have had Elisa instead, but I didn't have a chance to revel.

'I mean, the boy will sleep with any decent-looking girl he can get his hands on, so I just don't understand what's wrong with me,' she said tonelessly.

'Any girl?' I asked, still determined to hold on to the illusion that I might be his one and only.

'Well, pretty much any hot girl, which is why I can't understand why he doesn't respond to me. Maybe he just doesn't like his women thin.'

Ouch. Unintentional, but painful. I waited while she continued with her stock-taking.

'Let's see. Skye dated him, but that was years ago, way before he became who he is now. So did one of the List Girls – the pretty one – and that girl who was on the cover of *Marie Claire* last month, and a solid handful of the hottest girls at Condé Nast.' She continued to tick off names of beautiful and social girls, some that I recognized from years of idly reading the gossip columns and party pages, but I could barely hear her. Luckily, she only hit about a dozen before Kelly bounded from her office and called for me to enter her animal-print hell – the whole room was done in a hallucinogenic mixture of zebra, leopard, and tiger fabrics, replete with oversized furry pillows and a giant, spotted shag rug.

'Hey there, Bette. How is everything?' she said happily, closing the door and motioning for me to take a seat on a chair covered in what felt like actual skin and hair.

'Uh, great. It's been a great first week so far.'

'I'm so glad! I think so, too!' Biggest smile yet.

'Uh, yeah. Seriously, I'm so happy to be here, and I promise I'll get all this stuff down as quickly as possible so I can start actually contributing instead of just watching,' I said with what sounded to me like a reasonable level of sobriety and coherence.

'Uh-huh, that's nice. So tell me about last night!' She clasped her hands together and leaned forward.

'Oh, right, last night. Yeah, I went to dinner with Elisa and Skye and Leo and a couple others and we had such a nice night. It's a really great group of people you have here. Of course, I won't always let them keep me out so late. . . .' I laughed, trying to sound casual, since I wasn't exactly used to discussing nights out with my boss. Aaron most certainly hadn't been my go-to morning-after confidant, but Kelly seemed eager for it.

'You mean, you won't let them keep you out until the next morning . . .' She grinned and let her words trail off.

Ahem. I suspected we were toeing the line between personal and professional, and I wasn't about to cross it. 'It was a great dinner! I just love everyone who works here.' A slightly inane non sequitur, but it was the only thing that came to mind.

She leaned forward, brushing her side-swept bangs even more to the left, and placed her elbows on the rough-hewn wooden desk. 'Bette, dear, you can't expect to, ah, *spend the night* with Philip Weston and not have the entire world know about it. Here, look.' She thrust a piece of computer paper across the table. My hands shook as I took it.

I recognized it immediately as that day's edition of the column that Abby and Elisa had been talking about the night before, New York Scoop. It had been printed from the Scoop's website and the headline read: MYSTERY GIRL CHECKS INTO WESTON'S HOTEL. The story went on to detail how Philip had been 'accosted' at Bungalow 8 the previous evening by a 'pretty young thing' who some sources 'have fingered as a new hire at Kelly & Company. Keep it tuned right here to see if she resurfaces anytime soon . . .' The byline at the bottom of the piece read 'Ellie Insider.' *That's a stupid name*, I thought.

Despite the 'pretty young thing' semi-compliment that was

undoubtedly supplied to fill space, my stomach dropped and I looked at Kelly in horror.

'I'm working feverishly alongside half of Manhattan trying to figure out who Ellie Insider is. It's fucking brilliant. Do you believe how quickly they get things posted? I suppose that's the benefit of having it online, although I still can't help feeling that these, these, *blogs* are just little diaries for people who can't actually get published.'

'Kelly, it's so not what it looks like. I can explain. It's just that after dinner, we—'

'Bette, I know exactly what happened. And I'm thrilled!'

'You are?' I was certain this was just her convoluted way of firing me.

'Of course! Look, this is an ideal scenario. Philip Weston, Bungalow 8, a mention for the office. The only thing I ask is that next time you make sure the real Page Six is watching, too. This is a solid mention, but the column's still pretty new, and not completely up to par yet with its circ numbers.'

I opened my mouth to speak, but no words came out. She didn't seem to notice, though.

'He's amazing, isn't he? Just between you and me, I've always had a thing for him.'

'You have? For Philip?'

'Ohmigod, girl, who hasn't? He's splendid. Not only is he *all* boldfaced mentions *all* the time, he also happens to look amazing without a shirt.'

Her face had taken on the same hazy expression as Elisa's had earlier. 'Did you date him?' I asked, praying with all my energy that the answer was no.

'Good lord, I wish! Closest I ever came to sleeping with him was watching him take his shirt off at a charity auction where the organizers were selling a date with him. Three hundred other women and I went berserk when he yanked it over his head. Very *Coyote Ugly*, if you can picture it: wonderful and pathetic all at the same time.'

I let my guard down and forgot – for a split second – that I was talking to my boss. 'I saw that chest when he got out of the shower this morning, and it was every bit as beautiful as you say,' I added before I could realize what this implied.

Kelly's head snapped around, and she stared at me with an odd combination of envy and urgency. 'I'm assuming that when he calls you again, you'll go out with him, right?'

This didn't really sound like a question. 'Oh, I'm not sure he'll be calling,' I mumbled, realizing that absolutely no one would believe we hadn't slept together.

She peered at me intently and then broke into a wide grin. 'Bette, sweetie, you might be the last person to realize this, but in your own unique way, you're beautiful. And it's a widely known fact that no one loves beautiful girls more than Philip Weston. Of course he will call. And you'll say yes, right? And naturally, please invite him to all our events or stay out as late as you need to when you're with him.'

I could feel a weird sense of elation – like a high school crush – rising in my chest.

'Uh, sure. Okay, I'll keep that in mind.' Suddenly, I wanted to hug her.

'Great. I'm so excited for you! Definitely keep me updated. Should we get started?'

'Yes, let's,' I breathed, relieved to end this very strange discussion. 'You were going to tell me about The List, right?'

'Yes. The List. The single most crucial tool for ensuring a firm's success. We're nothing without the people we can provide for our clients, so I've spent years putting together one of the biggest databases in the industry. Pull your chair around so you can see.'

I yanked the furry stool to her side of the desk and settled in as she double-clicked an icon on her desktop. 'Here it is,' she purred. 'My baby. The most comprehensive list of tastemakers ever, anywhere.'

The screen resembled a search page you might encounter on a personals or apartment-rental website. You simply chose your search requirements, ticked their adjacent boxes, and hit Find. There were four main locations you could browse – New York, Los Angeles, Miami, and the Hamptons – but smaller, less complete lists existed for another dozen cities in the United States, and about two dozen abroad. The search criteria appeared endless. In a vertical row starting in the upper-left-hand corner, they were listed, in no particular order: Art, Literary, Film Production, Newspapers, Fashion, Record Label, Social, Young Social, Media Elites, Finance, Magazines, Architecture, Retail, Miscellaneous.

'You just key in the types of people you're looking for and the program provides you with all the information. Here, watch.' She quickly checked off 'Literary' and 'Young Social' and showed me the thousands of returns. 'We know everything about everyone. Full name, home address, work address, all phones, faxes, pagers, emails, country houses, beach houses, international addresses, birthdays, spouse information, and details on both the children and their nannies. There's also a subset – if you need to narrow it down even further – that tells you if a particular person is gay, straight, single, monogamous, or cheating, in addition to whether they party, travel, or get mentioned in gossip columns a great deal. It makes it pretty easy to hand-pick exactly who will be there when you know everything about their lives, you know?'

I just nodded, as there seemed no more appropriate response.

'Here, let's take your uncle, for instance.' She typed his name into a search field and up popped all his relevant info: Central Park West address and phone, office information, his exact title at the paper and the name of the column, the number of years he'd been writing, his nationwide readership, his birthday, and a short sentence about how he traveled frequently to Key West and Europe. Under 'cross-reference' he was described as 'Gay,' 'Literary,' 'Newspaper,' and 'Media Elite.' I noticed there was no Christian Coalition Reactionary category, but I said nothing.

'I've never seen anything like this.' I was unable to tear my eyes from the screen.

'It's incredible, isn't it? And that's not all. If you'll notice, there are no regular media people or celebrities in this database. We have separate ones for them since those are the two most crucial groups.'

'Separate ones?'

'Well, sure. Look.' She closed down the first program and clicked on an icon that read 'Press.' 'There are media elites – people like your uncle, Frank Rich, Dan Rather, Barbara Walters, Rupert Murdoch, Mort Zuckerman, Tom Brokaw, Arthur Sulzberger, Thomas Friedman, etcetera, etcetera, who of course you want at events because of their high profile, but you can't honestly expect them to cover anything. They're just like celebrities in their own right, which is why we need to have a completely separate database of real working media – all the people at the papers, magazines, TV, and radio who can actually give us the coverage we promise our clients. Of course, there's always overlap. You can have a socialite who also happens to work in magazines or a film exec who writes reviews for a local paper, so we just cross-list everyone.'

I took the mouse from her and scrolled through the separate fields, noticing that the media database was broken down by demographic, so you could best pitch the specific people covering music, design, travel, lifestyle, fashion, entertainment, gossip, celebrity, sports, or social engagements.

'This is absolutely incredible. How many are there total?'

'Between all three databases, probably close to thirty-five thousand. You haven't even seen the celeb one yet, which is our most important.' Another couple clicks and a list of the world's richest, most famous, and most beautiful people popped to the forefront.

'This is the industry list. With each celeb, we've also listed their current publicist, agent, manager, assistants, and family information, in addition to birthdays, current and upcoming projects, and preferences – everything from airlines to flowers, waters, coffees, liquors, hotels, designers, and music. We update this one pretty much hourly.'

She opened the profile for Charlize Theron and I saw that she had homes in South Africa, Malibu, and the Hollywood Hills; was dating Stuart Townsend; would only fly American Airlines first class or private jet; was currently shooting a movie in Rome; was signed on for another film in five months; and maintained a staff of four, with her agent temporarily also acting as her publicist.

'How do they all get updated? I mean, how could you possibly know all this stuff?'

Kelly threw her head back, clearly delighted by my shock. 'Elisa introduced you to the List Girls, yes?'

I nodded.

'It's not the most glamorous job in the world, but they've got the right connections, and we give them lots of perks to read every single publication known to man – in print and online – and take from that whatever they can to fill in the blanks. There are three of them, and they're all very socially connected family-wise, and they go out constantly anyway and meet people everywhere. Just this morning *New York* magazine came out with their Baby Power issue – the fifty kids in New York under the age of thirty who are the most accomplished in their fields. If they weren't in there already, every one of them has now been entered into our database.'

'Amazing. Really, Kell, it's amazing.'

'It sure is. Why don't you put a practice list together? Let's say we're planning a party for Asprey to celebrate the opening of their second store in the United States. It'll be held at the store on Fifth, and the company's main concern is that Americans simply aren't as familiar with the brand as the English are, and they're looking for more name recognition. Pull five hundred total fits: four hundred regular attendees and a hundred mixed of celebs and targeted press. Of course, an actual event like that would only have a hundred to a hundred fifty, max, but this will just be an exercise.'

It had suddenly occurred to me that I still hadn't dealt with my hangover, which was gearing up again in such a way that it demanded immediate attention.

'Sure, I'll have that to you on Monday?' I asked as cheerily as possible, standing up carefully to avoid any extra queasiness.

'Perfect.' Kelly nodded. 'Think about potential party favors, too. Oh, and Bette?'

'Hmm?'

'Do you have any plans to see Philip this weekend?'

'Philip? Who's Philip?' I thought she was still talking about The List, but apparently we'd transitioned seamlessly back to my personal life.

'Bette!' She giggled. 'That gorgeous super-stud whose bed you occupied last night? You will be seeing him, right?'

'Oh, right, Philip. It wasn't exactly like that, Kelly. It was more like—'

'Oh, Bette, stop right there. You don't owe me any explanations at all. It's your life, you know,' she pointed out, apparently seeing no irony whatsoever in the statement. 'I just hope you'll consider going out with him over the weekend, is all. Maybe have dinner at Matsuri or stop by Cain or Marquee?'

'Uh, well, I'm not sure he'll call me, but if he does, then well, I guess—'

'Oh, he'll call, Bette, he'll call. I'm glad to hear you're into the idea. Because frankly, you'd be crazy if you weren't! I'm headed out early today, so have a great weekend, okay?'

'Sure. Will do. You, too, Kelly,' I said, inching closer to the door, still not really believing that I had just promised my boss I'd continue sleeping with a guy I hadn't slept with yet. 'See you Monday.'

She picked up the phone, smiled, and gave me a thumbs-up. I beelined for my area, near Elisa, but was stopped several times on the way by people grinning at me in knowing ways or calling out 'Nice work' or 'Great work with Philip.' Elisa had gone out to lunch (read: a liter of Fiji water, a Baggie of baby carrots, and a half-dozen Marlboro Lights), according to a note she left on my computer, so I picked up the phone and called Penelope.

'Hey, how are you?' she asked.

'I'm fine. And you?' I responded in my detonation voice, so quiet and uptight that it gave the impression something might blow up at any second.

'Great. Thanks for inviting me to dinner last night. It was, uh, really interesting.'

'So you hated it?'

'No! Bette, I didn't say anything like that. I didn't hate it at all. It was just, uh, different from what we usually do. Hope you don't mind that I bailed early, but I was exhausted. How was the rest of the night?'

'Are you asking just to be polite or have you not seen the news today?' I mentally crossed my fingers that she hadn't heard.

'Yeah, I'm just being nice. Avery forwarded it to me first thing this morning. It's taken every last ounce of willpower not to call you. I want the full play-by-play. Start with "When I met him at Bungalow he was wearing a black ribbed shirt and black pants with a thirty-four-inch inseam and he bought me a Stoli Vanilla and Sprite." Proceed at that detail level, please.'

'Pen, I can't really get into it here,' I said tersely, looking up to notice that half of my coworkers were pretending to stare at their screens while listening to me intently.

'Bette! You can't be serious! You go and have sex with one of the hottest guys in the free world – Avery's always talking about how every female in Manhattan worships him – and you can't tell me about it?'

'I didn't sleep with him!' I all but screamed into the phone. Skye and Leo – in addition to a few assistants – jerked their heads up and grinned at me in unison.

'Whatever,' I heard someone else whisper.

Leo just rolled his eyes as if to say, 'Oh, dear God, we're not all *that* stupid.'

And for a minute I was flattered. So what if it was slightly slutty to meet someone and sleep with him that very night? Better everyone considered it a *possibility* that Philip Weston would deign to have sex with me, I suppose, than just assume he'd taken me in for the night out of pity and a sense of obligation and spent as little time as possible actually *in* the bed I occupied.

'Whoa,' Penelope was saying. 'Touchy, touchy. Okay, so you didn't have sex with him. I believe you. The only question I have now is, why the hell *not*? I'm sure you don't need me to remind you of your recent celibacy. What are you holding out for? He's supposedly incredible!'

I finally laughed for what I realized was the first time all morning. Seriously, what was the big deal? If I wasn't going to get fired for my rather public indiscretion – and that certainly didn't seem to be an option – then why not just enjoy it?

'I remember very little about what actually happened last night,' I whispered, placing my hand over the receiver, 'but I'll tell you whatever I can dredge up when I get home tonight.'

'Can't. Avery and I have dinner at his parents' house and I can't seem to talk him out of it. What about tomorrow night? Can we meet for a drink at the Black Door?'

'I'd love to, but I'm meeting the book club for dinner and drinks. Little Italy, I think.'

She sighed. 'Well, we should probably make a plan now for the weekend after next since I'm in St Louis for work the next two weeks. Are you around?'

It felt strange to have plans with people other than my book club, Will, or Penelope, but work had already begun to seep into my weekends, too. I checked my rapidly filling calendar. 'Yeah, totally, I just promised Kelly that I'd go with our group from here to scout a new location for the *Playboy* party. It's still four months away, but everyone's already panicking. Want to come?'

Penelope hesitated. I could tell she wasn't into the idea, but she couldn't really say no since she'd already admitted to being free. 'Uh, sure. That sounds great. We'll figure out the details this week. And of course, if you suddenly "remember" anything about last night, I'll take that, too.'

'Bitch,' I shot back.

She just laughed.

'You have fun with your future in-laws, you hear? Be sure to listen up when they tell you exactly how many grandchildren they want, broken down by gender and eye color. You do, after all, have certain obligations now. . . .'

It was good to hear her laughing again.

'Bettina Robinson, I'm not sure you're in a position to offer advice on such things right now, considering your rather tawdry exploits in the last twenty-four hours. . . . Talk to you later.'

'Bye.' I hung up the phone and decided that such a night and morning warranted a second bacon, egg, and cheese on a buttered roll. I still had to do that invitation list for five hundred and party favors, but I decided it could wait. My hangover could not.

9

Three weeks later – three weeks of list-making, wardrobe-building, party-going, and general immersion in the culture of Kelly & Company – I stood waiting for Penelope to arrive. The line outside Sanctuary looked absolutely unbearable. Whole hordes of girls smoothed their Japanese-reconditioned hair with manicured hands while the boys – revitalized from various steak dinners – gripped their forearms to keep them from tottering over sideways on their heels. The early November night was chilly, but no one seemed to notice that it wasn't July anymore. Skin – scrubbed, buffed,

85

waxed, moisturized, tanned, and glowing – was everywhere, from huge expanses of bronzed cleavage to slightly sparkling stretches of stomach to those inches of upper thigh that are rarely spotted away from the beach or the gynecologist's office. A few people swayed in time to loungy music emanating from behind the imposing steel door, and most seemed to twitter at the mere idea of what the night held: the sensation of that first martini hitting your bloodstream, the feeling of music pulsating through your hips, the cigarette smoke burning but delicious, the chance to press some of that perfect skin against someone else's. There was nothing quite as heady as a Saturday night in New York when you were standing outside the newest, chicest place in the city, surrounded by all sorts of glittering, pretty things, the kind of vibe where every fantasy was just waiting to unfold . . . if you could only get inside.

To my surprise, Will had been less than thrilled with the coverage of my non-one-night-stand three weeks earlier. I'd called after work to say hi, figuring he didn't even read New York Scoop and there was a good chance he hadn't seen it, but I was very, very wrong. Everybody, it seemed, had begun reading New York Scoop – and worse, they were reading it solely for Ellie Insider's column.

'Oh, Bette, your uncle has been champing at the bit, just waiting for your call. Hold on a second, I'll get him,' Simon said rather formally, not even bothering to ask how I was or when I'd next be over for dinner, as he always did.

'Bette? Is that really you? The celebrity herself deigns to call her old uncle, huh?'

'Celebrity? What on earth are you talking about?'

'Oh, I don't know, maybe just that little piece about my "mystery niece." Apparently your new boyfriend is rather fashionable, and so his, um, conquests are often recorded for posterity within the Scoop's highly journalistic pages. Did you not see it?'

'My boyfriend? You're referring to the illustrious Philip Weston, I'm guessing?'

'Indeed I am, darling, indeed I am. Not exactly what I had in mind when I encouraged you to get out there and meet someone, but what do I know? I'm just an old man, living vicariously through his beautiful young niece. If you find that whole British trustafarian thing appealing, well, then, far be it from me to say otherwise. . . .'

'Will! I should think you of all people would understand that you can't necessarily believe everything you read in the papers, you know? It didn't exactly happen like that.'

'Well, darling, since you seem to be a bit late to the game, everyone's been reading Ellie Insider lately. She's surely a conniving little wench, but she *does* always seem to have the scoop. Are you telling me you didn't go home with him? Or that it was a different new Kelly hire? Because if that's true, then I'd recommend having that corrected as soon as possible. I'm not sure that's the reputation you'd be looking to create for yourself.'

'It's complicated' was all I could manage.

'I see,' he replied quietly. 'Well, look, it's certainly none of my business. As long as you're enjoying yourself, that's really all that matters. See you at brunch on Sunday. We're in prime pre-holiday wedding season, so I imagine there'll be some real winners in Sunday's announcements. Wear your snarky shoes, darling.'

I'd agreed, but I felt unsettled. Something had changed – or shifted, at least – and I couldn't quite pinpoint it.

'Hey, Bette, over here,' Penelope called a bit too loudly as she settled up with the cabdriver and waved to me from the backseat.

I waved. 'Hi! Right on time. Elisa and crew are already here, but I didn't want you to have to come in alone.'

'Wow, you look great,' she said, putting a hand on my hip and examining my outfit from head to toe. 'Where'd you find clothes like that?'

I laughed, pleased that she had noticed. I'd only been working at Kelly & Company for a month, but it was long enough for me to get sick of looking like I was always dressed for a funeral. I'd thrown my drab suits in the back of my closet, ripped a couple pages out of *Lucky* and *Glamour,* and made a beeline for Barney's. Standing at the register, I'd mentally added up the years it was going to take to pay for all this stuff and then bravely handed over my credit card. When the salesperson gave it back, I could have sworn it was warm to the touch. In one afternoon I'd managed to kiss both dorkiness and credit health good-bye.

While it wasn't exactly couture, I was pretty happy with my new look: Paige Jeans that cost more than all my monthly bills combined; a silky, lace-lined lingerie top in kelly green; a tweedy, fitted blazer that didn't match anything but which the salesman, Jean-Luc, had declared 'ravishing'; and the classic Chanel clutch Will had bought me for my twenty-first birthday because apparently 'it's criminal to pass into womanhood without a single designer paving your passage. Welcome to what I hope will be a long life of shallow consumerism and brand worship.'

I had worked at CWK for five years, slaving away for eighty hours a week. Since I'd never had any time to spend money, I'd managed to build a little nest egg without really trying. After eight weeks of unemployment and one afternoon at Barney's, that nest egg had been seriously compromised, but my ass had never looked better in denim. Standing outside Sanctuary among the thin and beautiful people, I felt like I belonged. It had been worth it.

'Hi there,' I said, hugging Penelope's tiny frame. 'Do you like it? It's my "I've never been remotely cool but I'm trying real hard to be so now" look. What do you think?'

'I think you look hot,' she said, forever the good friend. 'Is someone planning on seeing a certain English deity this evening?'

'Hardly. I don't think Philip Weston calls girls who don't immediately fall into his bed with their legs spread. Actually, I don't think he calls girls who do, either. Whatever. He's beautiful, but he was unbelievably arrogant and full of himself.'

'And no one likes that, of course,' Penelope said with mock seriousness.

'Of course not,' I replied. 'Come on, everyone else is inside and it's freezing. Let's go in.'

'Have you seen this line? What's going on here tonight? You'd think they were handing out free lap dances or something.'

'I don't know too much except that it opened last night and is supposed to be the ultimate exclusive place, sort of a VIP room on steroids. Kelly wanted us to check it out in case it actually does live up to the hype. If it becomes the new place, we'll already have it booked for the *Playboy* party.'

Kelly & Company had been commissioned by *Playboy* over a year ago to put on the Manhattan portion of their never-ending Fiftieth Anniversary celebration, which would start in Chicago in January and eventually end in a blowout at the mansion in Los Angeles in March, making stops in Vegas, Miami, and New York along the way. It was going to be a massive undertaking – definitely our biggest project to date, and it pretty much dominated every workday. Kelly had gathered us around the day before to change the number on the countdown board to 164 and then asked for updates. The List Girls were already running simultaneous searches on all A- and B-list celebs, preparing to construct a final winning group. Meanwhile, the rest of us spent half of each day fielding calls from every imaginable person in every sector of the city looking to wrangle invitations and request invites for themselves, or clients, or both. Combine all the anticipation with Hef's paranoid insistence that all details (including – but not limited to – location, date, time, and attendees) be kept lockbox-quiet, and we had the recipe for total chaos.

'I looked it up on Citysearch today. They quoted the manager as saying they expected the clientele to be "upscale creative," which I sort of thought applied more to menus than people, but what do I know?' Penelope sighed.

I'd recently begun to understand that the concept of exclusivity was an organizing principle of life in Manhattan. Part of this was undoubtedly due to the sheer concentration of people on such a tiny island. New Yorkers instinctively compete for everything from taxis at rush hour to seats on the subway to Hermès Birkin bags to Knicks season tickets. Impenetrable co-op boards take years to navigate. Icy hostesses at the city's most desirable restaurants haughtily demand reservations six months in advance. 'If they let you in without a hassle,' people say, 'it's probably not worth going.' Since the days of Studio 54, and probably long before (if there even were nightclubs before then), club-goers have made getting into trendy nightclubs a competitive sport. And at the chicest places, like tonight, there are levels of access. Getting in the front door is just the beginning – any NYU sophomore in a tube top can manage that. 'The main bar?' I'd heard someone say in reference to Sanctuary. 'I'd rather be at TGI Friday's in Hoboken.' Elisa had provided explicit instructions to make our way directly to the VIP lounge, apparently the only place to find some 'real action.' Jagger and Bowie partied in Studio 54's legendary private rooms. Today Leo, Colin, and Lindsay hold court, unmolested by prying eyes. And everyone else clamors to get in.

I'd grown accustomed to being a non-VIP quite some time ago – it hadn't occurred to me that VIP was even a possibility for me. It had taken the opening of a VIP room outside of the confines of the nightclub arena to really stir my righteous indignation. In what I could only interpret as the first sign of the apocalypse, my dentist, Dr Quinn, had opened a VIP waiting room in his office. 'So the doctor's high-profile, important clients will have a place where they feel comfortable,' the assistant had explained. 'You can have a seat in our regular lounge.' I sat in Dr Powell's very uncool and very public waiting room, thumbing through a two-year-old issue of *Redbook* and silently willing the overweight gentleman next to me to cease cracking his gum. I gazed longingly at the door marked VIP and fantasized about the plush dental wonderland that surely lay beyond. I resigned myself to the fact that I would always be one of those people on the outside looking in. But there I was, a mere few months later, standing outside Sanctuary in my cool new clothes with a gaggle of fabulous friends waiting inside. It felt like my luck was changing.

Out of the corner of my eye, I saw a girl who looked exactly like Abby kiss the bouncer and make her way into the lounge, but I couldn't positively identify her from where I stood. 'Hey, you'll never guess who I saw the other night. I can't believe I forgot to tell you! Abby was at Bungalow that night you left after dinner.'

Penelope's head snapped toward mine. She hated Abby more than I did, if that was possible. She'd refused to acknowledge her presence since Abby had cornered her in an empty classroom sophomore year and told her not to take it personally that Penelope's father was sleeping with his secretary, that it was certainly no reflection on his love for her. Penelope had been so shocked she'd merely asked, 'How do you know?' and Abby had smirked in return. 'Are you serious?' she'd asked. 'Who doesn't know?'

'You saw that midget and didn't tell me? What'd she have to say for herself?'

'Her usual. She's now at the vortex of the media world, you'll be happy to know. Goes by Abigail now, not Abby, so of course I said "Abby" as many times as I possibly could. Had her boobs done and half her face rearranged, but she's still exactly the same.'

'Girl would walk over her own mother in spike heels if it helped her get ahead,' Penelope mumbled.

'Sure would,' I confirmed cheerfully. 'And you just might have the pleasure of seeing her here tonight. I think she just walked in.'

'Great. That's just great. Lucky us.'

I linked arms with Penelope and boldly walked to the front of the line, hopefully projecting some level of confidence. A highly manorexic black guy sporting a giant, fake Afro wig and a long-sleeved mesh T-shirt over hot pink Lycra tights peered at us through sparkle-encrusted eyelashes.

'Are you on the list?' he asked in a voice that was surprisingly gruff for someone who cross-dressed so expertly.

'Yep, sure are,' I said casually. Silence. 'Um, yes, we are on the list. We're here with Kelly & Company.'

No response. He held the clipboard but didn't consult it, and I decided he hadn't heard me.

'I spoke with the manager earlier today to arrange a visit? We're actually here to check out the venue for a potential—'

'Name!' he barked, wholly disinterested in my explanation. But as I spelled out my last name, four guys in seventies leisure suits and a girl in something that looked an awful lot like a flapper outfit walked directly in front of me.

'Romero, darling, move that silly rope aside so we can get out

90

of the cold,' the girl ordered, placing a hand gingerly on the bouncer's cheek.

'Of course, Sofia, come right in,' he cooed deferentially, and I realized that the flapper was Sofia Coppola. The entourage followed her lead and nodded their respects to the bouncer, who was glowing with pride and happiness. It took him a full three minutes to regain his composure and another two to remember that we were still there.

'Robinson,' I said, sounding definitely more irritated. 'R-O-B-I – '

'I can spell it,' he snapped, apparently now in a full-fledged snit. 'Yes, fortunately for you, I have you on the list. Absolutely no one is getting in tonight otherwise.'

'Mmm' was about all I could manage in reply to this fascinating piece of information.

He placed his hand on the velvet rope but didn't lift it. He leaned over and addressed Penelope directly, and none too quietly: 'Just FYI for next time, girls: you're really a bit more casual than we like to see here.'

Penelope giggled, obviously unaware that our new transvestite friend was *not* kidding.

'Hey, I'm just giving it to you straight,' he continued, his voice getting louder every second. A sort of silence had overtaken the previously fidgety and excited crowd, and I could feel fifty pairs of eyes staring at us from behind. 'We prefer to see a little more style, a little more effort.'

My mind began to race, in search of a snappy retort, but of course I managed to say nothing. Before I knew what was happening, a girl so young, so tall, and with breasts so enormous they'd only ever work in LA, came over and volunteered a brief but highly informative lecture on the current fashion situation.

'We especially like to see forties looks lately.' She smiled warmly.

'Huh?' Penelope said, verbalizing exactly what I was thinking.

'Well, it's just one option, of course, but it's quite effective. Black and white with bright red lipstick, you know? Perhaps some vintage Prada heels or something even chunkier. It's all about distinguishing yourself.' I heard a few people laughing appreciatively in the background.

It was at this point that I noticed that she looked like something out of *I Want a Famous Face* gone horribly awry.

What did I say? What did I do? Absolutely nothing. Instead of maintaining one iota, one tiny shred of self-respect, we proffered our left hands for the obligatory stamp and sort of shuffled shamefully past the velvet rope that had finally been lifted. The final indignity came just as the door was shutting behind us, when the cosmetically enhanced giraffe announced to the circus freak, 'It wouldn't be quite so bad if they just minded their labels.'

'Did that just happen?' Penelope asked, looking as dumbfounded as I felt.

'I think so. Just how pathetic were we? I'm almost afraid to ask.'

'There are actually no words for that level of pathetic-ness. It was like watching *Jeopardy!* – I knew all the answers, just ten seconds too late.'

I was about to suggest that we medicate ourselves with as much undiluted vodka as we could locate, but Elisa found us first.

'This place is so hot,' she breathed into my ear while waving hello to Penelope. 'Check it out. Far right, back corner, Kristin Davis. Far right, just in front of her, Suzanne Somers. Random, I acknowledge, but celeb nonetheless. Far left, not quite in the corner, more like twelve o'clock, Sting and Trudie Styler, making out. At the round leather couch in the middle, Heidi Klum and Seal, and Davide heard them say that Zac Posen is on his way.'

'Wow,' Penelope said, making an admirable effort to sound impressed, 'there are a lot of people here tonight. Bette? What do you say about getting a drink?'

'I'm not finished,' Elisa hissed, pulling my arm tighter toward hers and continuing to scan the room. 'Flirting with the waitress, by the side door, Ethan Hawke. Made significantly more awkward by the presence of Andre Balazs, Uma's new man, sitting with business associates at first banquette on the right. And look! That ugly little lesbian troll blogger who can't stop writing about how much blow she does every night is sort of lurking in the back there, watching them all. Tomorrow she'll have everything plastered all over her blog, making it sound like she was partying with everyone rather than spying all night long. Oh, and look! Right behind her, an assistant from Rush & Molloy. They rotate them constantly so no one ever knows who they are, but we have a source there who faxes over pictures and bios of the new ones right away. . . . Hmm, it doesn't look like Philip is here tonight. Shame. I bet you were wanting to see him, no?'

'Philip? Uh, no, actually, not really,' I mumbled somewhat truthfully.

'Oh, really? Does that mean he still hasn't called? How sad. I know what it's like, Bette. Don't take it personally – he obviously just has very strange tastes.'

I had spent three weeks dodging Elisa's questions, trying to appear nonchalant about Philip Weston. I was about to repeat that I couldn't care less that he hadn't called, that I hadn't even left my number as instructed, but I figured it wasn't worth it. This was clearly a sensitive point and best left alone. Besides, I didn't exactly adore the fact that I hadn't heard from him, number or not.

Penelope and I followed Elisa over to a small circle of white suede couches – a phenomenally stupid idea for a place where people do nothing but eat, drink, and hook up – and said hello to Leo, Skye, Davide, and someone Elisa introduced as 'the brains behind this entire production.'

'Hi, I'm Bette, and this is my friend Penelope,' I said, extending my hand to the Semitic-looking-yet-mullet-sporting guy Elisa had referenced.

'Yo. Danny.'

'Without Danny, we wouldn't be here tonight.' Elisa sighed, and everyone at the table nodded knowingly. 'He came up with the whole concept that is Sanctuary and put the whole project together. . . . Isn't that right, Danny?'

'Word.'

I was wondering why this short Jewish guy from either Great Neck or Dix Hills was attempting to sound as though he'd grown up on the playgrounds and basketball courts of Cabrini Green.

'Oh, so you were the one who hired that charming bouncer, huh?' I asked, and Elisa shot me a warning look.

Danny apparently sensed nothing amiss. 'Fag freak, but whatever. Gets his shit done. Keeps out the losers – all that matters to me.'

Mmm. Penelope nodded seriously in agreement and simultaneously nudged me, and I gnawed the inside of my cheeks to keep from laughing. Compared to two minutes ago, Danny was being downright verbose.

'So, Danny, what gave you the idea for Sanctuary?' Penelope asked, staring at him with wide, fascinated eyes.

He took a swig from his Stella Artois and peered at her as though he were trying to determine which language she'd just used, his eyes scrunched up in confusion, hand on his crinkled forehead, head shaking slightly from side to side. 'Dude. Everywhere else is so fucking stressful. The line at Bungalow's a nightmare and I can't stand all those fuckin' media types at Soho House. Figured we all need a place that could be, like, a y'know, what's the word? A place to chill.'

'A sanctuary?' I supplied helpfully.

'Right on.' He nodded, obviously relieved. The amount of product in his hair was nothing short of astounding.

Unfortunately, before this fascinating conversation could see itself to its logical end – most likely the one where Danny eventually remembered the name of his own club – I spotted an exceedingly familiar tan.

'Ohmigod, it's him,' I stage-whispered to our motley crew, immediately leaning my head in for both cover and consultation. Heads turned.

'Philip. Philip Weston is here. Just walked in with that, that, that *model*,' I spat out, not even remotely aware of how insanely jealous I sounded. And looked.

'Bette, is that jealousy I hear?' Elisa asked, leaning in to whisper in my ear. 'And here I thought you were immune to the Weston charms. Good to see you're a red-blooded American girl after all. Of course, just because you're interested doesn't mean he is. . . .'

'Dude! Philip! Over here,' Danny was calling, and before I'd even realized what was happening, Philip was kissing me hello on the mouth.

'Hi, love, I was hoping you'd be here. You can run, but you can't hide. . . .'

'Pardon?' was about all I could manage, since at this point I was fairly certain he'd meant to direct both the kiss and comment elsewhere. Like toward the knockout who was patiently waiting about three feet behind him, not looking the least bit distressed about anything.

'You didn't leave your number with my doorman. What do you call that here? Playing hard to get. Well, I always fancy a good game, so I decided to play along and find you myself.'

I saw Elisa collapse into the couch behind him, her mouth hanging open quite unattractively, shock flashing across her face.

'Play along?' I asked him.

'Girls don't exactly flee from me, love, if you know what I'm saying. Hey, mate, may I get a Tanq and tonic?' he said, addressing Danny as though he were our waiter.

'Right on, dude, coming right up,' Danny said, moving as quickly as one might expect only when the offer of drugs or girls was promised.

He turned around when Philip called, 'And hey, something for Sonja here, too.' He turned not to me but to the girl with infinite legs. 'Sonja, doll baby, what can I get for you? Ginger ale? Vegetable juice? Talk to me, honey.'

She stared back, uncomprehending, and I was almost – almost – amused by the idea that Philip had brought along one girl for accompaniment as he pursued another. He *was* pursuing me, wasn't he?

Elisa had returned to Davide's lap, apparently recovered from

Philip's unexpected arrival. I saw her very discreetly remove a small packet of white powder from her seafoam green Balenciaga bag and slip it to Skye, who immediately bolted in the direction of the ladies' room. Ever resourceful, Elisa then stuck a hand into the bag's side pocket and distributed a few tablets among the table's remaining people. Hands simultaneously found their way to mouths, and the mystery pills were quickly washed down with champagne and vodka and what Skye – our very own drink critic – had described as 'the only decent cosmopolitan in this entire fucking city.'

'Oh, Pheeeely, I think it will be nice to have the tom-ahto juices, *oui*?' Sonja said, biting her lower lip seductively.

'Hey, y'all, come and play. We've got more than enough to go around!' Elisa called over the Hotel Costes CD that might've passed for relaxed lounge music had it not been pumped out at decibels capable of drowning out a 747.

Danny left to fetch drinks for Philip and Sonja, while Penelope tried gamely to make conversation with an ever more wasted Elisa. I just stood there, acutely aware that I looked awkward and dumb, but not really possessing the faculties to move.

'So, Philip, introduce me to your, uh, your friend,' I managed, wondering what the protocol was when the guy whose bed you'd recently shared made the effort to track you down with his girl-friend in tow.

'Sure thing, love. Sonja, this is the smashing creature I was telling you about – the one who turned me down a few weeks ago, if you can believe it. She was completely blotto, of course; it's the only feasible explanation.' Sonja nodded, not necessarily comprehending anything. He rapidly switched to French and the only word I managed to catch was *name*, which I immediately assumed meant he was informing her he didn't know what mine was.

'Bette,' I said, extending my hand to Sonja while ignoring Philip.

'Son-yaaah.' She giggled, revealing shiny teeth with absolutely no nicotine stains.

'Sonja's folks have entrusted her to me for the week while she interviews at all the agencies,' he explained in his irritatingly adorable British accent. 'Our parents have neighboring villas in St Tropez, so she's always been like a little sister to me. Only fifteen. Can you believe it?' In all fairness, he was neither leering nor lecherous, but it felt as though he should have been.

I once again found myself in the rather uncomfortable position of being unable to speak or respond with any sort of consistency, and so I was delighted when Penelope announced that she was ready to go.

'I know we just got here,' she said quietly in my ear, 'but this just isn't my scene. Are you okay here by yourself? Your whole office is here. It should be fine, right?'

'Pen, don't be crazy! I'm coming with you,' I announced, mostly eager for an excuse to leave, with only a hint of desire to stay and talk to Philip.

Danny returned, leading a cocktail waitress over to us. Philip and Sonja received their requested drinks and I was thoughtfully provided with a mini bottle of Piper and a red-striped sipping straw. Penelope received nothing.

'Here, have a drink before we go,' I said, and thrust the bottle in her direction.

'Bette, I'm just done, okay? I really think you should just stay and—'

'AVERY!' Elisa shrieked all of a sudden, propelling her emaciated figure off the couch and into the arms of a tall blond guy wearing an aggressively preppy pink shirt. Both Penelope and I turned simultaneously to see her fiancé embracing my coworker as though they'd known one another for years. 'Come here. Y'all just have to meet my favorite party boy, Avery Wainwright. Avery, this is—'

Apparently the look on both our faces was enough to stop her mid-sentence, a feat I'd never before thought possible.

'Hey, honey, I didn't know you were coming here tonight,' Avery said, extracting himself from Elisa's signature arm-grip and enveloping Penelope in a rather awkward bear hug.

'I didn't know you were, either,' she said quietly, not quite meeting his eyes. 'You said you were going to dinner with the boys tonight.'

I wished I could scoop up Penelope and whisk her off to the Black Door, where we could drown that yucky feeling – he hadn't done anything technically wrong, but I knew her stomach was sinking anyway. But there was nothing to do but try and divert attention away from their two-person show.

'I did go to dinner with the boys. We all went to Sparks, and then most of them wanted to get home, but I decided to check this place out with Rick and Thomas. See, they're right over there,' he said quickly, the words tumbling out in the panicky tone of someone who'd just been caught.

Rick and Thomas were, in fact, located where he'd indicated. In the thirty seconds since they'd arrived, a group of very young girls had accepted their invitation to join them at their VIP table and were just beginning to shimmy and dance on the banquette. Penelope looked like she was ready to throw up. I could tell it was coming to her in waves, the realization that if she hadn't been there, Avery would most likely be grinding against one of those girls right now.

'Mmm,' she murmured, watching as Rick and Thomas sandwiched a girl between them and gyrated. 'I see.'

'Pen, come here, baby, it's not like that. They know those girls from work and they're just being friendly.'

'Work?' Her voice was steely and her eyes had turned to ice. Everyone was waiting for a colossal fight, so I began chatting up Elisa, Philip, Danny, and Sonja simultaneously and nudged Penelope to move a few feet away to spare us a scene.

'So, Sonja, what sort of agencies are you interviewing with?' I asked, wondering if Philip had perhaps meant 'schools' instead. She was really, really young.

'Oh, you know, the common ones. Elite, Ford, Wilhelmina. Phee-ly says I will make beautiful model.'

'Sure do, doll. Ever since this one was a mere tyke, trolling around the villa in nappies, I thought she was splendid. Jailbait, but splendid.' He was now officially leering.

'Gel-bet? What is gel-bet?' she asked us both, her eyes crinkling adorably.

'Nothing, doll. Why don't you sit right here and look ravishing and let me talk to Betty for a minute, okay?'

'You know, Betty is really cute, but I prefer Bette,' I said as nicely as I could manage.

'You are a randy one, aren't you?' He put his hands on my hips and pulled me close, but didn't make a move to kiss me. It was hard to concentrate on his flawlessly chiseled face when I could hear Avery pleading in the background.

'Honey, I don't know why she called me a "party boy." You *know* I like to go out. Hell, I wish you'd come with me more. Elisa's just a silly cokehead who happens to know where the good parties are, that's all.'

That bastard. He had the nerve to stand there and call Elisa a cokehead through clenched teeth and a lower jaw so jittery it looked like it was hooked up to electrodes. Penelope knew a lot of things the rest of us didn't – how to wrap presents, when to write thank-you notes, the best way to set a dinner table – but she was painfully clueless when it came to Avery, drugs, or Avery and drugs. Skye finally came back from the bathroom, her jaw all atwitter as well. The DJ switched from chill lounge music to OutKast, which apparently inspired Elisa to grab Davide and Skye and begin dancing on the banquettes. She rarely took her eyes off Philip, who had walked across the room, but he didn't seem to notice. Her stilettos began piercing neat, clean holes in the white suede, and I felt better with each little ripping sound.

But not for long. The voice behind me was unmistakable, and I immediately felt my stomach sink.

'Bette! So funny seeing you here!' Abby tugged on my arm, causing my champagne to splash on the suede.

'Hey, Abby,' I said as flatly as possible, looking around for a possible escape before even making eye contact.

'So, you and Philip are looking pretty hot and heavy, huh?' She winked and I suppressed an urge to scratch the grin off her face.

'Mmmm. What brings you here?'

She laughed and adjusted a five-inch heel, which did little to disguise her height. 'Does anyone need a reason to have a little fun? Ohmigod, is that Avery Wainwright? We haven't had a chance to catch up recently. That boy grew into a *very* handsome man, don't you think?'

'He's engaged,' I snapped. 'To Penelope. You remember Penelope, don't you?'

She feigned cluelessness. 'Hmm. Well, you know what they say . . .'

'No, what's that?'

'Nothing's final until the vows are exchanged.' She rubbed her hands together as though she was anticipating something very delicious or exciting.

At my reaction she said, 'Oh, Bette, calm down. I was just kidding!' A look of mock horror passed over her face. 'You should really work on that sense of humor, you know. Speaking of which—'

'Abby, it was really great bumping into you, but I've got to get back to my friends. Sort of a work night, you know?' I ducked out from behind her and began sliding away.

'Sure, honey, but let's get that lunch sometime soon, okay? I'd love to hear *all* about Philip and the new job and everything. Everyone's still talking about that mention in New York Scoop,' she called after me.

I wanted to make sure Penelope was holding up, but Avery had her cornered and neither looked thrilled, so I made my way back to our table, where Davide handed me a drink.

Penelope immediately walked over. 'Bette, I think we're going to head out,' she said wearily, sounding as though she'd rather kill herself than either stay or leave.

'You okay? Seriously, why doesn't Avery just stay here and hang out and you and I can go get something to eat? I wouldn't mind leaving before I do something I'll seriously regret, like going home with Philip and making mad, passionate love to him, even though I think he's the most obnoxious guy I've ever met.'

She sighed. 'No, thanks. I think we really need to get home. I'll call you tomorrow.'

I wondered if they'd sleep at all that night. Avery was so amped up on coke that it would take a horse tranquilizer to put him to sleep. Or maybe he'd start having flashbacks from all the acid he did in college and try to eat a parakeet or fly out a window. Poor, sweet Penelope.

'Bette, love, are you ready to leave?' Philip asked, draping his arms over my shoulders as though he were my long-term boyfriend instead of the guy I didn't want to want to sleep with. 'Let's go back to my flat. Maybe you won't be too drunk tonight to—'

'Uh, yeah, why don't you, me, and Sonja,' I said a bit more snottily than I intended, 'have a slumber party? Wouldn't that be fun!'

He slid his hand up the back of my lingerie top. 'What's with all the attitude? Seriously, love, you've got to relax. Come on, I'll put Sonja in a suite upstairs and then you and I can spend a little quiet time together, okay?'

Before I could respond, Philip was whispering to Sonja in French. She did little except nod enthusiastically, raise her perfect eyebrows, and giggle when he was finished. '*Oui, oui,* of course it is okay to spend the time alone together,' she said, providing us with her blessing to engage in slightly drunk, somewhat random sex.

'You know what, Philip?' I said, not knowing how to explain that I wasn't really up for tonight when I wasn't even sure myself. 'It's not right to put her in a hotel when she's just with you for a week. I mean, she's only fifteen. Don't you think you should keep an eye on her? She can't walk three feet without guys hitting on her, you know.'

He looked thoughtful, as though he was actually buying my whole 'concern for Sonja' thing. He nodded. 'Quite right, love. I'll take her home and tuck her in, and then we'll head to a hotel somewhere. Good call. Cheers,' he announced in the direction of the others, who merely glanced once in our direction and nodded in acknowledgment. Elisa stopped gawking long enough to give me a none-too-subtle thumbs-up.

I figured it'd be easier to drop them both off at the Archives and then redirect the cab to Murray Hill than argue about it, so I waved to Elisa and followed Sonja and Philip to the front door, feeling like the chubby, uncoordinated child of two Olympic athletes.

'Hey, guy, call us a cab, will you?' Philip called to the doorman, snapping his fingers in that general direction. It was undeniably obnoxious, but considering what an asshole the guy had been to us, it seemed perfectly acceptable to me. That was, until a closer look revealed that it wasn't the malnourished, wig-sporting Romero but the cute (and rude) bouncer from Bungalow 8. Sammy. He turned to look at Philip with a venomous expression and noticed me trying to hide off to the side. His eyes bore into mine with just a moment's recognition before he turned his attention back to the street and silently hailed a cab from the dozens that were flying past.

Sonja scooted in first and Philip dove in next to her, leaving me standing four inches from Sammy as he held the cab door open. I don't know why I got in with them, but I did. It was like my body was following some invisible script.

'Thanks,' I managed to say quietly, just as Philip said, 'Mate, I've got two gorgeous girls coming home with me, if you know what I mean. You mind being quick about this?' Sonja giggled and rested her delicate head on Philip's shoulder; Sammy looked at me one last time, expressionless, and slammed the door. Just as the cab pulled away, I looked at the restless line outside the club, the camera-ready paparazzi waiting for celebrities to exit, the crush to be inside like its own form of addiction. And even though I couldn't pinpoint why, I was quite sure I wanted to cry.

10

'How do you eat like that and stay so tiny?' I asked Penelope for the thousandth time since we'd met. We'd just settled into a booth at EJ's after an hour-long wait. I was famished enough to order one of everything on the menu, but I was enjoying my still-thin figure too much to jeopardize it now. I'd managed to cut out all trips to Dylan's and even most of my morning bacon, egg, and cheeses – with the occasional Slim Jim acting as my only real indulgence – and it was almost starting to feel normal to police myself with food. Which only made it all the weirder when Penelope ordered the way we always had – three-egg cheese omelet with bacon and hash browns, accompanied by a short stack of chocolate-chip pancakes and a baby fistful of oozing, melted butter. She raised her eyebrows when I ordered an egg-white omelet with spinach and tomatoes and two slices of dry whole-wheat toast, but she kindly refrained from commenting, with the single exception of a murmur: 'Elisa influence much?' I ignored her wan smile and changed the subject.

'Is everything okay with you and Avery?' I asked as sympathetically as I could, wanting very much to draw her out and not sound critical. I'd helplessly watched them leave Sanctuary, knowing how upset she was but feeling powerless to do anything but watch. When she'd called early this morning, I immediately ducked out of my standing Sunday brunch plans with Will and Simon and jumped in a cab downtown.

She avoided my eyes and instead concentrated on slicing her pancakes into small, even pieces. Slice, spear, mouth, repeat. I watched this cycle three times before she spoke. 'Everything's just fine,' she said tonelessly. 'Once he explained everything to me, I could see that last night was just a big misunderstanding.'

'I'm sure. It must have been surprising to see him there when you weren't expecting it,' I prompted, hoping to elicit some sort of acknowledgment from her.

She laughed without pleasure. 'Well, you know Avery. Likely to crop up just about anywhere, any time of the night. It's good one of us is social, I suppose, or else we'd drive each other crazy sitting in the apartment all the time.'

I didn't know where to go with that, so I just nodded.

'What about you? Looked like you were having fun when I left, talking to Elisa and Philip. Was it a good night?'

I stared at her, thinking about how awkward I'd felt with Elisa and Philip, as if I were a trespasser in a members-only world – a feeling that had become pretty familiar to me since I'd joined Kelly & Company. I thought about how I'd gotten in the cab and argued to be dropped off alone and how – much to my surprise – Philip hadn't argued back, not one bit. I thought about how empty my apartment had seemed when I got home, and how even Millington curled up beside me in bed didn't make me feel much better. And I looked at Penelope and wondered just when, exactly, we had grown so far apart.

'It was all right, I guess. I was hoping to hang out with you more . . .' I stopped short when I realized it sounded accusatory.

She lifted her gaze and looked at me sharply. 'I'm sorry, I wasn't expecting the situation with Avery. Also, I would have loved for it to be us, going out, like we used to, but you were the one who had us meet up with all your work friends to scout the location. It seems like they're omnipresent these days.'

'Pen, I'm sorry, I didn't mean for it to sound like that. I was just saying that I'd rather hang out with you any day. After you left, it just got worse. Philip was babysitting some girl from home and I

101

shared a cab home with them because I didn't want to start a big scene at the club, but then people saw me getting in the backseat, and I felt like shit. Oh, and Abby, too. It was just a giant mess and I wish I'd left when you did.'

'So did you go home with him? Where did the girl sleep?'

'No, I just got in the cab because it seemed easier than listening to him throw a fit. I made them drop me off first, but people watching would never know that.'

'Why didn't you go home with him? And who's "people"?' I could tell she was trying to keep everyone straight, but she hadn't even met all the players.

'Well,' I lied, 'I'm not sure I'm ready to get involved in Philip's world. He's tied in to just about everyone and everything at work, which makes it all even weirder.'

'I wouldn't know. You didn't introduce me,' she said lightly.

I felt the reprimand and knew she was right, but I didn't want to turn it into a big discussion. 'No? Last night was a little hectic. Trust me, you're not missing much. He's gorgeous, that much you saw, but otherwise he's your basic spoiled party kid, just with a fantastic accent. Damn shame he's so cute, though.' I sighed audibly.

'Well, that little speech sounds all well and good, my dear, but you should've seen your face when he walked in with that model. I thought you'd die. You like him, don't you? Admit it.'

I didn't know how to say that of course something attracted me to him, but something simultaneously repelled me. I didn't want to say aloud how flattered I was that someone like Philip could want someone like me, even if he didn't seem to be all that great of a guy. I didn't want to explain the entire situation at work, how I suspected Elisa might be jealous that Philip was interested in me, or how Kelly had seemed ready and willing to whore me out to Philip because it meant good things for the business. I just shrugged and salted my omelet, making sure to fix my coffee cup to my lips so I wouldn't have to say anything just yet.

Penelope understood that I wasn't going to get into it then. It was the first and only time in the nearly nine years we'd been friends that I could remember both of us sitting at a table and willingly withholding information from each other. She'd refused to tell me her real feelings about her relationship with Avery; I'd taken a pass on commenting on Philip. We sat in a comfortable enough but foreign-feeling silence until she said, 'I know I don't know the entire situation, and of course I know you're more than capable of handling everything yourself, but please, for me, just be careful? I'm sure Philip is a perfectly nice guy, but I've seen enough with Avery's friends and now your work friends to know that the whole scene just freaks me out. Nothing concrete, but I worry about you, you know?'

She placed her hand over mine and I knew we'd get back to our old selves at some point. In the meantime, we'd have to settle for thinking about each other from afar.

11

'Okay, kids, quiet down,' Kelly announced as she tottered into the conference room in the high heels she wore every single day. 'Did everyone have a chance to read their Dirt Alerts already?'

'Sure did,' piped up Leo from the other end of the glass table that looked like it belonged more in a W hotel than in an office. 'Seems like our favorite new staffer got herself another mention.'

I felt the familiar loopiness in my stomach begin its rounds. I'd been ten minutes late this morning and hadn't yet read the Dirt Alert, obviously a major misstep on my part. One of the assistants specifically got in every morning by six A.M. to create the day's Dirt Alert for all of us – a sort of survey of all the columns, papers, and stories that might, in some way, be related to our clients or industry – and place them on our desks by nine A.M., but everyone generally scanned all the websites when they first got up in the morning, skimming quickly between Drudge, Page Six, Liz Smith, Rush & Molloy, *USA Today*, *Variety*, New York Scoop, an assortment of blogs and columns, and a few of the bigger trade headlines. It's best to know early if something bad happened and your phone was going to ring off the hook, so the Dirt Alert was more of a formality than any sort of breaking news. The only really relevant information we got each morning was the Celeb Alert, which included information on who's in town, why they're here, where they're staying (and under what name), and how to best contact them to bribe or beg them to attend an event. Four straight weeks of logging on to analyze every imaginable website within five seconds of waking up – supplemented by a professional report a few hours later – and the one day I wasn't fully informed of all the late-breaking gossip, of course, was the only one that mattered.

'Um, I haven't had a chance to see it yet this morning. And besides, I can't imagine what could be in there, considering I was checking out Sanctuary this weekend – with all of you – right up until I went home. Alone,' I added quickly, as though I owed my coworkers this explanation.

'Well, let's see here,' Kelly said, picking up a printout of the online column. ' "New Kelly & Company employee seems determined to fit in with her hard-partying coworkers. Sources say the event planner's unnamed new girl – supposedly scoping out Sanctuary on Saturday night as a potential venue for the ultra hush-hush *Playboy* party – mixed business and pleasure when she left with Philip Weston and an unidentified model. Their final destination? We have our ideas.' . . .' Kelly let the last words trail off and turned to grin at me.

I felt myself turn crimson.

'What, exactly, is it implying? Because so far I haven't heard one remotely true statement. And who the hell wrote that?'

'Ellie Insider, of course. There's a picture of you climbing into the cab with Philip and this absolutely gorgeous girl, so I guess it's not hard to figure out what she's suggesting. . . .' Kelly continued smiling. She looked like she couldn't be any happier.

Was it utterly bizarre to be discussing this in our weekly staff meeting, called today supposedly to discuss work events?

'Kelly, I'm really sorry for any impact any of this stuff has had on you or the company. Honestly, I don't know why anyone would care, but in all seriousness, it's just not happening like—'

' "The newest It Girl, an associate at Kelly & Company." Do you realize how huge that is? Hopefully next time they'll use your name. They probably just couldn't confirm it in time since you're not on the industry roster yet.'

I noticed Elisa was having trouble smiling.

'Not only that, but it says the rest of us are hard-partying,' Leo chimed in proudly.

'And it plugs the *Playboy* party!' Skye added.

'I just don't know who would give them that information,' I muttered. 'It's not even true.'

'Bette, honey, I don't care if it's true, I just care that it's being covered. You've done wonderful things for the team in the short amount of time you've been with us. Plus, Danny will be thrilled about the plug for the club. Keep up the good work.' And with that, we moved on to one of Kelly's specialty brainstorming sessions.

'Okay, everyone, start talking. We've got the premiere for *Shrek 3* next month. Invites need to be out within two weeks. Skye's in charge of this one. What's the enticement?'

'I still don't understand why we agreed to do a premiere for a kids' movie,' Skye whined, which I noticed she did a lot at meetings. 'Why can't the studio handle their own premiere for that one?'

'That was a rhetorical question, right? We do premieres because they're easy and pay well. You know DreamWorks has their own internal PR, but as you also know, they're tied up with all the awards shows and bigger pictures' publicity, and besides, virtually all of the important press is in New York. We have relationships with people they don't.'

'I know, I know.' Skye sighed in a very unteamlike way. I saw Elisa shoot her a look, and she sat up a little bit straighter. 'It's just that kids' movies are so boring.'

'Well, Skye, if you're not interested in overseeing this, I'm sure Elisa or Leo or Bette or even Brandon wouldn't mind stepping in. I don't think I need to point out just how many celebs are having kids these days . . . Liv, Courteney, Gwyneth, Sarah Jessica, just to name a few. I hope you're not saying that their children are boring.'

'No, of course not. You can count on me – I'm up for it. We've done a dozen of these. Okay. Does anyone have the report on the *Harry Potter* premiere we did over the summer?'

'Yep, right here,' Leo said, pulling a stapled packet from a folder. 'Sunday afternoon in August, at Christie Brinkley's estate in Bridgehampton. Party started at eleven A.M., with the screening from twelve to one-thirty to allow everyone enough time to get back to the city. Children's entertainment included wading pools filled with ice and juice packs, horseback riding, a small petting zoo, a cotton-candy machine, a sno-cone maker, a few roving clowns. Adults were kept amused by highly attentive and attractive cocktail waitresses serving socially acceptable day drinks from a hidden bar inside – mostly mimosas, Bloody Marys, screwdrivers, champagne, margaritas, sangria, and the occasional frozen daiquiri or piña colada if requested. Matt Lauer, Susan Sarandon, Katie Couric, Aerin Lauder, Kate Hudson, Russell Simmons, and Courteney Cox all had children in attendance, in addition to hundreds of others who were slightly less recognizable but just as photogenic. Pics appeared in *People, US Weekly, Star,* Sunday Styles, *Gotham, W,* and a dozen online social pages, including but not limited to the New York Social Diary and Patrick McMullen's website. Warner Brothers was thrilled.'

'Okay, kids, so we've got the template, and we obviously know what works. Clearly we won't be in the Hamptons, but we should stick with the same format. I like the Clearview in Chelsea because they're pretty relaxed about having lots of action in their lobby,' Kelly said, efficiently checking things off a list. 'What else?'

'Well, for food, the usual kid favorites,' Elisa said. 'Pigs in blankets, quarter-sized burgers, candy hunts.'

'Make your own sundae,' Leo added without pause.

'Balloons, magicians, design your own cupcake, bubble machines,' Skye said without the least bit of enthusiasm.

'Guy in a monster Shrek outfit.'

'Face-painting the kids green.'

'Parents hate face-painting. Plenty of other stuff you can do. Maybe those mini-trampolines?'

'Are you kidding? Total liability. Might as well just have "Sue Me" in lights. Speaking of which, how about "Shrek" spelled out in a massive wall of green lightbulbs?'

Everyone nodded. I started to get slightly self-conscious about not having contributed anything, but I'd never been to a movie premiere and didn't know anything about them besides stars walking down the red carpet.

'What if we have a green carpet instead of a red one?' I offered before considering how stupid it sounded. I braced myself, but the faces at the table looked fairly happy.

'Fab idea, Bette! We'll have a green carpet and a giant green walk-and-repeat at the end where everyone can get photographed. Green carpet should definitely mean more pictures. Things sound like they're going smoothly there, so let's move on to what really matters. Where are we with the *Playboy* party?'

The color had returned to Elisa's face, and she appeared more composed. She stood with perfect posture in her Diane von Furstenberg wrap dress and pointed to the bulletin board with her Mason Pearson brush.

'As you can all see, we are just a few months away. After much scouting and debating, we have selected Sanctuary as our location. Leo, can you update us on the logistics?'

Leo looked at Elisa as if to say 'Since when am I answering to you?' but then cleared his throat and told the room he was interviewing production companies (who would handle everything from furniture to lighting) and should have the shortlist by the end of the week. 'I'm sure we'll end up with Bureau Betak,' he said. 'We always do.'

The meeting continued for another hour and a half (we covered gift bags, potential sponsors, and invitations) before we were released for lunch with the encouragement to go somewhere we'd 'see or be seen.' I begged out of going to Pastis with the group and roamed a few blocks east to a divey pizza joint where I surely wouldn't run into anyone from the office. As soon as I had wedged my body into a tiny booth near the restroom, I called Will at work and was surprised to find him at his desk.

'Why are you there?' I asked. 'It's not even deadline day.' Will only went to his office at the paper once or twice a week, less if he could help it.

'Hello, darling. I'm struggling a bit with this week's column.' He was quiet for a split second before adding, 'Lately, it seems I'm struggling a bit with *every* week's column.'

He sounded frustrated and resigned at the same time, two sentiments I wasn't accustomed to hearing from Will.

'Are you okay, Will? What's going on there?' I asked, forcing myself to forget my own problems for just a few seconds.

He sighed heavily. 'Nothing interesting, darling, that's for sure. Readership of "Will of the People" is way down this year. Another few papers dropped it from syndication. My new thirty-one-year-old editor has no sense of humor – keeps telling me that "today's readers" are more "socially sensitive" and that therefore I should strive to be more "politically correct." Naturally, I told him to fuck off, but he won't stay quiet for long. Then again, why would anyone want to read my column when they can read about pretty young party planners gallivanting about with rich, famous pretty boys?'

I felt like I'd been punched. 'You saw.'

'Naturally. Am I to assume there was any truth to that tawdry little write-up?' he asked.

'Of course not!' I wailed loud enough to cause the cashier to turn and glare at me. 'I saw Philip at Sanctuary this weekend, when I was there for work. We shared a cab home because it was less complicated. The other girl was his family friend. Childhood family friend. The whole thing could not have been less scandalous.'

'Well, then, it seems this Ellie Insider character is doing her job splendidly. Take comfort in the fact that they didn't use your name, darling. But don't think for a minute that it won't come soon.'

'Do you know who she is, Will? I mean, you must have met her somewhere along the line, don't you think?'

I heard Will chuckle and imagined the worst. 'Well, I've certainly heard lots of names bandied about, but there are no solid leads. Some people insist it's some socialite ratting out all her friends. Others seem to think it's an unknown with a few well-placed sources. For all we know, it could be that ex–fashion editor – oh, what was her name? The one who keeps busy penning nasty book reviews? I could see her writing trash like this.'

'It's just creepy. I'm about ready for whomever it is to start focusing on someone else, you know? Someone a little more interesting, who might actually be living a scandalous life? I definitely don't qualify.' I bit into a piece of pizza, possibly the most perfect slice in the world.

'I understand, darling, truly I do. But Philip qualifies, don't forget! I hate to go rushing off, but my column doesn't seem to want to write itself this week. Talk soon? Will we see you at dinner this Thursday?'

'Of course,' I said automatically before realizing that I was expected to attend the launch of a new Gucci fragrance that night. I knew I'd have to call back and cancel, but I just couldn't bring myself to do it now. 'Wouldn't miss it for the world. Talk to you later.'

I finished my little slice of heaven and ordered a second, which I also knocked off in record time. I was listlessly staring at a tattered copy of the *Post* someone had left on the table when my phone rang. HOME flashed on the caller ID.

'Hello?' I answered, wondering whether it was my mother or father – or both, since they often enjoyed the tag-team calling of first one, then the other, then all three of us talking from different extensions.

'Bette, is that you?' my mother practically shouted. 'Can you hear me?' Her voice was, as usual, louder than necessary. She was convinced that cell phones required above-average volume from all involved parties and therefore screamed whenever she called mine.

'I can hear you, Mom. Perfectly. How are you?'

'I can't really talk since I'm running into a scheduling meeting, but one of the girls at the clinic today said she saw your picture on some website. A picture of you and a famous boy and another girl? Or something to that effect.'

Impossible! My mother, who had only recently registered for her own email address, was now receiving information about the content of online gossip columns? I was quick to deny it. 'It was nothing, Mom, just a little photo of me at a work event.'

'Bette, that's wonderful! Congratulations! I can't wait to see it. I asked Dad to get online and print it out, but he couldn't seem to open the page or something. Save us a copy?'

'Of course,' I said meekly. 'Will do. But seriously, it's nothing important, just work stuff. I have to get back to the office, so can I call you later?'

'Sure, dear. Congrats again. Not at the job long, and already you're making headlines!'

If only she knew, I thought as I clicked off the phone. Thankfully, there was no chance my father would ever figure out how to register for the free account that New York Scoop offered to readers. As long as no one actually printed it out and showed it to them, I was safe. At least for now.

12

'I'd like to open tonight's meeting with a toast to Bette,' Courtney said, raising her mojito above her head.

I'd been reading a text message from Kelly politely requesting (read: ordering) that I 'put in an appearance' at the *Mr and Mrs Smith* premiere that was being overseen by Skye and Leo. The movie would end at exactly eleven o'clock, which meant I could stop by the after-party at Duvet and still be home by twelve-thirty and asleep by one A.M. – which would be the earliest night in weeks. I had just concluded my calculations when the sound of my name made me snap to attention.

'Me? What have I done to deserve a toast?' I asked distractedly.

The group stared at me as though unable to comprehend my stupidity. Janie spoke first. 'Excuse me, do you think we live in a vacuum? That our lives cease to exist outside this book club?'

I just stared, having a fairly good idea where this was headed, but still trying to prevent it from happening.

Jill mashed some limes with sugar in a bowl before spooning more of the muddled mixture into my drink. 'Bette, we all read New York Scoop, you know – hell, everyone reads it. And you appear to be the featured story every day. When on earth were you planning to mention that your boyfriend just happens to be *Philip Weston*?' She said his name with a slow deliberateness and everyone laughed.

'Whoa, girls, let's hold on a second here. He is *not* my boyfriend.'

'Well, that's not what Ellie Insider seems to think,' Alex chirped in. Her hair was an unsavory shade of puke green tonight and I marveled at the thought that even the East Village punk crowd was reading that horrific column.

'Yeah, that's true,' Vika added thoughtfully. 'You do seem to be with him quite frequently. And why not? He's wildly, undeniably, fabulously gorgeous.'

I thought about that for a moment. He was indeed gorgeous, and every woman between the ages of fifteen and fifty seemed to want him desperately, so what was so wrong with letting everyone think we were dating? Unless I told them, no one would really know that I hadn't been back to Philip's apartment since the first time I accidentally woke up there. In fact, they probably wouldn't even believe it if I explained that we only saw one another (and were subsequently seen together) because I was expected to stop by every Kelly & Company event – whether I'd worked on it or not. I'd run into Philip 'accidentally' almost every other night for weeks. After all, it was my job to throw the best parties, and it was Philip's self-designated responsibility to attend each and every one.

Why explain that even though we only chatted briefly at these events, he always seemed to throw his arm around my shoulders (or put his hand on my ass or his drink in front of my chest or his mouth on my neck) precisely when a photographer happened to stroll by? It appeared to anyone who was watching that we were inseparable, but what got labeled as 'lots of hot-and-heavy canoodling' was about as sexual as my nightly cuddles with Millington. Why, I wondered, would anyone possibly want to hear all of that?

I knew the answer. Because he was the It Boy du jour, and I was making out with him.

'He is cute, isn't he?' I asked. Philip Weston might be one of the more arrogant guys I'd ever met, but it was ridiculous to deny that I was absurdly attracted to him.

'Um, *yeah*. And let's not overlook the fact that he's the most perfect Harlequin guy you could imagine existing in real life.' Courtney sighed. 'I think I'm going to model the hero of my next novel after him.'

'After Philip?' It was difficult to envision any leading Harlequin man whining and bitching about his thread count, but I supposed the genre could use some updating for the new millennium.

'Bette! He's tall, handsome, and powerful. He's even foreign, for Christ's sake,' she pointed out while waving a copy of *Sweet Savage Love* and pointing to the hulking man in a loincloth on the cover. 'And better looking than Dominick, which is remarkable when you consider that Dominick is *drawn* to look as gorgeous as humanly possible.'

The girl had a point. Philip fit the ideal of the romantic hero more closely than any guy I'd met before – except for that small, nagging little problem of his personality.

I spent the rest of book club distracted, dreamily wondering if I'd see Philip later at the after-party and what might happen.

I ducked out of the meeting early and changed before heading to Duvet. Where, of course, the first person I saw upon walking inside was Mr Weston himself.

'Bette, love, come say hello to a few mates visiting from England,' he said, planting a brief but admittedly delicious kiss directly on my lips.

I couldn't help it; I looked over my shoulder. I had promised myself I'd be more aware of the photographers, but I saw nothing unusual, just the regular beautiful writhing masses.

'Hi,' I said, noticing (a) he looked even more like fictional Dominick when he was standing in front of me, and (b) Courtney was right: Philip was better-looking. 'Can I meet you over there in a minute? I've got to find Kelly and make sure everything's okay.'

'Sure, love. Will you bring me a cocktail when you come back? That'd be smashing!' And he scampered off to play with his friends, as happy as a little boy at the playground.

I managed to check in with Kelly, ask Leo and Skye if they needed anything, wave to Elisa as she made out with Davide, introduce myself to two potential clients (the much-worshipped designer Alvin Valley and someone who Kelly described to me as 'the most sought-after stylist in Hollywood'), and bring Philip a gin and tonic, all in less than an hour. So much for what might happen with Philip. He was busy entertaining his 'blokes.' The dull headache I'd managed to ignore since morning had suddenly become sharper, and I knew it couldn't be another late night. I slipped out the door shortly thereafter and was home by twelve-fifteen (a solid fifteen minutes ahead of schedule) and unconscious by twelve-thirty, after deciding that silly nighttime rituals like teeth-brushing and face-washing could easily be neglected. When my alarm went off six and a half hours later, I was not looking good.

I grabbed the Dirt Alert before rushing out and read it as I inhaled a large coffee and a buttered cinnamon-raisin bagel on the subway. Unsurprisingly, New York Scoop was the first clipping of the day's packet and, again, there was a huge picture – a close-up, actually – of Philip kissing me the night before. Only the back of his head was visible, but somehow the camera had zoomed in on my face and caught me with some sort of faraway, dreamy look caused by my eyes being only partially open while they gazed adoringly at him. Or drunkenly, depending on how one might interpret my half-blink. I probably should have expected it, but since I'd never even spotted a camera, the full-page photo made me physically recoil. That day's scoop was extra memorable. As predicted, I'd graduated from being 'Philip's gal pal' and 'the new girl' and 'party girl' and 'PR maven-in-training' to warranting my own identity. Right there, under the picture – just in case there was anyone left in New York State who didn't know my whereabouts at all times – was my name, spelled in big, bold letters, and a caption that read: APPARENTLY, SHE'S HERE TO STAY ... BETTINA ROBINSON KNOWS HOW TO PARTY. The feeling was a weird mixture of embarrassment at having anyone see me in such a state, indignation at the misrepresentation of it all, and a faint but persistent misery at the realization that I no longer had anything remotely resembling privacy.

The walk from the subway to the office felt six miles longer than the actual three blocks it was, and it was made incrementally worse when I overheard two perfect strangers talking about Philip's 'new girlfriend, what's her name?'

By the time I'd dropped my laptop bag on the circular table, the entire staff had surrounded me.

'I suppose you've all seen it already?' I asked no one in particular, flopping into a leather work chair.

'It's really nothing we don't already know,' Kelly pointed out, sounding disappointed. 'It just says here that one Mr Philip Weston has been seen so frequently in the company of one Ms. Bettina Robinson that it would only be fair to consider them an item.'

'An item?' I asked, incredulous. In my horror at seeing the picture and the caption, I'd simply forgotten to read the accompanying text.

'Oh, yes, it says here that an unnamed source claims that the two of you spend nearly every night together, after partying at all the hot spots like Bungalow and Marquee.'

'We are not dating,' I insisted.

'The pictures are right here, Bette. And it very much appears that you are, thank God.' Kelly turned her twenty-inch flat-screen Mac monitor toward the group so we could all enjoy the photos of Philip and me.

My personal and professional lives had become not only intertwined but completely dependent on one another. Any idiot could see that my connection with Philip had made me an accepted part of the team with a swiftness that made my head hurt.

'Well, it's just that *dating* is kind of a strong word,' I said awkwardly. Why did no one understand?

'Well, whatever you're doing, Bette, just keep on doing it. Do you know we've been hired to represent BlackBerry solely because you're dating Mr Weston?'

Solely? I thought.

'Surprise, Bette! We got a call from their internal PR company just this morning. They want us to introduce their new BlackBerry to New York's younger set, and picked us because we clearly have access to that world. BlackBerry's already huge, of course, with the Wall Street crowd, and everyone who's anyone – and most people who aren't – in Hollywood already has one, but they haven't hit as big with the younger crowd. We will do our best to change that, of course. And I'm happy to report that I'm putting you in charge of all the logistics, reporting to me only for approval.'

'In charge?' I stammered.

'Their account rep told us how much she'd love to have you planning and Philip hosting the event, so I think it works out perfectly!' she sang, not the least bit aware that Philip most likely still didn't even know my full name.

'Skye will help you with whatever you need' – a quick glance at Skye informed me that she wasn't thrilled with this pronouncement – 'and we'll all be here to support you. The party is scheduled for November twenty-second, which is the Tuesday before Thanksgiving, so you'd better get started immediately.'

I did a few mental calculations and realized that it was less than three weeks away. I said as much.

'Oh, Bette, stop stressing,' Elisa said with an exasperated eye-roll. 'It's nothing. Find a venue, get sponsors, order invites, work The List, and save all your presswork until that week. Anything that Philip hosts will be automatically covered, so this is not exactly going to be a lot of work.'

When the meeting finally ended, I ducked out with my laptop and headed to Starbucks in a panicky effort to figure out exactly what needed to happen for the BlackBerry event. I almost hoped Philip would make it some sort of quid pro quo that he'd host the event if I'd sleep with him . . . and then immediately felt pathetic. Everyone assumed we'd already consummated our relationship, but the reality was that we both seemed to avoid the situation entirely. Which wasn't difficult, considering he only seemed to want to mug for the cameras. He was great with the suggestive remarks, but he never really followed up on any of them, and he seemed almost relieved when I brushed him off and left alone each night. There hadn't been much time to think about it, but I figured he had some sort of top-secret girlfriend (or five) that he kept sequestered away and was content to let the general public think we were dating. It was vaguely insulting – I still wanted him to *want* to have sex with me – but we seemed to have an unspoken agreement to maintain the present arrangement.

I left a message with Amy Sacco's office asking if we could reserve Bungalow for the BlackBerry event, just as Penelope called on the other line.

'Hey, what's going on? What warrants the middle-of-the-day call? How's Aaron? Have you seen him lately?'

'Do you know how much the quality of my work life has improved since you left?' Penelope asked. 'No offense, but it's almost worth not having you around to never have him utter the word *powwow*. How's lover boy?'

'Oh, you mean my boyfriend? He's dreamy,' I said.

'Tell me,' Penelope said, trying to sound enthusiastic. I know she couldn't stand the thought of Philip, but she'd been kind enough not to say that outright . . . yet.

'Let's see. Things are, like, so amazing. We go to these wonderful parties where he spends at least a few minutes talking to me before flirting with every other girl there. Often I'm allowed to bring him his favorite cocktail – gin and tonic, for the record. I let him kiss me for the photographers and then we go our separate ways. No sex, by the way. We haven't even spent the night together since I passed out there the first time I met him.'

'Maybe he's just so overwhelmed by the amount of sex he's having with every model, actress, and socialite in London, Los Angeles, and New York that he's just physically exhausted? It's possible, you know.'

'Did I ever tell you what a good friend you are, Pen? Seriously, you always know exactly what to say.'

She laughed. 'Yeah, well, I don't have to spell out that I think you're not doing yourself justice. But enough, let's talk about me for a second. I have something to tell you.'

'You're knocked up and feel guilty about getting rid of it because you're engaged and old enough to take responsibility for your own actions?' I asked eagerly, leaning in closer to the phone as though she could see me.

She sighed, and I knew she was rolling her eyes.

'You're knocked up and it's not Avery's baby?'

When this elicited nothing but another exasperated sound, I decided on just one more.

'You're knocked up and—'

'Bette.' Her voice tightened and I could tell she wasn't enjoying this nearly as much as I was.

'Sorry. What's up?'

'I'm leaving.'

'You're what?'

'I'm leaving. Done. I'm finished.'

'Ohmigod, no.'

'Yes,' she said.

'It's definite?'

'Yes.'

'Are you serious? Just like that? Over? Are you okay with it?'

I was doing everything possible to contain my glee at the idea that she wouldn't be going through with the wedding, but it was difficult, especially since I knew she'd probably had to walk in on Avery and some girl, a scenario I'd already decided was the

114

only way she'd ever believe it. That aside, she sounded good. Maybe it was the best thing and she knew it.

'Honestly? I didn't expect this, but I couldn't be happier. I've wanted to do it for a long time and, well, I'm just so excited about what's next.'

I slowly took a sip of my coffee and contemplated this new information. 'You wouldn't be this excited if you hadn't met someone else. Who is he? I had no idea you and Avery were having trouble – how could you not tell me?' I choked out. 'What about the ring? You know, etiquette dictates that if you're the one to break off the engagement, you've got to give it back. Ohmigod, he isn't cheating on you, is he?' I pretended to be horrified at even the idea of it, as though it were just too impossible to even imagine. 'Is that bastard—'

'Bette, stop! I'm not leaving Avery, I'm leaving this job!' she hissed, trying not to be overheard by her cubicle mates.

Serious one-eighty – and a major disappointment.

'You're leaving UBS? Really? What happened?'

'Well, I kind of had no choice. Avery got accepted to UCLA for law school, so we're moving there. He doesn't start until January, but we figured we'd go now to get settled and learn our way around.'

'UCLA?'

'Uh-huh.'

'So you're not leaving Avery, you're leaving me?' I wail-whispered. The juicy story of my best friend cheating on her fiancé had become the story of my best friend moving to another coast.

'I'm not leaving you,' she said, sighing. 'I'm leaving this job and this city and going to California. Probably just for the three years, and then I'll be back. And we'll visit, of course. You'll love coming out there when it's February and you haven't left your apartment in twelve days because the temperature hasn't hit the double digits.'

'There aren't law schools on the East Coast? Avery really has to be so selfish as to drag you all the way out, out, *there*?'

'Oh, Bette, shut up and be happy for me. UCLA is a great school, and besides, I could use a change. I've lived in the city for five years since graduation, and eighteen before it. I'll be back, there's no getting around that. But for now I think it could be nice to do something different.'

It occurred to me right then that as a friend, I was required to express some sort of support, however lame it might come across.

'Honey, I'm sorry, this is just all so surprising – you didn't even mention he was applying out west. If this is what you want to do, then I'm excited for you. And I promise to try very, very hard to stop only thinking about how it will affect me, okay?'

'Yeah, he did the UCLA application at the last second, and I never thought he'd want to go there. But seriously, I'm not too worried about you. You've got a whole new crew now, and I have a feeling you'll be just fine without me. . . .' She let the words trail off, trying to sound casual, but we both knew this was the closest she'd ever get to saying something more important.

'Well, we'll have to have a great big going-away dinner for you guys,' I said with forced cheer, not quite acknowledging my opportunity to disagree.

'As you can imagine, our mothers are already on that. We're leaving sort of soon, so they planned a joint dinner at the Four Seasons on Saturday. You'll be there, right? It'll be dreadful, but you're obligated to attend nonetheless.' She cleared her throat. 'And, of course, Philip is always invited.'

'Pen! Of course I'll be there. And I'll certainly spare all of you Philip's company.'

My call waiting beeped with a 917 number I didn't recognize. I decided to answer it in case it was related to the BlackBerry party.

'I'm sorry, Pen, I've got to take this call. Can I call you later?'

'Sure, no worries.'

'Okay, I'll talk to you in a few. And congratulations! If you're happy, then so am I. Grudgingly, of course. But happy for you.'

We hung up and I clicked over right before the phone went to voice mail. 'May I speak with Bette?' I heard a gravelly male voice ask.

'Speaking.'

'Bette, this is Sammy calling from Amy Sacco's office. You called about a date you wanted to reserve the club?'

Sammy? Wasn't that the name of the Bungalow 8 bouncer? Could there be more than one Sammy in her employ? I didn't know that bouncers did office work.

'Yes, hi, how are you?' I said as professionally as possible, although he certainly didn't know my name or remember me as the cranky girl with no umbrella.

'Great. We got your message, and Amy asked me to call you back because she's tied up all afternoon.' The rest was drowned out by the screech of sirens.

'Sorry, I missed that. It's just the loudest siren I've ever heard. It must be eight fire trucks or something,' I screamed, trying to be heard over the wails.

'I hear it, too, only not just through the phone. Where are you now?'

'I'm at the Starbucks near Eighth and Broadway. Why?'

'That's weird. I'm literally across the street. I was just leaving class when I got the message from Amy to call you back. Hold on, I'm coming over.' He hung up, and I stared at the phone for a second before frantically yanking a lip gloss and brush out of my bag and sprinting for the bathroom, which, naturally, was occupied. I watched as he approached the front door and then bolted back to my table in a side nook, falling back into my seat before he even saw me.

There was no subtle way to fix anything right now since I needed to focus my energy on pretending to look both busy and indifferent, which was impossible. I knew I'd choke if I tried to drink or drop my phone if I pretended to be talking, and so I just sat, staring at my Filofax with such determined interest that I briefly wondered if it might just up and ignite from the intensity of my gaze. A quick mental survey of my physical state revealed a list of clichéd reactions – shaking hands, pounding heart, dry mouth – that could indicate only one thing: my body was telling me that I liked Sammy or, quite possibly, that I worshipped him. Which, if one cared to draw a parallel, was exactly how Lucinda felt right before her first one-on-one meeting with Marcello in *The Magnate's Tender Touch*. This was the first time I could ever remember feeling all tingly with nervous anticipation, just like the women in my books always did.

I felt him standing over me before I saw him, a sort of amorphous figure in all black. And he smelled good! Like freshly baked bread or sugar cookies or something equally as wholesome. He probably stood there for thirty seconds, staring at me stare at my Filofax, before I finally mustered the nerve to look up, just as he cleared his throat.

'Hey,' I said.

'Hey,' he said right back. He was unconsciously rubbing at what appeared to be a flour stain on his black pants, but he stopped when he noticed me watching.

'Uh, would you like to sit down?' I stammered, wondering why it was utterly impossible for me to make one intelligible or coherent statement.

'Sure. I, uh, I just thought it might be easier to do this in person since I was, uh, right across the street, you know?' It was comforting that he didn't sound much better.

'Yeah, definitely, it makes perfect sense. Did you say you were just coming from class? Are you taking a bartending course? I've always wanted to do that!' I was rambling now, but I couldn't help it. 'It just seems like it'd be the most useful thing, whether or not you actually work in a bar. I don't know. It'd be nice to know how to mix a decent drink or something. You know?'

He smiled for the first time, a megawatt ear-to-ear shiner, and I thought I might just cease living if he ever stopped. 'No, it's not for bartending, it's for pastry-making,' he said.

It didn't make much sense that the bouncer was into pastries, but I thought it was nice that he had outside interests. After all, aside from the nightly ego rush of rejecting people based on appearance alone, I imagined it got pretty boring.

'Oh, really? Interesting. Do you cook a lot in your free time?' I was only asking to be polite, which, unfortunately, came across loud and clear in my voice. I rushed on. 'I mean, is that a particular passion of yours?'

'Passion?' He grinned again. 'I'm not sure I would call it a "passion," but yeah, I like to cook. And I sort of have to, for work.'

Ohmigod. I couldn't believe he'd called me out for using that ridiculous word, *passion*.

'You *have* to?' It came out sounding downright snotty. 'I'm sorry, I didn't mean it like that. Where do you cook?'

'I'm studying to be a chef, actually,' he said, diverting his eyes from mine.

This was a new and interesting development. 'A chef? Really? Where?'

'Well, nowhere yet, really. I already graduated from CIA and I'm taking a few classes at night. Like pastry-making.' He laughed.

'How'd you get into that?'

'I'm not particularly into it, but it's good to know. Aside from making omelet dinners growing up when it was my turn, I didn't really ever cook. I lived in Ithaca for a summer in high school with a buddy and worked as a waiter at the Statler Hotel on Cornell's campus. One day the general manager saw me refilling a guest's coffee by holding the carafe almost four feet above the cup and freaked out – he loved it. He convinced me to apply to the hotel school there. He got me a few scholarships, and I worked the whole time – busboy, waiter, night manager, bartender, you name it – and when I graduated he hooked me up with a year-long apprenticeship at a Michelin-starred restaurant in France. It was entirely his doing.'

I was vaguely aware that my mouth was quite unattractively hanging open in shock at this information, but Sammy graciously saved me from myself by continuing.

'You're probably wondering why I'm working as a bouncer at Bungalow, huh?' He grinned.

'No, not at all. Whatever works for you. Um, I mean, it's just a different side of the hospitality industry, right?'

'I'm paying my dues now. I've worked in what feels like every imaginable restaurant in this city.' He laughed. 'But it'll be worth it when I finally open my own place. Hopefully it'll be sooner rather than later.'

I must have still looked confused because he just laughed. 'Well, clearly the first and foremost reason is the money. You can actually make a decent living piecing together a few security and bartending gigs, and I have a bunch of that stuff going on. It keeps me from going out at night and spending, so I stick it out. Everyone says there's nothing like opening a restaurant in this city. I've been told it's really important to know all the social politics, from who's sleeping with whom to who's really important and who's just pretending they're a player. It doesn't really interest me, but I don't exactly run with that crowd, so there's no better way than to watch them in their native environments.'

He clamped a hand over his mouth and peered at me. 'Look, I probably shouldn't have said all that. I didn't mean any offense to you and your friends, it's just that—'

Love. All-consuming and overwhelming love. It was all I could do not to grab his face and kiss him full on the mouth . . . he looked so horrified.

'Seriously, don't say another word,' I said. I moved my hand to touch his reassuringly, but I lost my nerve at the last minute and my fingers ended up awkwardly suspended above the table. Lucinda from *Magnate* would've been cool enough to pull off that move, but I, apparently, was not. 'I think it's really great what you're doing. I can't imagine some of the things you must see every night. Ridiculous stuff, right?'

It was all he needed to hear. 'Christ, it's incredible. All those people – they have so much money and so much time and don't seem to want to do anything but beg me to let them into these clubs every night,' he said. His eyes met mine.

'It's got to be kind of fun, though, isn't it? I mean, people fall all over themselves trying to be nice to you,' I managed, too distracted by his gaze to think straight.

'Oh, come on, Bette, we both know it's hardly like that. They kiss my ass because they need me, not because they know anything about me or like me as a person. I have a very short shelf life for respect and likability – namely, the few minutes between the time they arrive and the time they walk inside. They wouldn't remember my name if they saw me anywhere away from that velvet rope.'

The look of distress returned to his face, and I noticed how his forehead wrinkled when he frowned, and it only made him cuter. He sighed and I had a bizarre desire to hug him. 'I have such a big mouth. Forget everything I just said. I really don't take the job all that seriously, so I shouldn't make it sound like it's a bigger deal than it really is. It's just a means to an end, and I can put up with anything if it'll get me closer to my restaurant one day.'

I was desperate for him to keep talking, saying anything about anyone just so I could continue to watch his perfect face and examine the way his mouth moved and his hands gestured, but he was finished. When I opened my mouth to tell him that I understood exactly what he meant and had never really thought of it from that perspective, he gently cut me off. 'I guess you're just easy to talk to,' he said and smiled so sweetly that I had to remind myself to breathe. 'I'd appreciate if you didn't mention any of this stuff to anyone at your office. It's just easier for me to do what I need to do without everyone, well, uh, you know.'

I sure did know. Without everyone knowing where you came from and where you were going, trying to decide at every moment if you fell into their own personal 'worth knowing' or 'safe not to acknowledge' categories. Without everyone angling for position or trying to manipulate the situation to their own benefit or slowly but surely chipping away at your confidence because it made them feel better about themselves. Uncle Will was joking when he always said, 'If you can't have, discredit,' but most of this crowd weren't. Yes, I got it, loud and clear.

'Of course. Totally. I understand completely. I, uh, I think it's really cool what you're doing,' I said.

Another blinding smile. Ah! I tried to think of something, anything, I could say that would elicit another smile, but one of us finally remembered that we were there on business.

He seemed completely recovered from any moment of vulnerability when he said, 'I'm getting a coffee, and then we can figure out the event details. Can I get you something?'

I shook my head and pointed to my coffee cup.

'No grande sugar-free vanilla extra-hot no-whip skim latte?'

I laughed and shook my head again.

'What? You think I'm kidding? I actually order that fucking drink every time I come here.'

'You do not.'

'I do, I swear I do. I made it through twenty-some years of life being perfectly fine with a cup of regular coffee. Sometimes I had it light and sweet, and sometimes late at night I asked for it decaf, but it was definitely just coffee. Then a friend mentioned how good lattes were. Soon after that a girl from school announced that adding flavoring made it even better. The rest of it just followed, and it's gotten totally out of hand. I wish, just once, they'd refuse to make the damn thing, just say, "Get ahold of yourself, Sammy. Be a man and drink a goddamn cup of regular coffee." But they never do and, alas, neither do I.' And with that, he was off.

I watched as the barista flashed him an undeniable I'm-yours-for-the-taking smile. I don't think I blinked the entire time he was gone, and I audibly exhaled when he reclaimed his seat next to me.

'Okay, enough confessional for one day. Should we get this party worked out?' He brushed the back of his head, and I couldn't help thinking that I'd seen him do that a million times before.

'Sure. What first?' I sipped my coffee and concentrated on looking cool and professional.

'How many did you say the event is for?'

'I'm not exactly sure, since I haven't put together a finalized list yet' – or any list, for that matter, but he didn't need to know that – 'but I'm thinking it'll be in the area of a couple hundred.'

'And will Kelly & Company be bringing in its own people for everything or using ours?'

Again, not something I'd considered yet, but I tried to think back to past meetings and cobble together a semi-reasonable answer. 'Well, I'll definitely be securing some sponsors, so I think we'll do alcohol but use your bartenders. I'm assuming we'll be using your, uh, your . . .'

'Security?' he provided helpfully, somehow sensing my discomfort at using the word *bouncers*.

'Yes, exactly, although I'll have to check on that.'

'Sounds good to me. As of now, only Lot 61 is free that night, but Amy may want to consider rearranging the schedule. Who will be hosting?'

'Oh, uh, a guy named Philip Weston. He, uh, he's—'

'I know who he is. Your boyfriend, right? I've seen you guys to-gether a lot lately. Yeah, I'm sure Amy will be thrilled to hear that, so I wouldn't worry about Bungalow being free that night.'

'No, no, he's certainly not my boyfriend,' I said as quickly as possible. 'It's not like that at all. Actually, he's just this weird guy I sort of know who—'

'None of my business, that's for sure. Guy always seemed like kind of an asshole to me, but what do I know, right?' Was that bitterness I detected? Or wanted to detect?

'Yes, I suppose it's not any of your business, is it?' I said with such prissiness that he actually physically recoiled.

We stared at each other briefly before he looked away.

He took another sip of his coffee and began to gather his stuff. 'Well, then, this has been fun. I'll check with Amy and get back to you about the venue. Assume it's fine. Like I said, who wouldn't jump at the chance to have Mr British Royalty himself throw a party, right? He's going to have to start tanning now if he has any hope of being dark enough in time.'

'Thanks for your concern, I'll be sure to pass that along. In the meantime, you enjoy making your little puff pastries. I'll work out the details of the event on my own or directly with Amy, since as much as I enjoy being verbally attacked by you, I don't really have the time right now.' I stood up with as much steadiness as I could manage and began to lurch toward the door, already wondering how things had managed to go so terribly wrong in so little time.

'Bette!' he called just as I was about to pull open the door. *He's so sorry. He just had a really long day and is under a lot of stress lately and hasn't been getting enough sleep and he didn't mean to take it out on me. Either that, or he's so wildly, insanely jealous of the fact that Philip and I are dating that he simply couldn't refrain from saying something nasty. Or perhaps a combination of the two,* I thought. Either way, I would of course forgive him when he begged for me to understand and apologized profusely.

I turned around, hoping all the time that he would rush toward me with a plea for forgiveness, but instead he was holding up something and waving it. My cell phone. Which naturally began ringing before I'd reached the table.

He glanced down and I spotted the tightness in his face before he forced a smile. 'What a coincidence, it's the man of the hour. Shall I take a message for you? Don't worry, I promise to tell him we're on a jet on our way back from Cannes and not sitting at a downtown Starbucks.'

'Give that to me,' I snapped, wanting to kick myself for programming Philip's number into my phone while yanking it from Sammy's fingers and noticing only briefly how nice it was to touch his skin. I silenced the ringer and tossed it in my bag.

'Don't not answer on my account.'

'I'm not doing anything on your account,' I announced. I looked back only once as I stormed out, only to see him watching me and shaking his head. *Not exactly how the same scene would've played out in* The Magnate's Tender Touch, I thought with not a little remorse. But I cheered myself up slightly with the rationalization that all new relationships – even the fictional ones – have obstacles to overcome in the beginning. I would not give up hope on this one. Not yet.

13

The rest of the day after the Starbucks encounter passed in a blur as I alternately obsessed over my bizarre fight with Sammy and Penelope's news that she was moving. Both of these, combined with the reality that I was entirely responsible for planning an event that was to take place in two and a half weeks, made me want to curl up with Millington and watch back-to-back showings of *When Harry Met Sally* on TNT. By the time I arrived at home, my small-talk quotient was rapidly approaching zero, and I still had to traverse the entire lobby to reach the elevator, where I would surely be accosted by Seamus. I'd managed to press the button and was silently rejoicing in my victory when he materialized, as always, out of nowhere.

'Good day?' he asked with a huge smile.

'Um, yeah, it was fine, I guess. And you?'

'Fine sounds very different from good, Bette!' he was practically singing. What sort of vibe did I give off that said 'Talk to me'?

'I suppose it is different, but I think "good" would be an overstatement. It was definitively fine,' I explained, wondering if it'd be worth it to climb thirteen flights of stairs rather than wait for the elevator and endure the interim conversation.

'Well, let's just say I have a really good feeling it's going to get better,' he replied with what was, unmistakably, a wink.

'Mmm, really?' I said, desperately staring at the elevator doors and willing them to open. 'That'd be nice.'

'Yep, you heard it here first. I officially predict that your day is going to improve significantly within the next couple of minutes.' He said this with such certainty – and in that particularly rankling I-know-something-you-don't-know tone – that I actually looked up at him.

'Is there something I should know? Is someone here?' I asked, both horrified and curious as to who might be staking out my apartment, waiting for me to get home.

'Okay, well, I've said enough, that much is for sure!' he sang. 'It's none of my business, of course. Time for me to get back to the door.' He tipped his hat and turned on his heels and I wondered if there was any possible way to ask him nicely never to speak to me again.

I knew exactly what he'd meant when I stepped off the elevator and rounded the corner to lucky number 1313. Resting against the door were the most gorgeous flowers I'd ever seen. My first thought was that they'd been mistakenly left in front of my door and were actually left for someone else, but as I got closer, I could see my name written in black marker on the outside of the envelope that was nestled behind the cellophane wrapping. After accepting that it wasn't a delivery glitch, a second thought popped into my head immediately: they were from Sammy, who'd thought over everything that had happened earlier and wanted to apologize for his behavior. Yes! I knew he wasn't such a bad guy, and flowers were such a sweet, gentlemanly way of getting in touch to say he's sorry. *I'm sorry, too,* I mentally directed toward the flowers. *I don't know why I was so bitchy and nasty, especially since I haven't stopped thinking about you for one second since then. Yes, I'd love to meet you for dinner and put that whole stupid conversation behind us. And if you must know, I'm already beginning to envision you as the father of my future children, so we'd best be getting to know each other. How much our kids will love hearing that our lifelong love affair began with a fight and makeup flowers! It's almost so romantic I can't bear it. Yes, darling, yes, I forgive you and I apologize a hundred times myself and I know this will make us stronger.*

I heaved the arrangement upward and unlocked the door, so delighted with this surprise that I barely even noticed Millington wrapping herself around my leg. Flowers always featured prominently in romance novels, which made receiving such a first-rate bouquet even more wonderful. There were actually three dozen roses in shades of bright purple and hot pink and white, all clustered tightly together in a short, round bowl that appeared to be filled with some sort of sparkling glass marbles. Completely absent was any sort of adornment – no ribbons, bows, filler greenery, or ugly baby's breath; it screamed simple and elegant and very, very expensive. The card wasn't the ordinary sort, either. It was a heavy cream vellum and I couldn't tear it from the purple-lined envelope fast enough. But it took only a split second for my eyes to find the signature, and when they did, I thought I might pass out.

Doll, I'll absobloodylutely host the BlackBerry event! We'll make it the poshest party of the year. You're brilliant. Big kiss! Philip

What?! I reread it a few dozen times to make sure my brain was correctly processing the words, and then I read it again because

124

I still couldn't believe it. How did he know where I lived? How on earth did he know anything about the event when I hadn't even mentioned it yet? But more to the point, where was Sammy, with his declaration of undying love? I flung the card across the room, left the flowers on the kitchen counter, and flopped quite dramatically onto the couch. Within seconds, my cell phone and land line began ringing simultaneously, and a cursory check of each yielded even more disappointing results: Elisa on the cell and Uncle Will on the home phone. No Sammy.

I flipped open my cell and told Elisa to hold on before she could even speak and then clicked the portable on and said hi to Will.

'Darling, is everything all right? You're late, and Simon and I are worried that you're drowning your public-humiliation sorrows all alone. We both thought you looked great in that last New York Scoop photo! Let's get sloshed together! Are you on your way?'

Dammit! I'd forgotten all about dinner. Even though Thursday nights had been the standing plan since the day I'd graduated from college, I'd missed the last few weeks for Kelly events and had obviously completely flaked on tonight.

'Will! I'm sorry I'm late, but I was at the office until two minutes ago and I just ran home to feed Millington. I'm literally walking out the door this minute.'

'Sure, darling, of course. I'll buy that story if it's the best you're offering, but I'm not letting you out of tonight. We will see you soon, yes?'

'Of course. In just a few minutes . . .'

I hung up without saying good-bye and turned back to my cell phone.

'Hey, sorry about that. My uncle just called and I—'

'Bette! You'll never guess what! I have the best news in the whole world. Are you sitting down? Ohmigod, I'm just so excited.'

I didn't think I could handle another engagement announcement, so I just leaned back into the cushions and waited patiently, knowing that Elisa wouldn't be able to hold out for long.

'Well, you'll never imagine who I just spoke to.' Her silence indicated I was supposed to respond, but I couldn't muster the energy to ask.

'None other than our favorite gorgeous and no-longer-eligible bachelor, Mr Philip Weston. He was calling to invite the whole crew to a party and I just happened to answer and – oh, Bette, don't be mad, I just couldn't hold out – I asked him if he'd host your BlackBerry event and he said he'd love to.' At this point, she actually squealed.

'Really?' I asked, feigning surprise. 'That's great. Of course I'm not mad; that saves me from having to ask him. Did he sound excited about it, or just willing?' I didn't really care, but I couldn't think of anything else to say.

'Well, I didn't *technically* speak to him, but I'm sure he's totally thrilled.'

'What do you mean by "technically"? You just said that he called and—'

'Oh, did I say that? Oops!' She giggled. 'What I meant to say was that his *assistant* called and I ran the whole thing by her and she said of course Philip would be delighted. It's totally the same thing, Bette, so I wouldn't worry about it for a second. How great is that?'

'Well, I guess you're right because I just got flowers from him with a card saying that he's going to do it, so it seems like everything worked out.'

'Oooooooh, my god! Philip Weston is sending you flowers? Bette, he must be in love. That boy is just so amazing.' Long sigh on her part.

'Yes, well, I've got to run, Elisa. Seriously, thanks for figuring it out with him, I really appreciate it.'

'Where are you off to? You guys have a hot date tonight?'

'Uh, no. I'm just headed to my uncle's for dinner and then straight to bed. I haven't been home before two A.M. since I started this job, and I'm just ready to—'

'I know! Isn't it great? I mean, what other job would actually require that you stay out and party all night? We're so lucky.' Another sigh, followed by a moment for both of us to reflect on this truth.

'We are, yeah. Thanks again, Elisa. Have fun tonight, okay?'

'Always do,' she sang. 'And Bette? For all it's worth, you may have gotten this job because of your uncle, but I think you're doing great so far.'

Ouch. It was classic Elisa: a backhanded compliment meant to sound entirely sincere and positive. I didn't have the energy to start, so I said, 'You do? Thanks, Elisa. That means a lot to me.'

'Yeah, well, you're dating Philip Weston and, like, totally planning a whole event yourself. It took me almost a year to do that once I started.'

'Which one?' I asked.

'Both,' she said.

We laughed together and said good-bye and I hung up before she could insist that I attend another party. For that very brief moment, she actually felt like a friend.

After a quick scratch for Millington and an even quicker change

126

into jeans and a blazer, I shot one last bitter glance at the flowers and bolted downstairs to get a cab. Simon and Will were bickering as I let myself into the apartment and waited quietly in the ultramodern foyer, perched on a granite bench underneath a bright Warhol that I knew we'd covered in art history but about which I could recall not a single detail.

'I just don't understand how you could invite him into our home,' Simon was saying in the study.

'And I'm not sure what you don't understand about it. He's my friend, and he's in town, and it would be rude not to see him,' Will replied, sounding nonplussed.

'Will, he hates gays. He makes a living hating gays. Gets *paid* to hate gays. We're gay. What's so hard to understand?'

'Oh, details, darling, details. We all say things we don't quite mean in the public arena to generate a little controversy – it's good for the career. It doesn't mean we actually mean it. Hell, just in last week's column I had a moment of weakness, or perhaps hallucination, and wrote that pandering line about how rap music is its own art form, or something inane to that effect. Seriously, Simon, no one actually thinks I believe that. It's very much the same situation with Rush. His Jew-gay-black hating is strictly for ratings; it's certainly not reflective of his personal opinions.'

'You are so naïve, Will, so naïve. I can no longer have this conversation.' I heard a door slam, a long sigh, and ice cubes being dropped into a glass. It was time.

'Bette! Darling! I didn't even hear you come in. Were you lucky enough to witness our latest tiff?'

I kissed him on his clean-shaven cheek and assumed my usual perch on the lime green chaise. 'I sure did. Are you actually inviting Rush Limbaugh here?' I asked, slightly incredulous but not really surprised.

'I am. I've been to his home a half-dozen times over the years, and he's a perfectly nice fellow. Of course, I was never quite aware of how heavily medicated he was during those evenings, but it somehow makes him even more endearing.' He took a deep breath. 'Enough. Tell me what's new in your fabulous life?'

It always amazed me how he could be so cool and casual about everything. I remember my mother explaining to me as a child that Uncle Will was gay and that Simon was his boyfriend and that as long as two people are happy together, things like gender or race or religion don't mean anything at all (not applicable, of course, to me marrying a non-Jew, but that went without saying. My parents were as liberal and open-minded as two people could get when they were talking about anyone besides their own kid). Will and Simon visited Poughkeepsie a few weeks later and as we sat at the dinner table, trying to choke down fistfuls of sprouts and what felt like never-ending rations of vegetarian dahl, I had asked in my sweet ten-year-old voice, 'Uncle Will, what's it like to be gay?'

He'd raised his eyebrows at my parents, glanced at Simon, and looked me straight in the eye. 'Well, dear, it's quite nice, if I do say so myself. I've been with girls, of course, but you do soon realize that they just don't, ah, well, work for you, if you know what I mean.' I didn't know, but I was certainly enjoying the pained faces my parents were making.

'Do you and Simon sleep in the same bed like Mommy and Daddy?' I'd continued, sounding as sweet and innocent as I possibly could.

'We do, darling. We're exactly like your parents. Only different.' He took a swig of the scotch my parents kept on hand for his visits and smiled at Simon. 'Just like a regular married couple, we fight and we make up and I'm not afraid to tell him that even he can't pull off white linen pants before Memorial Day. Nothing's different.'

'Well then, that was an illuminating conversation, wasn't it?' My father cleared his throat. 'The important thing to remember, Bette, is that you always treat everyone the same, regardless of how they might be different from you.'

Booooring. I had no interest in another love-in lecture, so I settled on one last question: 'When did you find out you were gay, Uncle Will?'

He took another sip of scotch and said, 'Oh, it was probably when I was in the army. I sort of woke up one day and realized I'd been sleeping with my commanding officer for some time,' he replied casually. He nodded, more sure now. 'Yes, come to think of it, that *was* rather telling for me.'

It didn't matter that I was slightly unclear on the terms *sleeping with* and *commanding officer;* my father's sharp inhalation and the look my mother shot Will across the table were perfectly sufficient. When I'd asked him years later if that was actually when he realized he preferred men, he'd laughed and said, 'Well, I'm not sure that was the first time, darling, but it was certainly the only one that was appropriate for the dinner table.'

Now he sat calmly, sipping his martini and waiting for me to tell him all about my new and improved life. But before I could come up with something to offer, he said, 'I assume you've gotten the invitation to your parents' for the Harvest Festival?'

'I have, yes.' I sighed. Every year my parents threw their Harvest Festival party in the backyard to celebrate Thanksgiving with all their friends. It was always on Thursday, and they never served turkey. My mother had called a few days earlier and, after listening politely to the details of my new job – which to my parents was only slightly preferable to padding the coffers of a huge corporate bank – she'd reminded me yet again that the party was coming up and that my presence was expected. Will and Simon always RSVPd yes, only to cancel at the last moment.

'I suppose I'll drive us all up there Wednesday when you're done with work,' Will said now, and I barely managed to keep from rolling my eyes. 'How is everything going, by the way? Judging from everything I'm reading, you seem to have, ah, *embraced* the job.' He didn't smile, but his eyes sparkled, and I swatted him on the shoulder.

'Mmm, yes, you must mean the new little write-up in New York Scoop.' I sighed. 'Why are they after me?'

'They're after everyone, darling. When your sole mission as a columnist – online or otherwise – is to cover what's being consumed in the Condé Nast cafeteria, well, nothing should really surprise you. Have you read the latest?'

'This isn't the latest?' I felt the familiar dread begin to build.

'Oh, no, darling, I'm afraid to say it isn't. My assistant faxed it here an hour ago.'

'Is it awful?' I asked, not really wanting an answer.

'It's less than complimentary. For both of us.'

I felt my stomach flip. 'Oh, Christ. I can understand Philip, but for whatever reason they've made me their project, and there's not a damn thing I can do about it. Now they're including you?'

'I can hold my own, darling. I'm not thrilled, but I can handle it. As far as you're concerned, you're right. There's not much you can do, but I would certainly advise you not to do anything exceptionally stupid in public, or at least while you're in the company of this certain gentleman. But I'm not telling you anything you don't already know.'

I nodded. 'I just don't think my life is interesting enough to chronicle, you know? I mean, I'm no one. I go to work, I go out because I have to, and all of a sudden, my activities are fair game for public consumption.'

'Not yours – *his*,' Will pointed out, absentmindedly fingering the platinum ring that Simon called a wedding band and Will referred to as 'Simon's security blanket.'

'You're right. I just can't seem to extricate myself. He's omnipresent. And it's such a weird situation.'

'How so?' We both smiled when Simon swooshed by in an angry huff of ivory linen, and Will mouthed the word *snit*.

'Well . . . I don't actually like Philip as a person, but—'

'Darling! Don't let that stop you from dating someone! If *liking* the person was a requirement for having sex with them, well then, we'd all be in trouble.'

'See, that's the other thing. I'm not actually sleeping with him. Or rather, he's not sleeping with me.'

Will raised an eyebrow. 'I have to admit, that one puzzles me.'

'Well, at first it was because I didn't want to. Or at least that's what I thought. I just thought he was kind of a jerk, and even though I'm sure of it now, there's something that attracts me to him. Not in any kind of redeeming-quality way whatsoever, but he's certainly different from everyone else I know. And he's just not interested.'

Will was about to say something but stopped himself just as his mouth opened. He appeared to regroup for a minute and then said, 'I see. Well, ah, I have to say, I'm not actually surprised.'

'Will! Am I that much of a cow?'

'Darling, I have neither the time nor the inclination to spoon-feed you compliments right now. You know that's precisely not how I meant it. I just find it unsurprising since it's the men who talk about sex the most, the ones who make it such a crucial element of their identities, who actually define themselves by it, are usually the ones not performing up to par. With most people, when they're happy with that area of their lives, they're also happy to keep it private. All of this is by way of saying that I think you have the best situation possible right now.'

'Oh, really? Why's that?'

'Because from what you've mentioned before, it's important to your boss and colleagues that the Brit stay in the picture, right?'

'Correct. Your niece is a glorified prostitute, and it's all your fault.'

He ignored that comment. 'Well, it seems that it's an easy out, no? You can continue spending time with him as you – or your company – see fit, but you don't actually have to, ah, participate in anything unsavory. You're getting credit for minimal work, darling.'

That was an interesting way of looking at it. I wanted to tell him about Sammy, maybe even ask his advice, but I realized it was ridiculous to talk about my unrequited crush. Before I could broach the subject either way, my cell phone rang.

'Philip,' I announced, wondering, as usual, whether to answer it. 'He seems to instinctively call at the most inopportune times.'

'Answer it, darling. I'm going to find Simon and soothe his jangled nerves. That man is a walking basket case, and I'm afraid it's due in no small part to yours truly.' With that, he strolled out.

'Hello?' I said, pretending, as everyone does, that I had no idea who was calling.

'Please hold for Philip Weston,' a hollow voice replied. A moment later, Philip came on. 'Bette! Where are you? The driver said you're not home, and I can't imagine where else you'd be.'

There were a few things to process here, not the least of which was how I'd just been blatantly accused of having no life outside of him.

'I'm sorry, who's speaking?' I asked formally.

'Oh, stop banging on like that, Bette. It's Philip. I sent a car to your flat, but you're not there. Bungalow is blowing up tonight and I want to see you. Get over here,' he commanded.

'While I appreciate the sentiment, I have plans tonight, Philip. I can't make it,' I said for emphasis.

I could hear Eminem in the background and then muffled words from another male voice.

'Hey, some guy wants me to say hello for him. The fucking *bouncer*. Jesus, Bette, you must patronize this establishment more than I had originally thought. Man, what's your name?'

If I'd been given the choice at that moment, I would've chosen death over talking to Sammy through Philip. But before I could change the subject or ask him to move away so I could hear him better, Philip said, 'Are you listening to my conversation? Sod off, man.'

I cringed.

'Philip, thank you so much for the gorgeous flowers,' I blurted out, trying desperately to divert his attention. 'They were the most beautiful I've ever seen, and I'm so happy you'll be doing the BlackBerry party.'

'What?' More mumbled talking. 'The bouncer's called Sammy and he says he's working with you on a party or something. What's he talking about, Bette?'

'Yes, that's what I was just saying. The BlackBerry party.' I was screaming into the phone now, trying to be heard over the background noise. 'The one you agreed to do . . . the flowers . . . the note . . . any recollection?'

'Flowers?' He sounded genuinely confused.

'The ones you sent me just earlier today? Remember?'

'Oh, right on, love. I suppose Marta sent them. She's quite attentive to the details, sending shit at all the right times. She's my best girl.'

It was my turn to be confused. 'Marta?'

'My assistant. She runs my life, makes me look good. Works well, doesn't it?' I could almost hear him grinning through the phone.

'So did she tell you that she agreed on your behalf to host this party?' I kept my voice as steady and measured as was humanly possible.

131

'Not for a second, love, but that's all right. If she's keen on it, then so am I. She'll just tell me where to be and when. What?' he asked, sounding distracted.

'What?' I asked back.

'Hold on a moment, the bouncer wants to talk to you. He said it's about work.'

This was unacceptable. I'd almost – almost – forgotten that Sammy had been standing there listening to this entire exchange. He'd heard the bit about the flowers, and certainly how patronizing Philip had been during his charming pronouncement that the bouncer wanted to talk to me. 'Wait! Philip, don't just go and—'

'Hello, Bette?' It was Sammy. I couldn't even speak. 'You still there?'

'I'm here,' I said meekly. The flutter feeling described so vividly in all my books began immediately, and with great forcefulness.

'Hey, listen, I just wanted to—'

I cut him off without thinking and blurted, 'I'm sorry he sounds like such an asshole right now, but he really can't help it, since that's exactly what he is.'

There was a momentary silence and then a deep, appreciative laugh. 'Well, you said it, not me. Although I won't disagree with you.' Again I heard some sort of muffled exchange and then heard Sammy call out, 'I'll keep it right here for you, man.'

'What's going on?' I asked.

'Your boyfr – your, uh, your friend – spotted another, uh, a friend and went inside to say hello. He just left me with his phone. Hope he's not too upset if it gets accidentally run over by a cab. Listen, I really wanted to apologize for this afternoon. I don't know what got into me, but I had no right to say that stuff to you. We don't even know each other, and I was totally out of line.'

Here it was! My big apology, and he couldn't have sounded more sincere had he showed up outside my apartment and serenaded me in the adorable Calvin Klein boxer briefs I just knew he wore. I wanted to crawl through the phone and into his lap, but I managed to maintain some semblance of cool.

'Not at all. I'm sorry I snapped at you like that, too. It was just as much my fault, so please don't worry about a thing.'

'Great. So this won't get in the way of our professional relationship, right? Amy told me today that I'm going to be the primary liaison for your party, and I didn't want this to affect how well either of us does our job.'

'Uh, right.' Our jobs. Of course. 'Yes, yes, no problem at all.' I tried to hide my disappointment and obviously didn't do

132

well because he stammered right back, 'Uh, yeah, well, our jobs, and of course our, uh, our friendship. You know?' I could almost feel him blushing and wanted nothing more than to stroke his face with my palm right before wrapping my entire body around his.

'Right. Our friendship.' This was getting worse with every passing second, and I decided that no matter how nice it was to hear his voice, nothing good could come from continuing the conversation.

'Oh, Bette, I almost forgot to tell you! I spoke to Amy and she okayed you guys having Bungalow that night. It's in the books and there's no problem whatsoever. She just has a few requests for some of her people that she'd like included on the list, but otherwise you'll control the guest list entirely. She almost never agrees to that. Perfect, right?'

'Wow!' I said with forced enthusiasm. 'That's really great news. Thanks so much!'

Some girls started giggling in the background, one of them saying his name a few times, obviously trying to get his attention.

'Well, duty calls. I better get back to work. Good talking to you, Bette. And thanks for being so understanding about today. Can I call you tomorrow? To, uh, discuss the other details?'

'Sure, sure, that'd be great,' I said quickly, eager to hang up since Will had just walked back in, and he had ominously placed a sheet of paper in his lap. 'I'll talk to you then. Bye.'

'Was that your boyfriend?' Will asked, picking up his drink again and settling back into the chair.

'No,' I sighed, reaching for my own martini. 'It most definitely was not.'

'Well, not to rain on this little party here, but you'll have to read it at some point.' He cleared his throat and picked up the sheet. 'By Ellie Insider. She writes a paragraph about her trip to Los Angeles last week and all the movie stars with whom she partied. That's followed by a short ditty concerning her immense popularity with designers, to the point where they all clamor to dress her for events. We're up next. It's short, but not sweet. "Since any friend of Philip Weston's is a friend of ours, we realized we didn't know much about his new girlfriend, Bette Robinson. We do know that she's a graduate of Emory University, an ex-employee of UBS Warburg, and the new darling of Kelly & Company PR, but did you know that she's also the niece of columnist Will Davis? The once-favored arbiter of all things Manhattan has, admittedly, become a bit passé, but what must he think of his niece's very public antics? We're willing to guess he's less than pleased." That's all she wrote,' Will said softly, calmly tossing the paper aside.

I instantly had a queasy feeling, as though I'd just awakened from a nude-in-the-high-school-cafeteria dream. 'Oh, my god, Will, I'm so sorry. The last thing I ever wanted was to drag you into this. And what she said about your column is patently untrue,' I lied.

'Oh, Bette, darling, do shut up. We both know she's exactly right. But you can't control what these people write, so let's not worry about it for another moment. Come, let's dine.' He said all the right words, but the tension in his face said something else, and I was left with an odd feeling of sadness and nostalgia for the way things had been before my new and improved life.

14

'Tell me again why your mother is throwing you a going-away dinner when she's so pissed you're moving?' I asked Penelope. After a full day of list-checking and sponsor-calling for the BlackBerry party – which was now only four days away – it seemed like everything was shaping up nicely, and I'd retreated to Penelope's in the hope of discussing something, anything, that wasn't related to publicity. I was flopped on the floor of the bedroom that Avery and Penelope now shared, although it didn't appear that Avery had compromised much on combining their stuff: the king-sized waterbed rested on an imposing black platform, a frat boy–style black leather couch ate up what little room remained, and the only item that could qualify as 'decor' was an oversized and slightly discolored lava lamp. The apartment's pièce de résistance, however, was a fifty-five-inch plasma screen that hung from the living room wall. According to Penelope, Avery didn't know how to wash a dish or launder a pair of socks, but he carefully detailed his flat-screen with special nonabrasive cleaning solution every weekend. The last time I'd been over I'd heard Avery instruct Penelope to 'tell the maid to keep that surface cleaner away from my flatty. That shit fucks up the screen. I swear to God, if I see her go near my TV with that can of Lysol, she's gonna be looking for a new job.' Penelope had smiled indulgently, as if to say 'Boys will be boys.' She was currently packing Avery's clothes in the Louis Vuitton suitcases his parents had bought them for their engagement-party trip to

Paris while simultaneously bitching about the dinner that was to be held in their honor that night. I didn't inquire why Avery couldn't pack his own clothes.

'You're asking me? She said something asinine about "keeping up appearances" or something like that. Honestly, I think she didn't have anything else scheduled for tonight and couldn't bear the thought of staying home.'

'That's a really positive way of looking at it.' The empty bag in my hand reminded me that I'd just plowed through sixteen ounces of Red Hots in twelve minutes flat. My mouth alternated between numb and tingly, but that never slowed me down.

'It's going to suck and you know it. The best I'm hoping for right now is tolerable. What the hell is this?' she mumbled, holding up a bright blue T-shirt with yellow lettering that read I DO MY OWN NUDE SCENES. 'Eww! Do you think he's ever worn this?'

'Probably. Toss it.'

She threw it in the garbage. 'Are you sure you don't hate me for making you come tonight?'

'Pen! I hate you for moving, not for inviting me to your going-away dinner. I mean, I'm not exactly complaining about your parents picking up the tab for dinner at the Grill Room. What time should I get there?'

'Whenever. It starts at eight-thirty or so. Come a few minutes early, maybe, so we can do shots in the bathroom?' She smiled wickedly. 'I'm seriously considering bringing a flask. Is that bad? Ick. Not as bad as these . . .' This time she held up a pair of faded, well-worn boxers with a none-too-subtle arrow in fluorescent pink pointing directly to the crotch.

'A flask is definitely in order. What am I going to do without you?' I moaned pathetically. I had not yet come to terms with the idea that Penelope, who'd been my best – and only – girlfriend for the past ten years, was moving across the country.

'You'll be fine,' she said, sounding more certain than I would've liked. 'You've got Michael and Megu and your whole new crew at work, and you've got a boyfriend now.'

It sounded weird for her to mention Michael, considering we almost never saw him anymore.

'Puh-lease. Michael has Megu. The "crew" at work is precisely that – a bunch of people with mysterious access to huge piles of cash and a penchant for spending it on lots and lots of alcohol. As for the boyfriend remark, well, I'm not even going to dignify that.'

'Where's my favorite girl?' Avery called right after the front door slammed. 'I've been waitin' all day to get home and get that cute ass of yours into bed!'

'Avery, shut up!' she called, appearing only slightly embar-rassed. 'Bette's here!'

But it was too late. He'd already shown up in the doorway, shirtless, with his jeans unbuttoned and unzipped to reveal lime green seersucker boxers.

'Oh, hey, Bette.' He nodded in my direction, looking not the least bit distraught that I'd been witness to his seduction scene.

'Hey, Avery,' I said, diverting my eyes to my sneakers and wondering for the umpteenth time what, besides his admittedly flat stomach, Penelope saw in him. 'I was just heading out. Gotta get home and get ready for the big dinner tonight. Speaking of which, what does one wear to the Four Seasons?'

'Whatever you'd normally wear to dinner with your parents,' Penelope said as a very ADHD Avery starting shooting hoops with his balled-up pairs of socks.

'You might want to reconsider that. Unless, of course, you want me showing up in palazzo pants with a matching GIVE PEACE A CHANCE T-shirt. I'll see you both there tonight.'

'Right on,' Avery said, holding up two fingers in a sort of combination peace/gangster sign. 'Later, B.'

I hugged Penelope and let myself out, trying not to envision what would inevitably take place the moment I left. If I hurried home, there'd be time to drag Millington out for a quick walk and maybe even take a bath before dinner. I cabbed it home and chased Millington around the apartment for a few minutes as she made a concerted effort to duck me. She instinctively knew when I was planning to take her outside, and unlike any dog I'd ever met, she hated it. All that dust and pollen and ragweed – she'd be incapacitated for hours afterward, but I thought it was im-portant for her to get out every now and then. Otherwise it was around the block and back. I marveled at her metabolism. We'd just made it to Madison Square Park and managed to dodge the crazy guy who usually chased Millington with his grocery cart when I heard my name.

'Bette! Hey, Bette, over here!'

I turned to see Sammy sitting on a bench, drinking coffee, his breath visible in the icy air. With what appeared to be an absolute knockout of a woman sitting right next to him. Dammit. There was no escape. He'd obviously seen me and then watched as I looked right at him, so there was no conceivable way to pretend the whole thing had never happened. Plus, Millington decided to be social for the first time in her entire short life and took off toward them, yanking her Extend-a-Leash to its maximum capacity and hurling herself into his lap.

'Hey there, puppy, how are you? Bette, who is this cutie?'

'Charming,' said the brunette, eyeing Millington coolly. 'Of course, I prefer the Cavalier King Charles, but Yorkies can be appealing as well.'

Meow.

'Hi, I'm Bette,' I managed to say, extending my hand to the girl. I'd tried to smile warmly at Sammy, but I imagine that it looked like a grimace.

'Oh, formal, are we?' she said with a little laugh. She gave me her hand after making me wait three seconds longer than was comfortable. 'Isabelle.'

Isabelle was no less attractive up close, but she was older than I'd originally figured. She was tall and thin in the way that only the truly hungry can be, but she lacked that certain freshness of youth, that dewy-faced contentment that said 'I haven't gotten too beat up by the Manhattan dating scene – I still even hold out hope that I'll meet a good guy one day.' Isabelle had clearly given up the dream long ago, although I imagined that her size 2 Joseph pants combined with her gorgeous chocolate brown Chloe bag and obscenely pert breasts provided some sort of comfort.

'Uh, so what brings you here?' Sammy asked, clearing his throat with such awkwardness that it was obvious these two were not friends or siblings or coworkers. And more to the point, he wasn't volunteering any explanations.

'Walking the dog. Getting some fresh air. You know, the usual,' I said, realizing that I sounded more than a little defensive. For some reason my polite conversation skills had just evaporated.

'Yeah, same here,' he said, sounding sheepish and slightly embarrassed.

When it was clear that neither of us could think of anything else to say, I scooped Millington from Sammy's lap, where she was obviously enjoying being stroked – how I could understand! – mumbled a goodbye, and tore off in the direction of my apartment with a speed that bordered on humiliating. I could hear Isabelle laughing and asking Sammy who his little friend was, and it took every ounce of willpower not to whip around and suggest that next time she have her doctor adjust her Botox injection so she wouldn't have that telltale deer-caught-in-headlights expression.

So it was official, I thought, as I stood under the shower's scalding hot water: Sammy had a girlfriend. Or, rather, I suppose it was more appropriate to call her a woman friend, since the female in question couldn't conceivably be a day under forty. Of course he hadn't been jealous that day in Starbucks when he'd made fun of Philip. Feeling more ridiculous with every passing moment, I quickly dressed in one of the old, navy bank pantsuits that had been relegated to the back of my closet and spent not one second longer than necessary drying my hair and applying the faintest traces of concealer.

By the time I'd arrived at the Four Seasons, I'd almost managed to convince myself that I didn't care. After all, if Sammy really wanted to date someone with better clothes, more money, and a chest three times the size of mine, well, that was certainly his prerogative. Who needed someone that shallow, anyway? I was just working myself up to start a list of his many, many flaws (none of which were immediately apparent, but which certainly must exist somewhere) when my cell phone rang. It was Elisa, probably calling, as usual, to ask obsessively detailed questions about when, where, why, and with whom I'd last seen Philip, so I screened it and approached the maître d'. The phone rang again mere seconds later, and even though I switched it to vibrate, she sent a text message that read: 911. CALL IMMEDIATELY.

'Bette? Hey, have you found them yet?' Michael asked, walking toward me, looking haggard and slightly miserable. Penelope had told me he was on yet another huge M&A deal. All-nighters four days and running.

'No, are we the first ones here?' I kissed him on the cheek and thought about how long it'd been since I'd seen him. Weeks and weeks; so long I couldn't remember. 'Where's Megu?'

'She's at the hospital. I think Pen said they might all have a private table in the back, so let's go there.'

'Perfect.' I took the arm he offered and had an odd feeling of homecoming. 'You know, it's been forever since we've all hung out. What are you doing afterward? Why don't we talk Pen into going to the Black Door for a drink or six?'

He smiled even though it looked like it took all his energy and nodded. 'Definitely. We're all already in the same place, and when the hell does that ever happen? Let's do it.'

The table looked to seat about eighteen or twenty, but just as I was saying my hellos to Penelope's father, my phone began to vibrate again.

'I'm so sorry, please excuse me,' I said to Penelope's dad and bolted toward the door again to turn it off. Elisa again. Christ, what could be so important that she needed to take the full-stalk approach? I waited for it to stop buzzing and then flipped it open to turn it off, but she must have dialed again because I heard her voice emanating from my palm.

'Bette? Is that you? Bette, it's crucial.'

'Hey, listen, this really isn't a good time for me. I'm at my friend's—'

'You've got to get down here right away, Kelly's freaking out because—'

'Elisa, you didn't even let me finish. It's eight-thirty on a Saturday night and I'm just about to start dinner at the Four Seasons with my friend and her entire family and it's really important,' so I'm sure you can handle whatever Kelly's freaking out about.' I congratulated myself on being firm and setting boundaries, something my mother had been trying to teach me from age six.

She was breathing heavily at this point, and I heard the faint clinking of glasses in the background. 'Sorry, hon, but Kelly's not taking no tonight. She's at dinner with the BlackBerry people right now at Vento and she needs us to meet them at Soho House by nine-thirty, latest.'

'Impossible. You know I'd be there if I could. It's mandatory that I stay here for at least the next couple hours,' I said, hearing a waver in my voice. 'I mean, nine-thirty is ridiculously early, and I don't understand why, if she expected us to meet them, it has to be on a Saturday night, or why she couldn't have mentioned it beforehand.'

'Look, I hear you, but there's no way out. You're in charge of the party, Bette! They came into town early and Kelly thought a dinner meeting would appease them, but apparently they want to meet you . . . and Philip. Tonight. Since the party is so close, and apparently they're nervous.'

'Philip? You can't be serious.'

'You *are* dating him, Bette. And he *did* agree to host this event for us,' she said, sounding like a bossy older sister. I saw Penelope approaching me out of the corner of my eye and knew I was being horrifically rude.

'Elisa, I really—'

'Bette, honey, I don't want to pull rank here, but your job's on the line. I'll help as much as possible, but you've *got to be here*. I'll send a car to the Four Seasons in thirty minutes. Get in it.'

As the call cut off, Penelope threw her arms around my neck.

'I love your plan!' she said, grabbing my hand and walking me toward the table. I overheard Mr Wainwright talking loudly about a lawsuit he was overseeing to a rather subdued, dignified-looking woman, and I wondered if Penelope might not want to save her grandmother from her future father-in-law.

'Plan?'

'Yes, Michael told me about the reunion at the Black Door tonight. Such a good call! It's been forever since we've done that and' – she looked around – 'I'll need to drink heavily after this. You have no idea what Avery's mother did tonight. Took my mom and me aside and presented me, quite proudly, with a copy of

Fête Accompli!: The Ultimate Guide to Creative Entertaining and the entire Barefoot Contessa cookbook series. Oh, but it gets better. Not only did she highlight all of her suggestions for dinner-party themes, she also made notes by all of Avery's favorite dishes so I may properly instruct the cook. She made a special point of letting me know that as a general rule, he doesn't like any food that should be consumed with sticks, in her words.'

'Sticks?'

'Chopsticks. She said they "confuse him."'

'That's fantastic. She sounds like a real treat.'

'Yep. My mother just stood there, nodding. She did manage to comfort Avery's mom by pointing out how easy it would be for us to find household help in California, what with the hordes of Mexican immigrants. The "promised land of cheap labor," I think were her exact words.'

'Let's just remember never to allow our parents in the same room again, okay?' I said. 'They'd have a field day with this one. You remember what a disaster it was last time?'

'Are you kidding?' she said. 'How could I not?'

We'd cleverly kept our two sets of parents from being in the same place through four years of college, but during graduation it had proven impossible. Each was curious about the other and after much prodding from both mothers, Penelope and I had grudgingly scheduled a dinner for everyone on Saturday night. The stress began with the restaurant selection: my parents were rallying to try the all-organic raw-food bar that had published a number of famous cookbooks, while Penelope's parents insisted on going to their usual place when they visited – Ruth's Chris Steak House. We compromised on some high-end, pan-Asian chain that displeased everyone, and things only spiraled downward from there. The restaurant didn't serve my mother's type of tea or Penelope's father's favorite cabernet. As far as conversation topics went, politics, careers, and future plans for the graduates were out, since there were no shared opinions or ideas whatsoever. My father ended up talking to Avery for most of the meal and then making fun of him later; I spoke to my mother, Penelope talked only to hers, and her father and brother exchanged the occasional sentence or two in between gulps from the three bottles of red wine they killed together. It had ended as awkwardly as it started, with everyone eyeing each other suspiciously and wondering what their daughters saw in one another. Penelope and I had dropped them all at their respective hotels, hit the bars immediately, and proceeded to drunkenly imitate each one, all while swearing to never repeat that evening.

'Come here – talk to my father for me, will you? It's been a few decades since he's socialized outside the office and he doesn't seem to know what to do.' She seemed in reasonably high spirits, and I wondered how to tell her that I could only stay through drinks because I had to go to a party with the gorgeous bad boy I was supposedly dating.

'Pen, I'm so sorry to do this and I acknowledge that it's the shittiest, most selfish thing in the whole world, but I just got a call from work and I have absolutely positively no choice but to go because I'm in charge of this particular project and there are people in from out of town that my boss is currently with and she's insisting that I meet them and even though I told her that I was at something really, really important she basically threatened my job – through a third party, of course – if I'm not downtown in under an hour and I argued and argued, but she was adamant, so I'm planning to get down there and back as quickly as possible and of course I'm still up for the Black Door if you guys don't mind waiting for me.' Stop. Deep breath. Ignore death look on Penelope's face. 'I'm sorry!' I wailed loud enough to cause a few of the waiters to glance in our direction. I somehow managed to ignore the sinking feeling in my stomach, Michael's surprised look from a few feet away, and the reproachful stare from Penelope's mother for making the commotion.

'When do you have to leave?' Penelope asked calmly, her expression revealing nothing.

'In a half-hour. They're sending a car.'

She unconsciously twisted the small diamond stud in her right ear and gazed at me. 'Do what you need to do, Bette. I understand.'

'You do?' I asked, not quite believing her, but hearing no anger in her voice.

'Of course. I know you want to be here, and sure, I'm disappointed, but I know you wouldn't go unless it was really important.'

'I'm so sorry, Pen. I promise to make it up to you.'

'Don't worry about it. Go on, take that seat over there next to Avery's cute single friend and at least enjoy the time you have.' She was saying all the right things, but the tightness of her mouth made her words seem forced.

Avery's decidedly uncute single friend immediately started reminiscing about his wild and crazy frat days at Michigan while I quickly worked my way through drinks two and three. One of Penelope's friends from the bank, a girl I didn't know when I was there but who seemed to be with Pen all the time now, made an impromptu toast that was adorably funny and charming. I tried to suppress my bitterness when Penelope threw her arms around the girl, and I insisted to myself that it was my paranoia speaking and that no one was staring at me, thinking me an awful friend.

The half-hour passed in a split second. I thought it better to steal away than make a big production and explain myself to everyone, so I tried to catch Penelope's eye but simply left when it seemed like she was deliberately avoiding me.

On the sidewalk, I offered a dollar to a well-dressed man for a cigarette, but he refused and tossed me one for free, adding a pitiful headshake. There was no car in sight and I thought about going back in for a few more minutes, but just then a very familiar-looking lime green Vespa pulled up alongside the curb.

'Hey, love, let's do this,' Philip said, flipping up the screen on his helmet and plucking the cigarette from my fingers for a drag. He kissed me roughly on the mouth, which, incidentally, hung open from shock, and dismounted to get the second helmet from underneath his seat.

'What are you doing here?' I asked, inhaling sharply on my cigarette when he handed it back.

'What does it look like I'm doing here? It seems we are obliged to attend. So let us hurry this along, okay? Nice suit.' He looked me up and down and snickered.

His cell phone rang to the tune of 'Like a Virgin' – it was my turn to snicker – and I heard him tell someone we'd be there in ten minutes.

'I'm actually waiting for a car that Elisa's sending,' I said.

'Afraid not, love. Elisa sent me. We're going to pay a visit to my dear friend Caleb, and Elisa's going to bring the business blokes to us.'

This was not making any sense, but he did seem to be working on direct orders from Elisa. 'Why are we going to your friend's apartment?' I asked.

'He's having a little birthday gathering at his place. Costume party, actually. Let's go.' It was only then that I noticed he was in full seventies disco gear, from brown polyester bell-bottoms to a skintight white collared shirt and some sort of bandanna tied around his head.

'Philip, you just said we had to meet Kelly and the BlackBerry people. We can't be going to a costume party right now. I don't understand!'

'Hop on, love, and stop stressing. I'm handling it.' He revved the Vespa, if such a thing is possible, and tapped the seat behind him. I hopped on as gracefully as my pantsuit would allow and wrapped my arms around his waist. His rock-hard abs pushed back.

I still don't know why I turned around. I don't remember thinking anything was out of the ordinary – if you discount the fact that I was being kidnapped by a raging metrosexual celebrity on a Vespa – and yet I looked over my shoulder before we flew off, only to see Penelope standing on the curb. She was holding out her hand, my scarf draped limply over it, her mouth open, staring at my back. My eyes met hers for just the briefest moment before Philip revved the scooter and it shot forward, away from Penelope, leaving no time to explain anything at all.

15

'Will you just relax, love? I told you, I'm handling it.' Philip parked the Vespa on the sidewalk carpet outside a beautiful West Village apartment building and slipped the doorman some cash, which was met with a discreet nod. I was struck by the sudden realization that this was the first time Philip and I had been alone together since the morning I woke up in his apartment.

'Relax? You're asking me to relax?' I shrieked. 'Excuse me, sir, could you please hail me a cab?' I asked in the direction of the doorman, who immediately looked to Philip for permission.

'Bette, just chill the fuck out. You don't need a cab. The party's here. Now come inside, and let's get you a little drinky, okay?'

Drinky? Did I just hear that? This guy has shagged every attractive female in Manhattan between the ages of sixteen and forty-five and he says 'drinky'? I couldn't dwell on this disturbing development, though, as I had less than ten minutes to get to Soho House.

He continued. 'Elisa called and I told her I couldn't possibly go; I'm expected at Caleb's party. She asked if she could bring the BlackBerry people here, said that they'd think it was cool to see a "real downtown party" or some bullshit like that. So they'll be here any minute. This is where we're *supposed* to be, okay?'

I looked at him dubiously, wondering how this had all unfolded. Was Elisa diverting me deliberately? I considered that for a moment but then realized there was no way she could sabotage this party without Kelly knowing, and besides, why would she want to? Granted, she might have wanted Philip at one point, and maybe she'd seemed less friendly lately, but I figured it was just because we were all really busy at work, planning individual events in addition to laying all the groundwork for the *Playboy* party. All I wanted to do was call Penelope, explain that I hadn't lied to get out of her dinner so I could run off into the night with this sad excuse for a boyfriend. Philip had already strolled past the doorman and was waiting impatiently for me to join him, and as soon as we stepped into the elevator, true to form, he attacked me.

'Bette, I simply cannot wait to take you home later and shag you all night,' he crooned into my hair, his hands running all over my body and sliding under my shirt. 'Even in that silly getup you're hot.'

I pushed his grabby hands away and sighed. 'Let's just get through this, okay?'

'Why do you get your knickers in such a twist, love? Oh, I see now, you'd like it if I tried a touch harder. I am most willing to accommodate. . . .' And with that, he thrusted his entire lower half into mine with minimal skill and his characteristic tongue lashing. Had Gwyneth really endured such treatment? Was it actually possible he'd slept with so many girls only once that none had bothered to tell him that he had no idea what he was doing? It was sickening, as was the sudden realization that Philip only pursued me with this passion when he knew we couldn't go through with it. Tonight was no different; there was no risk of me tearing off my clothes and pleading for sex when the elevator doors would swing open at any moment. Which they did, directly into Caleb's penthouse apartment. A quick and subtle backhanded wipe across my face and neck removed most of the saliva, and I was as ready as I'd ever be.

'Philip, baby, come on over!' a lanky guy with long hair called from the couch, where he was hunched over a mirror, rolled-up bill in hand. What appeared to be a naked girl was draped across his lap. She stared up at him with a look that surpassed admiration and approached worship. He snorted quickly, effortlessly, handed the girl the bill, and then pulled his mask back over his face.

'Cally, Cal-man, this is Bette. Bette, Caleb, the thrower of this most fabulous party, and as of today, a gentleman no longer in his twenties.'

'Hi, Caleb, nice to meet you,' I said to the mask. 'Thanks for inviting me.'

All three of them looked at each other and then at me and started laughing. 'Bette, why don't you come join us here for a little taste, and then we'll head upstairs? Everyone's on the roof.'

'Uh, I'm good, thanks,' I said, unable to take my eyes off the girl. She finished the two small lines Caleb had left for her and rolled onto her back. Technically, she wasn't completely naked, if you counted the swatch of fuchsia silk that hung low on her hips and covered only the front of her pelvis, leaving her entire backside bare. The thong I thought she'd been wearing when I first saw her turned out to be nothing more than a tan line, and her breasts had long since broken free from their own silk constraints, a contraption shaped something like a bra but with no actual hooks, straps, or shape. She curled up in a ball with a happy smile and sipped her champagne, announcing that she was just going to party downstairs a little longer before joining everyone else.

'Suit yourself, babe,' Caleb said, motioning for us to follow him. We stepped back in the elevator, where he used a special key that allowed us to select the Terrace button. I almost passed out when the doors opened again. I don't know what exactly I'd been expecting, but this sure wasn't it. Perhaps I'd thought it was going to be like Michael's Halloween party, when a bunch of his friends from UBS and college had gathered in his fourth-floor walk-up. The kitchen table had held bottles of cheap booze and mixers and a few cereal bowls of candy corn, pretzels, and salsa. Some guy in drag announced that pizza was on the way to the assorted costumed revelers, who sat around talking about college, who had gotten engaged or promoted, and how badly President Bush was fucking up in Iraq.

This scene was very, very different. The rooftop itself looked like an exact replica of Skybar in LA, all sleek and chic and streamlined, with low-rider lounging beds and heat lamps and geometrical candelabras casting a soft glow over everything. A frosted-glass bar peeked out from behind some sort of intimidating vegetation, and a DJ booth had been installed in another corner, mostly out of sight so as not to block one inch of the incredible city views that spanned below us. Nobody seemed much interested in the Hudson right then, though, and I immediately understood why: the flesh on display was far more compelling than some river, and far more expansive.

There are parties and there are costume parties, and then there's what was unfolding on Caleb's rooftop, something that by definition would technically qualify as a costume party but what in reality looked more like a revival of *Hair* – plus La Perla lingerie, minus tacky sixties updos. I felt an immediate desire to strip off my shoes and suit and roam around in nothing but my bra and underwear, if for no other reason than an intense desire to remain as inconspicuous as possible. Even then I'd surely be wearing more clothing than any other woman here, but at least I wouldn't stand out quite so much.

Caleb had disappeared briefly and returned with a glass of champagne for me and a tumbler of something amber-colored for Philip. I downed it in one long gulp and gaped openly at the girl he'd brought over to meet us. The introduction was preceded by a long and very visual kiss during which both Caleb and the girl opened their mouths so wide and with such tongue enthusiasm that I almost felt like an equal participant.

'Mmm,' he murmured, playfully biting her neck after reclaiming his tongue from the depths of her face. 'Guys, this is . . . the most gorgeous girl at the party. How hot is she? Seriously, have you seen anything so stunning in your lives?'

'Gorgeous,' I concurred, as though she weren't there. 'You're absolutely right.' The girl apparently wasn't bothered that Caleb appeared to have forgotten – or never discovered – her name. Not so weird, I figured; it seemed like lots of people hung out together but didn't really know one another's names. The music was always too loud and everyone was usually wasted, but mostly it was because no one cared. 'I'll remember her name when I read it on Page Six,' I'd heard Elisa announce on the subject. This girl didn't seem to mind much, perhaps because she didn't appear to comprehend a single word we were exchanging. She just giggled and occasionally adjusted her outfit and concentrated very hard on touching Caleb as often and as suggestively as possible. Yet another guy in drag (this one sporting a full-body mask with bare breasts, shimmery eyeliner, and a black-and-white-checked head-dress à la Yasir Arafat) came over to announce that the cars would arrive in just a few minutes to take us to Bungalow 8 for Caleb's 'real' party.

'It will hopefully be an improvement over my rubbish birthday party last year,' Philip replied.

'Why rubbish?' I asked, not caring but trying to appear involved so my staring wouldn't be quite so obvious.

'The fuckwits at the door let everyone in, and within an hour it was overrun with B&T. Bad times.'

'Was,' agreed the she-male Arafat. 'Bad times all around. Tonight will be better. That big one, what's his name, Sammy's at the door. He's no genius, but he's not a complete fucking idiot, either.'

Sammy! I wanted to sing out his name, hug the guy who'd just uttered it, dance in little circles at the thought of seeing him. But first I had to get through this.

'So, what are you?' the turbaned guy asked me.

'She's going as an uptight bi . . . businesswoman,' Philip kindly answered on my behalf. And as I looked around, I wondered what it was about costume parties that always made guys dress like girls and girls dress like sluts. Regardless of the coolness of the party or the price of the alcohol served, it happened each and every time, without fail. I looked around for the scantily clad kittens, nurses, princesses, singers, French maids, cheerleaders, Catholic schoolgirls, devils, angels, or dancers, but these girls didn't bother with such repressive titles. None of their outfits were technically costumes, just an amalgamation of shiny fabrics and sparkly accessories designed to showcase some of the best bodies God had ever created.

A brunette reclining on one of the beds was wearing a pair of flowing magenta gypsy pants that billowed out from a low-slung belt and were gathered together at her ankles, the transparent material allowing us to view her diamond-studded thong, which was tucked between perfectly firm butt cheeks. On top she wore a diamond-studded bra that created cleavage in that flawless way that said, 'Look at me' but not 'I'm an aspiring Pamela Anderson.' Her friend, looking all of sixteen and lying next to her, playing with her hair, wore a pair of silver fishnets that stretched so far across her infinite legs that they looked partially shredded. She had pulled on a pair of red leather boy shorts over them, which dipped so low at the hips and so high at the thigh that she'd definitely needed to make a special request at the waxer's. The only accompaniment to the 'costume' were the silver fringe tassels hanging from the nipples of her apple-sized breasts and a giant tiara of multicolored feathers and fur that cascaded down her back. I've never had a single sexual impulse toward another woman in all my twenty-seven years, and yet I thought I would sleep with either one of them right then.

'They look like lingerie models, for chrissake,' I muttered under my breath to no one in particular.

'They are,' Philip responded, staring with what can only be described as lust. 'Don't you recognize Raquel and Maria Thereza here? They're Victoria's biggest girls this year, the youngest Brazilian crop ever.'

I was devastated to see that they don't airbrush nearly as much as I'd always convinced myself they did. We roamed around the glass-enclosed roof – only the ceiling was open to the sky – as Philip handed out high fives to Jimmy Fallon and Derek Jeter in quick succession and cheek kisses (always just missing the lips) to a long line of fashion-magazine editors, sitcom actresses, and Hollywood starlets. I was checking my cell to see if Elisa or Kelly had called when I spotted Philip massaging the back of the titty-tasseled girl, who I now recognized as the one who'd modeled the cotton bikini panties I'd recently ordered from the VS catalog and who I'd mentally blamed for misrepresentation when I'd put them on and looked in the mirror. The Hotel Costes soundtrack thumped out of some flattened, plasma-like unit that hung from one of the outdoor walls while people alternately danced, smoked, did drugs, munched sushi, and ogled each other. I kept checking the door for Elisa, worried they wouldn't find us on the terrace, and eventually sent her a text message with elevator instructions. At some point I accepted a drink from a gorgeous, shirtless waiter wearing a loincloth and heels, but I remained rooted near the door, making sure I could see everyone who arrived and left. There was a brief break in the fun when Caleb announced that a fleet of cars was waiting downstairs to transport everyone to the club, but then the partying continued straight through the elevators and into the two dozen Town Cars that lined the block as far as I could see.

'Philip, we can't leave this party!' I hiss-whispered as he tried to hustle me into the elevator. 'We're waiting for the BlackBerry people.'

'Stop fretting, love. Elisa rang to tell me that your boss rang to tell her that the meeting is canceled for tonight.'

I couldn't have heard that correctly. It was *impossible*!

'What? You can't be serious.' I couldn't even consider the possibility that I'd been forcefully removed from Penelope's dinner to tend to clients who didn't need tending.

He shrugged. 'That's what she said. Come on, love, you can call from the car.'

I wedged myself between Caleb and Philip and tried not to touch any of the exposed body parts of the girl who was lying across all our laps.

I dialed Elisa and nearly screamed with frustration when it went to voice mail. Kelly answered on the third ring, sounding vaguely surprised to hear from me.

'Bette? I can barely hear you. Anyway, the meeting's off for the night. We had a lovely dinner at Soho House and then had drinks by the pool, but I don't think they're quite used to New York partying. They went back to the hotel already, so you're off the hook. But they're very excited about this week!' She was screaming above music somewhere and didn't realize that even though she couldn't hear herself, I could hear her perfectly.

'Oh, well, okay. Um, that's fine. As long as you're sure—'

'Are you with Philip?' she shouted.

At the sound of his name coming through the phone, he squeezed my knee and started moving his hand upward.

'I am. He's right here. Do you want to talk to him?'

'No, no, I want *you* to talk to him. I hope you guys are at Bungalow. It's going to be a huge night – everyone will be there for Caleb's birthday.'

'Huh?'

'Lots of photogs, lots of opportunity . . .'

Despite the weirdness of Kelly's obvious pimping tactics, I liked my job – and Kelly – at that point. I knew I didn't ever want to go back to mutual funds. I wanted this BlackBerry party to be the best event of the year and I supposed it wouldn't hurt to take a few pictures with Philip before sneaking out and meeting Penelope and Michael at the Black Door. Besides, we were already heading there anyway, right? Despite my outrage at being yanked from Penelope's dinner, I tried to tell myself it wasn't that bad. . . .

'Sure thing, I hear you,' I said with faux cheeriness while removing Philip's hand from where it currently resided – my inner thigh – and tapping it the way a grandmother might. 'Thanks, Kell. See you Monday.'

The cars pulled up single file along Twenty-seventh Street and I saw that the line was almost a hundred people, all of whom stared, slack-jawed, as we exited the fleet of cars in our outrageous costumes. Sammy was standing off to one side while a man from the party wearing a long blond wig and very high heels yelled at him. I tried to get his attention as we cut in front of the entire line, but another bouncer approached us first.

'How many are you?' he asked Philip pleasantly, giving no indication that he knew who anyone was.

'Oh, I don't know, man, forty? Sixty? Who bloody knows?'

'Sorry, dude – not tonight,' the doorman replied, turning his back. 'Private party.'

'My man, I don't think you understand. . . .' Philip clapped him on the back and the bouncer looked like he might deck him, but then he noticed the credit card Philip was brandishing – the one and only Black Card. The negotiations began.

'I only have three tables right now. I'll let in six per table and an additional ten people, but that's the best I can do,' he said. 'Any other night, no problem, but tonight it's really out of my hands.'

This guy was clearly new and had no idea who he was dealing with, and Philip looked like he was ready to let him know. His voice tight and controlled, he got within three inches of the bouncer's face and said, 'Look, man, I don't give a toss what your problem is. Caleb is one of my closest mates and it's *his* party. Three tables is bullshit. I want six tables, starting with two bottles apiece, and everyone admitted. *Now*.'

I noticed Sammy finishing his conversation and tried to slink away from the front as quietly as possible so I could lose myself in the crowd; I was desperate not to let him see me with Philip. All around me, guys were working their cell phones, calling anyone and everyone they knew who might get the bouncer to release the velvet rope; girls approached the doormen with puppy eyes, stroking their arms and quietly making their pleas for admittance. Sammy walked toward Philip and caught my eye as I moved closer again to hear what was happening. I fervently hoped he would tell them all to fuck off, to take their money and party elsewhere, but he just looked quickly at me again and addressed the other bouncer.

'Anthony, let them in.'

Anthony, who'd already been surprisingly accommodating and nonconfrontational, appeared dismayed at this development and began to argue. 'Dude, they have like eighty fucking people. I don't care how much cash they got, it's my ass on the line if—'

'I said let them in. Clear out whatever tables you need to and give them whatever they want. Do it now.' And with that, Sammy glanced at me one last time and stepped inside the door, leaving Anthony to handle us.

'See there, mate?' Philip gloated, unable to help himself, assuming it was his fame that had secured our entrance. 'Do what the good man said. Take this card here and get us our goddamn tables. You can handle that, can't you?'

Anthony took the Black Card, his hands shaking with rage, and held the door open for the forty or so of us who had already arrived. The line quieted as we filed inside, and everyone tried to see the famous among us.

'There's Johnny Depp!' I heard one girl stage-whisper.

'Ohmigod! Is that Philip Weston?' asked another.

'He dated Gwyneth, didn't he?' one of the guys said.

Philip swelled with noticeable pride and directed me to the table that the maître d' had just emptied for us. The evicted party stood a few feet away, holding their drinks, their faces flush with shame as we took our seats around the banquette.

Philip pulled me onto his lap and rubbed my leg, kneading it in that way that tickles uncomfortably and hurts at the same time. He mixed me a vodka tonic using the $400 bottle of Grey Goose that was immediately deposited at our table, and greeted every single person who walked past by name, occasionally burying his face in my neck.

During one of these burrowings, he rested his chin on my shoulder and gazed at the model sitting next to me, legs crossed seductively, face in her hands, elbows on her knees, nipple tassels slipping slightly off-center.

'Just look at her,' he whispered, his voice husky, his eyes fixed on the youngest-looking girl of all. 'Look how she imitates the older models, watching how they move their hips, their eyes, their mouths, and doing exactly that because she knows it's sexy. She's just growing into that body of hers, doesn't quite realize what she possesses, and she's learning like a newly hatched chick. Isn't it smashing to watch?'

Mmm, absolutely smashing. Downright gripping, actually, I thought, but I just shook him off and announced I'd be right back. He nearly fell on her as I untangled myself from him, and I heard him complimenting her directly as I walked toward the front of the club.

Elisa was draped across an attractive man at a banquette near the door, her head and shoulders leaning against his chest while her bare feet – still red with sandal-strap lines – rested in Davide's lap. She didn't appear to be too concerned – or even aware of – the BlackBerry situation. I wasn't sure she was conscious or even alive until I got close enough to see her concave stomach rise and fall with the slightest motion.

'Bette, honey, there you are!' She mustered enough energy to make herself heard over the music even though she probably hadn't consumed enough calories that day to remain in a standing position. I decided to address the BlackBerry debacle another time.

'Hey,' I mumbled, displaying my lack of enthusiasm.

'Come here. I want you to meet the most talented skin-care therapist in Manhattan. Marco, this is Bette. Bette, Marco.'

'Aesthetician,' he immediately corrected.

I'd been on my way to thank Sammy, but there was no avoiding putting in at least a few minutes at their table. I sat down and immediately poured myself a vodka tonic. 'Hi, Marco, nice to meet you. How do you know Elisa?'

'How do I know Elisa? Why, I like to think I can claim responsibility for that flawless, *glowing* skin!' He held her head between his manicured fingers and thrust it toward me as though it were an inanimate object. 'Here, look. Do you see this evenness? Do you see the complete and utter lack of blemishes or discoloration? This is achievement!' He spoke with a slight Spanish accent and much flourish.

'Mmm, she does look great. Maybe you could help me out sometime,' I said, because I couldn't think of anything else.

'Mmm,' he said back, examining my face. 'I'm not so sure about that.'

I took that as my cue to excuse myself, but Elisa hoisted herself into a sitting position and said, 'Darlings, amuse yourselves for a few minutes while Davide and I say hello to a few friends.'

I looked up to see Davide lean forward so the table would obscure his hands. He deftly opened Elisa's white and gold Dior bag on the floor, removed a key from its ring, poured white powder from a tiny packet into the key's longest groove, and held it quickly up to his nose. His hand covered the entire key, and if you weren't watching very closely, it wouldn't look like anything more than a casual nose itch, perhaps a little allergy sniffle.

He refilled it within a second or two and passed it invisibly to Elisa, who also worked so quickly that I wasn't even sure what had passed under her nose or when. Another few seconds and the key ring was back in her purse and the two were jumping out of their seats, ready to work the room.

'They could at least have offered us some, don't you think?' Marco asked.

'Yeah, I guess so,' I said, not quite sure whether to announce that I'd never tried it, and while I was immensely curious, I was more scared.

Marco sighed meaningfully and took a long pull from his drink.

'Rough day?' I asked, again unsure of both how to proceed or escape.

'You can say that again. Elisa fucked up my schedule again. She knows how much I hate it when she passes out in my chair.' Another sigh.

'She passed out? Is she okay?'

His huge eye roll was followed by a long, exhausted exhalation. 'Look at her – does she look okay to you? Hey, I'm all about starving yourself – I've certainly had to do it myself a few times – but you've got to take responsibility for your actions! You *know* when you're about to pass out! There are little flashes of light before your eyes and you get really dizzy. Your body does this to let you know that it's time to take a bite of that PowerBar you should be toting around for occasions like this. You gotta heed the warnings, you know, and get the hell out of my chair, or else you're going to screw up my entire schedule.'

I wasn't quite sure how to respond to this, so I just sat and listened.

'These girls think they can come in after a long week of nose drugs and no food and just conk out in my chair and I'll take care of them. Well, that used to be okay, but I've got better things to do now. The way I see it, it's the same as some heroin junkie: I couldn't care less if you're using, man, just don't overdose in my home because then it becomes my problem. You know?'

I nodded. *The world is lucky to have a guy as sensitive as Marco,* I thought.

'People have it worse than I do, though,' he continued earnestly. 'Friend of mine's a makeup artist. He brings one case of makeup with him, and another of PowerBars and fruit-juice boxes because the girls are always conking out on him. At least when mine faint in the chair, I don't have to start all over. He also usually sees them right before big events, at their hungriest, since they've been on super-starvation to fit into their dresses. It's tough, man. They leave us to pick up the pieces.'

'Yeah, I hear that. Listen, it was really nice to meet you, but I've got to run and say hi to a friend. Will you be here for a few minutes?' I asked, realizing that if I didn't escape soon, it might never happen.

'Sure, whatever, great to meet you. Catch you later.' He nodded in my direction before leaning over to mix another drink.

I wanted to find Sammy and thank him for what he'd done, maybe explain that I was not there as Philip's date or his girl-friend or even by choice, but by the time I fought past the door crowd – which seemed to have expanded exponentially in the last hour – Sammy was nowhere in sight.

'Hey, have you seen Sammy?' I asked Anthony, trying to sound casual.

He appeared to have calmed down since our last interaction and shook his head while glancing over his clipboard.

'Nah, he headed out early to meet his girl. Left me here alone for one of the biggest parties of the year. Wouldn't usually do that, so it musta been important. Why, you gotta problem? I'll try and help you in a few when I get rid of some of these people.'

'No, no problem. Just wanted to say hi.'

'Yeah, well, he'll be back tomorrow.'

I bummed a cigarette from a guy in an emerald green prom dress and willed myself to go back inside. I didn't have to, though. The party had come to me.

'Bette! I was hoping I'd see you here!' Abby screeched as her behemoth breasts threatened to overtake her entire face. 'You should be inside keeping an eye on that boy of yours, don't you think?'

'Hey, Abby. I'd love to chat, but I was just leaving.'

'It's Abigail now, actually. Come inside and have one cigarette with me, okay? For old times' sake.'

I wanted to tell her that there had been no old times, but I was already feeling defeated by the mental image of Sammy curled up with Isabelle, the Botox beauty.

'Sure,' I said listlessly. 'Whatever.'

'So, tell me. How is everything with Philip? It's just so amazing that you two ended up together!' she said, leaning in conspira-torially.

'Amazing? Not really.' I tried to think of something, anything, to end the conversation.

'Bette! Of course it is! Now, I hope you don't mind if I ask you a personal question, but I've always been dying to know: How is he in bed? Because, as I'm sure you're aware, there are rumors that—'

'Abby, I don't want to be rude, okay? But I really need to leave. I cannot have this conversation now.'

She appeared completely unfazed. 'Sure, no problem. I know how tired you must be from the new job. Anyway, we'll be sure to catch up soon, right? Oh! And I just love what you did with that suit – only you could make something so average look so good!'

I backed away as though she were a rabid dog and began to stumble back to Elisa's table to collect myself. Instead, I headed to the bar and drank down a martini – mixed just the way Will liked them. It wasn't half-bad, actually, sitting and getting drunk solo, but when an entire horde of gorgeous and mostly naked girls commandeered my personal space, the temptation to leave was just too great to resist. No matter Kelly's photo ops – I just couldn't endure more of Philip's fascinating musings on the growth cycle of South American models or Marco's suggestions for the most efficient starvation techniques, so I texted both Philip and Elisa one line claiming sudden illness and collapsed into the back-seat of a cab. I looked at my watch – one-thirty in the morning. Would they still be at the Black Door? I got my answer when Michael slurred hello on the fifth ring.

'Sorry,' I said.

'Just got home,' he replied. 'You missed a good night. But the Black Door with Pen and Avery is a lot different from the Black Door with Pen and Bette!'

I began calling Penelope as soon as the meter began running and continued calling until I finally fell asleep, a little after three in the morning. It went to voice mail every time.

16

I resumed my calling seven hours later, desperate to explain to Penelope that it wasn't how it appeared, but no one was answering. Avery finally picked up the phone a little after noon, sounding groggy and slightly hung over.

'Hey, Bette, what's up?'

'Hi, Avery. Is Penelope there, please?' I had zero interest in exchanging any words with him past the required minimum.

There was a rustle and something that sounded suspiciously like a whisper before Avery said, 'Actually, she's at her parents' for brunch today. Can I leave her a message?'

'Avery, please put her on. I know she's there and I know she's upset with me and I want to explain everything. It's not really how it looked.' I was pleading.

154

His voice got lower and more conspiratorial; he was trying to talk so Penelope couldn't hear. 'Hey, Bette? Don't worry about it. I would've rather been at Caleb's party last night, too. Trust me – if there was any way I could've gotten out of that miserable dinner last night, I would've been right there with you. Pen's just over-reacting.'

Of course Avery would know about the party. I felt ill.

'It wasn't like that, Avery. I wouldn't have rather been—' I realized I was justifying my actions to the wrong person. 'Can you just put her on?'

There was some more rustling and a muffled call and then Penelope was saying hello as though she didn't know I was the one on the other end.

'Hey, Pen. It's me. How are you?'

'Oh, Bette. Hello. I'm fine, how are you?'

The conversation felt distinctly like dozens I'd had with my overly polite but slightly senile great-grandmother. Clearly, Penelope was every bit as furious with me as I'd feared.

'Pen, I know you don't want to talk to me right now. I'm sorry if Avery tricked you into picking up the phone, but I really want to apologize. It didn't go down last night the way it appeared.'

Silence.

'I got a call from work saying that some people from the BlackBerry account were in town unexpectedly and I had to go meet them. I'm in charge of their event this week, and there's just no way I could've refused to stop in and say hello.'

'Yes, that's what you said.' Her voice was ice-cold.

'Well, that's exactly what happened. I was planning to run over there for an hour and do my thing and then hopefully make it back before dessert. I was waiting for the car Elisa said she'd send when Philip showed up. Apparently Elisa sent him to get me instead of the car since the BlackBerry people wanted to meet him, too. I had no idea, Pen, seriously.'

There was a pause and then she said, very quietly, 'Avery said everyone saw you at some guy's birthday party downtown. That doesn't sound like work to me.'

I was more than a little creeped out by the 'everyone saw you' comment but rushed on to explain what had actually transpired. 'I know, Pen, I know. Philip told me that Elisa'd told him that we were going to meet Kelly there.'

'Oh. Did the meeting go well?' She sounded like she was thawing a bit, but this next part wasn't going to do much to help it along.

'No, I didn't even get to meet them. Apparently, they got tired and headed back to their hotel after having a drink with Kelly.

At that point, it was one A.M.! I couldn't get back to you. I'm so sorry, Pen. I left your going-away dinner because I thought I had no choice, and it all ended up being for no reason whatsoever.' It sucked, but at least it was true.

'Why didn't you come to the Black Door?' she asked. But then her voice softened. 'I knew you wouldn't have left just to go to some party,' she said. 'Avery kept insisting that you'd invented that whole work story because this was going to be the most amazing birthday party ever, but I didn't really think you'd do that. It just got harder to believe when I saw you ride off with Philip.'

I wanted to strangle Avery with the phone cord, but I was finally making progress with Penelope and had to concentrate on that. 'You know I'd never do that, Pen. There was nowhere else I wanted to be last night. And if it's any comfort, it was a horror of an evening. Absolutely, positively, undeniably *not* fun.'

'Well, I'm sure I'll read about it online this week.' She said it lightly and laughed, but I could tell she was still upset. 'Speaking of which, did you see this morning's edition?'

My heart skipped a very small beat. 'This morning? It's Sunday! What are you talking about?'

'Oh, it wasn't nearly as bad as some of the others. Don't worry,' she rushed to say. I knew she intended to make me feel better, but her statement had the opposite effect. 'Avery showed me a few minutes ago. It just has some snarky comment about how you were wearing a business suit to a costume party.'

It was incredible! Relatively speaking, the installment was totally innocuous, but for some reason it was even more upsetting than all the lies and misrepresentations about my nighttime activities: if I couldn't even make clothing choices without inviting public commentary, there was not a shred of privacy left.

'Great. That's just great' was about all I could manage to say. 'Well, as evidenced by the fact that I did indeed wear a suit to a costume party last night, you can see that I wasn't planning on leaving your dinner.'

'I know, Bette. We're past that, okay?'

We were about to hang up when I remembered that I hadn't invited Penelope to the BlackBerry party.

'Hey, Pen, why don't you come on Tuesday? Bring Avery if you want, or just come by yourself. It should be fun.'

'Really?' she asked, sounding pleased. 'Sure, that sounds great. You and I can finally sit down and catch up. It feels like it's been a while, doesn't it?'

'I'd love to, Pen. All I want to do is sneak off to some corner and make fun of everyone we see, but I should tell you now that I'm not going to have a free second. I'm in charge of the whole thing, and I just know I'll be racing around, dealing with a hundred things. I'd love for you to come by, but it won't be the best night for catching up.'

'Oh, right. Of course. I knew that,' she said.

'What about right after Thanksgiving?' I asked. 'We could have dinner alone, just the two of us, before you go.'

'Uh, sure. Why don't we play it by ear?' I'd lost her again; she sounded desperate to hang up.

'Okay. Well, uh, I'm sorry again about last night. I'm looking forward to next week . . .'

'Mmm. Have a good day, Bette. Bye.'

'Bye, Pen. Talk to you soon.'

17

When you're twenty-seven and the phone rings in the middle of the night, you're apt to think it's some guy drunk-dialing an invitation to come over and 'hang out' rather than a work-related disaster that will surely change your life forever. Not so the night before the BlackBerry party. When my cell phone blared at three-thirty in the morning, I was certain I would have to deal.

'Is this Betty?' an older woman asked as soon as I'd flipped open the phone.

'Hello? Who is this? This is Bette,' I said, still groggy even though I'd already bolted upright and had a pen in hand.

'Betty, this is Mrs Carter,' the woman's voice said.

'I'm sorry. Could you say your name again, please?'

'Mrs Carter.' Silence. 'Jay-Z's mama.'

Aha! 'Hi, Mrs Carter.' I thought about the way I'd separated the invites on the party list and how Mrs Carter was the only person who was cross-referenced as 'Celeb Mother.'

'We are just so excited to be hosting your son and his whole pos – uh, his friends tomorrow. Everyone's just really looking forward to it!' I said, silently congratulating myself on the feigned sincerity I heard in my own voice.

'Yes, dear, well, that's why I'm calling. Is this too late? I figured a big party planner like yourself would definitely still be awake at midnight. I wasn't wrong, was I, sweetheart?'

'Um, no, not at all. Of course, I am in New York, so it's three in the morning here, but please don't worry about a thing. You could call me anytime. Is something wrong?' *Please no, please no, please no,* I chanted silently, wondering what else I could add to the $150,000 paycheck, penthouse suites at the Hotel Gansevoort, and business-class plane tickets we'd thrown in for the man, his mom, his superstar girlfriend, and his nine closest friends. When I'd asked why they needed hotel rooms at all – even I knew Jay-Z had a palatial New York pad – his mom had laughed and said, 'Just book it.'

'Well, dear, my son just called and said he really doesn't see the need to take a flight that early tomorrow. He was hoping you could book us all on something later.'

'Something later?'

'Yes, you know, a flight that gets in later than the one already—'

'I understand what you mean,' I said a little too sharply. 'It's just that the event starts at seven and as of now you're all scheduled to land at two. If we make it any later, there's a chance you won't arrive in time.'

'Well, I'm sure you'll figure that all out, dear. I've really got to be getting some rest for our big travel day tomorrow – that LA-to–New York leg always tuckers me out – but just fax me the confirmation when it's all fixed. Ta-ta now.' And she hung up before I could say another word.

Ta-ta? Ta-fucking-ta? I threw my cell phone against the wall and felt absolutely no satisfaction when it made a weak bleating sound, right before the battery cover popped off and the screen went blank. Millington had buried her face under my pillow hoping to escape my wrath. I wondered if it wasn't too late in life to develop a severe and all-consuming addiction to tranquilizers. Or painkillers. Or both. Blessedly, the airlines were open all night, and I was dialing American from my land line before I could damage any more of my belongings.

The operator who answered sounded just as tired and hassled as I felt, and I braced myself for what would surely be an unpleasant interaction.

'Hi, I have an annoying question. I made reservations for a party of twelve to fly from LAX to JFK on your eight A.M. flight and I was hoping I could change them all to something just slightly later?'

'Name!' she barked, sounding not just disinterested, which I expected, but downright hostile. I wondered if she was going to 'accidentally' disconnect me just because she didn't feel like dealing. I could almost understand.

'Um, the reservation is actually under Gloria Carter. They're all flying business class.'

There was a moment of heavy silence before she said, 'Gloria Carter? As in *the* Gloria Carter? As in the mother of Jay-Z?'

How on earth people knew these things was a mystery to me, but I sensed a momentary advantage and went for it. 'That's the one. He's flying to New York to perform, along with a few friends and his mother. Of course, if you're based in New York and you could work this out, you'd be more than welcome to come by and hear him sing his set.'

She exhaled audibly and said, 'No way! Really? I'm actually working out of our call center in Tampa right now, but my brother lives in Queens, and I just know he'd love to go.'

'Well, let's see what we can do about changing that flight. I don't want them coming in too late – maybe just an hour or two later, max. Is that flight usually on time?'

'Honey, LAX to JFK is never on time.' I cringed. 'But it's usually not *too* bad. Let's see, I've got a flight leaving Los Angeles at ten A.M. arriving Newark at four. Would that work?'

'Yes, yes, that would work just fine. And you have twelve open seats?' I asked hopefully, thinking that this woman just might be the best thing that ever happened to me.

She laughed. Or, rather, cackled. A bad sign. 'Sure, I've got twelve seats open, but they're not all business. The best I can do is four in business, six in first class, and two in coach. You'll of course need to pay the difference for the first-class seats, which comes to, oh, let me see here . . . a total of seventeen thousand dollars. Does that work?'

It was my turn to laugh. Not that anything was actually funny, of course, but the only alternative was weeping. 'Do I have a choice?' I asked meekly.

'You sure don't,' she said, sounding suspiciously like she was enjoying this. 'And you should probably make up your mind soon because another business-class seat just disappeared.'

'Book it!' I practically screamed. 'Book it right now.'

I gave her my corporate card number, rationalizing that it was better than telling Mrs Carter there were no later flights and having them cancel altogether, and fell back under the covers.

When the alarm blared static a couple hours later, I felt like I'd spent the night curled up on a hard cement floor. Blessedly, I'd already packed my outfit for the night's party in a separate bag, so the only real task was to remain standing and fully conscious in the shower.

Figuring if there was ever a time to splurge for a cab it was now, I chased one halfway down my block and dove into it head-first. Not being stuck underground in the signal-free subway also allowed me to check a few of the morning's websites from my brand-new BlackBerry, a gift from the company's corporate department so I could 'familiarize myself with their product.' I pulled clips of the *Shrek 3* premiere, the Grey Goose relaunch, and of course the New York Scoop column featuring Philip, me, and my pantsuit.

Naturally, the cab got stuck in gridlock less than three blocks from my apartment, and naturally I decided – against the cabbie's advice – to remain in the temperature-controlled vehicle at all costs, regardless of how high the meter ran or how many minutes it took to cover an eighth of a mile. I needed to complete the check-list for the BlackBerry event. With Red Hots and an early-morning cigarette in hand (the cabbie had given me his blessing), I checked my cell phone to ensure that Mrs Carter hadn't left a message in the four hours since I'd last spoken to her. To my great relief, she hadn't called, but neither had Penelope, and that was disconcerting. My attempts to explain that it wasn't what it appeared, that Philip had just shown up and I hadn't lied to get out of her dinner, had sounded flat and pathetic even to my own ears, and I imagine to Penelope they sounded even less believable. The worst part of it all was that she and Avery had switched their tickets and were flying out tonight. I didn't understand what the big rush was – especially since Avery wouldn't be starting school for over a month – but I imagined it had something to do with Avery's eagerness to embark upon a brand-new West Coast party circuit. That and the fact that Penelope would do anything to avoid spending Thanksgiving with either her or Avery's parents. Penelope's mother had dispatched her own domestic staff to collect their boxes and suitcases and ship them ahead, and Avery and Pen were set to fly out of JFK, with their carry-ons and each other. Michael was planning to see them off, but it wasn't even an option for me.

The only message was from Kelly, a text reminding me to have my checklist filled out and on her desk first thing that morning so we could go over the last-minute stuff together. I unfolded its now-crumpled pages and pulled the pen cap off with my teeth. I stared at them for the few remaining minutes in the cab processing nothing. I'd have plenty of time before she got in, and the most important thing right now was to make sure Jay-Z and his entourage knew about the flight change and got on that plane with absolutely no problems.

A quick scan of the Dirt Alert revealed good news for once. Page Six had upheld their end of the bargain and written about my party in a way that made it sound exclusive, exciting, and really, really cool:

We hear that Jay-Z will be making a surprise appearance at tonight's party at Bungalow 8 to celebrate the launch of BlackBerry's redesigned handhelds. While Bette Robinson of Kelly & Company declined to confirm, watchers insist that boyfriend Philip Weston's friendship with the rapper ensures he's the mystery guest. In a related tidbit, Mr Weston and friends were spotted at a Saturday-night birthday party canoodling with Brazilian models, the youngest of whom was a mere fourteen years old.

I couldn't have been happier if they'd provided a web address for ordering the new BlackBerry: everything was exactly as I'd directed, and I knew Kelly would be deliriously excited when she saw it. I patted myself on the back, pleased with this mention, and thought back to one of Elisa's mini-lessons to me.

'Remember, there's a big difference between scoop and favor,' she'd said, spreading printouts of gossip columns all over the table at work.

I stared at them. 'What? What do you mean?'

'Well, look here.' She pointed to a couple of sentences from an on-set stylist who'd first noticed that Julia Roberts needed to have her costumes let out because, the girl assumed, Julia was newly pregnant. Page Six had been the first to talk to the stylist, who'd been the first to notice this shift. 'What is that – scoop or favor?'

'You're asking me?'

'Bette, you need to know these things. How else are you going to get our clients the coverage they pay us for?'

'I don't know . . . it's scoop,' I said, choosing one of the words at random.

'Right. Why?'

'Elisa, I appreciate that there's something important here, but I don't know what it is. But if you'd tell me rather than quizzing me, it'd probably save us both a lot of time. . . .'

She'd rolled her eyes dramatically and said, 'If you look carefully, there's a difference between "scoop" and "favor." Something juicy and revealing and slightly scandalous is "scoop." A celebrity spotting at a party or in public, or a mention of somewhere they've been, is a "favor." You can't ask the columnists for all favors without giving them scoop. Information is currency, and the more you have of it, the more favors you get.'

'So you're saying that some publicist out there wanted her client's name mentioned in the column and provided this bit about Julia Roberts in exchange?' It sounded so sordid, but it certainly made sense.

'Exactly. The publicist hand-delivered that stylist to Page Six and then made demands for coverage of her own.'

Well, that didn't seem too hard. Perhaps Page Six might be interested in knowing that quite a few of the city's most eligible bachelors had been keeping company with certain Brazilian girls who were not just underage, but who were years away from attending an R-rated movie without parental accompaniment. In fact, they *had* been interested, and when I followed up with the usual Tip Sheet we prepared for all the press – the blast-fax that went out with all the information about the party should anyone want to write about it – a researcher had expressed enthusiasm in possibly mentioning the BlackBerry party. Hmm, that wasn't hard, now was it? Morally abject and devoid of all integrity? Absolutely. But difficult it was not.

By the time Kelly had descended upon the office at nine, I'd completed the checklist and triple-checked that the plane-change fax had gone through to Jay-Z's compound and his mother's compound, as well as to his publicist, agent, manager, and a half-dozen other handlers. I marched into her office at ten after nine with an entire file folder of schedules, contact information, and confirmation numbers and planted myself in the zebra-print loveseat directly underneath the window.

'Are we all set for tonight, Bette?' she asked, scrolling rapidly through her inbox while slugging back a liter of Diet Coke. 'Tell me we're good.'

'We're good,' I sang, thrusting the *Post* under her nose. 'And even better, considering this.'

She scanned the piece hungrily, her smile growing ever larger with each word she read. 'Ohmigod,' she murmured, barely swallowing a mouthful of soda. 'Ohmigod, ohmigod, ohmigod. Was this you?'

It was all I could do not to do a little jig right there on the zebra-print shag carpet. 'It was,' I said quietly, confidently, although my insides were flipping with excitement.

'How? They never cover events *before* they happen.'

'Let's just say I listened very carefully to Elisa's valuable lesson on the concepts of scoop and favor. I think the BlackBerry people will be happy, don't you?'

'Fan-fucking-tastic, Bette. This is amazing!' She began reading it for a third time and picked up the phone. 'Fax this to Mr Kroner at BlackBerry immediately. Tell him I'll call him shortly.' She hung up and looked up at me. 'Okay, we're off to a perfect start. Give me an update on where everything stands.'

'Sure thing. Tip sheets went out ten days ago to all the usual dailies and weeklies.' I handed over a copy and continued while she surveyed it. 'We have confirmed attendance for writers or editors from *New York* magazine, *Gotham,* the *Observer,* E!, *Entertainment Weekly,* the *New York Post, Variety,* and the Styles section. I approved a few people from the monthlies as a gesture of goodwill, even though they'll never cover it.'

'What about the *Daily News*?' she asked. They were one of the papers that had just dropped Will's column, and I'd felt like a traitor for even contacting them.

'So far no one's RSVP'd, but I'd be shocked if someone wasn't there, so all the doormen have been instructed to allow admittance to anyone in possession of a business card from a legitimate media outlet.'

She nodded. 'Speaking of which, we *are* controlling the door, correct? I will not have any of the Grey Goose people trying to bring randoms, will I?'

This was a slightly sticky point. Grey Goose had offered to sponsor the event and put up thousands of dollars' worth of free booze in exchange for a logo on the invite and the press we'd promised would be there. They claimed they understood they wouldn't be permitted to allow guests who weren't prescreened by us and placed on the list in advance, but sponsors were notorious for dragging in dozens of their friends and associates because they thought it was their party, too. I'd discussed it with Sammy – unnecessary because he'd done hundreds of these and knew the drill – and he'd assured me that it wouldn't be a problem.

'Everyone will be trying their best to ensure that doesn't happen. Sammy is the best and most senior bouncer at Bungalow, and he'll be in charge of the door tonight. I've spoken with him.' *And simultaneously dreamed of draining the collagen right out of his girlfriend's lips,* I thought, but that was a different story.

Unlike Elisa, Kelly connected the name and the person immediately. 'Excellent. I always thought he was bright, at least as far as bouncers go. What VIPs do we have confirmed?'

'Well, obviously Jay-Z and crew. He requested that a whole contingent from his record label be invited, but most didn't respond to invitations, so I don't think many will show. Otherwise, we've got Chloe Sevigny, Betsey Johnson, Drew Barrymore, Carson Daly, Andy Roddick, Mary-Kate and Ashley, and Jon Stewart as definites. Also a handful of top-tier socialites. There might be more. When you've got an artist that big doing a private performance at a small venue . . . I'd be shocked if we didn't get unannounced visits from Gwen or Nelly or anyone else who might be in town and around. The door has been informed.'

'And who did the final vetting of the list?'

'I went over it with both Philip and Elisa, with Mr Kroner at

BlackBerry having final approval over everything. He seemed very, very happy with the projected attendees.'

Kelly finished off her bottle of Diet Coke and reached into the fridge underneath her desk to pull out another one. 'What else? Give me the quick rundown on decorations, gift bags, interviews, chain of command.'

I could tell we were nearing the end, and I was thrilled, not just because I desperately needed another coffee and perhaps a second egg-and-cheese, but because I knew I was nailing this party and Kelly was impressed. I'd been working on it all day, every day since it'd been thrown in my lap, and even though I could recognize the ridiculousness of what we were doing, I liked it. I'd almost forgotten what it felt like to work hard and do well, but it was damn nice.

'Samantha Ronson is DJing and knows to keep things upbeat. Bungalow is taking care of the decorations, with instructions to keep it minimal, chic, and very, very simple. I'll head over there this afternoon to check it out, but I'm really only expecting a few clusters of well-placed votives and, of course, the underlit palm trees. I think all the models we've got coming will be the primary attraction.'

At the word *model*, Kelly perked up even more. 'How many and who are they?' she asked with the efficiency of a drill sergeant.

'Well, I invited all the supermodels as guests, as always, and then we went with that new company – what's it called? Beautiful Bartenders. They hire out actors and models to tend bar and serve drinks. I saw a bunch of them working a Calvin Klein event two weeks ago and reserved a fleet of the guys, requesting that they all have long hair and wear head-to-toe white. They're magnificent and really make a statement.' *Did I just say that?* I thought.

'As for everything else, the interns are putting together the gift bags now. They've got airplane bottles of Grey Goose, MAC lipstick and eye shadow, a copy of the current issue of *US Weekly*, a gift certificate for thirty percent off at Barney's Co-op, and a pair of Kate Spade sunglasses.'

'I wasn't aware Kate Spade even made sunglasses,' Kelly said, now nearly finished with the second liter of Diet Coke.

'Neither was I. I guess that's why she wants them in the gift bag.' When she kept gulping, I figured I'd better wrap things up. 'So that's really it. I've touched base with Mr Kroner, and he understands exactly what he's to highlight and avoid when talking to the press, and I'll be there the entire night to oversee glitches. All in all, I expect everything should go very smoothly. Oh, and I've spoken with Philip and I think he understands that as host of this event, he shouldn't be drinking entire bottles of vodka, ogling preteens, or doing drugs openly or with reckless abandon. I can't guarantee he'll actually play by the rules, but I assure you that he's at least been informed as to what they are.'

'Well, we're all there to have a good time now, aren't we? So I'm sure if Philip wants to have a little fun, too, we won't be too uptight about that. *Just keep it away from the press.* Understood?'

'Of course.' I nodded solemnly, wondering how on earth I was supposed to keep the columnists and photographers away from the very person they'd been invited to see. I decided I'd deal with that later. 'And Kelly? I can't apologize enough about all that stuff in New York Scoop. I feel like I have a target on my back just because I'm supposedly dating Philip Weston. If I were paranoid, I'd think this Ellie girl was out to get me.'

She looked at me strangely, with an expression resembling pity, and I wondered if all the mentions were bothering her more than she'd let on. Kelly had brushed off every one of my apologies about the online column, swearing that any association with Philip Weston was a good one and that it had only succeeded in raising the profile of the company, but maybe she was tiring of the attacks. Which would make two of us.

'Bette, I have something to tell you,' Kelly said slowly. She pulled a new plastic liter bottle of Diet Coke from her under-desk fridge.

I could tell by the tone of her voice that this wasn't good. *Here it comes,* I thought to myself. *Here's where I get fired for something that's completely beyond my control. She looks so pained to have to do this – after all, she's got such loyalty to Will, but I've obviously left her no choice. In an industry that revolves around the press, I've failed miserably. It's actually her duty, her obligation, to fire me – she built this firm, and I walk in here and degrade it. How will I tell Will? Or my parents?* I had already begun calculating how long it would take me to rework my résumé and begin applying for other jobs when Kelly took a swig and cleared her throat.

'Bette, promise me that what I'm about to tell you will never leave this room.'

I audibly exhaled in relief. That didn't sound like the beginning of a firing speech.

'Of course,' I said, the words tumbling out in rushed eagerness. 'If you tell me never to mention it, then of *course* I won't.'

'I had lunch the other day with a woman from Ralph Lauren. I'm hoping very much to sign them – they'd be our biggest and most impressive account yet.'

I nodded as she continued.

'Which is why it's so crucial that you keep this under wraps.

If the information gets out – if you tell anyone – she'll know it's me, and we'll never get this account.'

'I understand,' I said solemnly.

'It concerns New York Scoop . . .'

'You mean Ellie Insider?'

Kelly looked at me. 'Yes. As you know, that's merely a pen name. She's gone to great lengths to keep her identity secret so she can move around freely and talk to people without their knowing. I'm not sure if this name means anything to you, but the column is actually being written by a girl named Abigail Abrams.'

I'm not sure how, but I knew a split second before she uttered the name that it was going to be Abby's. I'd *never* considered that the columnist was someone I'd known before – or even someone I'd met – but somehow, in that momentary flash, I was certain she'd utter Abby's name. The realization hadn't done anything to prepare me, however, and I couldn't do anything but stare at Kelly, my hands tucked under my legs and that same breathless, suffocating feeling I'd had in fifth-grade gym class when the red rubber kickball struck my stomach and knocked the wind right out of me. *How could I have been so clueless? How could I not have known?* I struggled to breathe and make sense of what Kelly was saying. All the awful things that had been written – all the exaggerations and embellishments and inferences and outright lies – had come from none other than Abby, the self-proclaimed *vortex* of the media world. *Why on earth does she hate me so much?* I kept thinking with irrational repetition. *Why? Why? Why?* Of course we'd never liked each other; that much was obvious. But what could inspire her to try to ruin my life? What had I done?

Apparently, Kelly had interpreted my shock as cluelessness because she said, 'Yeah, I didn't recognize the name, either. Some nobody, I guess, which is actually very smart on their part – no one can be suspicious of someone they don't know. The woman from Ralph Lauren is married to Abigail's brother, and she swore me to secrecy. I got the feeling she just wanted to tell someone. Or maybe she's testing my discretion. It doesn't really matter. Don't breathe a word of it to anyone, but just in case you run across that girl, you can make sure she gets the *right* pictures or information.'

I initially thought Kelly was telling me the columnist's identity so I could avoid her at all costs, but this was clearly not her intention.

She continued. 'Now you can feed her all sorts of stuff – be cool and casual and make it sound like scoop – and we'll have an even better shot at getting the clients covered.'

'Sounds good,' I croaked. I couldn't wait to get out of that office and reread every word Abby had written. How did she have any access at all? I thought bitterly about how she must have felt when she'd stumbled into a gold mine that first night at Bungalow 8, the night I'd met Philip. It was all starting to fall into place: she had been everywhere lately, always appearing out of the woodwork like a Pop-a-Weasel, ready with a nasty comment or a sneering look.

'Okay, enough of that. Don't worry about it too much right now. Just focus on making sure everything works for tonight. It's going to be great, don't you think?'

I murmured 'great' a few times and shuffled out of her office. I had already begun fantasizing about confronting Abby. There were a million possibilities, and each sounded delicious. It wasn't until I was back at the circular table, staring at my laptop, that I realized I couldn't do one damn thing about it. I couldn't tell anyone I knew, least of all Abby.

I tried to focus. After cutting out the Page Six clipping and taping it to the center of the office's shared circular desk, I logged on to see if the plane that would be bringing Jay-Z from LA to New York had actually left New York on time, which would highly increase the odds of its arriving in LA – and then coming back again – on schedule. So far, so good. I assigned two interns to take cars to Newark and stake out his arrival. This was not particularly necessary, since the Hotel Gansevoort was sending two stretch limos for them, but I wanted someone there to visually confirm that he'd arrived and gotten in his car without getting distracted by anything along the way. A quick call to Sammy – be still, my heart – confirmed that the setup was going smoothly. My to-do list complete, I tried to block out the thoughts of Abby's viciousness. It was late afternoon, and the only thing left to do was, well, absolutely nothing.

18

Not only was Jay-Z's plane on time, it was a few minutes early. He was polite and attentive. Nearly every single person who'd RSVP'd to the event showed up, and miraculously, the people who materialized at the door with no invite were all actually people we would've wanted to come. Mr Kroner spent the evening tucked away at a table with his associates, and we made sure the little RESERVED sign was displayed prominently for them and that a steady stream of pretty girls stopped by to say hello.

Most surprising was Philip. I'd been terrified he'd do something in a drunken state to embarrass me or the firm, but he'd kept his nose clean in every respect and even managed not to bury it in anyone's cleavage – at least not in front of any photographers, which is all that really mattered. I'd tried to warn him in a hundred different ways that, as host, he would need to be friendly to everyone, but my fear had been totally unfounded. From the moment he'd stepped inside the front door, he'd performed brilliantly. He'd rotated among all the groups assembled, shaking hands and nodding sagely with the corporate types, ordering rounds of shots for the bankers and mini-champagnes for the models, and back-slapping the celebrities with Clintonian charm. He strolled and smiled and carried conversations effortlessly, and I watched as men and women alike fell in love with him. It was instantly clear why gossip columns tracked him and why women everywhere swooned when he turned his attention to them. His ability to chat and joke and listen came so naturally that when he was near, people were left feeling like the volume had been turned down on everyone and everything except Philip Weston. They warmed to his touch, to his presence, and I found myself buzzing right along with everyone else. I couldn't deny that I was bizarrely drawn to him.

The only almost-disaster came when Samantha Ronson's flight from London was canceled and we were left with no DJ. At the exact same time, I'd received a call from Jake Gyllenhaal's publicist, asking if he could be placed on the VIP list for the evening. Having just read an article on do-it-yourself DJing, I asked Jake and the other confirmed celebs to bring their personal iPods and DJ for an hour each after Jay-Z did his twenty-minute set. It had been a huge success; each of the famous names had arrived with an iPod full of personal favorites, and soon everyone in attendance knew Jerry Seinfeld's all-time favorite dance song. Everything else had gone perfectly. There'd been no catfights over the gift bags, no brawls at the door, pretty much no uninvited drama to distract from the conveyance of the message: everyone young, hip, urban, and remotely cool is partying to celebrate BlackBerry, which must mean that BlackBerry itself is young, hip, urban, and cool. Therefore, you – whoever you are and wherever you're reading about this fabulous event – must own one so that you, too, may be young, hip, urban, and cool.

All in all, the event was a complete success. Kelly was happy, the client was thrilled (if slightly scandalized and extremely hung over – apparently Mr Kroner was unaccustomed to the sort of enthusiastic and committed drinking that had encompassed the entire evening), and the photogs had snapped, snapped, snapped just about every celebrity that our rotating staff of interns and coordinators physically threw in front of them. And then there was the effect the evening had on my love life.

Taking a break, I slinked outside under my usual pretense of wanting a cigarette. I found Sammy reading from another tattered paperback, Richard Russo's *Empire Falls*.

'Having fun?' he asked, lighting my cigarette. I'd cupped my hands around his lighter to protect the flame from the wind and felt a flutter in my chest when our skin touched. Was it lust, love, or just early-onset lung cancer? At that moment, it didn't seem to matter.

'Shockingly, yes.' I laughed, suddenly feeling that all was right and good. 'If you'd told me a few months ago that I'd be planning a party at Bungalow 8 with Jay-Z as the entertainment, I would've thought you were crazy. I hated banking. I'd sort of forgotten what it was like to *want* to do something well.'

He smiled. 'You obviously do this well. Everyone's talking about you.'

'Talking about me? I'm not sure I like the sound of that.'

He turned to check a few girls' names against the list and let them enter. 'No, no, all good stuff. Just that you've got this whole thing figured out and that you know how to put it all together. I can't remember the last time we had a party here that went this smoothly.'

'Really?' Part of me knew that this whole conversation was utterly ridiculous – we were, after all, talking about event-planning – but it was still really nice to hear.

'Sure. The question is, do you like it?'

'Well, *like* is a strong word for just about anything, don't you think?' He laughed and I had to physically bury my hands in my coat pockets to keep from grabbing his face. 'It's a far cry from the Peace Corps, for sure, but it's okay for now.'

His face clouded over almost immediately. 'Yeah' was about all he could manage.

'So, what are you doing for Thanksgiving?' I blurted out, not realizing that it might sound like I was asking him out when all I really wanted to do was change the subject. 'Going anywhere with your girlfriend?' I added casually to show him I knew the situation.

He gave me another uncomfortable look, followed by some obvious squirming, sending the message loud and clear: I had overstepped my bounds.

'I, uh, I didn't mean anything by—'

'No, no worries,' he cut in, leaning backward against the door as though he felt dizzy. 'It's just that, well, it's kind of complicated. Long story. Anyway, I'm actually going home this weekend. My old man's not doing so well, and it's been a couple months since I made it up there.'

'Where's home?'

He looked at me curiously, as though he were trying to read my face, and then said quietly, 'Poughkeepsie.'

Had he said that he was born and raised in Laos, he could not have shocked me more. Was he toying with me? Kidding? Had he found out that I was from Poughkeepsie and going home this weekend and thought this was funny somehow? A quick check of his face – smiling sweetly as he watched me process this – indicated no.

'Poughkeepsie, New York?' was about all I could manage.

'The one and only.'

'That's crazy. I'm from there—'

'Yeah, I know. I just didn't ever know if you knew. I remember you,' he said softly, looking out across Twenty-seventh Street at, as far as I could tell, absolutely nothing.

And, of course, it all came back then. Not that there were so many clues, but there had always been the sense that he was familiar. The time we'd stood right here and he'd joked that one of the girls who'd just gone inside needed a lesson in hippie chic since her flowing caftan was all wrong, and that she should head upstate to be schooled by the pros. That day in Starbucks when he'd brushed his hand up the back of his head and I'd sworn I'd seen that before. The very first night at Penelope's engagement party, when he wouldn't let me in and I couldn't shake the feeling that he was staring at me, almost waiting for me to say something. It was all so obvious now. Samuel Stevens, the guy in high school who was too gorgeous for his own good. The guy everyone assumed was gay because he was big and beautiful and didn't play a sport, but who instead kept mostly to himself while working at a few well-known local restaurants. The guy who came across as conceited and arrogant when we were teenagers and too young to realize that he was intensely shy, a loner, someone who didn't feel quite right with any one group of kids. The guy who'd sat at the table diagonally across from me in shop class, always focused on the wooden serving trays or gumball machines we were learning to make, never flirting or spacing or sleeping or whispering with his tablemates. The guy every girl should have loved but actually hated because he was somehow beyond her, already looking ahead, past the idiocy of high school and social hierarchies and seemingly unaware that anyone else existed. I did a quick calculation and realized that I hadn't seen him in nearly twelve years. I was a freshman and he a senior when we had that one shop class together before he graduated and vanished altogether.

'Mr Mertz's shop class, 1991, right?'

He nodded.

'Ohmigod, why didn't you say anything before now?' I asked, pulling out another cigarette. I offered him one and he took it, lighting first mine and then his own.

'I don't know, I probably should've. I just figured you had no idea. I felt kind of weird not saying something at first and then too much time went by. But I remember, when everyone else was sanding and chiseling, you'd always be writing – letters, it looked like – line after line, page after page, and I always wondered how anyone could have so much to say. Who was the lucky guy?'

I'd mostly forgotten about the letter-writing; I hadn't written one of those in years. It was easier now that I no longer heard my parents asking me what I had done for the world that day. They'd taught me how to write letters when I was old enough to put sentences on paper, and I'd instantly loved it. I wrote to congressmen, senators, CEOs, lobbyists, environmental organizations, and, occasionally, the president. Each night at dinner we'd discuss some great injustice and the following day I'd write my letter, letting someone know my outrage about capital punishment or deforestation or foreign-oil dependence or contraception for teenagers or prohibitive immigration laws. They were always chock-full of self-importance and read like the obnoxious, self-righteous missives they were, but my parents were so lavish with their approval that I couldn't stop. They tapered off at the end of high school, but it wasn't until some guy I was hooking up with freshman year in college picked one off my desk and made some offhand comment about how adorable it was that I was trying to save the world that I stopped entirely. It wasn't what he said so much as the timing. My parents' lifestyle was already less appealing. I had traded the alternative, peace-on-earth persona for a significantly more mainstream college social life pretty damn fast. Sometimes I wondered if I'd been just a little too thorough in my rejection. There was probably a happy medium somewhere, but banking and – let's be honest – party-planning hadn't exactly put me back on the track to selflessness.

I realized that Sammy was watching me intently as I recalled that time and said, 'Guy? Oh, they weren't to a boyfriend or anything like that. Guys didn't exactly dig the dreadlock/espadrille thing I had going back then. They were just, you know, letters to . . . I don't know, nothing special.'

'Well, I always thought you were pretty cute.'

I immediately felt myself blush.

For some reason, this made me happier than if he'd announced his undying love for me, but there was no time to savor it because my cell phone bleated with a 911 text message: *Doll, where R U? Need Cristal ASAP.*

Why Philip couldn't just ask one of the three dozen male model/waiters wandering around for that very reason was beyond me, but I knew I should check on things.

'Listen, I've got to get back in there and make sure everyone is drunk enough to have fun but not so trashed that they'll do anything stupid, but I was wondering: do you need a ride home tomorrow?'

'Home? To Poughkeepsie? You're going?'

'I couldn't possibly miss the annual Harvest Festival.'

'Harvest Festival?' He once again paused to open the velvet rope, this time to let in a couple who weren't coordinated enough to walk but still seemed in possession of enough faculties to grope each other.

'Don't ask. It's something my parents do every year on Thanksgiving Day, and my presence is required. I'm pretty positive my uncle will bail – he always comes up with some pressing obligation at the last minute – but he'll lend me his car. I'd be happy to give you a ride,' I said, fervently praying that he'd accept and not want to invite his aging significant other.

'Uh, sure. I mean, if you don't mind, that'd be great. I was just planning on taking the bus up Thursday morning.'

'Well, I was planning to go tomorrow after work, so if you could go Wednesday instead of Thursday, I'd love to have the company. I always want to drive the car off the road right around Peekskill.' I cheered myself silently for finally managing to maintain a normal exchange with this boy.

'Yeah, I'd really like that,' he said, looking pleased. Of course, I'd be pleased, too, if I didn't have to endure a four-hour Greyhound ride for a trip that normally takes two hours. I assured myself it was my companionship that convinced him and not just the chance to escape the gross stickiness and claustrophobia of the bus.

'Great. Why don't you meet me at my uncle's apartment at, let's see, maybe around six? He's on Central Park West, northwest corner of Sixty-eighth Street. Is that okay?'

He had just enough time to say that he was really looking forward to it before Philip materialized outside and literally dragged me back inside by the arm. I didn't much mind, though, considering what I had to look forward to the next day. I floated happily around the room, accepting compliments from everyone on staff and listening as guests talked about what a 'great scene' we had going on that night. When the party began to wind down around two, I pleaded yet another headache to Philip, who seemed happy to remain behind with Leo and a bottle of Cristal. At home, I curled up in bed with a Slim Jim and a brand-new Harlequin. It was the most perfect evening I could remember.

19

I could barely contain my excitement as I waited for Sammy in the lobby of Will's building. That day had dragged on interminably. Never mind that Kelly had bought the entire office breakfast in celebration of the previous night's success, or that she'd brought me into her jungle lair to tell me that she was so impressed with the evening that she was officially making me second-in-command of the *Playboy* party, reporting directly to her. Elisa's face tightened when the announcement was made; she'd been there a year and a half longer than me and clearly had expected to oversee the company's biggest event. But after a few remarks about how she was happy to 'give someone else a chance' at overseeing what would surely be total chaos, she plastered on a happy face and proposed celebratory drinks. Newspapers and websites that weren't even at the party had covered it, breathlessly writing how the 'slew of celebs and socialites' had come out to fete the 'hottest new urban accessory.' It almost didn't register when a box arrived directly from Mr Kroner's office with enough BlackBerries to stock an entire wireless store, the note sounding so effusive I was almost embarrassed. I barely even noticed the few lines in New York Scoop that announced I'd been spotted sobbing in a corner as Philip made out with a Nigerian-born soap star, and I didn't get the least bit upset when Elisa confided to me that she'd 'accidentally' gotten a ride with Philip on his Vespa because 'she was so drunk and she and Davide had gotten in a fight but that nothing – *nothing, I swear on your life and mine* – had happened.' No, none of that had even really registered because none of it made the minutes any shorter or got me in the same car with Sammy any faster. When he walked through my uncle's lobby's door wearing a pair of broken-in jeans and a very snuggly sweater, a duffel bag slung over his shoulder, I didn't know if I'd be able to keep my eyes on the road long enough to get us out of the city.

'Hey,' he said when he saw me sitting on the bench, pretending to examine the paper. 'I can't tell you how much I appreciate this.'

'Don't be ridiculous,' I said, standing on tiptoe to kiss him hello on the cheek. 'You're the one doing me the favor. Hold on a sec, I'll have my uncle come down with the keys.'

Will had agreed to lend me his Lexus for the weekend only after I'd sworn to uphold the story he'd fabricated to explain his absence. Even though I was just giving Sammy a lift to his parents' house, he insisted that Sammy be fully apprised of the cover story as well.

'You promise you've got the details down, darling?' he'd asked nervously upon relinquishing the keys as the three of us stood in his underground garage.

'Will, stop stressing. I promise I won't give you up. I shall endure the suffering alone. As always.'

'Humor me. Let's go through it one more time. When she asks you where I am, what do you say?'

'I simply explain that you and Simon couldn't bear the idea of spending an entire weekend in a solar-powered house where there's never enough hot water and the all-natural, undyed sheets are itchy and nothing's really ever clean since chemicals aren't used, so instead you decided you'd rather admire the harvest from your comped beachfront suite in Key West. Oh, yeah, and that you find it quite dull when the dinner-table conversation consists solely of ecopolitics. Is that about right?' I smiled sweetly.

He looked helplessly at Sammy and coughed a few times.

'Don't worry, sir, Bette's got the story down,' he assured him, climbing into the passenger seat. 'Simon had a last-minute request to fill in for one of the missing musicians, and you felt it wouldn't be right to leave him alone on the holiday, as much as you'd like to see everyone. You would've called them yourself, but you're on a tight deadline for your bastard of an editor and will call next week. I'll get her up to speed on the ride.'

Will released the keys into my open palm. 'Sammy, thank you. Bette, I want you to pay close attention to the empowerment lectures – women can do anything, you know – and try not to feel too bad for little old me, kicking back poolside with a daiquiri and a paperback.'

I wanted to hate him, but he looked so happy with his alibi and his sneaky plans that I didn't do anything but hug him and turn on the car. 'You owe me for this. As usual.' I tucked Millington's Sherpa Bag in the backseat and tossed a Greenie inside so she wouldn't cry or whine while we drove.

'You know it, darling. I'll bring you back one of those kitschy fringed T-shirts, or maybe a coconut candle or two. Deal? Drive safely. Or don't. Just don't call me if anything happens, at least not for the next three days. Have fun!' he called, blowing kisses in the rearview mirror.

'He's great,' Sammy said as we worked our way slowly through traffic up the West Side Highway. 'Like a little kid who got out of school by pretending to be sick.'

I stuck *Monster Ballads* (ordered from an 800 number in an insomniac three A.M. fit) in the six-disc changer and skipped through until I found Mr Big's 'To Be with You.' 'He is really great, isn't he? I honestly don't know what I would do without him. He's the only reason I'm normal today.'

'What about your parents?'

'They're sixties throwbacks,' I said, 'and they take it very seriously. My mother cried the first time I shaved my legs, when I was thirteen, because she was afraid I'd subjugated myself to the male-dictated cultural expectations of female beauty.'

He laughed and started to settle in, stretching out his legs and putting his hands behind his head. 'Please tell me she didn't talk you out of that particular practice?'

'No, she didn't, at least not now ... although it took me until college to shave again. They once insisted that I alone was responsible for disrupting an entire ecosystem because I bought a snakeskin keychain. Oh, and then there was the time I wasn't allowed to go to the biggest slumber party in fourth grade because they noticed that the parents of the girl hosting it refused to recycle their newspapers. They thought it was a potentially evil environment for a child to spend twelve hours in.'

'You're joking.'

'I'm not. It's not to say they're not really great people, because they are. They're just *really* committed. Sometimes I wish I were more like them.'

'I sure didn't know you well in high school, but I remember you being more like that than, uh, than this New York thing.'

I didn't quite know what to say.

'No, I didn't mean it like that,' he hastened to say. 'You know, you just always gave the impression of being really involved in so many causes. I remember you wrote that editorial on a woman's right to choose in the school paper. I overheard some of the teachers talking about it in study hall one day – they couldn't believe you were only a freshman. I read it after I listened to them and I couldn't believe it, either.'

I felt a little frisson at the thought that he'd read and remembered my article, as though we all of a sudden had an intimate connection.

175

'Yeah, well, it's hard to maintain. Especially when it's something chosen for you, and not something you come upon yourself.'

'Fair enough.' I could see him nod out of the corner of my eye. 'They sound interesting.'

'Oh, you have no idea. Luckily, even though they were hippies, they were still *Jewish* hippies, and didn't much love the deprivation lifestyle. As my father still constantly points out, "One is no more convincing coming from a place of poverty than coming from a place of comfort – it's the argument that matters, not the material trappings or lack thereof."'

He stopped sipping his coffee and turned to look at me. I could feel his eyes on my face and knew that he was listening intently.

'Oh, yes, it's true. I was born on a commune in New Mexico, a place I wasn't totally convinced was an actual state until I saw the 2000 electoral map on CNN. My mother loves recounting how she gave birth to me in their "marriage bed" before all the commune's children, who'd been brought in to watch the miracle of life unfold before their little eyes. No doctors, no drugs, no sterile sheets – just a husband with a degree in plant science, a touchy-feely midwife who coached with yogic breathing, the commune's chanting guru, and two dozen children under the age of twelve who most likely went on to remain virgins well into their thirties after witnessing that particular miracle.'

I don't know what it was that kept me talking. It had been years and years since I'd told that story to anyone – probably not since Penelope and I met during orientation week at Emory, smoked pot in the bushes by the tennis courts, and she admitted that her father knew his office staff better than his family and that she'd thought her black nanny was her mother until she was five years old. I figured there was no better way to cheer her up than to show her just how normal her own parents were. We'd laughed for hours that night, stretched out in the grass, stoned and happy. Though my boyfriends had met my parents, I'd never talked to anyone about them like this. Sammy made me want to tell him everything.

'That's absolutely incredible. How long were you there? Do you remember it?'

'They only lived there until I was two or so, and then they moved to Poughkeepsie because they got jobs at Vassar. But that's where my name came from. First they wanted to name me Soledad, in honor of the California prison that housed Berkeley protestors, but then their shaman or someone proposed Bettina, after Bettina Aptheker, the only female member of the Steering Committee of Berkeley's Free Speech Movement. I refused to

176

answer to anything but Bette when I was twelve and "The Wind Beneath My Wings" was a hit and Bette Midler was actually cool. By the time I realized I'd renamed myself after the redheaded singer of a sappy Top 40 inspirational, it was too late. Everyone calls me that now, except my parents, of course.'

'Wow. They sound so interesting. I'd love to meet them sometime.'

I didn't know quite how to respond to that – it might be a bit unnerving for him if I were to announce that they were his future in-laws – so I asked him about his parents. Nothing came to mind when I tried to recall Sammy from high school, and it occurred to me that I had no clue about his home life. 'What about you? Anything juicy about your family, or are they actually normal?'

'Well, calling them normal seems like a bit of a stretch. My mom died when I was six. Breast cancer.'

I opened my mouth to apologize, to murmur something ineffectual and clichéd, but he cut me off.

'Sounds really shitty, but I was honestly too young to really remember. It was weird not having a mom growing up, but it was definitely harder for my older sister, and besides, my dad was pretty great.'

'Is he okay now? You mentioned something about him not being well.'

'No, he's okay. Just lonely, I think. He was dating a woman for years, and I'm not totally clear on what happened, but she moved to South Carolina a couple months ago and my dad's not taking it well. I just thought a visit would be good for him.'

'And your sister? What's her story?'

'She's thirty-three. Married with five kids. *Five* kids – four boys and a girl – do you believe it? Started right out of high school. She lives in Fishkill, so she could see my father all the time, but her husband's kind of a prick and she's busy now that she's going back to school for nursing, so . . .'

'Are you guys close?' It was strange to see this all shaping up, a whole world that I never knew existed for him, that I could never have imagined existing when I saw him slapping backs with the various moguls and moguls-in-training at Bungalow 8 every night.

He seemed to think about this for a second as he popped open the can of Coke he pulled from his backpack, offering me a sip before he took one.

'Close? I don't know if I'd say that, exactly. I think she resents that I left home to go to college when she already had one kid and another on the way. She makes lots of comments about how I'm Dad's reason for living and at least one of us has a chance of making him proud – you know, that sort of stuff. But she's a good girl. Christ, I just got heavy there. Sorry about that.'

Before I could say anything, let him know that it was okay, that I loved hearing him talk about absolutely anything, a Whitesnake track came on and Sammy laughed again. 'Are you serious with this music? How do you listen to this shit?'

The conversation continued easily after that – just chitchat about music and movies and the ridiculous people we both dealt with all day long. He was careful not to mention Philip, and I returned the favor by steering clear of Isabelle. Otherwise, we talked as though we'd known each other forever. When I realized we were only a half-hour outside of town, I called to let my parents know that I was dropping someone off and would be there shortly.

'Bettina, don't be ridiculous. Of course you'll bring him by for dinner!' My mother all but shrieked into the phone.

'Mom, I'm sure he wants to get home. He's here to see his family, not mine.'

'Well, be sure to extend the invitation. We never get to meet any of your friends, and it would make your father very happy. And of course, he's more than welcome at the party tomorrow. Everything's all set and ready to go.'

I promised her I'd relay the information and hung up.

'What was that all about?' he asked.

'Oh, my mother wants you to come over for a late dinner, but I told her you'd probably want to get home to your dad. Besides, the stuff they try to pass off as food is atrocious.'

He was quiet for a second and then said, 'Actually, if you don't mind, that'd be really nice. My old man isn't expecting me until tomorrow, anyway. Besides, maybe I could help out in the kitchen, make that tofu a little more palatable.' He said this tentatively, trying to sound indifferent, but I sensed (prayed, hoped, willed) that there was something more.

'Oh, uh, okay,' I said, trying to come across as cool but instead sounding mortally opposed to the idea. 'I mean, if you want, it'd be great.'

'Are you sure?'

'Positive. I'll give you a ride home afterward, and I promise not to keep you trapped any longer than absolutely necessary. Which will still be long enough for them to try to convert you to a meat-free lifestyle, but hopefully it'll be bearable.' The awkwardness was over. I was ecstatic. And slightly terrified.

'Okay, that sounds good. After the stories you've told me, I feel like I have to see them now.'

My mother was sitting on the porch swing wrapped in multiple

178

layers of wool when we pulled into the driveway, which bisected the nearly six acres of land they'd lived on for a quarter-century. The hybrid Toyota Prius they kept for emergencies (I often wondered what they'd think if they knew that Hollywood's entire A-list drove them, too) sat in the driveway, covered by a tarp, since they rode bicycles 99 percent of the time. She threw down the book she was cradling in her mittened hands (*Batik Technique*) and ran to meet the car before I'd even put it in park.

'Bettina!' she called, yanking open the driver's-side door and clasping her hands together excitedly. She grabbed my arm and pulled me out into an immediate hug, and I wondered if anyone besides my mother or my dog would ever be so happy to see me. We stood there for a moment longer than was necessary and I immediately forgot how much I'd dreaded this visit.

'Hi, Mom. You look great.' And she did. We had the same long, unmanageably thick hair, but hers had turned a beautiful shade of gray, and it literally shimmered as it hung down her back, parted straight down the middle as it had been since she was a teenager. She was tall and delicately thin, the type of woman whose determined expression is the only clue that she's not quite as fragile as she appears. As usual, she wore no makeup, only a turquoise sun pendant on a whispery silver chain. 'This is my friend, Sammy. Sammy, my mother.'

'Hello, Mrs Robinson.' He paused. 'Wow, that sounds weird, doesn't it? Although I suppose you're used to it.'

'I sure am. "Jesus loves me more than you will know." Either way, please just call me Anne.'

'It's really nice of you to invite me over, Anne. I hope I'm not intruding.'

'Nonsense, Sammy. You both made our whole night. Now come inside before you freeze.'

We followed her through the simple pine doorway after pulling a sneezing Millington from her Sherpa Bag and walked back to the small greenhouse they'd installed a few years earlier 'for contemplating nature when the weather wasn't cooperating.' It was the only modern feature of the whole rustic house, and I loved it. Totally out of place with the rest of the log-cabin theme, the greenhouse had a minimalist Zen feel, like something you'd discover tucked away in the spa of the latest Schrager hotel. It was all sharp-angled glass with leafy red maple around the perimeter and every imaginable species of plant, shrub, flower, or bush that could conceivably thrive in such an atmosphere. There was a pond, slightly larger than a golf-course sand trap, with a smattering of floating lily pads and a few teak chaise longues off to the side for relaxing. It opened out into a huge, treed-in back-yard. My father was correcting papers at a low wooden table lit by a hanging Chinese paper lantern, looking reasonably well put together in a pair of jeans and Naot sandals with fuzzy socks ('No need to buy those German Birkenstocks when Israelis make them just as well,' he liked to say). His hair had grayed a bit, but he jumped up as spryly as ever and enveloped me in a bear hug.

'Bettina, Bettina, you return to the nest,' he sang, pulling me into a little jig. I stepped aside, embarrassed, and kissed him quickly on the cheek.

'Hi, Dad. I want you to meet my friend, Sammy. Sammy, this is my dad.'

I prayed my dad would be normal. You could never tell exactly what he'd say or do, especially for a private laugh from me. The first time my parents came to the city after I'd graduated from college, I brought Penelope out to dinner with us. She'd met them at graduation and once before – she probably barely remembered a thing about them – but my dad didn't forget much. He'd kissed her hand gallantly after I reintroduced them and said, 'Penelope, dear, of course I remember. We all went out for dinner, and you brought that sweet boy. What was his name? Adam? Andrew? I remember him being very bright and very articulate,' he deadpanned without a hint of discernible sarcasm.

This was my father's subtle way of inside-joking with just me. Avery had been so stoned at dinner that he'd had trouble responding to simple questions about his major or hometown. Even though he hadn't seen Avery or Penelope in years, my father would still occasionally call me and pretend to be Avery's fictional dealer, asking me in a faux-baritone voice if I'd like to purchase a pound of 'some really good shit.' We thought it was hysterical, and he clearly couldn't resist taking a quick shot now and then. Penelope, being accustomed to clueless and absentee parents, had not detected a thing and simply smiled nicely. My dad knew nothing of Sammy, so I figured we were safe.

'Pleasure, Sammy. Come sit and keep an old man company. You from around here?'

We all sat. My father poured the Yogi Egyptian licorice tea that my mother brewed by the bucket as Sammy carefully arranged his large frame on one of the oversized beaded floor cushions scattered around the table. I flopped between him and my mother, who folded her legs Indian-style so gracefully that she appeared to be twenty years younger.

'So what's the plan for the weekend?' I asked cheerily.

'Well, no one will be coming until late tomorrow afternoon, so you're free until then. Why don't you guys see what's going on at the university? I'm sure there's a good program or two,' my mother said.

'The campus ballet troupe is performing an early Thanksgiving matinee tomorrow. I could arrange for tickets if you're interested,' Dad offered. He had taught ecology at Vassar for so long and was such a beloved professor on campus that he could arrange just about anything. My mother worked for the campus health clinic's emotional health department, dividing her time equally between hotline work (rape crisis, suicide, general depression) and rallying the university to adopt a more holistic approach to students' problems (acupuncture, herbs, yoga). They were the pet couple of Vassar, just as I knew they'd been the pet couple at Berkeley for so many years in the sixties.

'Maybe I'll check it out, but you're forgetting that Sammy is here to visit his family,' I said, giving them both what I hoped were warning looks to lay off. I spooned some of the unprocessed brown sugar and passed the dish to Sammy.

'Speaking of which, what was Will's excuse again for not being able to make it?' my mother asked nonchalantly.

Sammy stepped up before I could intervene, not realizing that my parents had long been onto Will's pitiful stories and lies, that it had become a favorite family pastime to tell and retell the new and creative fibs he crafted. He and my mother were close, despite the small detail that she was an annoying hippie liberal who refused to affiliate with a political party and he was an annoying conservative Republican who defined himself by one. Somehow they talked weekly and even managed to be affectionate when together, although each loved viciously mocking the other to me.

Sammy spoke up. 'Wasn't it something about Simon's work?' he said to me. 'The Philharmonic called Simon at the very last minute to fill in for an ill musician. They gave him no choice, really. He just couldn't say no,' he blurted out before I could screw it up. He was loyal, I had to give him that.

My mother smiled first at me and then at my father. 'Is that so? I thought he said something about an emergency meeting with his entertainment lawyer at their offices in New Jersey.'

Sammy flushed, immediately convinced he'd somehow gotten the story confused. Time to intervene.

'They know Simon's not filling in for anybody, Sammy, and they know you know it, too. Don't worry, you didn't give anything away.'

'That was sweet of you, Sammy, but I simply know my dear

brother too well to believe the stories anymore. Where are they off to? Miami? The Bahamas?'

'Key West,' I said, topping off everyone's mugs.

'You win,' my father conceded. 'Your mother bet me he'd cancel at the last minute and blame it on Simon. Frankly, I'm delighted he finally moved past that tired old deadline excuse.' They both cracked up.

'Well, I'd better get dinner going,' my mother announced. 'I went to the farmers' market today and got all their winter specials.'

'May I help you?' Sammy asked. 'It's the least I can do after lying to you. Besides, it's been a while since I've been in a home kitchen – I'd really appreciate it.'

My parents peered at him curiously.

'Sammy's a chef,' I said. 'He studied at the Culinary Institute of America and is planning to open his own restaurant someday.'

'Really! How interesting. Do you currently cook anywhere in the city?' my father asked.

Sammy smiled shyly, looked down, and said, 'Actually, I started doing Sunday brunch at Gramercy Tavern a few months ago. It's a serious crowd. It's been a really good experience.'

I felt a jolt go through me. Who was this guy?

'Well, in that case, come with me. Can you do anything interesting with zucchini?' my mother asked, linking her arm with his once he hoisted himself up from the floor cushions.

Within minutes Sammy was at the stove, while my mother sat quietly at the table, staring at him in wonderment, unable to disguise her delight.

'What are you making?' I asked as he drained a pot of noodles before adding a splash of olive oil. He wiped his hands on the apron my mother had provided (which read IN ACCEPTANCE, THERE IS PEACE) and surveyed his progress.

'Well, I thought we'd start with a pasta salad with roasted carrots, cucumbers, and pine nuts, and maybe some zucchini antipasto. Your mom said she wanted something casual for the entrée, so I was thinking of trying curried chickpea sandwiches on focaccia and a side of stuffed red peppers with rice and escarole. How does everyone feel about baked apples with freshly whipped cream and this sorbet here for dessert? I have to say, Mrs Robinson, you picked some fantastic ingredients.'

'Gee, Mom, what were you planning on making?' I asked, loving the expressions on both their faces.

'Casserole,' she said, never taking her eyes off Sammy. 'Just throw it all together and bake it for a few minutes, I guess.'

'Well, that sounds great, too,' Sammy was quick to say. 'I'd be happy to do that if you'd prefer.'

'No!' my father and I shouted simultaneously. 'Please continue, Sammy. This is going to be a real treat for us,' Dad said, slapping him on the back and taking a taste of the chickpea mixture with his fingers.

Dinner was amazing, of course, so good I didn't make a single nasty comment about the lack of meat or the abundance of organic food, but that was mostly because I didn't even notice. All my concerns about the potential awkwardness of Sammy sharing the table with my parents had evaporated by the time we finished our pasta salad. Sammy glowed from the constant praise everyone lavished on him, and he became chatty and happy in a way I'd never seen. Before I knew what had happened, I was clearing the table alone and my parents had sequestered Sammy back in the greenhouse and were showing him the much-dreaded naked-in-the-bathtub baby pictures and all the things I'd supposedly accomplished in my life that no one besides the people who'd given birth to you could conceivably care about. It was almost midnight when my parents finally announced they were going to bed.

'You two are more than welcome to stay and visit, but your father and I need to get to sleep,' my mother announced, while stamping out the last stub of her clove cigarette, a treat they shared when they were in a festive mood. 'Big day tomorrow.' She extended her hand to my father, which he took with a smile. 'So nice to meet you, Sammy. We just love meeting Bette's *friends*.'

Sammy leapt to his feet. 'Nice to meet you both as well. Thanks for having me. And good luck with the party tomorrow. It sounds great.'

'Yes, well, it's a tradition, and we hope to see you there. Nighty-night,' my father said cheerily, following my mother into the house, but not before he leaned in and whispered a fervent thank-you to Sammy for allowing him one edible meal.

'They're great,' Sammy said quietly when the door had closed. 'After the way you described them, I was honestly expecting circus freaks. But they couldn't be more normal.'

'Yeah, well, it depends on your definition of *normal*, I guess. You ready?'

'Uh, sure. If you are.' He sounded hesitant.

'Well, I figured you'd want to get home, but I'm totally up for hanging out if you are,' I said, holding my breath the entire time.

He appeared to think about this for a minute and then said, 'How do you feel about hitting the Starlight?'

It was official: he was perfect.

I exhaled. 'Great call. It's only the best diner on earth. Do you love it as much as I do?'

'More. I used to go there by myself in high school, if you can even believe how humiliating that is. I'd just sit there with a book or a magazine and a cup of coffee. It broke my heart when the original wart lady left.'

The Starlight had been the epicenter of our high school social life, the place I'd spent the better part of my teenage years, hanging out with my friends who, like me, weren't quite pretty or cool enough to be considered popular, but who could still confidently claim superiority over the dorks and losers (mostly the horrifyingly antisocial math and computer types) who unwillingly occupied the rungs beneath us. The social hierarchy was strictly maintained: the cool kids monopolized the smoking section, the severely socially challenged played video games at the two booths all the way in the back, and my crowd (assorted hippies, alternative punk kids, and the socially striving who hadn't quite made the big leagues yet) held the half-dozen tables and the entire counter space in between. The guys would sit in one booth, smoking and discussing – quite suavely, and with the strong suggestion of expertise – whether they'd sacrifice blow jobs or sex if forced to decide at gunpoint, as we, their loyal girlfriends (who weren't doing much more than kissing any of them), gulped coffee and analyzed in great detail which of the girls at school had the best clothes, chest, and boyfriend. Starlight was the Poughkeepsie version of Central Perk, only slightly stickier and with fluorescent lights, brown vinyl booths, and a waitstaff where each employee, incredibly, possessed either a sprouting facial wart or a missing finger. I loved the way some people remain devoted to their childhood bedrooms or summer-vacation spots, and I returned, like a homing pigeon, every time I went back to town. The idea of Sammy there alone made me sad and nostalgic.

We settled into the least sticky booth we could find and pretended to examine the plastic menus, which hadn't changed in decades. Even though I was stuffed, I debated between cinnamon toast and fries and then decided that carb-loading was acceptable outside the Manhattan city limits and got both. Sammy ordered a cup of regular coffee. One of my favorite waitresses, the woman with the longest hair of all growing from the wart near her lip, had snorted when he'd asked for skim milk instead of cream, and the two were now involved in some sort of glaring contest across the room.

We sipped coffee and chatted and picked at the food.

'You never mentioned you were doing brunch at Gramercy Tavern. I'd love to come by.'

'Yeah, well, you never mentioned that you were salutatorian of your class. Or that you won the Martin Luther King Award for cross-cultural community service.'

I laughed. 'Boy, they didn't miss a thing, did they? I thought it was lucky you graduated three years before me so you wouldn't remember any of that stuff, but I should've known better.'

The waitress refilled Sammy's mug and let a little of the coffee splash for good measure.

'They're proud of you, Bette. I think that's so nice.'

'They *were* proud of me. It's different now. I don't think my newfound ability to draw celebs to Bungalow 8 and get written about in gossip columns was exactly what they had in mind for me.'

He smiled sadly. 'Everyone makes compromises, you know? Doesn't mean you're any different from the person you were back then.'

The way he said it made me want to believe it. 'Can we get out of here?' I asked, motioning for the check, which, regardless of how many people were in the party or what was ordered, always amounted to exactly three dollars per person. 'I think I need to conserve my energy for tomorrow's festivities, which I'm hoping to convince you to attend. . . .'

He left a twenty dollar bill on the table ('To make up for all the nights I left really shitty tips after sitting here for hours') and put his hand on my back to direct me out. We detoured long enough for him to win me a small stuffed pig from the claw game in the foyer – the one that sat just past the rotating pie display. I hugged it to me and he told me it was the best two bucks in quarters he'd ever spent. The ten-mile drive to his house was quiet, and I realized that in all the years I lived in Poughkeepsie, I'd never been to this part of town. We were both contemplative, with none of the chitchat or joking or confiding that we'd shared during the past nine hours we'd spent together – nine hours that felt like five minutes. I pulled into the short, unpaved driveway of a small, tidy Colonial-style home and put the car in park.

'I had a great time tonight. Today, tonight, the whole thing. Thanks for the ride and for dinner – all of it.' He didn't look like he was in any rush to get out of the car, and I finally allowed myself to entertain the idea that he might just kiss me. Any Harlequin novel would've surely pointed out how the electricity crackled between us.

'Are you serious? I should be thanking you! You're the one who kept us from enduring an entire night of vicious food poisoning, you know,' I blurted out. Then I tucked my hands underneath my knees to keep them from shaking.

And then he was climbing out. Just like that. He simply opened the door and grabbed his duffel from the backseat and waved, mumbling something about calling me tomorrow. The disappointment stung like a slap to the face, and I put the car in reverse as quickly as possible, needing to leave before I started crying. *Why on earth would you think he's even remotely interested in you?* I asked myself, going back over the night in my head. *He needed a ride and you offered him one and he was nothing except perfectly friendly. It's your own delusion and you need to get over it immediately before you make a complete ass of yourself.* As I turned to back out of the gravelly driveway, I saw a figure approaching the car.

He was talking, but I couldn't hear him through the closed window. I rolled it down and hit the brakes.

'Did you forget something?' I asked, trying to keep my voice from quivering.

'Yes.'

'Well, hold on a sec. There, the back door's open, so—'

I didn't get to finish. He reached in through the driver's-side window and across my lap and I was briefly frightened until he grabbed the gearshift and put the car in park. He then unbuckled my seat belt, yanked open the door, and pulled me from the car.

'What? I don't know—'

But he silenced me by taking my face in his hands in exactly the way that every girl wants and no guy ever does. Just like on the cover of *Lustfully Yours,* if I was recalling it correctly, the picture that had symbolized for me the ultimate in romantic make-outs. His hands were cool and strong and I was convinced he could feel my face burning, but there was no time to worry about it. He leaned in and kissed me with such softness that I could barely respond, had no choice but to stand there and let it happen, too shocked to even kiss him back.

'I promise I won't forget that next time,' he said with what I swear was the kind of gruffness you'd only ever hear in a movie. He gallantly held my door open for me and motioned that I was to sit down again. Happy I needn't rely on my own legs for support anymore, I collapsed clumsily into the seat and grinned as he shut the door and walked off toward the house.

20

I had just finished stringing the last succotash-shaped paper lantern when my mother finally caved and asked me about Sammy.

'Bettina, honey, Sammy seems like a lovely boy. Your father and I enjoyed meeting him last night.'

'Yeah, he does seem nice.' I was going to make her work for this one and enjoy every second of it.

'Will he be joining us for the party?' She placed a hummus platter next to a tray of mixed olives and stood back to admire her work before turning her attention to me.

'I don't think so. I know he'd like to, but we're both only here for the weekend, and I think he needs to spend some time with his dad. He mentioned they might go out for steaks or something.'

'Mmm, is that so?' she asked in a tight voice, visibly trying not to comment on what she was surely envisioning to be a frenzied orgy of meat-eating. Sammy had only said that they'd go out for Thanksgiving dinner, but it was too easy and too much fun to drive her crazy. 'Maybe he'd like to stop by afterward and sample some of our finest local produce?'

'Yes, well, I'll definitely pass along that sexy invitation.' I was upset when Sammy had called to say he couldn't make the party, and even more so when he mentioned that he wouldn't be riding back to the city with me. After thanking me quite politely for the ride the day before, he explained that he had to work Saturday night and would be taking the bus back. I thought about leaving early, too, but knew my parents would be upset, so I just wished him a good night and hung up.

'Hey, Bettina, come and help me with this, will you?' My father was lovingly arranging a pile of sticks and firewood in a complicated woven pattern. The pièce de résistance of every Harvest Festival was the ceremonial bonfire, around which everyone would gather to dance, drink wine, and 'serenade the harvest,' whatever that meant.

I bounded over, feeling especially unfettered in a pair of worn-out cords from high school, a zip-up wool sweater, and a thickly piled fleece pullover. It felt weird and wonderful, a relief from the flimsy little tank tops and the skintight, ass-lifting, thigh-binding, must-have jeans I now wore religiously. My feet were swathed in fuzzy angora socks and tucked into a pair of mushy-soft Minnetonka moccasins. Rubber-soled. Beaded. With fringe. They'd been a horrifying fashion abomination in high school, but I'd worn them nonetheless. It felt slightly impure to wear them again now that they were splashed all over the pages of *Lucky*, but they were too comfortable to reject on principle. I took a deep breath of the late November air and felt something strangely akin to happiness.

'Hey, Dad, what can I do?'

'Grab that pile by the greenhouse and drag it over here, if you can,' he grunted while heaving a particularly huge log over his shoulder.

He tossed me a pair of oversized work gloves – the kind that had long ago turned black from so much dirt – and waved in the general direction of the wood. I pulled on the gloves and relocated the firewood from one area to another, one log at a time.

My mother announced that she was going to shower but had left a pot of Yogi Egyptian licorice tea in the kitchen. We sat and poured and drank.

'So tell me, Bettina. What is your relationship with that fine young fellow from last night?' Dad asked, trying to sound casual.

'Fine young fellow?' I said, more to buy time than to poke fun. I knew they both desperately wanted to hear that Sammy and I were dating – and God knows no one wanted that to be true more than me – but I couldn't bring myself to explain the entire situation.

'Well, of course you know your mother and I dream of you ending up with someone like Penelope's fellow. What's his name?'

'Avery.'

'Right. Avery. I mean, it would be delightful to have a never-ending supply of really good grass, but barring a dreamboat like him, this Sammy fellow seems all right.' He grinned at his own joke.

'Yeah, well, nothing too exciting to report. I just sort of gave him a ride up here, you know?' I didn't want to get into it – it felt like I was a little old to be telling my parents about something that currently qualified as little more than a crush.

He sipped his tea and peered at me over the top of his Veterans for Peace mug. Neither of my parents was a veteran of anything, as far as I knew, but I didn't say anything. 'Okay. Well then. How's the new job going?'

I'd managed not to think about work for a full twenty-four hours, but I suddenly felt a frantic need to check my messages. Luckily, there was no cell reception at my parents' house, and I didn't bother to call my number from their land line.

'It's actually pretty good,' I said quickly. 'Much better than I expected. I like my coworkers for the most part. The parties are still fun, although I can see how that can get old really fast. I'm meeting a ton of new people. Overall, it seems like a good plan for right now.'

He nodded once, as though processing, but I could tell he wanted to say something.

'What?' I asked.

'No, nothing. It's all just very interesting.'

'What's so interesting about it? It's just events PR. It's not what I'd call fascinating.'

'Well, of course, that's precisely what I mean. Don't take this the wrong way, Bettina, but we – your mother and I, that is – are just somewhat surprised that you chose this route.'

'Well, it's not UBS! I almost gave Mom a heart attack when she found out that one of their clients was Dow Chemical. She wrote me letters every day for three weeks accusing me of supporting deforestation, lung cancer in children, and somehow – although I'm still not clear how – the war in Iraq. Don't you remember? She was so panicked, I finally had to get excused from that account. How can you be upset that I have a new job?'

'It's not that we're upset, Bettina, it's just that we'd thought you were ready to do something, something . . . meaningful. Maybe grant-writing. You've always been a wonderful writer. Weren't you talking about Planned Parenthood there for a while? What happened with that?'

'I mentioned a lot of things, Dad. But this came along, and I'm enjoying it. Is that so bad?' I knew I sounded defensive, but I hated this conversation.

He smiled and placed his hand over mine on the table. 'Of course it's not so bad. We know you'll find your way eventually.'

'Find my way? How condescending is that? There's nothing wrong with what I'm doing—'

'Bettina? Robert? Where are you? The girls from the food co-op just called, and they're on their way. Is the bonfire all set?' My mother's voice reverberated through the wooden house and we looked at each other and then stood.

'Coming, honey,' my father called.

I placed both our mugs in the sink and brushed past my father as I ran upstairs to exchange one pair of baggy pants for another. By the time I'd run a brush through my hair and rubbed some Vaseline on my lips (the very same lips that Sammy had kissed a mere twenty hours earlier), I could hear voices in the backyard.

Within the hour the house was packed with people I didn't know. Aside from a handful of neighbors and university people whom I'd known for years, there were large groups of strangers milling about, sipping hot cider and sampling the baba ghanoush.

'Hey, Mom, who are these people?' I asked, sidling up to her in the kitchen as she mixed more lemonade. The sun had just set – or rather, the sky had darkened, since there hadn't really been any sun that day – and some sort of klezmer band had begun to play. A man wearing sandals similar to my father's whooped happily and began hopping in a way that could just as easily have indicated a ruptured hernia as the desire to dance. Not your typical Thanksgiving dinner.

'Well, let's see. Lots of new people this year. We've had more time to socialize since your father's only teaching one class this semester. The group sitting at the table is from our food co-op – did you know we switched to a new one a couple months ago? Ours was getting so fascist! Oh, and those two lovely couples we know from the Saturday green market over on Euclid Street. Let's see. There are some folks we met during the weeklong silent vigil to abolish the death penalty last month, and a few from our committee on building sustainable ecovillages. . . .'

She continued chatting as she filled the ice trays and stacked them neatly in the freezer. I leaned against the counter and wondered when, exactly, I'd lost touch with my parents' lives.

'Come, I want to introduce you to Eileen. She works at the crisis hotline with me and has been a savior this year. She knows all about you, and I'm dying for you two to meet.'

We didn't have to search for long because Eileen appeared in the kitchen before we could balance the pitchers on trays to carry them out back.

'Oh, my, this must be Bettina!' she breathed, rushing toward me, her fleshy arms jiggling. She was pleasantly fat, her overall roundness and huge smile giving her a trustworthy appearance. Before I could even think about moving, she had gathered me up like an infant.

'Oh! I'm so glad we finally met. Your mother's told me so much about you – I've even read some of the fantastic letters you wrote in high school!' At this point I shot my mother a death look, but she just shrugged.

'Really? Well, that was a while ago. Of course, I've heard such good things about you, too,' I lied. I'd only first learned the woman's name thirty seconds ago, but my mom seemed pleased.

'Humph! Is that so? Well, come here. Sit right down next to Auntie Eileen and tell me what it's like to be so famous!'

The 'Auntie Eileen' bit was a tad much, considering she looked to be a mere decade older than me, but I played along and planted myself at the kitchen table. 'Famous? Not me. I sort of work with famous people – I'm in public relations – but I certainly wouldn't describe myself that way,' I said slowly, now convinced that Eileen had me confused with someone else's daughter.

'Girlfriend, I may live in Poughkeepsie, but no one reads more tabs than me! Now don't you hold back for a single second. What's it like to go out with that god Philip Weston?' Here she took a sharp intake of breath and feigned fainting. 'Come now, don't leave out a single detail. He's the most gorgeous man on the planet!'

I laughed uncomfortably, running escape routes through my head, but I didn't get really upset until I saw my mother's face.

'Pardon?' she asked. 'Philip who?'

Eileen turned to her in disbelief and said, 'Anne, just *try* and tell me you don't know that your flesh and blood is dating the world's most desirable man. Just *try*!' she screeched. 'The only reason I didn't ask you about it directly was because I knew I'd be meeting Bettina tonight, and I wanted to relish every juicy detail directly from the horse's mouth!'

My mother couldn't have looked more surprised if I'd hit her, and I gathered in those short few seconds that my parents, thankfully, hadn't read the latest installments by Abby.

'I, uh, I wasn't aware you had a boyfriend,' she stammered, most likely feeling doubly betrayed – not only had her daughter omitted some crucial information, but this lapse in the mother-daughter relationship was now on display for her coworker. I wanted to hug my mom and pull her away and try to explain everything, but Eileen kept hammering me with questions.

'Does he have an explanation for why he and Gwynnie broke up? That's what I've always really wondered. Oh, and has he ever personally met the Queen of England? I imagine so, what with his family being royalty and all, but I wonder what that must be like?'

'Royalty?' my mother whispered, holding on to the counter for support. She looked like she wanted to ask a million questions, but all she managed was, 'What about the boy from last night?'

'He was here?' Eileen instantly demanded. 'Philip Weston was here? In Poughkeepsie? Last *night*? Ohmigod . . .'

'No, Philip Weston was not here. I gave a friend a ride home, and he stopped in to meet Mom and Dad. I'm not technically dating Philip. We've just gone out a couple of times. He's friendly with everyone I work with.'

'Oooooh,' Eileen breathed. This was clearly a good enough explanation. My mother didn't look quite as thrilled.

'You've gone out a few times with whom? Weston something or other? Do you mean, as in the famous English Westons?'

I was a little bit proud that even my mother had heard of him. 'The one and only,' I said, glad that things were finally smoothing over.

'Bettina, you *are* aware that the Westons are notorious anti-Semites? Do you not remember that situation with the Swiss bank accounts from the Holocaust? And as if that isn't bad enough, they're reputed to employ South American sweatshops in a couple of their business ventures. And you're *dating* one of them?'

Eileen quickly noticed that the conversation had begun to nose-dive and quietly slipped out.

'I'm not dating him,' I insisted, although the denial sounded ludicrous in light of the fact that I'd just admitted to going out with him.

She peered at me as though seeing my face for the first time in months and shook her head slowly. 'I never expected this from you, Bettina, I really didn't.'

'Expected what?'

'I never thought that a daughter of mine would associate with these types of people. We want you to be everything you are – smart and ambitious and successful – but we also tried to instill in you some level of social and civil consciousness. Where did it go, Bettina? Tell me, where did it go?'

Before I could answer, a man I'd never seen before rushed into the kitchen to announce that my mother was needed outside to take a picture for the local paper. For the last five years my parents had been using their annual party as a fund-raiser for battered women's shelters in the area, and it had become such a Poughkeepsie institution that both the local and school newspapers covered it. I watched as the photographer posed my parents, first in the greenhouse and then by the bonfire, and I spent the rest of the night getting to know as many of their friends and coworkers as I could. Neither my mom nor my dad mentioned my job or Philip Weston again, but the weird feeling lingered. Suddenly, I couldn't wait to get back to the city.

21

The week after Thanksgiving was brutal. My parents' concerns were weighing on me. Philip was calling nonstop. And although I told myself there was no reason to worry, I hadn't yet heard from Sammy. I'd passed a couple of days dreamily reliving The Kiss, remembering the way Sammy had pulled me from the car, and wondering when he'd finally get in touch, but this was starting to lose its charm. To make matters worse, Abby hadn't stopped writing about me even though I hadn't been in town for a full five days. The whole thing had been a blur, but I knew for a fact that Abby had not been present at my parents' Harvest Festival, which was why it was so distressing to see my name jump out from the headline of New York Scoop. TROUBLE IN PARADISE? ROBINSON RECOUPS IN HOMETOWN. Abby had gone on to comment on how my 'sudden absence' was noteworthy because Philip and I had been 'inseparable,' and the fact that I'd 'fled' to my parents' house upstate obviously indicated some major relationship trouble. There was even an extra-special line implying that my 'weekend away from the party circuit' *might* have something to do with the need to 'detox' or perhaps 'lick rejection wounds.' She ended the piece by encouraging everyone to stay tuned for more details on the Weston/Robinson saga.

I had torn the first sheet from the stapled packet, balled it up, and thrown it as hard as I could manage across the room. Relationship trouble? Detox? *Rejection?* Even more offensive than the implication that Philip and I were dating was the suggestion that we weren't. And detox? It was bad enough being portrayed as an out-of-control party girl, but it was almost more embarrassing to be the person who couldn't handle it. The whole thing was becoming too ridiculous to comprehend. It took three straight days to reassure Kelly (and Elisa, who seemed particularly concerned) that Philip and I were not fighting, that I was not in Poughkeepsie scouting potential rehab clinics, and that I had no intention of 'dumping' Philip for any reason anytime soon.

I'd now spent most of December attending as many events as possible, mugging with Philip and generally inviting nasty commentary from Abby (who was only too happy to oblige), and everything had returned to some twisted version of normal. Kelly had placed us on a rotating holiday schedule; since we all couldn't take off at the same time, I'd agreed to work a cocktail party for Jewish professionals on Christmas Eve in exchange for having New Year's Eve off. I was looking forward to spending New Year's with Penelope in Los Angeles, finally taking her up on her offer to visit and buying my ticket the moment I learned my work schedule. Christmas was two weeks away, and our Monday-morning staff meeting was more frantic than ever. I was daydreaming about how Pen and I would soon be catching up over Bloody Marys in shorts and flip-flops, beachside, in the middle of winter, when Kelly's voice broke into my thoughts.

'We've accepted a new client I'm really excited about,' Kelly announced with a huge smile. 'As of today we officially represent the Association of Istanbul Nightclub Owners.'

'There's nightlife in Istanbul?' Leo asked, examining what appeared to be a flawless cuticle.

'I didn't know they allowed clubs in Syria!' Elisa exclaimed, looking shocked. 'I mean, Muslims don't even drink, right?'

'Istanbul's in Turkey, Elisa,' Leo said, looking pleased with himself. 'And even though it's a Muslim country, it's really, really westernized and there's, like, total separation of church and state. Or mosque and state, I guess I should say.'

Kelly grinned. 'Exactly, Leo, that's exactly right. As you all know, we're ready to expand to international clients, and I think this will be a perfect start. The association is made up of nearly thirty club owners in greater Istanbul, and they're looking for someone to promote the city's active night scene. And they've chosen us.'

'I didn't know people went to Turkey to party,' Elisa sniffed. 'I mean, it's not exactly Ibiza, is it?'

'Well, that's precisely why they need our assistance,' Kelly said. 'It's my understanding that Istanbul is a cosmopolitan city, really very chic, and they have no problem drawing all sorts of fabulous Europeans who love the beaches and clubs and cheap shopping. But tourism has suffered since nine-eleven and they want to reach out to Americans – especially young ones – and show them that partying in Istanbul is just as accessible as going to Europe, more affordable *and* exotic. It's our job to make them *the* destination.'

'And how, exactly, are we going to do that?' Leo asked, studying the buckle on his Gucci belt and looking supremely bored.

'Well, for starters, you'll have to get acquainted with what we're trying to promote. Which is why you'll all be spending New Year's in Istanbul. Skye will stay behind with me to keep things running here. You leave December twenty-eighth.'

'What?' I almost shouted. 'We're going to *Turkey*? *In two weeks*?' I felt a combination of horror at telling Penelope I wouldn't be coming to LA and excitement at the prospect of going somewhere so amazing.

'Kelly, I agree with Bette. I'm not sure that's such a good idea. I, like, don't make it a habit to visit war-torn countries,' Elisa said.

'I wasn't saying that I didn't want to go,' I whispered meekly.

'War-torn? Are you stupid?' Skye asked.

'I don't mind war-torn, I just don't think it sounds all that appealing to go to some third-world country where the food's dangerous, the water's unsafe, and you can't get decent room service. For New Year's? Really?' Leo said, looking at Kelly.

'See, this is part of the problem,' Kelly said, keeping her cool far better than I would have in her position. 'Turkey is a Western democracy. They're trying to join the EU. There's a Four Seasons and a Ritz and a Kempinski right in town. There's a Versace boutique, for chrissake. I have the utmost confidence that you'll all be perfectly comfortable. Your only requirement while you're there is to check out as many clubs and lounges and restaurants as humanly possible. Take cute clothes. Drink the champagne they'll give you. Shop. Lay out. Party as often and as much as you can manage. Ring in the new year together. And, of course, entertain your guests.'

'Guests? The nightclub owners, you mean? I am not fucking whoring myself out to some Turkish club owners, Kelly! Not even for you,' Elisa said, folding her arms across her chest in a show of moral fortitude.

Kelly grinned. 'That's funny.' She paused for emphasis. 'But fear not, young Elisa. The guests to which I'm referring are a carefully selected group of tastemakers from right here in Manhattan.'

Elisa's head snapped to attention. 'Who? Who's coming? What do you mean? We'll have fabulous people with us?' she asked.

Davide and Leo perked up, too. We all sat, leaning slightly forward, waiting for Kelly to give us the full scoop. 'Well, we haven't gotten final confirmations from everyone yet, but so far we have commitments from Marlena Bergeron, Emanuel de Silva, Monica Templeton, Oliver Montrachon, Alessandra Uribe Sandoval, and Camilla von Alburg. It helps that there's nothing really major planned here for New Year's Eve – everyone's looking for something to do. You'll all fly via private jet and stay at the Four Seasons. The client will take care of everything: cars, drinks, dinners, whatever you'll need to show them – and the photographers – a good time.'

'Private jet?' I murmured.

'Photographers? Please tell me you're not sending us over there with a planeload of paparazzi,' Elisa whined.

'Just the usual; there won't be more than three, and all are freelance, so they won't be tied down to any one publication. Throw in three – maybe four – writers, and we should get some fantastic coverage.'

I considered this information. In less than two weeks, I'd be en route to Istanbul, Turkey, charged with drinking, dancing, and lounging by the pool of one of the world's nicest hotels, my only real assignment having to keep a carefully selected handful of socialites and scenesters plied with enough alcohol and drugs to ensure that they were drunk enough to look happy in pictures but still coherent enough to say something remotely intelligible to the reporters. The party pictures would be splashed across all the weekly tabloids and papers when we got home, and the captions would all describe how everyone who was anyone partied in Istanbul, and no one would even realize that we'd been paid to bring the party there, complete with handpicked photogs to shoot it and writers to describe it. It was brilliant, and personified our industry's motto – STAGE IT, THEN PAGE IT – to perfection.

But then an image of Penelope flashed in my mind and I almost choked: How could I do this to her again?

'Bette, I took the liberty of asking the association to book you and Philip into the honeymoon suite. It's the least I could do for my favorite darling couple!' Kelly announced with obvious pride.

'Philip's going?' I croaked. Ever since Sammy's kiss, my faux relationship with Philip had felt even weirder.

'Well, of course he's going! Most of this was his idea! I was telling him about our new client at the BlackBerry event and he offered his services, said he'd be happy to take a group of his friends over to party if it would be helpful. He even volunteered his father's jet, but the association had already planned to use their own. Bette, you must be so happy!'

I opened my mouth to say something, anything, but Kelly had already moved to the conference-room door. 'Okay, kids, we've got a lot of work to do over the next couple weeks. Elisa, I'm putting you in charge of liaising with the client and the guests to confirm and reconfirm all the travel details – make sure everyone knows where and when they'll be going and what they need. Leo, you're to focus on keeping in touch with writers and photogs and their editors; put together a quickie press release and a tip sheet and get them whatever stock photos of our guests you can scrounge up. Davide, start putting together folders on the group you'll be hosting. They're all in the database, of course, so pull their profiles and get the team their social histories, likes, and dislikes as quickly as possible, and then follow up with the Four Seasons so we can ensure they have the right waters and wines and snacks personalized in each room. I don't think there are any major romantic conflicts, but make sure. Aside from the fact that Camilla used to fuck Oliver, and Oliver is supposedly sleeping with Monica now, I think it's a fairly nonincestuous group of people, which should make it easier.'

Everyone was furiously taking notes, and the List Girls, who'd been permitted to sit in the back of the room to watch the meeting, were staring at us in wonderment.

'Kelly, what should I do?' I called as she turned to leave.

'You? Why, Bette, the only thing you need to worry about is Philip. He's the key to all of this, so you just concentrate on keeping him as happy as possible. Anything he wants, get it for him. Anything he needs, provide it. If Philip's happy, his friends are, too, and this whole project will be a walk in the park.' She winked just in case any of us weren't exactly certain what she meant and then skipped back to her desk.

Leo and Skye and Elisa chattered happily and decided to lunch at Pastis to continue their planning, but I begged off. I couldn't get a waking-nightmare image out of my head: Philip outstretched on the balcony of a lavish honeymoon suite wearing only silk boxers and performing all sorts of yogic contortions while a photographer snapped pictures from our shared bed and Penelope looked on from afar.

22

I finally got through to Penelope on Tuesday night. She seemed far away, both in the physical sense of the distance and in the time difference, but it went beyond that. She swore that she'd forgiven me for leaving the night of her going-away party, but it didn't feel like she'd gotten over it. I still hadn't told her about the Sammy kiss or the situation with my parents at the Harvest Festival, or even how Abby was behind the horrible New York Scoop articles. Three months ago, that would have all been incomprehensible, and now here I was, about to make it much, much worse. Possibly irreconcilable.

I'd been working up the nerve to call Penelope for the past three hours while simultaneously thinking about Sammy, wondering if he was home, preparing to break up with his girlfriend so he and I could be together. He always seemed so happy to see me at Bungalow that I knew he'd do the right thing – which was, of course, to end things with Isabelle and embark on what would surely be a long and happy love affair with me.

Finally my fingers followed my brain's command to dial, and before I could hang up for the thousandth time, Penelope answered.

'Hi! How are you?' I asked, much too enthusiastically. I still didn't have my exact wording down and was trying to buy as much time as possible.

'Bette! Hi. What's up?' She sounded equally enthusiastic.

'Not much. The usual, you know.' I decided then to pull the Band-Aid off quickly: one rip instead of long, slow torture. 'I've got something to tell you, Pen—'

She cut me off just as I was formulating my first words. 'Bette, before you say anything, I have something awful to tell you.' She took a deep breath and then said, 'I can't spend New Year's Eve with you.'

What? How was this happening? Did she somehow already know about the Turkey situation? Was she so upset that she'd decided to cancel on me first? She must have interpreted my confused silence as anger because she rushed on.

'Are you there? Bette, I'm so sorry, I can't even begin to explain to you how sorry I am. My parents just called to tell us that they've rented a villa at Las Ventanas for the week between Christmas and New Year's. I told them I already had plans for New Year's, but then they said that they'd invited Avery's parents and brother, too, so we all have to go, and I have no choice. As usual.'

This was too good to be true.

'Really? You're going to Mexico instead?' I was asking just to make sure I had the story straight, but to Penelope I must have sounded very, very angry.

'Oh, Bette, I'm so, so, so sorry. Of course I'll reimburse you for the ticket you can't use, and I'll buy you another to come back as soon as you can. Just please forgive me. If it's any comfort, my New Year's is going to be an absolute nightmare. . . .' She sounded so distraught that I wanted to hug her.

'Pen, don't worry about it—'

'Really? You're not mad?'

'If we're all being honest here, I was calling to tell you that I couldn't come out there over New Year's. Kelly wants to send us all to Turkey.'

'*Turkey?*' She sounded confused. 'Why Turkey?'

'Work, if you can believe it. We got a new client – some night-club owners' association – and they want us to promote the nightlife in Istanbul. We're basically exporting the party to them and making sure it gets covered here. They figured New Year's was the perfect time to start.'

She started laughing and said, 'So you just made me go through that whole sob story when you were calling to cancel on me, anyway? You're such a bitch!'

'Um, excuse me, you just straight-up told me not to come visit you, so I don't see where you get off calling me a bitch.' We were both laughing, and I felt like a huge weight had been lifted.

'In all seriousness, though, that sounds so cool,' she said. 'Are you going to have time to sightsee while you're there? I've heard people describe the Hagia Sofia as a transcendent experience. And the Blue Mosque. The Grand Bazaar. A sightseeing boat ride down the Bosporus! My God, Bette, it sounds incredible. . . .'

I didn't want to tell her that the only daytime activities I'd seen on the itinerary so far were hot-stone massages, or that the only boat ride scheduled was a booze cruise, so I just murmured along with her and tried to change the subject. 'I know, it should be great. What's going on with you?'

'Oh, not much,' she said. 'This and that, you know?'

'Penelope! You recently moved across the country, if I recall. How is it out there? What's going on? Tell me everything!' I lit a cigarette and pulled Millington onto my lap, all set to hear how fabulous sun-drenched LA was, but Penelope's tone was clearly not thrilled.

'Well, so far it's okay,' she said carefully.

'You sound miserable. What's going on?'

'I don't know.' She sighed. 'California's fine. Nice, actually. Really nice. When you get past the whole wheatgrass smoothie garbage, it's really not a bad place to live. We've got a great apartment in Santa Monica, a couple blocks from the beach, and it's fantastic being so far away from our parents. I don't know, it's just . . .'

'It's just what?'

'Well, I thought Avery would calm down a little when we got out here, but he immediately hooked up with a whole crew of Horace Mann kids who moved out here after college. I hardly see him anymore. Since he doesn't start classes until mid-January, he's got another whole month of nothing but time to go out all night, every night.'

I didn't say what I was thinking: typical. 'Oh, honey, I'm sure he's just getting used to a new place. Things will slow down once he starts school.'

'I guess. You're right, I'm sure. It's just that, well, he . . .' She paused. 'Never mind.'

'Penelope! What were you about to say?'

'You're going to think I'm the most evil person ever.'

'Let me remind you, my friend, that you're talking to someone who's quote-unquote dating a guy for strictly professional reasons. I don't think I'm exactly in a position to judge anyone right now.'

She sighed. 'Well, I checked Avery's Yahoo account the other night when he was at the Viceroy, and I found a few emails that are rather unsettling.'

'You guys have access to each other's email accounts?' I asked, horrified.

'Of course not. But his password was hardly difficult to figure out. I typed in the name of his bong, and voilà! Instant access.'

'His bong? What did you find?' I certainly didn't think she was evil for hacking into his account. I tried for months to watch as Cameron typed in his password, but he was always too fast.

'I know I'm probably overreacting, but there are some very cute emails to a girl he used to work with in New York.'

'Define *cute*.'

'He went on and on about how she could hold her liquor better than any other girl he's ever met.'

'Wow, he's a real Don Juan, P. The guy could write a book on seduction.'

'Right? I know it sounds ridiculous, but they actually sounded flirty. He signed them "xoxo."'

'Oh, God. Is he gay? He's definitely not gay, is he? What straight guy on earth does that?'

'Well, he sure hasn't ever done that with me. It just creeped me out. I casually asked him last night when he got home at three in the morning if he still keeps in touch with anyone from work, and he said no just before he passed out. Am I overreacting? This morning he was so sweet and offered to take me shopping, spend the day together. . . .'

I didn't quite know what to say. The wedding was still more than eight months away, and it sounded like Penelope might – just might – realize before it was too late that Avery was a supreme jackass and not worth her entire married future. I'd happily fan the fire whenever possible, but she'd have to come to that conclusion herself.

'Well,' I said slowly, picking my words with the utmost care. 'It's normal for every relationship to have its ups and downs, right? That's why people get engaged first. It's just that. An engagement. If you discover something about him that you don't think you can live with forever, well, you're not married, and—'

'Bette, that's not what I'm saying,' she said sharply. Oops. 'I love Avery, and of course I'm marrying him. I was just talking to my best friend about what I'm sure is a ridiculous, unfounded, paranoid suspicion. It's clearly my own issue, not Avery's. I just need to be more confident in his feelings for me, that's all.'

'Sure, sure, Pen. I totally understand. I didn't mean to imply otherwise. And of course I'm always here for you, just to listen. I'm sorry I said that.'

'Whatever, I'm just emotional right now. A little homesick. Look, thanks for listening. I'm sorry about all this stuff. How's everything with you? Philip? Is he good?'

How had things gotten so out of control that my best friend not only asked about Philip but also had no idea that Sammy even existed? It was unfathomable to think that I could kiss someone like Sammy and not have Penelope know about it within thirty seconds when we were working together all day and hanging out at the Black Door at night, but it'd been forever since we'd done that. Or at least it felt like forever.

'It's complicated. Everyone thinks we're dating – even him, probably – but we're really not,' I said, knowing full well that I was making no sense but not having the energy to explain everything.

'Well, it's probably not my place, but I'm not sure he's right for you, Bette.'

I wondered what she'd say if she knew what my mom had told me about the Westons.

I sighed. 'I know that, Pen. I'm just overwhelmed right now, you know?'

'Not really,' she said. 'You haven't exactly explained it.'

'It's just that this job has sort of infiltrated the rest of my life. My boss isn't so great at making distinctions between what happens in the office and what goes on everywhere else, so there's a lot of overlap. Does that make sense?'

'No. What does your boss have to do with your personal life?'

'It's not just that. Will got me this job and expects me to do well. He called in a huge favor for it. And I am doing well, I think, whatever that means. But the whole Philip thing is sort of tied in.' I knew I was being positively nonsensical, that I could be speaking an African clicking language for all the clarity I was providing Penelope or myself, but I just didn't have the energy.

'All right,' she said hesitantly. 'I have no idea what you're saying, but I'm always around, you know? I'm only a phone call away.'

'I know, honey, and I appreciate that.'

'Again, I'm so sorry about New Year's, but I'm glad you'll be doing something so much more fabulous. I'll read about it in all the papers. . . .'

'That reminds me! I haven't told you. . . . How could I have forgotten this? You know how New York Scoop has been writing all those nasty things about me?'

'Yeah, they've been hard to miss lately.'

'Well, any idea who's writing them?'

'Of course. It's some stupid pseudonym, right? Ellie something?'

'Yeah, and you know who that is?'

'No, should I?'

'That, my dear Pen, is Abby. Vortex. That whore has been following me around and printing all that stuff under a fake name.'

I heard a sharp intake of breath. 'Abby is behind all that? Are you sure? What are you going to do about it? You need to shut her down.'

I snorted. 'You're telling me! Kelly told me weeks ago, but I was sworn to secrecy! I've been obsessing over it, but we're always so rushed and I forgot to tell you. Isn't it crazy? I never thought she hated me *that* much.'

'It *is* weird. I know she's not your biggest fan – or mine, for that matter – but this seems excessively mean, even for her.'

'All I want to do is confront her, and I can't. It's incredibly aggravating.' I glanced at the clock on the cable box and jumped off the couch. 'Ohmigod, Pen, it's already eight. I hate to run – I'm hosting the holiday book club tonight and I have to get everything set up.'

'I don't know why, but I love that you still read that stuff. You are such a romantic, Bette.'

I thought of Sammy and almost said something but decided to skip it at the last second.

'Yeah, you know me, always hopeful,' I said lightly.

I felt slightly better when we hung up. I should've spent the evening Googling and reading about the people we'd be taking with us to Turkey, but I couldn't bear to cancel book club if it wasn't absolutely necessary. It took me a full hour to arrange the apartment for the girls, but when the intercom buzzer first rang, I knew it would be worth it.

'I've decided to honor tonight's Latin theme,' I announced after everyone had settled in. We were reading *Bought by Her Latin Lover*, and the cover featured a tall man in black tie (presumably the Latin lover) embracing an elegant woman in an evening dress on the deck of what looked like a yacht. 'We have here one pitcher of sangria, and another of margaritas.'

They clapped and cheered and poured.

'In addition, I have chicken quesadillas, mini burritos, and some killer chips and guac dip. And for dessert, Magnolia cupcakes.'

'What do pink-frosted cupcakes have to do with our Latin theme?' Courtney asked, plucking one off the serving tray.

'That was, admittedly, random – I can't think of a Spanish dessert I'd prefer to a Magnolia cupcake,' I said. Just then Millington gave a little bark from her hiding spot in the corner. 'Baby, come here. Come here, good girl,' I called. She obliged and strolled over, giving everyone a view of the tiny sombrero she wore for the occasion.

'You didn't.' Jill laughed, scooping Millington up and admiring her hat.

'Oh, I did. Got it at that baby-costume store in midtown. See, it comes with a chinstrap so it stays on. How great is that?'

Janie helped herself to another quesadilla and absently scratched Millington. 'Bette, to think you went from a hesitant early member who refused to host to the Martha Stewart of the club. . . . Well, I just have to say, it's very impressive.'

I laughed. 'I guess my job is seeping into other areas of my life, huh? I can pull together an event in my sleep at this point.'

We ate and drank first, working up a decent sangria buzz so we'd be able to discuss with complete frankness how much we'd loved the night's selection. By the time Vika pulled her well-worn copy from her messenger bag, we were fairly far gone.

'I'll read the summary from the website,' she announced, unfolding a printout. 'Everyone ready?'

We all nodded.

'Okay, here goes. "Spanish millionaire Cesar Montarez wants Rosalind the moment he sees her; this electrifying attraction is like nothing he's ever felt before. But Cesar has little respect for money-hungry women – mistresses or trophy wives. Rosalind is determined she'll never be either, until Cesar discovers that she has secret debts. Now he can *buy* her as his *mistress* . . . and Rosalind has little choice but to pay his price. . . ." Wow. Certainly sounds hot. Thoughts?'

'It's just so romantic when he spots her at that seaside restaurant. He just *knows* she's the one. Why aren't normal guys like that?' Courtney asked.

I'm sure Sammy is like that, I thought, my mind drifting.

We all weighed in on our favorite characters, plot twists, and sex scenes, which inevitably led to conversation about our own lives – work stories and a few family complaints, but mostly men.

It was almost midnight when the buzzer rang from the lobby.

'Yes?' I asked, pressing the button on the intercom.

'I have a Philip Weston here to see you, Bette. Should I send him up?'

'Philip? He's here? Right now?' I didn't realize I'd said that out loud until Seamus sang back, 'Sure is, Bette.'

'I have company,' I said, panicked. 'Can you ask Philip to call when he gets home?'

'Bette, love, ring me up. My mate here – what's your name? Seamus? Good bloke! We're sharin' a pint and talking about what a good girl you are. Now be a good girl and ring me up.'

I glanced down at my ripped jeans and tattered T-shirt and wondered what on earth Philip could want at midnight. It would be obvious with a normal guy, but Philip had never drunk-dialed – never mind drunk-visited – and I actually felt queasy.

'What the hell.' I sighed. 'Come on up.'

'Ohmigod, Philip Weston is here? Right now?' Janie asked, sounding breathless. 'But we all look like hell. *You* look like hell.'

She was right, of course, but there wasn't time to do anything about it.

'Bette, don't think you're getting off this easy. We'll leave, but you better be prepared to explain yourself at the next meeting,' Vika warned.

Courtney nodded. 'You've been denying that the New York

Scoop columns are true, but now Philip Weston shows up at your apartment in the middle of the night? We deserve every juicy detail!'

There was a knock, followed by a dull thud in the hallway. I opened the door, and Philip reeled inside.

'Bette, love, I'm a tad pissed,' he slurred, slumping against the wall.

'Yes, I can see that. Come on in,' I said, half dragging, half supporting him as he shuffled in, and the girls parted down the middle to clear a path.

'Philip Weston,' Janie breathed.

'The one and only.' He grinned and scanned the room before flopping backward onto the couch. 'Dollface, where did all these smashing girls come from?'

Courtney stared at him for a full ten seconds before turning to me and saying, quite pointedly, 'Bette, we're going to clear out for now. Everyone, let's go and leave Bette and Philip to, uh, to themselves. I'm sure she'll tell us *all* about it at the next meeting. Speaking of which, what's on deck?'

Alex held up a copy of *The Taming of the Dark Lord,* tilted so only we could see it, and said, 'I nominate this.'

'Done,' I said. 'We'll read that for next time. Thanks for coming, guys.'

'Oh, no, thank *you*,' Janie said as I hugged everyone good-bye.

'Can't wait to hear about this one,' Jill whispered.

When they'd all gone, I turned my attention back to the drunk Englishman on my couch. 'Coffee or tea?'

'Gin and tonic sounds ab fab, love. I'd fancy a little nightcap right about now.'

I put the teakettle on and sat down on the chair opposite him, unable to get any closer because the stench of alcohol was overwhelming. It was emanating from his pores in that special way guys have when they've been drinking all night, enveloping everything within a five-foot radius in that distinctive frat-boy-freshman-year-floor stench. He still managed to look adorable, though. His tan was so solid it wouldn't allow him to look as green as he probably should, and his spiky hair was mussed in the most perfect way.

'So where were you tonight?' I asked.

'Oh, here and there, love, here and there. Bloody reporter following me around all night with her bloody cameraman. I told them to bugger off, but I think they followed me here,' he mumbled, reaching out for Millington, who glanced at him, growled, and bolted. 'Come over, pup. Come on and say hello to Philip. What's wrong with your dog, love?'

'Oh, she's always been particularly wary of tall, drunk Brits wearing Gucci loafers without socks. Honestly, it's nothing personal.'

For some reason, he thought this was hysterically funny and nearly rolled off the couch in fits of laughter. 'Well, then, if not her, then why don't you come over here and give me a proper greeting?'

The kettle howled as I walked to the stove to pour our tea. I caught a glimpse of Millington cowering on the floor of the dark bathroom, shaking slightly.

'Love, you really shouldn't have gone to so much trouble,' he called, sounding slightly more coherent.

'It's tea, Philip. It's just boiling water.'

'No, love, I meant your clothing choice. Seriously, I'd shag you no matter what you were wearing.' He collapsed into another laughing fit and I wondered how it was possible for someone to be so clever.

I placed a mug in front of him, and he pinched my ass in return.

'Philip.' I sighed.

He placed his hands around my hips with surprising strength and pulled me onto his lap.

'Everyone thinks you're my girlfriend, love.' He was slurring again.

'Yeah, weird, isn't it? Especially since we've never actually been, ah, intimate.'

'You don't go banging on about that, do you?' he asked quickly, looking alert for the first time since he'd walked in.

'Banging on about what?'

'Come closer, doll. Kiss me.'

'I'm right here, Philip,' I said, breathing through my mouth.

He slid his hand under my T-shirt and started stroking my back. It felt so nice that I managed to forget for a split second that it was a drunk Philip doing it and not Sammy. Without thinking, I wrapped my arms around his neck and pressed my mouth to his. I didn't immediately realize that he'd opened his own mouth to protest, not to kiss me back.

'Whoa, love, try to keep your knickers on.' He pulled back in shock and looked at me like I'd just torn off all my clothes and jumped on him.

'What's the problem? What?' I asked. I refused to let him off the hook this time – I had to know once and for all that it wasn't my imagination or some half-assed excuse. I wanted confirmation that, for whatever reason, he would rather die than touch me.

'Of course I fancy you, love. Where's that G and T? Why don't I tuck into that for a moment, and then we can talk?'

I climbed off him and retrieved a bottle of Stella Artois from the fridge. I'd bought it a year ago because I'd read in *Glamour* that you should always keep a cool beer in the fridge in case an actual guy ever materializes in your apartment, and I silently applauded the good folks on their editorial staff. By the time I'd returned, however, Philip appeared to be unconscious.

'Philip. Hey, look, I have a beer for you.'

'Argh.' He groaned, his eyes fluttering, a telltale sign that he was faking it.

'Come on, get up already. You may be drunk, but you're not asleep. Why don't I put you in a cab?'

'Mmm. I'm just going to have a little sleep, love. Argh.' He swung his loafered feet onto my couch with surprising agility and hugged an accent pillow to his chest.

It was just after two when I threw a blanket on the snoring Philip, retrieved Millington from the space between the bathtub and the sink, and tucked us both under the covers without bothering to undress or turn off the lights.

23

The day had finally arrived: we were set to leave that evening for Turkey. I'd arrived at the office to collect a few last-minute things, only to find a fax from Will. The cover sheet simply read 'Ugh,' and attached was a clipping from New York Scoop. The headline read: IS MANHATTAN'S FAVORITE PARTY BOY GAY OR JUST CONFUSED? Byline: Ellie Insider, obviously. Knowing who she was made it even worse. The text laid it out in no uncertain terms:

Philip Weston, heir to the Weston fortune and member of the British Brat Pack in New York, raised eyebrows last week when he was spotted at the Roxy, the notoriously flamboyant Chelsea nightclub. Weston, who has been linked in the press to various Vogue *fashion editors, Brazilian models, and Hollywood starlets, was spotted snuggling with an unidentified male in the club's VIP room, sources say. When Weston apparently realized that he'd been sighted, he hastily Vespaed to the home of his current fling, Bettina Robinson, an associate at Kelly & Company (see sidebar). Weston's publicist refused to comment.*

See sidebar. See sidebar. See sidebar. I read those two words nearly a dozen times before I could bring myself to glance to the right. Sure enough, there was a picture of me, snapped at Bungalow 8 the very first night I'd met Philip, pressed against him suggestively, my head thrown back in obvious ecstasy while I appeared to be literally pouring champagne down my throat, seemingly unaware of either the camera or Philip's hands cupping my ass. If I'd needed any proof of how trashed I'd been that night aside from the blackout, well, this was it. Headline: WHO IS BETTINA ROBINSON? Byline: Ellie Insider. Inside the one-column, page-length box was a bulleted list of my biographical details, including the date and place of my birth (thankfully, it merely read 'New Mexico'), schools, degrees, position at UBS, and relationship to Will, who was described as 'the controversial national columnist whose readership catered exclusively to the white, rich, and over-50 crowd.' It was a nightmare, naturally, but so far it was accurate. It wasn't until my eyes forced their way to the bottom paragraph that I thought I might vomit. Abby had found someone to go on record as saying that I'd 'certainly been well-acquainted with many guys' beds as an undergrad at Emory' and that there had been 'accusations of academic integrity issues, but no one knew for sure.' Someone else was quoted as describing how I had 'been plotting to take over Kelly & Company' even though I had no previous PR experience. When asked by Abby to elaborate, the 'source' merely intimated that 'everyone knew she never actually wrote her own papers and was known for "cozying up" to her male TAs in the classes she found particularly challenging, which, if I must say, were probably most of them.' The final sentence of the short paragraph implied that I'd aggressively pursued Philip from the moment I'd met him in order to become a boldfaced name myself and further my new career.

My first reaction, of course, was to hunt Abby down and subject her to a creatively torturous death, but it was difficult to consider any particulars because I was having trouble breathing. I gasped quite dramatically for a few moments. In some weird way I appreciated Abby's self-awareness: if she had just attributed all those things to herself instead of to me, I would have applauded her honesty. But this insight was brief, vanishing the moment Kelly appeared at the doorway of her office, clutching a copy of the paper and grinning so maniacally that I instinctively backed away in my rolling chair.

'Bette! You saw it, right? You read it, didn't you?' she asked frantically, rushing toward me with all the grace and enthusiasm of a linebacker.

She interpreted my dulled reaction time as a denial and literally threw the paper on my desk. 'Didn't you at least read the Dirt Alert?' she shrieked. 'The girls called me at home this morning to tell me about this one.'

'Kelly, I, uh, I'm just sick about this—'

'You minx! Here I was this whole time thinking you were this good little worker bee, slaving away at a bank, living a decidedly unfabulous life, and now I find out that you're a secret party girl? Bette, seriously, I can't tell you what a shock this is. We'd all had you pegged as, well, as a little reserved, shall we say – no offense, of course. I just didn't think you had it in you. God only knows where you've been hiding the last couple years. Do you realize you're a full *sidebar*? Here, read it.'

'I've read it,' I said numbly, no longer shocked that Kelly was delighted instead of horrified at such coverage. 'You know none of that stuff is true, don't you? You see, the girl who wrote that actually went to school with me and she—'

'Bette, you're a sidebar. Say it after me. Sidebar. In New York Scoop! There's a huge picture of you, and you look like a rock star. You *are* a star, Bette. Congratulations! This *so* calls for a celebration!'

Kelly scampered off, presumably to plan an early-morning champagne toast, while I was left to consider the possibility of simply flying to Istanbul and staying there forever. Within minutes my phone was ringing off the hook with all sorts of unsavory calls, each hideous in its own special way. My father called immediately to announce that even though they were home on winter break, one of his students had emailed the article to him; this was followed by my mother saying she'd overheard some volunteers at her crisis hotline wondering when I would ever own up to the fact that I was dating a Jew-hating slave driver, and did I want to talk to someone about what appeared to be my 'promiscuity/self-worth' issues? A woman left a message offering her services as my publicist, kindly mentioning that this would never have happened had I been on her watch, and a couple gossip columnists from small, local papers across the country wanted to know if I would submit to phone interviews to discuss such crucial issues as my opinions on Brad and Jen's breakup, my favorite party spot in New York, and my evaluation of Philip's sexual orientation. Megu called on Michael's behalf to say that if I wanted to talk about anything, they wanted me to know that they were both there for me. Elisa called from a cab on her way to the office to congratulate me on my sidebar status. So did Philip's assistant,

Marta. Simon called while I was riding in a Town Car to the airport. He declared, rather endearingly in light of our earlier conversations, that not one respectable person read New York Scoop, and not to worry because he was sure no one would ever even see it.

I decided to ignore everyone, but then I remembered that I was leaving the country and couldn't really avoid calling my parents one last time to say good-bye. I opted for my father's cell phone, figuring that it wouldn't be on and I could leave a message for both of them, wishing them a happy new year and telling them I'd call upon my return. No such luck.

'Well, look who it is. Anne, come here, our famous daughter's on the phone. Bettina, your mother wants to talk to you.'

I heard some shuffling and a couple of beeps as they accidentally bumped numbers on the keypad before my mother's voice rang out loud and clear.

'Bettina? Why are they writing all those things about you? Is it true? Tell me what's what because I don't even know what to tell people when they ask. I certainly never would've thought a single word of it was valid, but ever since I heard about that Weston boy . . .'

'Mom, I can't really get into it now. I'm on my way to the airport. Of course it was all lies – how could you think otherwise?'

She sighed, and I couldn't tell if it was out of relief or frustration. 'Bettina, honey, you can understand how a mother might wonder, especially when she finds out her daughter suddenly lives a strange and mysterious life.'

'It might be strange, Mom, but it's not mysterious. I promise. I'll explain it all when I get back, but right now I have to get a move on or I'll be late for the flight. Say good-bye to Dad for me. I'll call you guys when I'm back on Sunday, okay? I love you.'

There was a moment of hesitation while she decided whether or not to push the issue, and then another sigh. 'All right, we'll speak to you then. See as much as possible, dear, and be safe. And try to keep your private life out of the public eye, okay?'

All in all, it had been one solidly shitty morning, but thankfully I had a new problem to take my mind off the sidebar: Louis Vuitton. Lots of it. Carts full of it, actually, more trunks and rolling suitcases and valet cases and garment bags and carry-on duffels and clutch purses sporting the interlocking LVs than could surely reside in the flagship store in Milan or the behemoth boutique on Fifth Avenue. Apparently, everyone on board had gotten the memo that Louis Vuitton was the luggage of choice. Three porters in burgundy uniforms were struggling to move it from the subtly named Million Air terminal to the belly of the Gulfstream, but their progress was slow. Elisa, Davide, Leo, and I had taken a limo from the city to Teterboro a few hours early to make sure everything was ready for the arrival of the helicopter that was bringing Philip and his group from the Wall Street helipad to the airport.

Meanwhile, since I was blessed with stimulating and challenging tasks like overseeing the loading of the Louis Vuittons and ensuring that there was a sufficient supply of Evian facial misters onboard, I didn't have much time to stress about being portrayed as a lying, cheating prostitute in what was now the hippest, most coveted gossip sheet available, one that had found its way into the hands of every single one of my friends, coworkers, and family members. We were nearing our scheduled five o'clock departure time – with everyone onboard except one of our last-minute invites, a socialite and her 'guest' who'd called to say they were stuck in traffic at the Lincoln Tunnel – when the first crisis arose.

There were so many suitcases that the porters couldn't fit all the luggage on the plane. 'We're at full capacity on the flight today,' one of them told me. 'You can figure that Gulfstream Fives can usually handle six average-sized or four oversized pieces per person, but this group has gone way over.'

'How far over?'

'Well,' he said, crinkling his forehead. 'Y'all average four over-sized bags apiece. One gal has seven, including a trunk so big we needed to bring a crane from the hangar to haul 'er onboard.'

'What do you propose we do?' I asked.

'Well, ma'am, the best-case scenario would be to eliminate some bags.'

Knowing full well that we'd be resorting to the worst-case scenario, I thought I'd try to be cooperative and see if anyone was willing to part with some possessions. I climbed aboard the jet, borrowed the intercom handset from the copilot, and explained our situation over the loudspeaker. Not surprisingly, it was met with jeers and catcalls.

'You've, like, got to be kidding,' Oliver said, laughing hysterically. 'It's a fucking private plane, for chrissake. Tell them to figure it out.' Oliver was accustomed to making such decrees: he was the founder of a hedge fund so hugely successful that *Gotham Magazine* had named him Manhattan's Most Desirable Bachelor of 2004.

'If you think for one single second I'm going without my shoes, you're very mistaken,' Camilla, a cosmetics heiress, called out between sips of Cristal. 'Four days, twelve outfit combinations, and two possible shoe changes per outfit. No way I'm leaving anything behind.'

'I want every last one of those trunks put on this plane,' announced Alessandra. 'If I remembered to bring empty trunks for all the stuff I buy, then the least they can do is figure out how to get them there.' Her mother was a notorious shopper, a woman infamous for spending millions a year on clothes and shoes and bags, Imelda Marcos–style. Clearly, that apple didn't fall far from the tree.

'Stop worrying so much, love. Come over here and have yourself a little drinky. Let the crew handle that – it's what we pay them for.' This was from Philip, of course, who was sprawled on one of the cream-colored leather couches, his checkered Armani shirt opened one button too far. Elisa appeared equally unconcerned as she perched on Davide's lap, concentrating intently on hooking her iPod to the speakers in the cabin's stereo system.

Fair enough. If no one else cared, neither did I. Besides, as long as they didn't leave behind my single silver Samsonite, it really wasn't my problem. I accepted a glass of bubbly from a flight attendant whose perfect figure was only accentuated by her navy uniform and listened to one of the pilots – who also looked like a movie star, complete with chiseled Brad-esque jaw and subtle highlights – give us the rundown on the flight. It was only slightly unnerving to survey both passengers and crew and realize that all involved looked like they had stepped directly out of an episode of the *Fabulous Life Of,* except for yours truly.

'Flying time should be ten hours with minimal turbulence as we cross the Atlantic,' the pilot said with a heart-stopping grin and some sort of indeterminate European accent. *No one that good-looking should be responsible for our lives,* I thought. Someone slightly uglier and not as cool was likely to drink less and get more sleep.

'Hey, Helmut, why don't we divert this baby to Mykonos and call it a day?' Philip called out to the pilot.

Cheers went up all around.

'Mykonos?' asked Camilla. 'That's, like, *so* much more appealing than Beirut. It's at least civilized. There's a Nobu there.'

Helmut laughed again. 'Just say the word, kids, and I'll take 'er wherever you want to go.'

A woman's voice rose above the others. It was coming up the stairs from the tarmac. 'We're going to Mykonos?' we heard her ask someone, though we couldn't yet see who it was. 'I thought we were going to Istanbul. Jesus Christ, my fucking publicist can't get anything right. I was all set to buy a Turkish carpet!' she wailed.

It occurred to me that this must be Isabelle, our missing socialite with no job and certainly no apparent need for a publicist. Just as I was mentally congratulating her for knowing that Istanbul was in Turkey, a couple strolled aboard and looked around – a couple that just so happened to consist, as couples often do, of two people. It took my brain a second to register that the male half of this particular couple was none other than Sammy. My Sammy.

'Isabelle, honey, of course we're going to Istanbul, just like you were told. The boys are only joking – you know how they get when you mention the Greek Islands! Leave your stuff right there and come have a drink.' Elisa rushed to comfort the woman I immediately recognized from the park. 'And introduce us to your gorgeous friend.'

At this Sammy appeared to freeze, looking so rigid and uncomfortable I thought he might collapse. He hadn't seen me yet, hadn't taken in the entire group, but he did manage to mutter something. 'I'm Sammy. From Bungalow 8?' he said, his voice strangely high-pitched.

Elisa stared at him blankly while Isabelle struggled to haul aboard a massive Louis Vuitton duffel. She smacked him on the shoulder and nodded toward the bag, which he effortlessly lifted and placed under one of the leather banquettes.

'Bungalow? Did we meet there one night?' Elisa asked with a confused expression. I flashed back to the half-dozen times I'd gone there with her and watched as she had flirted with Sammy, hugged him, thanked him, and generally acted as though they were the best of friends. As far as I could tell, though, this wasn't an act; she really had no clue who he was.

By that point everyone's attention had been diverted to the unfolding awkwardness and all must have been wondering why, exactly, this very attractive guy looked so damn familiar when they just couldn't place him.

'I work there,' he said quietly, looking her directly in her face.

'At Bungalow 8?' Elisa asked, appearing more baffled than ever. 'Oh, I get it! You mean you spend so much time there that it's become like an office to you! Yeah, I totally know what you mean. It's like that for us, too, isn't it, Bette?' She giggled and sipped and appeared relieved to have solved the puzzle.

A jolt went through Sammy at the sound of my name, but he kept his gaze on Elisa's face, as though he were physically unable to divert his eyes. A full ten seconds passed before he turned his head slowly and looked at me. The smile that followed was sad but not surprised.

'Hey,' he said, but it came out sounding more like a whisper. Isabelle had settled in next to Elisa and everyone else had resumed chatting, which only served to make the moment feel intensely intimate.

'Hi,' I said, trying to stay casual while my mind frantically tried to process this new development. When Kelly had given us the final list for the group, she'd mentioned that Isabelle Vandemark had agreed to come only if she could bring her assistant. Naturally, Kelly had agreed. Did that mean that Isabelle wasn't Sammy's girlfriend? I had to know.

'There's a seat right here,' I said, waving in the general direction to my left. 'If you need one.'

He glanced at Isabelle, who was talking to Elisa, and tentatively began stepping over legs and carry-ons to make his way toward me. He stood in stark contrast to the flamboyant Leo and the meticulously dressed Philip, somehow more masculine and vulnerable at the same time. When he fell into the leather armchair next to mine, it felt like all the air had been sucked out of the plush cabin.

'Bette,' he started, talking so quietly I had to lean forward to hear him. 'I had no idea you were going to be here. I'm sorry about this. I really didn't know this was your trip.'

'What? She just told you that you guys were going to Istanbul for a few days?' I asked, holding back tears.

'Yes, if you can believe it, that's exactly what happened. She mentioned something last week about wanting me to go with her on some sort of press junket, but she didn't tell me we were definitely going until yesterday. I didn't really ask any questions. I just kind of packed my bag.'

'You just go wherever she tells you to go? What about work? What about school? I don't understand how you can just leave everything because she wants you to. No one else here has a job, it's not so weird that they just jet off to Istanbul when they feel like it. Does that mean you quit?'

He looked sheepish at first, and then his face hardened. 'No, they understand at work. Sometimes these things come up.'

'Oh, well, that makes sense,' I said nastily. 'Now you're being perfectly clear.'

'Bette, I'm sorry, it's complicated. She's complicated.'

I softened a bit when I saw how miserable he was. 'Look, Sammy, I'm sorry. It's none of my business. I'm just surprised, that's all.' It occurred to me that, unfortunately, he owed me no explanation whatsoever. Since The Kiss, I'd only seen him out at night. One of those times he was being hassled by a group of khaki-clad bankers who weren't pleased to be neglected on the sidewalk line. He'd merely glanced at me, smiled thinly, and lifted the rope so I could pass by.

'Let's forget it for now, okay? I've had a hell of a day trying to get her here,' he said and closed his eyes.

I thought about the horrifying Dirt Alert, but refrained from one-upping him on bad days.

The crew worked out the luggage situation and after a few frighteningly abridged safety instructions from the flight attendant, we lifted off into a moonless sky. Within minutes, Elisa began divvying up a small mountain of pills on the coffee table in front of her and auctioning them off, Sotheby's-style.

'Uppers, downers, what can I get everyone? Do we want to party or sleep?' she asked the already-bored group. 'This is off the record, right?' She turned to one of the reporters, who just nodded listlessly.

'Sleep,' Isabelle whined. 'I had the most hellish week ever, and I'm exhausted.'

'Definitely sleep,' Leo agreed, kicking off his Prada sneakers and cracking his powdered toes in the air.

Davide nodded, and even Philip concurred that it might be wise to sleep on the flight since their sole task for the next four days was to party.

'You guys are no fun!' Elisa baby-talked, shaking her head in a show of mock disappointment. 'But if that's what everyone wants . . . how can I help?'

'What do you have?' Emanuel, the Argentinean billionaire, asked with little interest. He appeared barely able to lift his face from the bowl-sized martini glass he was holding with both hands.

'You name it, I got it. Just tell me what you need. We have to get rid of all this before we land, anyway. I saw *Midnight Express* and I want no part of that,' she announced.

'Yeah, you don't muck around with the Turks and drugs,' Philip said agreeably. 'The concierge'll take care of us when we get there, but I wouldn't advise bringing in anything yourself.'

'I'll take a couple Valium,' Leo announced.

'Xanax for me.'

'Do you have any Ambien? If I take two and a drink, I should be good.'

'How about Percocet? Can you hook that up?'

Everyone patiently waited their turn as Elisa went around the cabin, providing each person with a custom order, managing to produce every brand and dosage that had been requested. Only Sammy and I passed, but no one seemed to notice. I lit a cigarette in an effort not to appear too angelic, but that didn't exactly pass for imbibing with this crowd. Sammy excused himself, saying he had a headache, and asked Philip if it was okay for him to lie down in the bedroom.

'Not my plane, man, so help yourself. Just don't mind if I ask you to leave in a little,' Philip said affably while managing to leer lecherously in my direction.

I cringed but made myself raise my footrest and focus for a few minutes on *Pulp Fiction*, which had begun playing on a wall-sized plasma screen. Just as I was getting into it, managing to put Sammy out of my mind for solid thirty-second increments, Elisa scampered over.

'Okay, so I'm, like, still pretty unclear,' she said, ripping the foil off a new pack of Marlboro Lights. 'Who *is* that guy?'

'What guy? Sammy?'

'Isabelle's guy. What does he mean, he *works* at Bungalow?'

'He's the bouncer there, Elisa. You've seen him probably a thousand times.'

'The bouncer? What's the *bouncer* doing on our trip?' she hissed. Almost immediately, her expression changed from disgust to understanding. 'Oh, I get it. He's one of the Downtown Boys. Yes, that makes perfect sense.'

'I don't think he lives downtown,' I said, trying to remember if I even knew where Sammy lived.

She stared at me disdainfully. 'Bette, you *know* Downtown Boys. They're the company that hires out gorgeous guys as bartenders or security or waitstaff at private parties and events. You ordered all those pretty boys to work the BlackBerry party, right? Well, Downtown is *way* more exclusive. And it's an open secret that they're available to their clientele for *whatever* needs they may have.'

I looked at her. 'What are you saying?'

'Just that I wouldn't be surprised if Isabelle keeps Sammy on some sort of retainer to escort her to events, work her parties, *keep her company*. Things like that. Her husband isn't exactly interested in her social obligations.'

'She's married?' This was the best news I'd heard all day.

'Are you serious?' Elisa asked, stunned. 'Do you think she's the most seen socialite in Manhattan because she's charming? Her husband is some sort of Austrian viscount – not that Austrian royal titles are so hard to come by – one of the *Forbes* Top 100 Richest People every year since the early eighties. Hell, probably forever. What, did you think that bouncer was her boyfriend?'

My silence said everything.

'Ohmigod, you did. That's so cute, Bette! You honestly think someone like Isabelle Vandemark dates bouncers?' She was laughing so hard she almost choked. 'That is such a great visual! She may be fucking him, but she sure isn't *dating* him!'

I briefly considered burning her with my cigarette, but I was too elated by what I'd just learned to hate Elisa that much. She grew bored after a few minutes and went back to drape herself across Davide, who couldn't seem to divert his eyes from Isabelle's chest, and she tried to flirt with Philip, who was deep in conversation with Leo about the merits and pitfalls of having the pedicurist razor your dead foot-skin instead of merely scrubbing it with a pumice stone. The photographers and reporters were mostly keeping to themselves, playing Texas Hold 'Em at the large dinner table and throwing back tumblers of bourbon. Everyone else was unconscious, or close, and before I'd even gotten to the scene where Travolta plunges the needle into Uma Thurman's chest, I was fast asleep as well.

24

It wasn't until almost two o'clock the next afternoon that I had my first second alone. We flew through the night, landed at eleven o'clock Thursday morning, and immediately climbed from the cool leather plushness of the Gulfstream to the cool leather plushness of a fleet of limousines, sent courtesy of the Association of Nightclub Owners – or ANO, as Mr Kamal Avigdor neatly abbreviated it. Mr Avigdor had obviously received the memo regarding the appearance qualifications of our little group and was beautiful in the most classic way. He waited with two strikingly pretty girls – his assistants, he claimed, but each had probably done a round or two in the role of girlfriend – on the red carpet that had been laid on the tarmac, a warm smile lighting up his welcoming face. His black suit was tight and fitted in the way only European guys can get away with, and his monochromatic green shirt-and-tie combo only illuminated his dark skin, dark hair, and green eyes. Naturally, he'd accessorized everything perfectly, with Ferragamo loafers, a Patek Philippe watch, and some sort of buttery soft man-purse that would have made any normal man sob with humiliation but somehow managed to make him look even more masculine. I estimated him to be somewhere in the thirty to thirty-five range, but I wouldn't have been the least bit surprised to learn he was ten years older or younger. Most impressive of all, he'd greeted each person by name as we'd disembarked.

Elisa, Leo, Davide, and I rode into town with Mr Avigdor – who insisted quite adamantly that we call him Kamal – while the others ducked into the limos behind us. He gave us the whole rundown on the weekend, assuring us that our only collective responsibility was to show our guests a fantastic time. He would take care of everything else. We were to let him know if they wanted anything, anything at all ('And by anything, I most certainly mean anything – boys, girls, leather goods, hard-to-find food or drink items, "recreational substances" – anything') and he would ensure that it found its way to the appropriate person. The itineraries he handed us looked more like lists of restaurants and clubs than any sort of schedule; the days were completely blank, leaving time for the 'beauty rest, spa treatments, shopping, and sunning that everyone will surely require,' but the nights were jam-packed. For three nights, starting at eight o'clock each evening, we'd be fed dinner at a fabulous restaurant, work our way through two fabulous lounges, and end up at a superfabulous, ultra-exclusive night-club, where we'd remain until close to dawn, just like the young Turks and visiting Europeans. New Year's Eve differed from the other nights only in that we were to conduct a champagne toast – on national TV – at the stroke of midnight. Photographers would document every minute of the fabulous fun, and Kamal expected that the resulting publicity would help just as much in Turkey as in America; after all, who doesn't want to party at the very same place Philip Weston did?

Check-in went smoothly with only a half-dozen complaints about the rooms ('too close to where the maids keep their cleaning shit'; 'not nearly enough towels to dry this much hair'; 'so not interested in having a view of a *mosque*!'), and everyone was in good spirits when we reconvened at the impressively elegant champagne brunch held in our honor on the hotel's rooftop overlooking the majestic Topkapi Palace. I managed to sneak away after an hour and walked the few blocks to the Grand Bazaar, where I planned to roam and gape at everyone and everything. I entered through the Nuruosmaniye Gate to cries of 'Miss, I have what you look for,' and wandered aimlessly through the cavernous building, weaving in and out of the overflowing stalls, taking in the limitless amounts of beads and silver and rugs and spices and hookahs and merchants who sipped and smoked, sipped and smoked. I was in the process of haggling with a little man who couldn't have been a day younger than ninety for a powder blue pashmina when I felt a tap on my shoulder.

'You realize you're fighting over approximately forty cents, don't you?' Sammy asked, grinning like he'd just discovered a very big secret.

'I know that!' I said indignantly. Of course I didn't.

'So why are you doing it?'

'You're obviously not very familiar with the culture around here. You're expected to haggle. They actually find it insulting if you don't.'

'Oh, really? Mister, what price are you asking for this scarf?' he asked, addressing the hunchback seller in the softest voice imaginable.

'Six dollars, U.S., sir. It is of the finest quality. From the south. Made by my own granddaughter just a week ago. It is beautiful.' The man smiled to reveal a fine spread of toothless gums that somehow made him look even friendlier.

'We'll take it,' Sammy announced, pulling some Turkish lira from his wallet and placing them gently in the man's paper-thin hand. 'Thank you, sir.'

'Thank *you*, sir. A beautiful pashmina for a beautiful girl. Have a nice day,' he said merrily, clapping Sammy on the back before returning to his water pipe.

'Yeah, you're right.' Sammy grinned at me again. 'He looked really insulted to me.' He wrapped the scarf around my neck and gathered my hair into a bundle to lift it up, letting it fall on top of the silky soft material.

'You didn't have to do that!' *But I'm so glad you did,* I thought.

'I know. I wanted to, to apologize for crashing your trip. I really didn't know you'd be here, Bette. I'm sorry about that.'

'Sorry for what?' I said lightly. 'Don't be ridiculous, you have nothing to apologize for.'

'Have coffee with me? I've been in the country for hours and I still haven't had Turkish coffee. I'm excited at the idea that it won't be skim or extra-hot or no-whip or sugar-free or blended. What do you say?'

'Sure. My book here says the best place is a few hallways over.'

'Your book?'

'*Lonely Planet*. How can you go anywhere without a *Lonely Planet*?'

'You're such a dork,' he said, pulling on the end of my pashmina. 'We're staying at the Four Seasons, getting shuttled around by private drivers, and have unlimited spending accounts, and you're following your *Lonely Planet*? Amazing.'

'Why, exactly, is that so amazing? Maybe I want to see a few things that aren't on the spa-oceanfront-dinner-members-only club circuit.'

He shook his head, unzipped his backpack, and rooted around inside. 'This is why it's amazing,' he said, pulling out his own copy of the exact same book. 'C'mon, let's go find that stall.'

We claimed a couple of miniature stools around a tiny table and hand-motioned for two cups of coffee, which came accompanied by a small plate of sugar cookies.

'Can I ask you something?' I said, slurping the thick liquid from the small cup.

'Sure. Ask away.'

'What is your relationship with Isabelle?' I asked, trying to sound casual.

His face tightened. He said nothing, just stared at the tabletop and ground his teeth.

'Forget it, it's none of my business,' I added quickly, desperate not to ruin the moment.

'It's complicated,' he said.

'So you've said.' I watched a tiny kitten leap from the ground to the top of a huge rug pile, where the teenage girl tending the stall fed it a dish of milk. 'Well,' I finally said, 'it's your deal. Let's just enjoy our coffee, okay?'

'She pays me to spend time with her,' he said softly, moving his eyes to meet mine as he took a sip.

Well, I wasn't exactly sure what to do with that information. It wasn't a total shock, considering what Elisa had said, but the way he stated it, so calmly, with that matter-of-fact way that I was discovering was very, *very* Sammy – well, it just sounded so strange.

'I'm not sure I understand. Does this have something to do with working for one of those agencies that hire all the hot guys to bartend and stuff?'

He laughed out loud. 'No, I never went that route, but I do appreciate your thinking that I could meet their attractiveness quotient.'

'Then I really don't understand.'

'A lot of times people meet us at Bungalow and then hire us to work their private parties, stuff like that. I was bartending there last summer, and Isabelle was around a lot. I guess she took a liking to me. It started out that she'd pay me a few grand a night to tend bar at her dinner parties or meet and greet guests at her charity benefits. When she was named co-chair of the New York Botanical Garden's annual benefit, she decided to take on a full-time assistant. I guess I was the natural choice because I could, uh, do other stuff as well.'

'Other stuff? She pays you to sleep with her?' I blurted before I could even consider what I was saying.

'No!' he said sharply, glaring at me with a steely look. 'Sorry. It's hardly weird that you would wonder that. I'm a little sensitive about it. The short answer is no, I'm not sleeping with her, but the more truthful one is that I'm not sure how long I can get away with that. I certainly didn't think that was an aspect of this in the beginning, but it's becoming pretty clear that it's expected.'

'What about her husband?' I asked.

'What about him?'

'Doesn't he care that his wife has hired a gorgeous young guy to hang out at her home, help her with her assorted fund-raising activities, accompany her on romantic weekend getaways to Istanbul? You'd think he wouldn't be thrilled.' I got a little tingle from indirectly calling him 'gorgeous.'

'Why wouldn't he be thrilled? As long as she's discreet and doesn't embarrass him and is available when he needs her for his work functions, I imagine he's psyched not to have to go to all her social shit and tell her how hot she is and discuss at length whether he prefers her in Stella McCartney or Alexander McQueen. He's the one who signs my checks, actually. He's a decent guy.'

I didn't quite know how to respond to any of this, so I sat, trying to think of something inoffensive to say.

'It's just a job that happens to pay really, really well. If I ever want to open my own place, I can't turn down a six-figure salary for hanging out with a pretty woman a few hours a week.'

'Six figures? Are you *kidding*?'

'Not in the least. Why else do you think I would do this? It's beyond humiliating, but I've got my eyes on the prize. Which, incidentally, might be closer than I thought.' He popped a cookie in his mouth and chewed.

'What do you mean?'

'Well, nothing's definite, but a few guys from CIA approached me last week about going in with them and opening a place together.'

'Really?' I moved closer. 'Tell me about it.'

'Well, it'd be more of a franchise situation, I guess you'd say, rather than a whole new place. It's by the people who own Houston's, and there are a few of them already on the West Coast. They say they do really well. It's a pretty basic American menu – not really any chance to do anything creative, since the concept and the menu are nonnegotiable, but it would be all mine. Or at least, mine and theirs.' He sounded about as excited as someone who'd just been told they had a sexually transmitted disease.

'Well, it sounds great,' I said, trying to inject my voice with some level of enthusiasm. 'Are you excited about it?'

He appeared to think about this for a few seconds and then sighed. 'I'm not sure *excited* is the right word, but I think it's a good opportunity. It's not quite what I had in mind, but it's a step in the right direction. It's crazy to think I'd be able to incorporate my own personal vision for a place at this point in my career – it's just not realistic. So to answer your question, do I have some burning desire to own one-third of an Upper East Side Houston's restaurant? Not really. But if it'll allow me to stop working at Bungalow 8 and act as a decent stepping-stone, then yes, I think it's worth it.'

'Fair enough,' I said. 'It sounds like a great opportunity.'

'For now.' He stood up, bought two more coffees, and placed one in front of me. 'Okay, your turn.'

'My turn for what?' I asked, although I obviously knew where this was going.

'What's your deal with Mr Weston?'

'It's complicated.'

He laughed again and rolled his eyes dramatically. 'Uh-huh, that's cute. Come on, I just gave you the whole sordid story. How on earth did you end up dating him?'

'What do you mean by that?'

'Nothing, other than the two of you seem really – well, really different.'

'Different how?' I knew exactly what he was saying, but it was fun to watch him squirm.

'Oh, come on, Bette, cut the bullshit. I know what it's like to come from Poughkeepsie and join the cool crowd in New York, okay? I get it. What I don't get is how you could actually like him. You might be able to hang with this crew, but that doesn't make you one of them. Which, by the way, is a very good thing.'

I considered this for a moment before I said, 'I'm not really dating him.'

'Every gossip column in Manhattan spots you together everywhere. Hell, I see you with him at Bungalow constantly. You might not call it dating, but I don't think he's quite figured that out yet.'

'I honestly don't know how to explain it because I'm not sure I understand it myself. It's almost like Philip and I have this mutual, unspoken understanding to pretend we're together even though we've never even really hooked up.'

His head jerked up. 'You what? That's impossible.'

'It's not impossible. I'd be lying if I said I didn't wonder why he doesn't seem interested, but I assure you, we haven't gone down that road. . . .'

Sammy finished off his second little cup of coffee and appeared to contemplate this. 'So what you're saying is that you've never had sex with him?'

I looked at him and was pleased to see that he cared.

'Not even close. And in the interest of full disclosure, I've actually tried to seduce him a few times. There's always an excuse – too much to drink, a late night with another girl. It's beyond insulting when you think about it, but what can you do? The amount of time I spend with him has a direct effect on my responsibilities at work. Kelly's thrilled with the publicity he brings the company, and all I have to do is smile for a few pictures. I never thought I'd be doing this, but we have this fairly bizarre unspoken agreement: I act like his girlfriend and he gives me a huge bump at work. It's creepy, but in a weird way, it's totally equal. We're both getting something we want from it.' It was a relief to say aloud what I hadn't yet described to anyone.

'I didn't hear a word you just said.'

'Great. Thanks for listening. You're the one who asked, you know.'

'I sort of tuned out after you said you've never slept with him. You're *really* not dating him?' he asked, spinning his empty cup in little circles with his thumb.

'Sammy, you've seen the way Philip is. He's not capable of dating anyone. I have absolutely no idea why he's picked me, and frankly, it's okay for my ego. But I could never be with someone like that. Even if he does have dynamite abs.'

'Dynamite abs, huh? Better than these?' And before I knew what was happening, he pulled up his shirt to reveal one tight stomach.

'Damn,' I breathed, reaching out a hand to pat the ripples. 'I might have to concede this one to you.'

'Might?' he asked, letting his shirt drop but taking my hand and pulling me closer. 'Come here.'

We kissed for real this time, getting as close to each other as the mini-stools would allow, touching faces and hair and necks while we tried to move even closer.

'It is not done here,' a small man said, knocking twice on the tabletop. 'It is not right.'

We pulled away, embarrassed by the reprimand, and straightened ourselves. Sammy apologized to the man, who merely nodded and moved on, and then turned to look at me.

'Did we just have our first public make-out?' he asked.

222

'Sure did.' I laughed, delighted. 'And I think that was more than a make-out. It might have even qualified for all-out necking. In the Grand Bazaar of Istanbul, no less.'

'What better place is there?' he said, stepping aside to let me stand. I started walking ahead of him out of the café, but he pulled on my hand. 'I'm not kidding around here, Bette. I'm not playing with you.' He looked at me.

'I'm not either, Sammy.' I thought I might choke on the words, but his smile allowed me to breathe again.

'I'd like to hug you right now, but I don't want to get flogged for public indecency.' Instead, he draped his arm over my shoulders. 'Let's just get through the rest of this trip, okay? We'll sneak away when we can, but we shouldn't get caught.'

I nodded, although all I really wanted to do was slip a week's worth of Valium into Isabelle's and Philip's respective beverages and watch them flail for a bit before settling into a nice, peaceful, permanent rest. But no! That wasn't quite fair. Neither was deserving of actual death. I silently conceded to spare both their lives if they boarded one-way flights for the sub-Saharan African village of their choosing. That would be acceptable.

It took us over an hour to traverse the five-block stretch of road back to the hotel. We made out, grabbed, touched, and groped in every hidden doorway we could find, utilizing every private or deserted alleyway, foyer, tree, or bench that would shield us from disapproving eyes for a few minutes. By the time the golden yellow exterior of the Four Seasons was visible from the street, I'd managed to establish beyond a reasonable doubt that Sammy wore Calvin Klein boxer briefs.

'You go in first. Do what you have to do to get through the next few days – except touch Philip Weston in any way, shape, or form. I loathe the idea of you sharing a room with him.' He curled his mouth down in a show of disgust and shivered a bit.

'Oh, yeah, and I'm thrilled with the thought of you crawling into bed next to Isabelle, all the while telling her how gorgeous she looks in her new La Perla.' The mere thought made me nauseated.

'Go,' he said, pressing his mouth to mine. 'I'll see you at dinner tonight, okay?'

'Okay,' I said, giving him a quick kiss back. And then, despite myself, I stammered, 'I'll miss you.' I grinned at the hotel doorman and literally skipped through the lobby to the elevator, and then from the elevator to my room. I barely even noticed Philip sprawled on the bed, wearing only a towel and a silk eye mask.

'Where were you, love? I'm completely knackered. This hangover's killing me, and you left me here all alone,' he whined. 'Why don't you put together a cold compress for me? That'd be brilliant.'

'Why don't you get your own cold compress, Philip?' I asked merrily. 'I'm just dropping off this stuff on my way to the spa. Take an Advil or two and be dressed and ready in the lobby by seven forty-five, okay?' I slammed the door hard to make the loudest possible noise and skipped all the way to the slick marble of the hotel's Turkish bath. I told the spa receptionist to add a massage, pedicure, and tall glass of mint tea to my scrub-down and slowly undressed in the eucalyptus-scented steam room, thinking of Sammy.

25

Since we were a dozen people with nothing to do but drink and hang out, we sat at dinner that first night and played pop-culture trivia. It wasn't called that, of course, nor was there any mention of actually playing a game – never mind a trivia game – because that would be very uncool, but the way we shot questions back and forth indicated that it was, undeniably, just that. It reminded me of the way Michael and Penelope would fire off *Beverly Hills, 90210* questions to each other. 'Who was the original owner of the Peach Pit After Dark?' Michael would ask, leaning forward as though he couldn't be more serious. 'Um, like everyone doesn't know that? Rush Sanders, Steve's dad. Given!' Penelope would say with an exasperated eye roll. They'd continue for hours ('What hotel did Dylan live in with his father, Jack?' 'What is the name of the character in the inaugural season who accidentally shot himself at his own birthday party?' 'True or false: Donna slept with Ray Pruit?'), each intent on proving they knew every scene, every character.

I could hardly claim intellectual superiority over Elisa and Marlena just because they could name all the members of Madonna's Kabbalah group, especially when my own best friends could state when, exactly, Mel Silver cheated on Jackie (Kelly's mom), and I could recall the names of Trista and Ryan's wedding planner and Angelina Jolie's adopted Cambodian son on command. That said, I'd never seen a group who appeared so comprehensively bored, indifferent, and uninterested play something with such fervor.

'Oh, like everyone on earth doesn't know that Marc Anthony

had two kids before he married J.Lo. That is, like, the most elementary information possible, but can you tell me the location of the court where he filed for divorce?' Alessandra practically shouted at Monica.

She huffed. 'Puh-lease. You're joking. If you ever read anything in your life you'd know that he filed in the Dominican Republic to speed things up. What you probably don't know – because it's hardly out there for the masses to read in those rags they publish every other day – is the name of the boat George keeps at his Lake Como house.'

'George?' Oliver asked, as everyone leaned closer.

'Clooney,' Marlena said. 'Who else?'

'Ohmigod, I can't even listen to this anymore,' Leo whined. 'You're all so pathetic.'

I silently cheered Leo for his good sense, but I was premature.

'You all think any of this is relevant? Name three people Jade Jagger used to date, and tell me which jewelry company she currently works for.'

Philip sighed and then listlessly clapped Leo on the back. 'Leo, chap, challenge us. That was singularly the worst question I could ever think of – especially since every single person here was at the grand opening of the Garrard store.'

It went on like this through the entire meal, and it wasn't until dessert that we'd begun wondering what a Turkish nightclub would look like.

'Well, I'm sure not covering up any more than this. I know it's a Muslim country and all that, but I'm dressed as conservatively as my wardrobe will permit,' Isabelle announced, casting her eyes down to her outfit. Her halter dress looked as though it were made of metal; it left her entire back bare, and part of her ass, although anything truly obscene was covered, and it did actually reach to her knees. In front it dipped down to her belly button, but the material still clung to her perfect breasts just next to the nipples. Upon closer inspection, I decided she must've taped it there. Silver, open-toed stiletto sandals and an alligator clutch completed her look.

'Do you think they even have Cristal there?' Davide asked with urgency. 'They do have bottle service, don't they, Bette?'

I was about to tell him that he would probably survive the night regardless of the presence or lack of magnums of Cristal, but Kamal, who'd been listening quietly with no expression whatsoever, leaned in conspiratorially. 'Friends, I assure you that you will find everything to your satisfaction. Tonight's venue will surely please you, as we have arranged it all.'

'So, Kamal, let's talk girls. What's the deal with Turkish girls?'

Philip asked. Davide laughed appreciatively and Elisa made a big show of rolling her eyes in my direction. I caught on quickly that this is how girlfriends were supposed to act and rolled mine right back.

'Hypothetically speaking?' Kamal asked. He thought for a moment and then said, 'Mr Weston, I think you will find Turkish girls the very same as American or British or anywhere else – some are, shall we say, more willing, while others come from good families and want no part of that.'

'And which ones are we most likely to make the acquaintance of tonight, Kamal? The willing ones or the ice queens?'

Philip had clearly won Kamal over because he began to grin and play along. He took a giant swig from his tumbler before arranging his features in something approximating a serious expression and saying, 'The former, Mr Weston. I predict you will encounter more of the former category this evening.'

Philip grinned right back and held up his hand for a high-five, which Kamal instantly accommodated. 'That will be acceptable, Mr Avigdor. Thank you.'

Not surprisingly, no bill ever appeared on the table, and by the time we piled onto the boat – a yacht, maybe, or perhaps a sailboat – that would transport us down the Bosporus to Bella, I was slightly buzzed and somewhat enjoying the night. In an effort to distract myself from watching Isabelle paw Sammy, I'd gone from person to person, persuading them to pose for the photographers for a half-hour upon arrival at the club, followed by another half-hour of on-the-record partying where anything they said or did could be reported by the writers we'd brought along. However, after that, the work would be officially over and everyone could party to any level of debauchery they desired without worrying too much about those pesky COKE AND HOOKERS! headlines. There was still the Turkish media to be wary of, but I didn't predict they'd pose much of a problem, and Kamal promised to keep them out of the VIP areas. All in all, most everyone seemed satisfied with the arrangement, and the crew appeared almost excited as the boat docked at a red-carpeted pier.

'Are all the men going to stare at us?' Elisa asked Kamal, her eyes wide with worry.

'Stare at you? Why? Of course, they will notice your beauty, but I don't think they will make you uncomfortable,' he said.

'Well, if they're only used to seeing women wearing burkas, I imagine we'll stand out,' she said thoughtfully.

Sammy shot me a look – one of many that evening, since we'd sat across from each other at dinner – and I managed to stifle a laugh, although not without a snort. She whipped around and glared at me. 'What? Do you feel like having a bunch of peasants staring at you all night? I didn't have to fly all this way for that – we could've just gone to New Jersey!'

Kamal kindly ignored her as he helped us off the boat and introduced us to another group of men, all of whom appeared to be good-looking and really, really successful. They were the rest of our clients, and each had between two and four knockout girls hanging on their every word. Much to Elisa's and Isabelle's surprise, these girls were not wearing burkas. They weren't even really wearing bras, if we were going to be technical. The amount of naked female flesh on display was almost blinding, and we hadn't even made it inside yet.

One of the new men introduced himself as Nedim and announced, quite grandly, that he owned Bella, the sprawling complex of entertainment that stretched before us. It had its own marina to allow celebrities and visiting VIPs to bypass the whole door situation; guests could merely step off their boats and fall directly onto a banquette, where anything they could even think to desire would be immediately provided. Nedim managed to look like every other club owner I'd ever met: he was the classic chain-smoking, vintage T-shirt and retro sneaker wearing, spiky-haired guy who no one would ever notice if he didn't drive the requisite red Porsche and comp bottles of champagne.

'Ladies, gentlemen, welcome to Bella,' he announced, sweeping his arms grandly, 'the premier nighttime destination in Istanbul. Bella rests, as you can see, on the Bosporus River, right at the dividing point between Europe and Asia, and our clientele certainly reflects that international feel. Come with me, please, and prepare yourself to enjoy all that Bella has to offer.'

He escorted us to a massive round table perched right on the water inside a roped-off section of the club that screamed 'VIP.' Only the flimsiest teak gate separated us from the river, and even that reached only two and a half feet high, a potential drunken disaster if I've ever seen one. The view was incredible: both small and large boats cruised slowly across the murky water, passing in front of a beautifully lit mosque with minarets that appeared to reach the sky. The floors were a shiny dark wood, almost black, and the banquettes were satin brocade with strings of gold filigree woven throughout. It was entirely open-air except for a few white canvas sheets that billowed out in the wind and lent the whole place an air of sexy exoticism; the only light came from Turkish-style glass lanterns and hundreds of tea lights in beaded votive holders. Roughly hewn bowls of mini apricots and pistachios rested on every available surface. It was undoubtedly the sexiest place I'd ever been, far more naturally chic than all the cool spots in New York or Los Angeles, but without that signature self-awareness that places seemed to develop when they knew they were hot.

A fleet of stylish waiters instantly surrounded the table and took our drink orders. Within a half-hour, everyone was pleasantly buzzed, and by the time midnight rolled around, Elisa and Philip were dancing on the tables. They looked pretty comfortable with the grinding groove they had going. It suggested something romantic – and recent. The photographers clicked away, but Nedim and crew kept them so plied with booze and girls and God knows what else that they missed a shot of Marlena straddling a famous Turkish soccer player who also belonged in the VIP area. I managed to separate them before anyone noticed and convince them that they'd be much happier in her room at the Four Seasons, and they didn't even protest when I escorted them to a waiting Town Car out front and instructed the driver to take them back to the hotel. I'd just hung up with the hotel's concierge – who assured me he'd whisk them to Marlena's room and keep out any photogs or reporters – when Sammy appeared at my side.

'Hey, where've you been hiding?' he said, wrapping his arms around me from behind and kissing my neck. 'I managed to keep track of you all night, and then you were just gone.'

'Hi there,' I said.

He glanced around to make sure he didn't see Isabelle or Philip or anyone with a camera. 'Let's get out of here,' he said gruffly. 'They're all so drunk, they'll never notice.' Again he kissed my neck, this time more roughly, and for the first time I had an inkling that Sammy wasn't just a nice guy. Thankfully.

'I can't, Sammy. I want to, but I can't. I've got to keep my eye on everyone here – it's literally my only responsibility.'

'It's almost two. How much longer can they really keep this up?'

'You of all people know the answer to that. Until daybreak, easily. Maybe we can figure something out later at the hotel, but right now I've got to go back in there.'

He let his arms drop by his sides and sighed loudly. 'I know this is how it has to be. It just sucks. You go in first, and I'll come in a couple minutes.' He started to run his fingers through my hair but abruptly pulled them away at the sound of his name.

'Sammy? Are you out here? Have you seen my boy – my, uh, my assistant?' Isabelle's shrill voice echoed over the water. I turned to see her asking one of the uniformed security guards who'd been watching us carefully to make sure no one harassed us.

'Jesus Christ,' Sammy muttered, moving away from me. 'What, she can't find the bathroom herself? I've got to run.'

'Just wait, I'll handle this,' I said and squeezed his hand. 'Isabelle, over here! He's over here.'

Isabelle's head swiveled, and when she saw us, she looked at first relieved and then confused. She ignored me completely while addressing Sammy. 'I've been looking for you forever,' she whined, obviously forgetting I was standing there, and then dropping the whine when she remembered.

'Sorry to steal him from you, Isabelle. Marlena and the guy she was with were pretty trashed, and Sammy was kind enough to help me put them in a car. We were just on our way back in.'

This seemed to mollify her, although she still hadn't acknowledged my presence. She was staring at Sammy, and he was intently focused on his feet.

'Okay, well, I'm going to see how everyone's doing inside,' I said cheerily. I made my way to the door, but not before I overheard Isabelle's voice change from whiny to viciously cold.

'I don't pay you good money to neglect and abandon me!' she hissed.

'Oh, save it, Isabelle,' Sammy said, sounding more exhausted than annoyed. 'I was helping her out for five minutes. I was hardly abandoning you.'

'Well, how do you think it feels to be sitting all alone in there while my guy runs off to help someone else?'

Unfortunately, I had to walk through the door and couldn't hear Sammy's response. The VIP area was completely empty by the time I fought through the hordes of commoners. American rap and hip-hop had given way to some sort of Turkish trance music, and it seemed the entire space was pulsating with barely concealed bodies. Camilla, Alessandra, and Monica had all found men – a soccer player from Real Madrid, an anchorman for CNN International, and an English playboy who claimed to know Philip from their boarding-school days – and were tucked away with them in various dark corners around Bella, under the watchful eye of Nedim and the other owners. I spotted Elisa and Davide standing next to the dance floor, gesturing wildly to each other. I figured they were fighting, until I got close enough to hear. They weren't actually arguing or having any kind of exchange at all: both were so obviously high on coke that they were talking *at* the other one, each so caught up in the importance of their own ideas that they shouted enthusiastically over the other's voice. As usual, the photographers and reporters had claimed a little table for themselves, away from the rest of us, and seemed once again to be drowning themselves in hard alcohol. Six empty packs of cigarettes were littered around them, and they barely glanced up when I asked if they needed anything. I didn't see Leo, but Philip wasn't hard to locate – I merely looked for the blondest girl in the room, with the biggest boobs, and then moved my eyes a few inches to the right. He had his arm around her waist as they both stood in front of the DJ stand. She looked vaguely familiar, but I couldn't place her from behind. As I waited for them to turn around, I watched as Philip removed a giant wad of cash from the back pocket of his AG jeans and thrust it toward the skinny DJ, who maintained the requisite DJ earphone-pressed-to-shoulder stance.

'Hey, mate, how much will it cost for you to play something with some bloody words?' he asked as the girl giggled and swigged from her drink. 'I can't listen to this Turkish shit anymore.'

The DJ palmed the cash and made it disappear under one of the machines on his table. He beckoned to another kid sitting in the booth and said a few words to him. The second guy turned to Philip and said, 'What you want to hear? He will play you anything.'

'Tell him we want a little Bon Jovi or Guns n' Roses.'

The helper translated and the DJ nodded, appearing puzzled. Within ten seconds 'Paradise City' was blaring from the speakers and Philip was mock-smashing his head to the beat. When he spotted me, he leaned in to whisper something to the girl and she nodded and scampered off.

'Hey, love, how much better are these tunes?' he asked, checking his reflection in the glass of the DJ booth.

'Was that Lizzie Grubman?' I asked, finally figuring out why she looked so familiar.

He resumed hitting his head against an imaginary wall. 'Apparently she and Tara Reid heard about our posh party here this weekend and wanted to have a look for themselves.'

'She's, uh, she's pretty,' I said lamely, knowing I should be happy, professionally speaking, that Lizzie Grubman and Tara Reid had followed our group to Istanbul.

'Face like a crocodile handbag,' he said, grabbing me and pulling me onto the dance floor. 'Come on, love, loosen up a little. Let's have a dance.'

I sneaked away after a few minutes and went back to Elisa, who seemed to have calmed a bit. She was sitting on Davide's lap, chattering quietly as he massaged her shoulders and took long drags off the joint that hung from his lips.

'Hey, do you think you can handle things here? I think a bunch of people went back to the hotel, and I should probably make sure everything's in order there.'

'Sure, whatever. You worry too much, Bette. Everyone's having a great time. Where's Leo? Just tell him you're going back and we'll see you at the hotel, okay?' She giggled as Davide exhaled the pot smoke in her face.

'Excellent. Will do. I'll see you tomorrow.'

'Yeah, whatever. I don't plan to see daylight tomorrow, but I'll find you when we wake up. Oh, where's Philip?' she asked, trying very hard to sound casual.

'Philip? Last I saw, he was dancing with Lizzie Grubman and Tara Reid.'

'What? They're here?' She leapt off Davide and plastered on a huge smile. 'I'm totally going to say hi. See you later, Bette.'

I looked around for Leo, but when I couldn't find him anywhere, I figured he'd met a guy and had retired to his room for playtime. Nedim offered to escort me back to the hotel in his Porsche, and I was tempted to accept until he let his hand brush against my lower back while smiling suggestively and saying he'd give me a tour of Istanbul's late-night hotspots. I declined politely and took a Town Car. The woman at the front desk greeted me by name and briefed me on who had returned so far and when.

'Oh, wait, there is a message for you.' She handed me a piece of folded paper, which I immediately opened, expecting some disaster. MEET ME IN ROOM 18 WHEN YOU GET BACK was written in bold print, all caps. There was no signature, but a plastic room key was enclosed.

I briefly considered my options. The note had to be from Sammy. He'd somehow arranged for a room away from Isabelle so that we could spend some private time together. It was, if I dared to think about it, the most exciting romantic gesture of my lifetime. I was buffed and polished from the spa that morning, and now my secret boy had called. It didn't get better than this.

The elevator ride seemed to last forever, and by the time I knocked on the door, I was shaking with excitement.

It took almost a minute for it to open, a minute that felt like a month, and I had a fleeting, horrifying thought that it wasn't Sammy at all, or that maybe the note was intended for someone else. A dozen possible misunderstandings flashed through my mind in the thirty seconds I stood there, rooted to the carpet, quietly panicking and wondering how I could possibly be expected to function if it wasn't him, if he wasn't waiting inside, preparing to tear my clothes off and throw me on what would surely be a king-sized bed tricked out in all its Four Seasons, down-filled, Frette-covered glory. *Oh, please,* I prayed to some unknown entity, *oh, please let it be him and let him want me as badly as I want him and also make it so that he has –*

The door swung open, and Sammy pulled me inside immediately, pressing his mouth to mine even before kicking the door shut. 'I want you so badly,' he breathed, moving his mouth over my face, my neck, my shoulders as he pushed aside the straps of my dress before he got frustrated and pulled the entire thing over my head.

Those were the last words either of us bothered with. We collapsed on the bed, which delivered every inch of fabulousness I'd imagined, and attacked each other with a ferocity that would have scared me if it hadn't delighted me so much. It was impossible to tell whose limbs belonged to whom, and I lost all awareness of time or place or where, exactly, I was being touched. It was a total sensation overload – the weight of his body, the smell of his deodorant, the way the hair on my arms and the back of my neck stood on end every time his fingers ran down my back. It was, I had to admit, a sex scene straight out of a Harlequin – maybe better. It wasn't until someone knocked at the door that I even noticed the dozens of candles strewn about or the two glasses of red wine that sat untouched or the great Buddha Bar soundtrack playing from the bedside Bose CD player.

'Who knows you're here?' I whispered, climbing off him and collapsing all in one motion.

'No one but the front desk. I put it on my personal credit card.'

'Could Isabelle have heard you?'

'No way. She took a fistful of Ambien to get over the time difference. She won't be awake for another two days.'

We continued to debate this for another few minutes, until I realized that night had eased its way into morning and I'd better be getting back to my rightful room if I didn't want to deal with lots and lots of questions.

He pulled me on top of him again and began kissing my earlobe, earring and all. 'Don't go. Not yet, at least.'

'I've got to, I'm sorry. You don't want this to be public yet, do you? Not like this.'

'I know, I know, you're right. Not like this. We'll have all the time in the world together once we're back in New York.'

'You aren't going to be able to get rid of me once we're home,' I whispered. My short, beaded dress was bunched up in a tiny ball on top of the desk, but I managed to get it on with some semblance of dignity before falling back into the bed. The thought of putting on any sort of undergarments was unbearable; after freeing my strapless bra from its resting place on the headboard, I tossed it and my underwear into my purse.

He yanked a sheet from the bed we'd destroyed and wrapped it around his waist as we walked to the door. 'Bette, thank you for an amazing night,' he said, holding my face in both his hands, making it feel small and delicate and absolutely gorgeous.

I stood on tiptoe to wrap my arms around his neck one last time. 'It was perfect,' I said.

And it was perfect, everything I'd hoped it would be, until the very second I opened the door and was greeted by the brightest, most aggressive flashbulb I'd ever experienced. It continued rapid-fire as I stood, frozen, too shocked to move.

'Oh, hey, sorry about that. Wrong room,' said John, one of the photographers we'd toted along.

'What the hell is going on?' Sammy asked.

'Let me handle it,' I said. 'Stay here.'

I stepped into the hallway and pulled the door shut behind me. 'What was that? What are you doing?' I practically shrieked.

'Hey, honey, I'm sorry about that. No worries, really, I didn't see a thing,' he said unconvincingly. He was the slickest of the group and had made me nervous from the very beginning – most of his work consisted of paparazzi-style pictures that he sold to the tackiest tabloids for the highest bid. Kelly had insisted it would be good to have him along because the photo editors loved everything he submitted.

'Why were you staking out my room? Uh, his room, I mean. I've spent all morning going around to everyone to discuss tonight's schedule, so you see, there's nothing really interesting there.'

'Look, I don't care who you're screwing.' He chuckled loudly and with great gusto. 'Of course, I imagine I could find someone who'd be interested to know that Philip's girl didn't spend the night with him, but you've been real good to us this trip, so we'll just forget that ever happened.'

Bastard. He was openly leering at my outfit and what I imagined to be a face full of smeared makeup and that general, all-night-sex look that simply could not be denied.

'Besides,' he continued, unsnapping the flash from his camera and tucking it into a black shoulder bag, 'what I *thought* was going on in there would've been far hotter than you banging Isabelle's guy.'

'Pardon me?' I wanted to strangle him for suggesting that anything could be better than the night I'd just had, for the fact that he didn't believe my ridiculous story about scheduling, and because he had the nerve to state that Sammy belonged to Isabelle.

Naturally, I couldn't think of one remotely insulting or clever thing to say.

'Well, let's just say that sources indicated the possibility of a little private party between your boyfriend and some of his closest friends.' He raised his bushy unibrow and pulled his lips taut against his teeth in an effort to smile.

'By "boyfriend" I mean Philip Weston,' he added with a grin.

I swallowed my anger. 'Mmm, while that all sounds really fascinating, I have to get back upstairs now to continue my rounds, so if you'll excuse me . . .' I pushed past him in my bare feet, with my sandals in one hand and my purse in the other, and beelined for the elevator.

The more I thought about it, the less nightmarish it seemed, especially since he didn't seem particularly fascinated by the scandal – or lack thereof – of Sammy and me. *And why should he be?* I reasoned. The man spends his life following insanely famous celebrities and documenting all the drama they manage to create, so why should he be the least bit interested in some insignificant publicist who appeared to be doing some extracurricular bed-hopping? And not even with someone famous! Of course, there was the issue of Philip. And if Kelly found out that I'd been caught keeping Isabelle's friend-for-hire company, she wouldn't be happy. Isabelle might insist I be fired. But I was getting ahead of myself; it seemed unlikely that John would leak anything. Only Abby seemed interested in my whereabouts, and there was no way even she had tentacles that reached all the way to Istanbul. I realized that was part of why I'd gotten so upset when I saw the photographer – for a blissful twenty-four hours, I'd forgotten what it felt like to feel stalked and spied on and vulnerable. Since Abby was a solid five thousand miles away, I didn't have that constant, creepy feeling that someone was trying to expose my private life to the general public. I took a deep breath and reminded myself that it could be far worse, and gave thanks that Abby was in an entirely different country.

As I approached, I saw that the door to Philip's and my suite was slightly ajar – only noticeable if you actually stood right next to it and looked – and I heard some muffled noises coming from inside. It was just after eight in the morning – practically the middle of the night, considering I hadn't returned to the hotel until three and Philip was still at Bella when I left – and I immediately understood that the supposed threesome most likely *was* going on, only it was happening in my room. The idea of knocking briefly crossed my mind, but instead I pushed the door open.

I rounded the corner from the sitting room and strolled through the French doors to the bedroom, only to see Leo sprawled on his back, naked, on the bed. It took another second or two for me to realize that the mop of hair that was currently bobbing up and down in the general area of Leo's exposed pelvic region – his bare ass saluting me – belonged to Mr Philip Weston. Before I could even react, Leo spotted me.

'Hey, Bette, what's up?' Leo asked nonchalantly, making no attempt to cover himself or Philip.

At the sound of my name, Philip's head snapped around, exposing the few inches of Leo's naked body that I hadn't yet seen. 'Oh, hey, babe, how are you?' he asked, wiping his mouth delicately with a pillowcase. 'Where were you all night?'

'Where was I all night?' As usual, I could merely mimic.

'I waited forever, love,' he whined, bounding off the bed like a little boy on Christmas morning and shrugging on a robe. I realized that this was the first time I'd seen him completely naked.

'Forever, huh?' I responded brilliantly.

'Well, if you'd come home when you should've, I don't think Leo would've ended up in my bed. Do you, love?'

I laughed out loud. Now *that* was funny. 'Oh, Philip. Please! You haven't wanted to sleep with me in – '

'Relax, doll, just calm down a bit. Leo here showed up a few minutes ago and just passed out. I must've had a sleep, too. We were daft to drink so much, but at least we slept it off.'

I was laughing uncontrollably now. 'Are you serious? Are you saying I didn't just see what I know I just saw?' Had either of them had the courtesy to appear the least bit embarrassed by what had just happened, I might – might – have been able to deal with it.

'Hey, guys, I'm going to order some coffee and orange juice, maybe a few croissants. I feel a wicked hangover coming on,' Leo announced. He still made no attempt to cover himself, instead grabbing the remote and scrolling through the hotel's movie offerings.

'Good call, mate. I fancy a double espresso, a few aspirin, and an extra-tall Bloody Mary,' Philip said.

'Is this happening?' I asked, wondering at what point my night – my entire life – had veered into the twilight zone. It felt like I was living in some sort of alternate reality, but apparently I was living there alone.

'Hmm?' Philip asked, dropping his robe again in front of both of us as he stepped into the shower, leaving the bathroom door wide open. 'Leo? Tell your coworker here that Leo and I are just mates.'

Leo managed to extract himself from the tangle of covers, which looked as though they'd been put through the paces for hours already, and pulled on his jeans sans underwear. 'Of course, Philip. Bette, we're just friends, honey. You want something to eat?'

'Um, no thanks. I, uh, I think I'm going to get some breakfast downstairs, okay? I'll see you both later.' I grabbed a clean pair of jeans, a T-shirt, and a pair of flip-flops, tossed them in a plastic hotel laundry bag, and sprinted out of the room, feeling slightly queasy as I left Philip and Leo to their domestic tranquillity.

I went to kill some time in the lobby restaurant and get a snack before I could safely go back to my room, but just as the waiter brought a full coffee service and a basket of the most amazing-looking pastries and muffins, Elisa stumbled in and collapsed into the seat across from me.

'I can't fucking sleep, and I'm ready to kill myself,' she announced.

I panicked the moment I saw her, convinced that she already knew what had happened. I figured no one would be awake at that hour, but her knotty hair and black-circled eyes and jumpy hands indicated that she'd probably done way too many drugs to even entertain the idea of sleep, so she'd come down to wait it out.

'Hey, sure, have a seat,' I said, trying to sound nonchalant.

The waiter brought her a cup and saucer. Her glassy eyes fixated on them for a moment, as though she'd never before seen either, but she recovered and poured herself some coffee. Then she eyed me suspiciously.

'You're up early. Where's Philip?' she asked, finishing off the entire cup in one gulp.

'Philip?' I tried to laugh casually, but it sounded more like a choke. 'Oh, he's sleeping, I think. I don't know why I'm up so early. Must be the time difference.'

'Time difference?' She snorted. 'If that's your only problem, just take a Xanax. I feel like shit.'

'Here, have something to eat. You look like you could use some food.'

Another snort. 'That muffin is equivalent in fat and carbs to at least two Big Macs. No, thank you.' She poured another cup of black coffee and finished it off.

'Is Davide upstairs?' I asked, not out of any genuine interest but because I felt I had to say something.

'I don't know where he is. Lost track of him around three in the morning. Probably went home with some Turkish chick.' She sounded neither upset nor surprised by this.

I just stared at her.

She just sighed. 'Philip would probably never do that to you, right? He's such a great guy . . .'

I nearly spat out my orange juice but somehow remained composed. 'Mmm,' I murmured. 'Have you ever heard anything about Philip being . . . well, uh, about him being interested in . . .'

She gave me a glazed stare. 'Interested in what?'

'Oh, I don't know . . . guys?'

This elicited a gasp, and her mouth fell wide open. 'Philip Weston? Gay? Are you joking? Bette, how can you be so naïve? Just because he happens to have a fabulous sense of style and drive a Vespa and do yoga does not, in any way, mean he likes guys.'

No, I thought to myself, *of course it doesn't. But what about the fact that I walked in on him a half-hour ago while he was performing oral sex on our very gay and very out coworker?*

'Right, no, I hear what you're saying. It's just that—'

'Bette, when are you going to appreciate that boy? Any girl in her right mind would do anything and everything she could to keep him, but you don't seem to understand that. So apparently there was some scandal around here this morning.' She switched tacks so quickly I barely had time to process that what she was saying might concern me.

'Scandal? With one of our group? Did anyone see it?'

She looked me in the eye and for a moment I was sure she knew the entire story. But then she just said, 'I'm not sure exactly. One of the photographers – that fat one, what's his name? – mentioned that he may have snapped a few "interesting" shots of someone in a compromising position. Any idea who it was or what happened?'

I chewed my croissant deliberately and fixed my gaze on the front page of the *International Herald Tribune*. 'Hmm, no, I haven't heard a thing. Should we be worried? I mean, we wouldn't want anything truly damaging to get out.'

Elisa poured a third cup of coffee and allowed herself a single packet of Equal this time. Her hands shook from the effort. 'I guess we'll just have to wait and see, won't we? I'm going to try to sleep – I've got to be back down here in a couple hours for my scrub in the Turkish bath. I hear it's even better for your skin than a laser peel. See you later.'

I watched her hobble out on stilt-skinny legs and tried to figure out what, exactly, had made that interaction so weird. But the mention of a scrub reminded me of my own appointment, so I finished breakfast and hit the spa for my pre-sightseeing massage, adding on a paraffin pedicure for good measure. This one I had earned.

26

'I have to say, I think this one's my favorite,' Will announced, passing me a computer printout across the table. He didn't sound particularly amused. He'd taken it upon himself to put together a little collection of all the newspaper clippings that had mentioned my name since I'd started at Kelly & Company and we were reviewing them together, over brunch. The week before, I'd returned from Turkey and what I'd thought was an incredibly successful trip. No one had seemed the least bit clued in as to what had *really* happened with either Philip or Sammy. It was becoming obvious that I'd relaxed too soon.

Abby was apparently omniscient. Somehow she must've gotten in touch with John, the fat photographer, because she'd managed to take a tiny, partial truth and weave it into a hideous lie. She'd published this particular gem on Friday, and this time I thought Kelly would have a heart attack:

> Publicist Bette Robinson is generating some publicity of her own, sources say, while running a press trip to Istanbul last month. Mostly known for her relationship with Philip Weston, Robinson was reported to be intimately involved with Rick Salomon – better known as the guy who brought us the Paris Hilton sex tape – in the same hotel where she also shared a room with Weston. Can readers look forward to a remake of this famous sex tape, this time featuring everyone's favorite party planner in place of everyone's favorite partier? Stay tuned.

The photo accompanying the darling little write-up was the one taken of me as I opened the door of Sammy's room, holding my sandals in one hand and running the other through my ratty, bed-head hair. My mouth hung open unattractively, and my makeup was smeared under my eyes. I looked just as slutty as Paris, minus her fab body and clothes. A figure had been blurred out in the background; upon closer inspection, it was clearly a male with a sheet tied around his waist, but identifying him beyond that was impossible. It was Sammy, of course – the bastard photographer had just spent five straight days with him and knew that perfectly well, but he clearly hadn't bothered to provide that information when he sold the picture to Abby. I imagined she'd spent little time trying to figure out who the guy was before picking someone particularly damaging at random and assigning him the role of my illicit, late-night paramour.

For the first time since I'd begun working for her, I saw that Kelly was not pleased with the coverage. She'd asked me, fairly, if there was any truth to the claim, and then followed up with questions about why Abby had it out for me. I assured her that I'd never met the Hilton sex-tape guy and certainly hadn't had sex with him – either on camera or off – and she seemed to believe me. Oddly enough, it never occurred to her to ask who the guy was if it wasn't Mr Paris Hilton, so I hadn't needed to lie. After this brief question-and-answer session, Kelly instructed me to settle any animosity with Abby since this kind of publicity was no longer helpful. She reminded me that we were a mere four weeks from the *Playboy* party, and there was to be no negative publicity, true or not, surrounding my private life between now and then. I assured her that I completely understood and vowed I'd put an end to it, although as of yet, I had no realistic plan for doing so. I knew I had to call Abby and confront her directly, but the thought of even hearing her voice made me sick with dread.

Philip, of course, had kept his mouth shut; only I knew he was relieved the photo was of my indiscretion – even if he did look like a loser whose girlfriend openly cheated on him, or, as Will had called him, a cuckold. At least it wasn't a shot of his little visit to the other team. Philip and I had yet to even mention anything that had happened that first night in Turkey. Not a word. Nada. Things had resumed their normal pattern for the rest of the trip. Two days of spa treatments and late-night debauchery. Eyeing but not touching Sammy (Isabelle's Ambien didn't last long enough) and generally making sure all the guests remained satisfied and out of trouble. We finished out Turkey like we had started – pretending to be together – although had anyone bothered to look closely, they would've noticed that I didn't so much as nap in Philip's room.

In the week since we'd been home, Philip and I had seen each other out, and neither of us denied it when people assumed we were together. After the chaos of the photo, the 'reconciliation' gave me some wiggle room with Kelly. But I needed a low-drama way out of this 'relationship' – not just because of the tabloid pressure, but because I really liked Sammy.

The good news was that every daily and weekly that mattered had dedicated massive spreads to the group's carefully orchestrated debauchery, and a very happy Association of Nightclub Owners was certain there would soon be an unprecedented number of

American partiers. Only New York Scoop had printed the ugly photo of me. Kelly seemed okay once she heard Philip and I had 'made up.' Sammy had been extremely apologetic, although Isabelle kept such a tight leash on him that we'd had little contact since the trip. The only people who seemed truly devastated were my parents.

My mother was so hysterical when she called that I had to hang up on her mid-conversation and have Will call her back to explain that you can't believe everything you read, especially when it comes to gossip columns. He managed to placate her slightly, but it didn't change the rather unsettling fact that even if I hadn't been sleeping with the Hilton sex-tape guy, my parents had still seen a photo of me taken right after I had quite obviously slept with someone. They didn't understand what I was doing professionally or personally . . . or why. While there'd been absolutely nothing good about the situation, the worst of it seemed to be over, and the only one who still seemed obsessed with it was Will.

It was Sunday, exactly one week after we'd returned from Turkey, and I was at my usual brunch with Will and Simon. I was bemoaning the lack of fact and truth in the piece when Will interrupted me.

'Bette, darling, stop using the word *truth* when referencing gossip columns. It makes you sound naïve.'

'Well, what am I supposed to do? Just be totally fine with the fact that that vengeful bitch can make up whatever she wants about me and they'll print it? It's a miracle and a blessing that I still have my job.'

'Is that so?' He raised his eyebrows and sipped from his Bloody Mary, his pinky extended.

'You're the one who practically mandated I take this job, if I remember. Said I needed more friends, to go out, to have a life. Well, I've done just that.'

'This,' he said, holding up the picture for emphasis, 'was not what I meant. And you know it. Now, darling, I'm happy to support you in anything that makes you happy, but I don't think it's a stretch of an observation to say that this is not it.'

Well, that one silenced me momentarily.

'So what do you propose I do?' I asked. 'You thought banking was a bore, and now you're disapproving of the job *you* picked for me because some girl I knew in a previous life has it in for me? That seems unfair.'

He sighed. 'Yes, well, darling, get over yourself. You're a big girl now, and I'm sure you'll find something a little more – how shall I put it? – *discreet* than your current lifestyle. Planning parties and going out, having a drink or two, a little romp with a cute boy is one thing, and I'm fully supportive of that. But dating some spoiled brat to please your boss, getting your name and face plastered across every rag in this city, and – not least – forgetting your old uncle's birthday because you were too busy acting as an international babysitter for a group of B-list stars and socialites is not quite what I had in mind when I recommended that you take this job.'

Will's birthday. January 2. I'd forgotten.

Will motioned for the waiter to bring him another Bloody Mary. 'Darling, excuse me for a moment. I'm going to take this mobile phone outside and see where Simon is. It's unlike him to be this late.' He placed his napkin on his chair and crossed the cavernous room in a few easy strides, looking every bit the distinguished gentleman.

When he returned, he was smiling and composed. 'How is your love life, my dear?' he asked, as if we'd not been talking about Philip at all.

'Haven't I said it enough? I have no interest in Philip.'

'Darling, I wasn't talking about Philip. Whatever happened to that hulking boy with whom you drove to Poughkeepsie? I rather liked him.'

'Sammy? How could you have liked him? You only met him for thirty seconds.'

'Yes, but in those thirty seconds he showed he was perfectly willing to lie on my behalf. Now, that's a quality person if there ever was one. So tell me, is there no interest there at all?' He peered at me with an intensity Will rarely displayed about anything.

I weighed whether or not to tell him the entire Istanbul story and then buckled. At least one person in my life should know I wasn't a complete tramp. 'Um, yeah, I guess you could say that,' I mumbled.

'Say what? That you are interested in him? Or you're not?' He winked.

I took a deep breath. 'He was the guy in the picture. You just couldn't see him.'

Will looked like he was trying to suppress a huge smile. 'He was in Turkey with you? How did you arrange that, my dear?'

'It's sort of a long story, but suffice it to say that I didn't know he was going to be there.'

Will raised an eyebrow. 'Really? Well, I'm pleased to hear that. I am sorry it had to end up in the gossip columns, but I'm glad the two of you have, ah, cemented your relationship.'

I listened to Will prattle on for a bit about how he always envisioned me being with someone like Sammy – the strong, silent type – and how it was about time I found myself a proper boyfriend who understood what was really important. And oh, by the way, how does he lean politically? I happily answered all of his questions, content to talk about Sammy if I couldn't be with him. We'd just tucked into our omelets when Will brought up the single subject I wanted to forget.

'Well, at least now there's a good reason why I couldn't see my own niece until she'd been back in the country for a week. I'd be offended if you were simply out gallivanting for work every night, but now that there's a boyfriend in the picture . . . New relationships must be coddled, and the beginning is the best time! Oh, how I remember the beginning! You just cannot get enough of each other. Every moment you're apart feels like torture. Which lasts about two years, of course, at which point things do a full one-eighty and you try to wrangle every possible moment alone. But you've got plenty of time before that happens, darling. So tell me, how has it been?'

I speared my eggs and pushed them around the plate before dropping my fork altogether. 'Actually, we haven't seen each other since we've been back,' I said, realizing how awful that sounded. 'It's not like there's anything wrong,' I added quickly. 'He's really busy talking to some people about opening up a restaurant – which is not his ultimate goal but seems to be a really good opportunity right now – and we've talked on the phone a few times, but I've also been so crazed getting everything together for the *Playboy* party and, well, you know how it is.'

I heard the words come out of my mouth and knew I sounded like a delusional girl trying to convince herself and everyone else that some guy really was interested, even though all outward signs indicated otherwise. It was beyond upsetting that I hadn't seen Sammy since we'd gotten home, but it was true that both of us had been extraordinarily busy, and besides, it was hardly unusual not to see a new guy for a week in New York City. Plus, I reminded myself, he had called three times in seven days, and he always said what a great time he'd had with me in Turkey, that he couldn't wait for things to calm down so we could go on a real date. I'd read enough romances to know that the worst possible thing I could do would be to push or demand. So far everything had unfolded organically, and while it would've been nice to have seen him once or twice in the past week, this was not a major cause for concern. After all, I was quite sure we had a long and beautiful future together, so what would be the point of rushing things now?

'Mmm, I see.' Will looked troubled for a moment but then

uncrinkled his forehead. 'I'm sure you know what you're doing, darling. Any plans to see him again?'

'Actually, yes. I have to stop by an *In Style* party tomorrow night, and he'll be working. He asked me to get coffee with him afterward.'

This seemed to satisfy Will. 'Excellent. Do send him my best.' He folded his hands together and leaned forward like an eager girlfriend waiting for the latest update. 'I command you to invite him to brunch next Sunday,' he said as Simon finally arrived.

'Sammy? Ooh, great idea! It'll just be the four of us. Give us a chance to really meet this young man,' Simon chimed in. Clearly, my big secret relationship with Sammy was nothing of the sort.

'As great as that sounds, guys, Sammy cooks brunch on Sundays at Gramercy Tavern, so he can't come to ours. Maybe another time,' I added when they looked crestfallen.

'Well, perhaps we'll make our way over there,' Will said half-heartedly. 'I hear it's a decent meal.'

Simon nodded unenthusiastically. 'Yes, why don't we? That sounds quite nice. At some point . . .'

And finally, blessedly, the conversation shifted to their upcoming trip to the Caribbean, and I was left to sit silently, feigning interest while I dreamed about my romantic, late-night coffee date with my new boyfriend.

27

Monday was a blur. I was so excited to see Sammy after work that I floated through the day in a dream-like state. I recalled not one subject that we discussed during the morning meeting, and even though I'd sat through the entire thing, I had to ask one of the List Girls to make me a copy of the notes she took so I could familiarize myself with what had been covered. The office was in full mobilization mode now that the *Playboy* party was rapidly approaching, and even though I was officially in charge, I couldn't concentrate. I ducked out at lunch to get a manicure. At three, I announced I was grabbing coffee, but I actually bolted to the tailor to pick up the sexy cocktail dress I'd gotten over the weekend, which was now newly shortened. By the time six o'clock rolled around, I started mumbling lies and weaving unintelligible stories about my parents, Uncle Will, a sick friend – anything that would allow me to leave early and have a full couple of hours to get home, decompress, and groom myself to within an inch of sanity. I emailed Kelly and Elisa that I'd be able to check out the *In Style* party that night and report back the next day, and then I walked out of the office at exactly six-thirty.

The evening disappeared in a whirlwind of primping activity (including shaving, scrubbing, plucking, filing, brushing, painting, and moisturizing), and by the time the cab pulled up to Bungalow, I was nearly breathless with anticipation. Will had hustled me off to Bergdorf's after brunch the day before and insisted on buying me the gorgeous Chaiken dress. It had a magical empire waist that made my own midsection look nonexistent, a skirt that flowed gracefully down to my knees. I'd never before owned a single item quite that gorgeous or expensive; from the moment I'd zipped it on an hour earlier, I just knew that the night was going to be special.

Sammy's expression as I stepped out of the taxi didn't disappoint. I watched him as his eyes covered the distance from my sparkly silver heels to the super-glam chandelier earrings Penelope had bought me for my last birthday. His smile grew wider until he finally finished looking and said, 'Wow.' It was followed by something that sounded like a low moan, and I thought I might die of happiness.

'You like it?' I asked, resisting the urge to twirl around. By some miracle, we were alone on the sidewalk, the last of a group of smokers having just ducked back inside.

'Bette, you look absolutely beautiful,' he said, and it sounded like he actually meant it.

'Thanks! You look pretty good yourself.' *Breezy and light*, I kept reminding myself. *Keep it breezy and light, and leave him wanting more.*

'Are we still on for later?' he asked, giving a 'one-second' gesture to two girls who'd just approached the velvet rope.

'Sure. I'm up for it if you are. . . .' My words were casual, but it took tremendous control for me not to choke with hopefulness.

'Definitely. If you don't mind waiting, I can probably be out of here by one. One-fifteen, latest. I know a good place nearby.'

I breathed a sigh of relief that he wasn't going to cancel. No matter that one A.M. was still a solid four hours away, or that I'd be a zombie at work the next day. None of it mattered one tiny bit because in a survivable period of time, I was going to be tucked into a corner booth with my head resting on Sammy's strong, solid shoulder, sipping my tiny espresso and laughing girlishly at the delicious things he'd be whispering in my ear – things like how it was time that each of us end whatever 'situations' we had with Isabelle and Philip so we could be together, fully and with honesty; how he'd never met anyone who understood him as well as I did; and how it was so incredible that we'd known each other as kids back in Poughkeepsie. He'd tell me that it wouldn't be easy – us being together, what with the social and professional pressures we'd both face – but that we had something worth fighting for, and he was ready and willing. I would pretend to think this all over, nodding occasionally and cocking my head at certain words, as if to say, 'Why, I can see what you mean,' and when I finally looked up at him and agreed that yes, this was all sounding like a good idea, he would pull me toward him and kiss me, at first softly and then with more urgency. From that moment on we'd be together in every sense of the word, best friends and lovers and soul mates, and while there'd surely be challenges, we'd get through it all side by side. I'd read the same story play itself out so many times in my novels that I could barely believe I finally had my own real-life version.

'Sure, that sounds great.' And before he could change his mind or say another word, I gracefully (I hoped) sashayed past him, opened the door myself, and glided into the packed room.

One o'clock rolled around with surprising swiftness. I capitalized on my good mood by circulating around the room, chatting first with Elisa and then Davide and then a few guys I knew peripherally through Avery. Nothing could ruin my night, not even catching a glimpse of Abby, skulking in a darkened corner beside the bar. She caught me looking at her and before I realized what was happening, she was standing next to me, hugging me in greeting. I pulled myself away and took a step back, examined her face as though I were trying to place it, and then simply turned around and walked away. For a split second she called out my name and tried to follow me, but I stuck my right hand in the air as I walked in the opposite direction, and by the time I reached Kelly & Company's table, she had disappeared. I'd just calmly poured myself a glass of champagne when Sammy walked over and motioned that he could leave.

We walked for nearly ten blocks before reaching a tiny diner that still had Christmas candles in its windows. He held the door for me and then chose a small corner booth – just like I'd envisioned. I blew on my hands to warm them, and when I wrapped them around my mug of hot chocolate, Sammy placed his own over mine.

'Bette, I have to ask you something,' he said, his eyes meeting mine directly.

I nearly gasped but was able to control my breath. *Ask me something? Ask me what? Ask me if I am dating anyone else because you think now would be a good time to stop? Ask me if I can actually see myself being your lifelong partner? The answer is yes, yes, of course, Sammy, but isn't it a tad early for that discussion?* I was considering all of these possibilities and more when he said, 'I need to ask for your patience.'

That sort of brought things to a grinding halt. *My patience?* I didn't know for sure, but that didn't sound like the opening of a commitment conversation to me. At least not the way it happened in any self-respecting romance novel.

As usual, any previous command I had of the English language had vanished.

'My patience?' I repeated.

'Bette, I want to make this work – more than anything – but I need you to be patient with me. I got a phone call this morning that blew me away.'

'What kind of phone call?' I asked. This was *definitely* not good news.

'From a lawyer. Some partner at a huge firm in midtown. He said he represented some investors who might be interested in backing a new restaurant. Apparently, they have a stake in a bunch of different businesses, but no restaurants right now. They're looking to get behind a hot new chef – his words, not mine – and they're considering a few different options. He asked if it sounded appealing to me.'

Well, I don't know what I was expecting, but this wasn't it. Luckily, I remembered that I was expected to react. 'Congratulations!' I said automatically. 'That's just great news, don't you think?'

He looked relieved. 'I do – of course I do. It's just that if I want to pursue this, I'm going to be crazy busy. They want me to write up a pitch covering all my ideas on possible spaces, themes, decor, even preferred prep and sous and pastry chefs. I'd have to give them all that – and three entirely different menu proposals – in the next month.'

I finally understood the 'patient' part.

He continued, 'I barely have any time as it is with work and class, but this is going to take every possible free second I can find. The good news is that it'll allow me to put the brakes on the whole Isabelle situation, which is a huge relief, but I'm going to be busier than ever. I wouldn't ever ask you to wait for me, but, well, if there's any way you could understand that—'

'Don't say another word,' I said, leaning in toward him across

246

the table. 'I understand completely, and I couldn't be happier for you.' I forced myself to say what I knew was right, and when I was rehashing the conversation later on, back in my own apartment with Millington on my lap, I congratulated myself on getting the words out. It wasn't what I'd hoped to hear, that much was sure, but like every single heroine I'd ever read about, I would fight for what I wanted.

I managed to smile at Sammy even though he looked genuinely distraught. 'You'll be great,' I said. We held hands across the table, and I squeezed his as I said this. We finished our drinks and I held back the tears until he put me in a cab. This was just another small obstacle to overcome, and I was willing to do it. Anything worth having was worth working for, and Sammy was worth having. If patience was what it took, then patience was what I had. Sammy and I were clearly meant to be together.

28

'Okay, everyone, this is it. Quiet down now, and let's get started!' Kelly had just inhaled her fourth Diet Coke and ordered her fifth as we settled in for our final meeting before the *Playboy* party. We were at a secluded sectioned-off table at Balthazar, Kelly's favorite lunch place and her preferred venue for working meetings before big events. The food had just arrived; Kelly pushed aside her Niçoise salad and stood up from the table, shaking slightly with caffeine nerves.

'As you all know, tomorrow is D-day. We'll run through the checklist together, but this is a mere formality. Why, you may ask, is this a mere formality? Because everything – *everything* – will be executed without a hitch. If there is *ever* a time for perfection, it's tomorrow night. And just in case there's any doubt in anyone's mind, it will be fucking *perfect*, because I won't have it any other way.'

We were all nodding, accustomed to Kelly's pre-event pep rallies, when there was a slight commotion at the door. Our table turned to look, along with everyone else in the restaurant. Leo spoke first.

'Ashlee and Jessica Simpson with' – he strained his neck to assess the accompanying group – 'that kid, what's his name? The one Ashlee was dating on and off? Ryan something? And the girls' father.'

'Who's on it?' Kelly barked.

'Got it,' Elisa snapped back.

She pulled her cell phone from her massive peacock blue Marc Jacobs Stella bag and began scrolling through numbers. She found the one she was looking for and pressed Send. Ten seconds later she was talking rapidly as we all listened.

'Hi, this is Elisa from Kelly & Company. Yeah, exactly. Anyway, I just got word that the girls are in town, and we would love to host them at our *Playboy* party tomorrow.' It was assumed that the person on the other line knew all about the party. After all, who didn't?

Elisa smiled and gave Kelly a knowing look while pointing at her phone. 'Yes, of course. No, I understand entirely. We'll be willing to provide a completely private fifteen-minute arrival window so they won't share the carpet with anyone else, and naturally they'll be escorted to their own table in the VIP section.'

She paused to listen and then said, 'The girls will have a personal concierge all night, so anything they need can be arranged immediately. I can guarantee they'll be subjected to absolutely no interviews; however, if they'd be so kind as to pose for a few select photographers, it would be our pleasure to cover the cost of their hotel suites, hair and makeup, transportation, and, if required, wardrobe selection.'

Another pause, and then a frown. 'Yes, of course they'll both be there. Mm-hmm, I'd be happy to set that up for you.' Her excitement had subsided and she was now clearly faking it. 'Great! I'll be in touch first thing tomorrow morning so we can arrange all the details. I so look forward to seeing them tomorrow night. Fabulous! Ciao!'

'Well done!' Kelly said as our group broke into light applause, reminding me again that Kelly was, as far as bosses go, pretty great. 'What was their final request that you said we could accommodate?'

Elisa gritted her teeth. 'Oh, the publicist mentioned how both girls have crushes on Philip Weston. She wanted to know if he would come over and meet them.'

Kelly screeched. 'Of course! Too easy! Bette, you and Philip will greet those girls the moment they walk in and show them to their seats. Tell Philip to flirt, flirt, flirt. Elisa, have Bette call and follow up with the publicist tomorrow, okay? Speaking of which, Bette, how are we doing with your end?'

I could feel Elisa staring at me, and I sensed the look wasn't filled with love. 'Uh, everything seems to be in order.' My focus was the midnight surprise. I'd been working on it nonstop for the past month, ironing out every minute detail, and I was finally confident it was going to be spectacular. Kelly had approved my plan but insisted it stay between us, since she didn't want to risk anything being leaked to the press. As a result, no one but the two of us and Hef himself had any idea what was happening at midnight. 'The midnight show is a go – I expect everything will run smoothly there.'

Elisa yawned loudly.

I continued. 'I've credentialed all the press with passes that are impossible to copy, alter, or fake, and each will be sent by messenger to its recipient exactly one hour before start time. Here are copies of the press grid' – I paused here to pull out a stack of papers and pass them around the table – 'with every reporter and photographer who will be in attendance; what, if anything specific, they're most interested in covering; who they tend to feature the most; the people and places each will or will not be able to access; and, of course, their drink preferences.'

Kelly nodded and studied the sheet. 'Are escorts listed on here?'

'Certainly. Everyone from the office will take turns, according to my schedule, escorting various members of the press to ensure they're exposed to the people we'd like them to meet.'

'I had a final meeting yesterday with the production company we're using, and I'm comfortable with how that side is shaping up,' Elisa interjected. 'Their plans for bar layout, bartenders, lighting, risers, music, decorations, and catering all seem to mesh with our instructions and the client's preferences.'

Kelly pushed the lettuce around on her plate and then changed her mind, choosing to sip her chardonnay instead. 'Okay, that's good,' she murmured. 'But back to this press situation for a minute. Bette, did you touch base with all the photo editors to let them know they have our full cooperation with anything they might need?'

'I did. I had a couple of the interns call them at the beginning of the week, and they reached everyone by Wednesday. All in all, I think we're in great shape.'

The lunch meeting continued like this for another hour before Kelly gave us the rest of the afternoon off to go home, attend grooming appointments, try to relax, and mentally prepare ourselves for the following evening. I'd already planned to stay in that night – with Millington and a huge bowl of extra-buttered microwave popcorn – and watch bad movie after bad movie on TNT, so I was ecstatic to hear that I had the afternoon off, too. Of course, the extra time would mean even more opportunity to think about Sammy. It hadn't been too much of a problem the past couple of weeks because I'd been swamped with prep work, but I shuddered to think of how much I could obsess if given a little free time.

Kelly paid the check and everyone was saying good-bye when Elisa pulled me aside.

'Can I talk to you for a minute?' she asked.

'Sure, what's going on?'

'Look, I know that things have gotten a little weird between us, but I really think we should do our best to work together tomorrow night. Neither of us wants to spend the whole night *working*, so we need to figure out a system where only one of us is on and the other can relax. And then switch. You know?'

I was surprised to hear her acknowledge that there was tension between us, but I was glad she no longer seemed so annoyed. 'Sure, sounds good. I can't imagine there's going to be much time tomorrow to do anything besides *deal*, but we can try, you know?'

This was apparently all she needed to hear. 'Great. That sounds great. See you tomorrow, Bette!'

I watched as she tightened her fringed scarf around her emaciated neck and ducked into the cold street. *Strange girl*, I thought, watching her hail a cab. I waited until her taxi had pulled away before heading outside myself. I had all afternoon to myself for the first time in recent memory, and I didn't want to waste a single second of it.

29

I'd just finished *You've Got Mail* and was halfway through *Can't Buy Me Love* when the phone rang. I was surprised to see Penelope's number come up on caller ID – surprised and thrilled. I'd given her the bare-bones rundown on Sammy, but she had no idea how much I adored him. I'd managed to read between the lines of her upbeat soliloquies to determine that Avery wasn't around a whole lot, that she still hadn't found a job, and that the couples they were hanging out with weren't exactly her type, but she wouldn't admit any of this outright. Left with not much to say, we emailed each other silly forwards and texted stupid things and spoke very occasionally about safe subjects, but I couldn't remember the last time I'd received a good, old-fashioned, late-night call from my best friend.

'Hey, B, how are you? Sorry to be calling so late, but the time difference really sucks and I figured you might still be up. Avery's out of town again and I don't really have anyone else out here to call and bother, so you're the lucky winner tonight!'

Her voice sounded hollow and I wished we were closer. 'Pen, I'm so glad you called! How are you?'

'I didn't wake you, did I?'

'Hardly. Just watching bad movies. What's going on with you? It's so good to hear from you.'

'Is your British trust-fund boyfriend there?' she asked.

Had everything been normal, Penelope would have already analyzed a hundred times over with me what Sammy's 'being patient' meant, and would have reassured me repeatedly that it was only a matter of time before he and I would be together. Now, despite knowing about Sammy, she didn't even seem to understand that I wasn't actually dating Philip.

'Pen, he's not my boyfriend, you know that. Philip and I are expected to go to the *Playboy* party together, but only for the photos.'

'Right, of course. When is that? That's a big deal, right?'

'It's tomorrow night! It's stressful because we've been working on it forever now and I'm pretty much first-in-command, after Kelly. But so far it seems like everything's in line. If the photographers behave themselves and the Bunnies all show up, we should be okay.'

We continued on like this for a few minutes, neither of us acknowledging that we had huge knowledge gaps about each other's lives.

'So what do you plan to do about Abby and the fact that she keeps printing those lies about you?' she asked, sounding like the old Penelope for the first time all night.

I'd been trying not to think about it, but when I did, the anger – the feeling of being violated – was enough to drive me mad. 'I still can't figure out why she hates me so much. It's torture not being able to confront her. Do you think people really believed that I was having an affair with the Hilton sex-tape guy? I don't even know his name!'

'No one does,' she said, clucking quietly. 'I have no idea what her problem is, although I guess it's not such a stretch to imagine her printing all this trash about you when she used to steal people's papers in college and pass them off as her own, right? Do you remember sophomore year when she skipped her grandmother's funeral because they were interviewing new columnists for the paper? The girl is seriously disturbed. Avery always said she's the type who'd sell out her own parents to get ahead, and I think he's right. He slept with her, of course, so I guess he'd know.'

'What? Avery had sex with Abby? I didn't know that.'

'I'm not totally sure, but I'm assuming he has. All of his friends did. Hell, every guy we know did her in college. I think I'd rather not know for sure, but if I had to bet . . .'

I swallowed a wave of nausea at the thought and mustered the energy to say, 'So how is that fiancé of yours, anyway? You said he was out of town?'

Her sigh said more than any of the words that followed. 'He's fine, I guess. I haven't seen a lot of him, that's for sure. I thought it would change once he was back in school and had to be on campus every day, but it's only given him more free time to stay out late. He's met a whole new crew of friends, so I guess that's good.'

'Do you like any of their girlfriends?'

She snorted. 'What girlfriends? They're all twenty-two-year-old kids, right out of school. He acts like he's the godfather and they're his acolytes. It's slightly disturbing, but how can I say anything?'

Well, that made two of us. I tried to steer the conversation to something more neutral. 'I'm sure it's just a period of adjustment. Are you guys at least exploring the city? I know LA's no New York, but there's got to be something to do there, right?'

'I go to the beach occasionally. Shop at Whole Foods, signed up for yoga, doing the whole Jamba Juice thing. Interviewing a lot. I know something will come up, but so far there's been nothing interesting. Avery'll be back the day after tomorrow, so maybe we'll take a little road trip to Laguna. Or Mexico again – that was nice. If he doesn't have to study the entire time.' She sounded so listless that I wanted to cry for her.

'Where is he, honey? How long has he been gone?'

'Oh, he's just back in New York for a few days. Family business of some sort – a meeting with his trust administrator and accountant or something like that. I'm not sure what, exactly, but I had an interview today, so he said he could handle it alone and there was no reason for me to fly all the way across the country.'

'Got it. Well, I wish you were here to come with me to the *Playboy* party. I'd put you on Bunny patrol, have you scout the room and make sure all their tails stay attached. Sounds awesome, huh?'

'Sure does. Bette, I miss you a lot.'

'I miss you, too, Pen. And if you feel like it, get on a plane and come home for a visit. You didn't move to Guam, you're just on the left coast. If you're feeling a little homesick, we'd love to see you for a visit. Maybe you and me and Abby can go out for lunch and then read in the paper the next day that we were both seen having sex with the Giants' entire defensive line. Doesn't that sound fab?'

She laughed and I wanted to hug her. 'To tell you the truth, I'm not necessarily opposed to having sex with the entire team. That's not bad, is it?'

'It's sure not, honey, it's sure not. Listen, I've got to try and sleep a little because tomorrow's going to be brutally long, but can we talk when the party's finally over?'

'Sure. It's just so good to hear your voice. Good luck getting through tomorrow night with no major scandals. I love you, B.'

'I love you, too, Pen. Things are going to get better from here, I promise. I miss you, and I'll talk to you soon.'

I placed the receiver back on its base and crawled into bed to finish the movie, happy just knowing that Penelope and I would somehow be okay.

30

'Check, one-two-three, check. Can everyone hear me? Count off. One . . .' I called into my earpiece, waiting for everyone else to call their numbers and let me know that the headphones were working. When Leo called out number sixteen, I knew we had everyone, and I took a deep breath. Guests were just beginning to show up and I was frantically trying to stem the tide of problems that wouldn't seem to stop. All my cool confidence and perfect plans from the day before were starting to seep away, and it was getting harder to quell my panic.

'Skye, can you hear me?' I hissed into the microphone that crawled stealthily out of my ear and stopped right above my top lip.

'Bette, honey, I'm right here. Calm down, everything's just fine.'

'I'll calm down when you tell me that the step-and-repeat is finally finished. It looked like shit ten minutes ago.'

'I'm standing outside, and it's all good. Thirty feet of *Playboy* Bunny logos on cardboard, just waiting for celebs to step in front of it for pictures. They put the finishing touches on it just a minute ago, and it should be dry in another few minutes. No worries.'

'Elisa? Do we have the final schedule for press set up and with security? Sammy from Bungalow 8 is in charge of the VIP entrance, so he needs to know which photographers are allowed where.' I was barking orders like a lunatic and hating the sound of my own voice with every passing minute. I hadn't hesitated when I'd said Sammy's name, though, and that was progress. He'd kissed me on the cheek when I'd arrived a few hours earlier and whispered 'Good luck,' and it was all I could do not to faint. The only thing getting me through the night was the knowledge that we would be in the same room for the next six hours.

'Check. *ET* and *Access Hollywood* have prime placement. E! was still wavering on whether they were coming – they're pissy they didn't get the exclusive – but if they send someone, we're ready. All of those plus CNN, MTV, and a guy who's doing a party documentary for Fox and has clearance from some big-name studio head are being allowed inside; regular tabloid paparazzi will remain outside. Everyone's been briefed on who's who and who's VIP enough to use this entrance. There's just one question. Who's Sammy?'

I couldn't very well point out over the mic that Sammy was hooked up to our system and listening to every word we were saying – nor that the mere sight of him set my nerves on fire. 'Elisa, very cute. Just give him the list, okay?' I prayed she would drop it at that, but in her hunger-induced perma-haze, she persevered.

'No, seriously, Bette. Who's Sammy?' she whined. 'Oh, wait, he's head of the production crew, right? Why does he need a finalized VIP list?'

'Elisa, Sammy is in charge of security tonight. We weren't thrilled with the idea of using Sanctuary's gestapo door people, so Sammy was kind enough to help us out. He should be out front, going over the last-minute details. Just get him a list.' I thought that would be the end of it, but of course Elisa wasn't finished.

'Oh, wait! Sammy. Isn't he that guy Isabelle was keeping on commission? Totally! I remember now. He was in Istanbul with us, wasn't he? She had him racing around like a slave all weekend. You thought they were—'

'What? Elisa? I can't hear you. I'm talking to Danny right now, so I'm muting my headphones. Back in a few.' I tore the headphones off and collapsed on one of the banquettes, trying not to imagine what Sammy had just thought of that little exchange.

'What up?' the ever-articulate Danny asked from his post at the bar. He was ogling the Bunnies as they scampered from place to place, preparing themselves for the onslaught of grabby men and jealous women.

'Nothing, nothing. I think we're actually ready, don't you?'

'Word.'

'Is there anything you can think of that I'm missing?'

He downed his third beer in five minutes. 'Nope.' He belched.

I looked around and was pleased with what I saw. The club had been transformed to the perfect space for celebrating fifty years of centerfolds. We had two entrances set up, one for VIPs and one for everyone else, each shrouded in a black tent with plenty of red carpet and logos. The security guys would all be wearing suits and subtle earpieces so as to remain as inconspicuous as possible. After entering an outside tent, each guest would be admitted to a long hallway shrouded in black, which culminated in a sweeping staircase adorned with filmy black curtains. Upon climbing the stairs and stepping through the curtains, they'd find themselves on a raised stage of sorts, a platform where everyone could watch as they descended the stairs into the main room. An eighty-five-foot bar occupied the left side of the room, where thirty-five female bartenders in hot pants, bikini tops, and bunny ears would be mixing drinks all night long. The wall behind the bar was covered in a floor-to-ceiling collage of *Playboy* centerfolds from the last fifty years: each was in full color and blown up to double poster size, and they were stuck together in no apparent pattern (save for the abundance of pre–bikini wax shots). We'd placed the VIP area on the far right side, a roped-off section of black velour banquettes and RESERVED signs resting next to the bottle chillers on each glass table. Gleaming from the exact center of the room was a circular stage shaped like a massive, multitiered cake. The bottom two tiers would provide dancing space for the Bunnies at the midnight performance, and the top level would be uncovered to reveal our surprise guest. A huge, 360-degree dance floor wrapped around the cake-shaped stage and was adorned with low velour benches around its perimeter.

'Hey, how is everything?' Kelly asked, twirling to show off her ultra-tight, ultra-short, barely opaque wrap dress. 'You like it?'

'You look amazing,' I said and meant it.

'Bette, I'd like you to meet Henry. Henry, this is one of my brightest stars, Bette.'

A pleasant-looking but entirely nondescript man of about forty – medium height, average build, brown hair – reached out his hand and revealed one of the warmest smiles I'd ever seen. 'So nice to meet you, Bette. Kelly's told me a lot about you.'

'All good, I hope,' I said without an ounce of creativity. 'Having fun, I hope? Things should really get going soon.'

They both laughed and looked at each other with such enthusiastic affection that it was impossible not to hate them.

By ten o'clock the party was fully under way. Hef took up the two most prominent VIP tables with his six girlfriends and drank Jack Rabbits, some combination of Jack Daniel's and Diet Coke. Scattered at tables around him were assorted celebs and their entourages: James Gandolfini, Dr Ruth, Pamela Anderson, Helen Gurley Brown, Kid Rock, Ivanka Trump, and Ja Rule all appeared content enough with the unlimited drinks and the platters of bunny-shaped chocolates and strawberries that we'd provided for them. The commoners were just starting to hit that point where they'd had a few drinks and were ready to dance, and the Bunnies were in full circulation, brushing up against every guy and most of the girls in the room. They were captivating to watch. Nearly two hundred of them in bunny ears, black satin bustiers, and thongs pulsated through the room, shaking their bottoms to emphasize their bunny tails and pushing their pelvises forward to show off the little horse-race ribbons that announced their names and hometowns. What the men didn't realize was that the real party was in the down-stairs ladies' room, where the Bunnies gathered to smoke, chat, and make fun of the gaping men. They had to unzip their bustier outfits and completely climb out of them in order to pee, and they weren't able to get dressed again without help. I leaned against a wall, staring, waiting for a stall to open, as one blond girl reached out and cupped another Bunny's huge, pillow-like breasts with two hands. She admired them for a few seconds before asking – boobs still in hand – 'Real or created?'

The fondled one giggled and gave a little shimmy. 'Girlfriend, these are entirely store-bought.' Then she squatted, leaned forward, and mashed her breasts as tight as they'd go against her chest while motioning for the fondler to zip her up. When she straightened up again, the black satin barely covered her nipples, and she looked like she might just topple forward from the weight imbalance. They finished their sneaked cosmos, left the empty glasses on the sink, and half-ran, half-hopped back upstairs to rejoin the party.

When I made it back myself, I did another cursory check over the headphones with everyone to see that all was progressing as planned, and there were blessedly few emergencies: a fallen disco ball that hadn't hit anyone, a couple of minor fights that Sammy and his crew had already dismantled, and a shortage of maraschino cherries due to hungry Bunnies who were reportedly grabbing them from behind the bar by the fistful. Elisa seemed to be sober and in control of the VIP lounge, while Leo had managed to keep his pants on long enough to patrol the bar and dance floor. There was only an hour to go until the midnight surprise and it was time for me to focus on that.

The surprise midnight performance had been my baby, something I'd been working on especially hard since returning from Turkey, and I was desperate for it to go well. At that moment, only Kelly, the head PR person from *Playboy,* and Hef himself knew what to expect, and I couldn't wait to see everyone's reactions. I was just getting ready to triple-check with Sammy and his staff at the door that they knew to refuse admission to Abby if she tried to get in when I heard his voice crackle on the headset.

'Bette? Sammy here. Jessica and Ashlee just pulled up.'

'Copy, I'll be there in a second.' I grabbed a gin and tonic from the main bar to bribe Philip with, but I couldn't find him anywhere. Not wanting the sisters to go unescorted, I sent the announcement out over the headset for anyone who saw Philip to meet me at the front door, then dashed there just as they were stepping out of the Bentley we had sent to fetch them.

'Hi, guys,' I said, rather ungracefully. 'We're all so glad you could make it. Come on in, and I'll show you around.' I guided them down the red carpet, squinting through the flashbulbs.

They posed like pros for their required fifteen minutes, jutting out their hips and putting their arms around each other and walking jauntily in their matching five-inch silver heels before following me past Sammy (who winked) and straight to the VIP section. I beckoned to the gorgeous guy we'd hired to attend to their every need and bolted off to find Philip, who had, as of yet, remained elusive.

Although I radioed out numerous SOS messages and patrolled the room myself a number of times, I couldn't seem to find him anywhere. I was just getting ready to send someone into the men's room to see if he was inside doing God knows what when I glanced at my watch. It was five minutes to twelve, and the show would be starting any minute. I raced upstairs and signaled the DJ, who cut off 'Dancing Queen' halfway through and played an electronic drumroll. This was the signal. Hef extricated himself from his gaggle of girlfriends and climbed slowly to the second tier of the stage, tapping once on the microphone before booming, 'Thank you all for coming.' He was cut off by the frantic, screaming cheers of the crowd, who clapped and yelled and chanted, 'Hef, Hef, Hef!'

'Yes, thank you. Thank you all so much for coming to celebrate with me and my crew' – he paused briefly to wink at the crowd, which invited all-out hooting – 'fifty years of important stories, celebrated writers, and, of course, beautiful girls!' The crowd continued to holler throughout the speech, reaching an almost deafening level when he thanked everyone for a final time and made his way back to the front-and-center tables where his women awaited. A few people thought it was over and started to head back to the bar or the dance floor, but they froze in place when the DJ began to play 'Happy Birthday to You.' Before anyone realized what was happening, a tiny, circular stage – just big enough for one person to stand on – began to rise from the center of the cake. It moved upward until the shadow of a woman could be seen behind the sheer curtain that covered it as everyone stood, rooted to the floor, their necks craning toward the ceiling. When the mini-platform stopped about three stories above the crowd, the gauzy white material simply melted away and standing there in a tight, shimmering, beaded purple evening gown with a fur boa was Ashanti, looking ravishing. She proceeded to sing in a low, throaty voice the sexiest rendition of 'Happy Birthday to You' I'd ever heard. It was an obvious tribute to Marilyn Monroe's famous performance for JFK, only Ashanti dedicated her performance to Hef, calling him 'the president of pussyland,' and when she finished, the room went wild. Gold glitter confetti rained down while the crowd cheered and every Bunny in the room – all eighty-five of them – kicked chorus line–style around the lower level of the stage. The DJ immediately segued into 'Always on Time' and the dancing immediately escalated from excited to frenzied. I heard a guy behind me scream into his cell phone, 'Dude, this is the party of the fucking century!' and more than a few newly formed couples began making out on the dance floor. Except for the 'pussyland' comment, everything had gone exactly as I'd planned – probably even better.

Elisa and Leo and Sammy had already reported into the headsets that it was a huge hit; even Kelly had managed to grab a headset and shriek her approval into it. The euphoria lasted another whole seven or ten minutes, until everything started barreling downhill at warp speed, threatening to take me with it. I was roaming through the VIP lounge looking for Philip when, tucked away in the darkest corners of the roped-off section, I spotted a very familiar blond head bobbing between a pair of Bunny-like breasts. I looked around frantically for a camera, hoping, praying that one would snap a picture of Philip nibbling this girl's cleavage and plaster it across every paper in the city so I could finally, blessedly, be finished with him. It seemed strange to see him being this intimate with a girl so soon after seeing him being *that* intimate with a guy, but it was an easy out for me, and one I wanted. I realized this was my chance: I would gladly play the part of betrayed girlfriend if it meant having a reason to be done with him once and for all. I leaned over to tap him on the shoulder, eager to put on an indignant public performance, but I physically recoiled when the boy turned around and snapped, 'What the fuck do you want? Can't you see I'm busy here?'

It wasn't Philip. No British accent, no chiseled jaw, no I've-been-a-very-bad-boy grin. Much to my surprise, the face that stared back at me, the one contorted with anger and annoyance, belonged to someone else I knew well: Avery. His jaw went slack when he saw me. 'Bette,' he whispered.

'Avery?' I couldn't move, couldn't think, couldn't come up with a single appropriate thing to say. I was vaguely aware that the girl was peering at us both with some sort of smug look, but it was hard to make her out in the dark. Besides, nearly her entire mouth was swollen from kissing, and lipstick was smeared across her chin and cheek. But after I studied her for fifteen seconds, I realized I knew her, too. It was Abby.

'Bette, this is, uh, this isn't what it . . . Bette, you know Abby, don't you?'

He was noticeably perspiring and waving his hands in some sort of spastic, counterclockwise pattern, motioning to the girl while simultaneously trying to pretend she wasn't there.

'Bette! Great to see you again. Saw that piece about you the other day,' she trilled. Her hand worked its way quite deliberately over Avery's back, rubbing and kneading while I watched every movement, and she watched me watching her.

I continued to stare, still at a loss for words, realizing that Abby still assumed I was clueless about her professional identity. It was all too horrible to process, and since I couldn't decide which one to confront first, I just stood there. Apparently, Avery took this as an indication that he should keep talking. 'Penelope knows I'm in New York, and of course she knows I like to go out a lot, but um, I'm not sure it'd be the best thing for her to know about, uh, about this. She's, um, she's had a lot to adjust to with the move and everything and I think it'd be most, ah, most *considerate* to her if we didn't upset her any more, you know?' He slurred nearly every word.

Abby chose this moment to lean over and begin licking his earlobe, closing her eyes in feigned passion after looking directly at me. Avery brushed her away like a gnat and stood up, placing an arm underneath my elbow and leading me away from the table. He was approaching blackout drunk, but he still managed to move rather deftly.

I allowed myself to be led away for a second before I snapped back to reality and tore my arm from his grip. 'You bastard!' I hissed. I'd wanted to scream, but nothing came out.

'Is there a problem here?' Abby asked as she sidled up next to Avery.

I stared at her, nearly scared of my hatred. 'Problem? No, why would you say that? No problem at all. It's funny, though, I have this sneaking feeling that you won't be writing tomorrow about how you threw yourself at someone else's fiancé – someone you've known for more than eight years now. No, I imagine tomorrow's little column will have no mention of you or Avery at all. Rather, it'll be some charming little story about how I was stealing tips off the bar or doing drugs with the dancers or having group sex with the photographers, right?'

They both stared at me. Abby spoke first.

'What are you saying, Bette? You really are making no sense.'

'Oh, is that so? Interesting. It's rather unfortunate for you that I know you're Ellie Insider. You want to know why that sucks for you so much besides the fact that it's a really stupid fucking name? Because I won't rest until everyone else knows, too. I'll call every reporter, editor, blogger, and assistant in this entire city and tell them who you are and how you lie. But I'll have the most fun telling your editor the whole story. Throw the words *libel* and *lawsuit* around, just for fun. Maybe she'd be interested to hear how you nearly got kicked out of school for stealing other people's papers? Or perhaps she'd find the story of the night you slept with not one, not two, not three, but *four* guys from the lacrosse team amusing? Hmm, Abby, what do you think?'

'Bette, listen, I – ' Avery appeared not to have heard a word of what I'd said, clearly concerned only with how this would affect his own life.

'No, Avery, *you* listen,' I hissed with more venom in my voice than I'd ever heard as I turned away from Abby and toward him. 'You have one week from today's date to tell Penelope. Do you hear me? One week, or she hears it from me.'

'Jesus Christ, Bette, c'mon, you have no idea what you're saying. Hell, you have no idea what really happened. Nothing was going on.'

'Avery, listen to me. Can you hear me? One week.' I turned to walk away, silently praying he wouldn't call my bluff and make me tell her. It'd be hard enough to tell my best friend that her dirtbag fiancé had abandoned her in a new city to come home for a weekend of drinking and cheating, but it would especially suck having to do so when our own relationship was still a little rocky.

I'd made it a few feet when I felt Avery's arm wrap around my elbow and tighten. He yanked so hard I tripped and would have hit the ground facefirst had he not yanked me upward and pushed me onto a banquette. His face was two inches from mine, his hot, boozy breath heating my skin, and he sounded quite co-herent when he whispered, 'Bette. I will deny every fucking word you say. Who's she going to believe? Me, the guy she's *worshipped* for the last decade, or you, the friend who ditches her going-away party to hang out with some guy? Huh?' He leaned in even closer, hovering over me with his entire body and his face contorted into a pained, threatening expression, and I briefly wondered if knee-ing him in the balls would be appropriate. I wasn't really concerned for my safety so much as disgusted by his closeness, but I didn't have to make the decision; before I could work my knee into strike position, Avery's entire body seemed to float backward.

'Can I help you with something?' Sammy asked Avery as he held him upright by the back of his shirt.

'Dude, get the fuck off me. Who the hell are you?' Avery spat, looking drunker and meaner than I'd ever seen him before. 'This is none of your fucking business, you hear?'

'I'm security, and it is my fucking business.'

'Well, this is my friend here, and we were having a conversa-tion, so back the fuck off.' Avery straightened up in a failed attempt to recoup a shred of dignity.

'Oh, really? That's funny, because your *friend* looked pretty fucking unthrilled to be part of your "conversation." Now get out.'

I watched the two of them go back and forth as I rubbed my arm, wondering who would be the first to use the word *fuck* three times in a single sentence.

'Dude, chill out. No one asked for your assistance, okay? I've known Bette for a long fucking time now, so step aside and let us finish. Don't you, like, have drinks to serve or something?'

For the briefest moment I thought Sammy would hit Avery, but he pulled himself together, took a deep breath, and turned to me. 'Are you okay here?' he asked.

I wanted to tell him everything, explain that Avery was Penelope's future husband and tell him how I'd seen him with another girl and that other girl happened to be Abby, who happened to be Ellie Insider, and even though I always knew he was a cheating bastard, I'd never seen him so belligerent before. I wanted to throw my arms around Sammy's neck and thank him over and over again for watching out for me and stepping in when he thought I was in trouble and ask him his advice on what to tell Penelope and how to deal with Avery.

For just a moment I thought about doing just that – screwing the party, the job, what Abby would surely write the following day, just grabbing Sammy and walking away from all of it. But of course he knew what I was thinking, could see it on my face, and he leaned over and discreetly whispered, 'Stay cool. We'll talk about it later, Bette.' I was attempting to calm down when Elisa and Philip came ambling over, their arms linked.

'What's going on here?' Philip asked, appearing wholly disinterested with the entire scene.

'Philip, stay out of this, it's nothing,' I said, willing them both to disappear.

'Why don't you call your fucking goon off me, Elisa?' Avery whined after pouring himself another drink. 'This big meathead got himself involved where it's none of his business. I was having a little chat with an old friend and all of a sudden he went ballistic. Does he work for you?'

Having already lost interest in the whole situation, Philip drunkenly flopped onto the couch and immersed himself in mixing a gin and tonic. Elisa, however, did not like to hear that the hired help was bothering one of her favorite party boys.

'Who are you?' she asked Sammy.

He looked at her and smiled as if to say, Are you kidding, you idiot? We recently traveled to a foreign country together for five full days, and now you have no idea who I am? When he was met with a blank gaze, he merely said, 'I'm Sammy, Elisa. We've met a few dozen times at Bungalow 8, and we were in Istanbul together. I'm in charge of security tonight.' His voice was strong and even, without a hint of condescension or sarcasm.

'Mmm, that's really interesting. So what you're telling me is that because you work the door at Bungalow a few nights a week and serve as a boy toy to Isabelle Vandemark, you all of a sudden think you're justified in treating one of our friends – a VIP at that – this rudely?' It was obvious that she was tipsy and enjoying her demonstration of power in front of the whole group.

Sammy peered at her, expressionless. 'With all due respect, your friend was bothering my . . . was physically assaulting your coworker here. She didn't seemed pleased with his attentions, so I encouraged him to focus them elsewhere.'

'*Sammy?* Is that your name?' she said nastily. 'Avery Wainwright is one of our closest friends, and I know for a fact that Bette would never be uncomfortable around him. Shouldn't you be, like, breaking up fights in the bathroom or telling all those bridge-and-tunnel kids lined up outside that they're not welcome here?'

'Elisa,' I said quietly, unsure of what to say next. 'He was just doing his job. He thought I needed help.'

'Why are you defending him, Bette? I'll see to it that his superiors know he initiated an incident with one of our VIPs.' She turned to Sammy and held up an empty bottle of Grey Goose. 'In the meantime, make yourself useful and get us another bottle.'

'Elisa, honey, she's defending him because she's fucking him,' piped up a girl's voice from behind us. Abby. 'At least that's my guess. Philip, you can't be too psyched about that, now can you? Your girlfriend's fucking the Bungalow bouncer. Hot stuff,' she laughed.

Philip chuckled, none too eager to engage me in a who's-sleeping-with-whom tell-all. 'She is not.' He chuckled, stretching his legs out on the glass table. 'She may not be faithful to me, but I don't think we have to accuse her of shagging the staff. Bette, you're not shagging the staff, are you, love?'

'Sure she is.' Abby giggled. 'Hey, Elisa, why'd you never clue me in on that one? It's so obvious – you must have known. I can't believe I never saw it before.'

It was like getting hit over the head with a shovel. *Why'd you never clue me in on that one?* Everything became suddenly and horribly clear. Abby knew where I was and who I was with at all times because Elisa told her. It was that simple. End of story. The only part I didn't quite understand was why Elisa would do that in the first place. Abby wasn't so confusing: she was an all-around nasty, vengeful, mean-spirited girl who would sell out her own dying mother – or sleep with a friend's fiancé – if it meant furthering her career or her reputation by an inch. But why Elisa?

Elisa, having no idea what else to do, started to giggle and sip her champagne. She glanced at me only once – long enough for me to know it was true – and then looked away before I could say a word about it. Avery had begun pleading again, and Sammy had turned to walk back to the door with a disgusted look on his face. Only Philip was either too drunk or too indifferent to really understand what was happening. He persevered.

'Are you, babe? Are you having a romp with the bouncer?' Philip prodded, absently playing with Abby's hair as she watched me intently, a look of distinct pleasure on her face. It was only then I wondered if he, too, had known about Elisa and Abby's little alliance all along. Or worse – had he been involved with them, looking for some public heterosexual confirmation himself? It was too horrific to even imagine.

'Hmm, an interesting question, Philip,' I said as loudly as I dared. Avery, Elisa, Philip, Abby, and Sammy all turned to look at me. 'I think it's interesting that you're so fascinated with whether or not I've had sex with "the bouncer," as you put it. It can't be because you're jealous. After all, you and I have never progressed beyond a wet and rather sloppy make-out.'

Philip looked as though he might die. Everyone else looked confused.

'What? Oh, come on now, people, please! You all know everything about everyone, and you never even suspected that this self-proclaimed God's gift to New York women actually prefers men? Well, believe it.'

Everyone started speaking at once.

'Yeah, right,' Elisa said.

'Bette, love, why are you talking such rubbish?' Philip asked with a calmness in his voice that didn't match his expression.

A shout from an unidentified floater came out over my headphones that P. Diddy had just arrived unannounced, having come from an earlier party somewhere nearby. Normally, this arrival would have been cause for celebration; however, considering that tonight an entourage of one hundred people joined him, it was a disaster. Apparently, he was extremely unhappy that he'd been kept waiting so long at the door, but since Sammy had been inside, the second-in-command security guy hadn't wanted to make any decisions. Did we tell him he couldn't come in because we were already too crowded? Tell him he could choose ten friends and have the VIP table of his choice, but the rest of his group had to leave? Figure out how to toss out a hundred current partiers to accommodate his crew? And who, exactly, was going to be the lucky chosen conveyer of this news? No one was exactly jumping at the chance.

Before we could get squared away on the Diddy disaster, one of the interns called me with the news that high-profile boy-band guests were in the process of being arrested for buying drugs in the bathroom – the very same bathroom where one of New York's finest had briefly stopped at the end of his shift doing crowd control outside. The disturbing part of this information was obviously not the incident itself but the fact that, according to the intern, it was currently being captured by no fewer than five paparazzi – pictures that would, of course, overshadow in the tabs all the good stuff we'd hoped to promote.

The third call came from Leo. He informed me that somehow – and no one knew how – the production company had miscalculated during their ordering and had just run out of champagne.

'It's impossible. They knew how many people would be here. They knew our main concern over liquor and beer was champagne. Bunnies drink it. Girls drink it. Bankers drink it. The only way to keep girls somewhere late is to give them champagne. It's only twelve-thirty! What are we going to do?' I was screaming over the decibel-crushing sound of an Ashlee Simpson song.

'I know, Bette, I'm on it. I sent a few of the bartenders out in search of as many cases as they can find, but it's not going to be easy at this time of night. They can buy a few bottles at liquor stores, but I don't know where they're going to find mass quantities now,' Leo said.

'Bette, I need to know what you want me to do with, uh, with our waiting VIP,' the panicked floater at the door called over the headphones. 'He's getting restless.'

'Bette, are you there?' My earpiece crackled and Kelly's voice came booming through. She'd grabbed someone's headset again and was beginning to piece together what was happening. The usual nice boss lady was gone and she'd been replaced by a demonic monster. 'Are you aware that we have kids here getting arrested on drug charges? People do not get ARRESTED at our parties, do you hear me?'

She cut out for a moment, but then came through loud and clear. 'Bette! Can you hear me? I need you at this door pronto! Everything's falling apart, and you're nowhere. Where the hell are you?'

I watched as Elisa removed her headpiece – out of some deliberate sabotage or just plain wastedness, I couldn't tell – and flopped down next to Philip, where she began to vie with Abby for his attention. Why fight when you can drink? I was just working up the energy to deal with all the problems I cared so little about when I heard one final comment.

'Hey, mate? Yeah, you right there.' Philip, who was now cradling Abby under one arm and Elisa under the other, was calling out to Sammy. Avery sat babbling incoherently at his side.

'Yeah, man?' Sammy asked, still not quite sure Philip was addressing him.

'Be a good chap and bring us a bottle of something. Girls, what will we have? Bubbly? Or would you prefer some vodka drinks?'

Sammy looked like he'd been slapped. 'I'm not your waiter.'

Apparently Philip found this hysterical because he convulsed with laughter. 'Just get us a drink, will you, mate? I'm less interested in the details of how it happens.'

I didn't wait to see if Sammy would hit him or ignore him or retrieve the bottle of vodka. I wasn't thinking about much besides how comfortable a bed would be right then and how little I cared if P. Diddy brought one guest or a hundred or even showed up at all. It occurred to me that I'd been spending nearly every minute of every day and night with some of the worst people I'd ever met, and I had nothing to show for it but a shoebox full of clippings that humiliated not only me but also everyone I loved. As I stood there watching a photographer snap away at a mugging Philip and listened to even more problems ring out over the earpiece as though they were huge international crises, I thought of Will and Penelope and the book-club girls and my parents and, of course, Sammy. And again, with a sense of calm I hadn't felt in many months, I simply removed my headset, placed it on the table, and said quietly to Elisa, 'I'm finished.'

I turned to Sammy and, not caring who heard what, said, 'I'm going home. If you want to stop by later, I would love to see you. I'm at 145 East Twenty-eighth Street, apartment 1313. I'll wait for you.'

And before anyone could say anything, I turned away. I walked across the dance floor, past a couple who appeared to be having actual intercourse near the DJ, and straight on to the door, where a horde of people seemed to be swaying with the music. I saw Kelly out of the corner of my eye, and a few List Girls who were flirting with some of P. Diddy's group, but I managed to slip quietly past them and onto the sidewalk. The crowd there threatened to overtake the street, and no one was paying any attention to me. I made it halfway down the block without talking to anyone and was just opening the door to the cab I'd hailed when I heard Sammy call my name. He ran toward me and slammed the cab door shut before I could get inside.

'Bette. Don't do this. I can handle myself in there. Go on, head back inside, and we can talk about all this later.'

I stood on tiptoe to kiss his cheek and raised my arm to hail another cab. 'I don't want to go back inside, Sammy. I want to go home. I hope I'll see you later, but I've got to get out of here.'

He opened his mouth to protest, but I got in the cab. 'I can handle myself, too,' I said with a smile as I sat down. And I pulled away from the entire surging nightmare.

31

By two-thirty in the morning, there was still no sign of Sammy. My phone was ringing off the hook with calls from Kelly and Philip and Avery, but I ignored them all. I'd calmed down long enough to draft a letter of apology to Kelly, and by three I'd come to the conclusion that Elisa – unlike Abby – was not necessarily evil and malicious, just very, very hungry. When four rolled around and I still hadn't heard from Sammy, I began to fear the worst.

I fell asleep sometime around five and almost cried when I woke a couple of hours later to no messages and no Sammy.

He finally called at eleven the next morning. I thought about not answering the phone – decided that I wouldn't, actually – but just seeing his name on the little screen was enough to demolish my willpower.

'Hello?' I said. I was aiming for breeziness, but the noise that came out sounded like it resulted from a lack of oxygen.

'Bette, it's Sammy. Is this a bad time?'

Well, that depends, I wanted to say. *Are you calling to apologize for last night, or at the very least to offer some explanation of why you never came by? Because if that's the case, then this is the best time imaginable – come on in so I can whip you up a fluffy omelet and rub your sore shoulders and kiss you all over. However, if you're calling with even the slightest implication that something might be wrong – with you, with me, or worst of all, with us – then perhaps you should know that I'm very, very busy right now.*

'No, of course not. What's up?' That sounded laid-back and unconcerned, right?

'I wanted to see how it all worked out last night. I was so worried about you – you just left in the middle of everything.' He made no mention of my invitation for him to come over, but the concern in his voice more than made up for it. Just knowing he was interested started me talking, and once I started, I couldn't seem to stop.

'It was a shitty thing for me to just walk out of there in the middle of everything – really immature and so unprofessional. I should've stayed and seen the night through no matter how bad it was. But it was like I wasn't even in my own body. I just left. And I'm glad I did. Do you have any idea what happened last night?' I asked.

'Not really, but I do know that I seriously dislike those people, Bette. Why did that kid Avery have his hands all over you? What was going on?'

And so I explained everything. I told him how I'd found Philip and Leo together in Istanbul. I described the situation with Abby/Ellie, and how she'd gotten all her information from Elisa. I said that Elisa had seemed particularly competitive lately, and that I knew she wanted Philip, but I was shocked that she would do that to me. I told him all about Penelope and Avery, from their first meeting until the day they got engaged, and then I told him I'd found Avery making out with Abby. I confessed that I'd been skipping dinners at Will and Simon's and canceling a fair number of Sunday brunches because there always seemed to be something more pressing to do. I told him that I hadn't returned even one of Michael's phone calls asking to meet for a drink because I'd been too busy and didn't really know what to say. I admitted that my parents were so disappointed they could barely talk to me anymore, and that I had virtually no idea what was going on in my best friend's life. And I apologized to him for trying to hide or deny that we had been together because I was thrilled about it, not ashamed.

He listened and asked a few questions, but when I mentioned him, he sighed. Bad sign. 'Bette, I know you're not ashamed – I know it has nothing to do with that. We both agreed it would be best to keep this quiet considering our current situations. Don't be so hard on yourself. You did the right thing last night. I'm the one who should be apologizing.'

I untied a plastic bag of Red Hots and poured some into my hand. 'What are you talking about? You were great last night.'

'I should've punched that kid's face in,' he said. 'Plain and simple.'

'Which one? Avery?'

'Avery, Philip, what does it matter? It took every ounce of willpower not to kill him.'

This was the right thing for him to say, so why did my stomach still feel like it was on the floor? Was it because I wondered how worried he could have been that he didn't call for ten hours? Or that I still hadn't heard him mention a word about us getting together? Or maybe it was simpler, and I was just stressed about my unexpected unemployment – the reality of looking for yet another job was beginning to set in. I'd always known that banking wasn't for me, but it was disconcerting to try an entirely different industry – one that was undeniably more fun – and realize that I wasn't cut out for that, either. As if on cue, Sammy asked what I might do next, and I told him that Kelly had graciously offered me a few freelance projects when I'd called to apologize that morning, but she'd accepted my resignation without argument. I added that maybe it was time to suck up my pride and join Will. As my mind wandered, I realized I hadn't even asked what was happening with his restaurant.

When I pointed this out, he was quiet for a moment before he said, 'I have some good news.'

'You got it!' I shouted without thinking. Then I prayed for a second before adding, much more tentatively, 'Did you get it?'

'Yeah, I got it,' he said, and I could hear his smile. 'I turned in the pitch and the menu proposals in under two weeks. The lawyer said his clients were impressed. They chose me as their head chef, and they bought a little space in the East Village.'

I could barely speak from excitement, but he didn't seem to notice.

'Yeah, it's all going to happen very quickly. Apparently, some restaurant was all set to open, but the investors pulled out at the last second. Some sort of corporate scandal that trickled down, I think. Anyway, these silent investors stepped in and bought the place on the cheap. They began looking for a chef immediately, and they want to open as soon as possible. Can you believe it?'

'Congratulations!' I said with genuine enthusiasm. 'That's so amazing. I knew you could do it!' I meant it, of course, but the moment the words were out of my mouth, my gut switched tracks entirely. I hated myself for even thinking it, but this didn't sound like good news for us.

'Thanks, Bette. That means a lot to me. I couldn't wait to tell you.'

Before I could even consider editing my words, I blurted, 'But what does this mean for us?'

There was a moment of awful, hideous, all-pervasive silence, and yet I still didn't get it entirely. I knew we were meant to be together. The obstacles were not insurmountable, just stepping-stones to a stronger relationship.

When he finally did speak, Sammy sounded defeated, and not a little sad. 'I'm going to be married to this project' was all he managed to say, and the moment he uttered those words, I knew it wasn't happening. 'It' meaning 'us.'

'Of course,' I said automatically. 'This is the opportunity of a lifetime.'

It was at that point that a romance hero would say, 'And so are you, which is why I'm going to do everything in my power to make this work,' but Sammy didn't say that. Instead he spoke quietly. 'So much is timing, Bette. I have too much respect for you to ask you to wait for me, although of course part of me hopes you will.'

Damn you! I thought. *Just ask me to wait and I will, ask me to understand that things will be difficult but that when this period is over, we'll be happy and in love and together. Please stop with the dreaded respect line – I don't want you to respect me, I want you to want me.*

But I said none of this. Instead I wiped away the tears that dropped to my chin and concentrated on keeping my voice steady. When I finally did speak, I was proud of my composure and my articulateness. 'Sammy, I understand what an amazing chance this is for you, and I couldn't be any more excited for you than I am right now. You need to concentrate all your time and energy on making this restaurant fantastic. I promise that I'm not mad or upset or anything, just so incredibly happy for you. Go. Do what you need to do. I just hope you'll invite me to dinner when your place is inevitably the hottest restaurant in New York. Keep in touch, okay? I'll miss you.'

I placed the phone quietly on the receiver and stared at it for nearly five full minutes before I really started to cry. He didn't call back.

32

'Tell me again how my life will improve one day?' I said to Penelope as we sat in my living room. I was stretched out on my couch in full sweatpant mode, as I had been for nearly three and a half months, with no genuine desire to ever again put on street clothes.

'Oh, Bette, honey, of course it will. Just look how fabulously my own life is shaping up!' she sang sarcastically.

'What's on tonight? Did you remember to TiVo last week's *Desperate Housewives*?' I asked listlessly.

She threw down her copy of *Marie Claire* and glared at me. 'Bette, we watched it when it was on the actual television last Sunday. Why would we need to TiVo it?'

'I wanna watch it again,' I whined. 'Come on, there's got to be something decent to watch. What about *Going Down in the Valley*, that porn documentary on HBO? Do we have that saved?'

Penelope just sighed.

'What about *Real World*?' I pulled myself upright and began punching keys on the TiVo remote. 'We've got to have at least one shitty episode, even an old one. How can we not have any *Real Worlds*?' I was nearly in tears by that point.

'Christ, Bette, you've got to get ahold of yourself. This is just not okay anymore.'

She was right, of course. I'd been wallowing for so long that it had become standard. This period of unemployment didn't much resemble my first one; there were no blissful mornings spent sleeping in or exhilarating trips to the candy store or long walks exploring new neighborhoods. I wasn't trying to find a job – either enthusiastically or halfheartedly – and I was currently supporting myself (barely) by taking on some sympathy freelance fact-checking work from Will and a few of his associates. I tore through it in my flannel bathrobe on my couch each morning, and then felt perfectly justified in rotting the rest of the day. The fact that Penelope – who had every reason to be in far worse shape than I – was becoming more functional every day had begun to alarm me.

I hadn't heard from Sammy since our last conversation, the morning after the *Playboy* party, which had been three months, two weeks, and four days ago. Penelope had called minutes after I'd hung up with Sammy to tell me that she'd just spoken to Avery and 'knew everything.' Avery had called her during the party to admit that he'd been really, really drunk and had 'accidentally' kissed a random girl. That morning she was upset but still making excuses for him. Finally I'd worked up my nerve and told her the full story. When she confronted him, Avery admitted he'd been sleeping with Abby for some time, and that there'd been others as well.

Penelope had then very calmly instructed the housekeeper (who just so happened to be Avery's parents' engagement gift to the happy couple) to pack all of her possessions and ship everything back to New York. She booked two last-minute, first-class plane tickets on Avery's credit card, called for the largest and most luxurious stretch limo she could find, and proceeded to drink herself into champagne oblivion in the first-class cabin while stretched out across both seats. I'd met her at JFK and dragged her directly to the Black Door, where I joined her in getting blind drunk. For the first few weeks she stayed with her parents, who, to their credit, did not once tell her to forgive him or take him back, and when she couldn't take living at home anymore, she moved onto my couch.

Finally together, we had been miserable, heartbroken, and unemployed, and so were the perfect pair: we shared a bathroom, multiple bottles of wine, and the rent, and we watched a horrifying amount of exceptionally bad TV. Everything had been perfect until Penelope had gotten a job. She'd announced last week that she'd be reverse-commuting to a boutique hedge fund in Westchester, and that she would be moving to her own place in two weeks. I'd known our extended pajama party couldn't last forever, but I couldn't help feeling a teeny bit betrayed. She was doing so well that she even mentioned that the guy who'd interviewed her had been really, really cute. It was now stunningly obvious: Penelope was moving on, and I was destined to be a wretch forever.

'How long do you think I have to wait before I can go check out the restaurant?' I asked for what must have been the thousandth time.

'I've already told you, I'm happy to put on a disguise and

sneak in there with you. Very discreet – he doesn't even know me! Healthy? Maybe not. But definitely a good time.'

'Did you see the piece in *The Wall Street Journal*? They worship the place. It calls Sammy one of the best new chefs of the last five years.'

'I know, honey, I know. That certainly seems to be the consensus, doesn't it? Aren't you happy for him?'

'You have no idea,' I whispered.

'What?'

'Nothing, nothing. Yes, of course I'm happy for him. I just wish I was happy *with* him.'

Sammy had opened his restaurant – a charming little Middle Eastern fusion place that in no way resembled a franchise – two months earlier, to little fanfare. I wouldn't have even known if Will hadn't casually mentioned it at one of our Thursday-night dinners, but from that moment on, I tracked every new development. At first there hadn't been much information: a biography of the chef and some details on the quick opening. Apparently, the adorable twelve-table Italian joint on the Lower East Side had been the pet project of a prominent former investment banker who'd been targeted by Eliot Spitzer and ultimately sentenced to two to three years in a federal prison. The guy had to liquidate his assets to pay the massive fine to the SEC. Since the entire place had just been gutted and renovated and the entire kitchen fitted to perfection, Sammy could open for business almost immediately. At first there were some scattered customer reviews on various websites and a small mention of the restaurant in a piece about neighborhood gentrification. But then something happened: Sammy's restaurant went from Neighborhood Solid to Citywide Spectacular in a matter of weeks.

According to the most recent *WSJ* Lifestyle article, people in the neighborhood went early and often, and Sammy was able to keep the doors open while his menu came into its own. By the time Frank Bruni went to review it for *The New York Times*, Sammy had hit his stride. Bruni gave him three stars, virtually unheard of for an unknown chef and his very first venture. The other New York papers and magazines immediately followed with ecstatic reviews of their own. *New York* magazine published a typically understated article proclaiming Sevi 'The Only Restaurant That Matters.' He'd gone from being a total unknown to New York's must-get-reservations-or-die-a-horrible-death-in-C-list-purgatory restaurant. The only catch with that was that Sammy didn't take reservations. For anyone. Under any circumstances. According to every interview I read of him

– and trust me, I read them all – Sammy insisted that everyone was welcome, but no one was getting any sort of priority treatment. 'I've spent so many years determining who's allowed in and who's not, and I'm just not interested anymore. If they want to eat here, whoever they are, they can come on down like everyone else,' he was quoted as saying. It was his one and only requirement.

'But no one will go if they can't make a reservation!' I'd shrieked to Penelope when I'd first read about it.

'What do you mean no one will go?' she'd asked.

'You have to have some horribly bitchy reservationist who insists that there's nothing available for the next six months if they want to eat after five or before midnight.'

She laughed.

'I'm serious! I know these people! The only way anyone will ever eat there is if he makes them believe they're not welcome. The fastest way to fill those tables is to tell anyone who calls that they're fully booked and then promptly raise all entrées by eight dollars and all drinks by four. Hire waiters who think they're above waiting tables and a hostess who looks all the guests up and down disapprovingly as they arrive, and he'll have a *chance*.' I was only half-kidding, but it didn't much matter: his policy clearly worked.

The review in *The Wall Street Journal* had gone on to describe how the New York restaurant scene had lately been dominated by a slew of high-profile restaurant openings and superstar chefs, how there were five such restaurants in the glittering new Time Warner Building alone. Somewhere along the way, people had grown weary of all the pomp and circumstance. They longed for a wonderful meal in a simple restaurant. And that was precisely what Sammy's place offered. I was so proud of him, I nearly cried every time I read a new write-up or heard someone mention it, which was pretty damn frequently. I was dying to see it for myself, but I couldn't deny that Sammy had most definitely *not* picked up the phone to invite me.

'Here,' she said, handing me my folder of delivery menus. 'Dinner's on me. Let's order something, and then maybe go get a drink.'

I stared at her as though she'd suggested spontaneously hopping a flight to Bangladesh. 'A drink? *Outside*? You're joking.' I flipped through the menus disinterestedly. 'There's nothing to eat.'

She snatched the folder out of my hands and pulled out a few menus at random. 'Nothing to eat? There's Chinese, burgers, sushi, Thai, pizza, Indian, Vietnamese, deli, salad bar, Italian . . . that's just these. Pick something, Bette. Pick it now.'

'Seriously, Pen, whatever's good for you works for me.'

I watched as she dialed someplace called Nawab and ordered two chicken tikka masalas with basmati rice and two baskets of chapati. She put the phone down and turned to me.

'Bette, I'm only going to ask you one last time: What do you want to do this weekend?'

I sighed meaningfully and resumed my position on the couch. 'Pen, I don't care. It's not a big birthday. I already have to do the book-club ritual, which is more than enough. I don't know why you're so insistent that we need to do something – I'd much rather just forget it's happening.'

She snorted. 'Yeah, right. Everyone says they don't care, and everyone cares a lot. Why don't I put together a little dinner on Saturday night? You, me, Michael, maybe a few people from UBS? Some of the girls from your book club?'

'That sounds nice, Pen, it really does, but Will said something about dinner on Saturday. We're going somewhere good, I can't remember where. Want to come?'

We chatted until the food came and I managed to haul my larger-by-the-minute butt off the couch to the little kitchen table for chow time. As we spooned the thick, spicy chicken chunks onto plates of rice, I thought about how I was going to miss Penelope. It was a great distraction having her around, and more to the point, things between us were finally back to normal. I watched her as she waved her fork around to punctuate a funny story she was telling, and then I stood up and hugged her.

'What was that for?' she asked.

'I'm just going to miss you, Pen. I'm going to miss you a whole lot.'

33

'Thanks, everyone. You guys really are the best,' I said as I hugged each person standing in the circle around me. During our special birthday book-club sessions, we met to eat cake and do a couple of group shots. My birthday cake was white chocolate mousse, and the accompanying shot was an old-school lemon drop, complete with sugar packets and sliced lemons. I was slightly buzzed and feeling good after our mini-celebration, one that had concluded with the presentation of a hundred-dollar Barnes & Noble gift card.

'Enjoy dinner tonight,' Vika called after me. 'Give us a ring if you want to meet up after you leave your uncle's.'

I nodded and waved and made my way downstairs. I was thinking about how I'd have to start taking people up on offers to go out again. It was only one in the afternoon, and I didn't have to be at Will's until eight, so I settled in at a little table on the patio at the Astor Place Starbucks with a vanilla latte and a copy of the *Post*. Some habits die hard, so, as usual, I flipped to Page Six and was stunned by what I saw: a large piece on Abby, complete with a picture. It said that New York Scoop had just canceled her 'Ellie Insider' column and dismissed her for falsifying her résumé. Details were sketchy, but according to an unnamed source, she'd listed herself as a graduate of Emory University when she was, in fact, three credits shy of graduation. She did not actually possess a B.A. I'd dialed Penelope before I'd finished reading the piece.

'Ohmigod, have you read Page Six today? You must see it. *Now*.'

While I hadn't exactly forgotten about Abby, I hadn't made good on my vow to ruin her life, either. She hadn't written another word about me since the night of the *Playboy* party, but I didn't know if that was because my threats had her worried or because now that I no longer worked at Kelly & Company or dated Philip, I didn't warrant any mention at all. There was also the possibility that her affair with Avery had ended. Either way, I hadn't stopped praying for her demise.

'Happy birthday, Bette!'

'Huh? Oh, yeah, thanks. But listen, have you seen the *Post* yet?'

She laughed for a full minute, and I got the distinct feeling I was missing something. 'My gift to you, Bette. Happy twenty-eighth!'

'What are you saying? I don't understand what's going on. Did you have something to do with this?' I asked with such hopefulness it was almost humiliating.

'You might say that,' she said coyly.

'Pen! Tell me this instant what happened! This might just be the best day of my life. Explain!'

'Okay, calm down. It was all very innocent, actually – it just sort of fell into my lap.'

'What did?'

'The information that our dear friend Abby is not a college graduate.'

'And how, exactly, did that happen?'

'Well, after my ex-fiancé told me he was screwing her—'

'Correction, Pen. He told you he was screwing *someone* – I told you he was screwing *her*,' I added helpfully.

'Right. So anyway, after I found out they were screwing, I had the inclination to write her a little letter and tell her what I thought.'

'What does this have to do with her not graduating?' I was too eager for the dirt to endure the extraneous details.

'Bette, I'm getting there! I didn't want to email her because there's always the potential that it'll get forwarded to a million people, but her address in New York is unlisted – she must think she's some kind of celebrity, and people would just beat down her door to catch a glimpse of the star herself. I called New York Scoop, but they wouldn't give it out. That's when it occurred to me to call Emory.'

'Okay, I'm following so far.'

'I figured that as a fellow graduate, I'd have no trouble getting her address from them. I called the alumni center and told them I was looking for a classmate, that we'd lost touch but I wanted to invite her to my wedding.'

'Nice touch,' I said.

'Thanks, I thought so. Anyway, they checked their records and told me they had no one under that name. I'll save you all the gory details, but basically a few more minutes of digging revealed that while darling Abby matriculated with us, she didn't manage to graduate with our class – or ever.'

'Jesus. I think I see where this is going, and I could not be more proud right now.'

'Well, it gets better. I was on the phone with a girl at the registrar's office. She swore me to secrecy and then told me that the reason Abby withdrew three credits short was because the dean of arts and sciences found out Abby was sleeping with her husband and suggested that she withdraw immediately. We never knew because Abby never told anyone; she just stuck around campus until the rest of us graduated.'

'Amazing,' I breathed. 'And yet not at all surprising.'

'Yeah, well, it only took a few minutes from there to set up an anonymous Hotmail account, let the good folks at New York Scoop know that their star columnist wasn't a college graduate, and give them a little clue as to why she'd departed without a degree. I called their offices every day asking for her until I was told yesterday that she was no longer with the paper, at which time I sent a helpful little anonymous tip to Page Six as well.'

'Ohmigod, Penelope, you evil bitch. I didn't think you had it in you!'

'So, as I said before, happy birthday! I found out about it months ago, when I wrote the letter, but I thought if I waited, it would make a fine birthday present. Consider it my gift to you. And myself,' she added.

We hung up, and I was unabashedly elated, imagining Abby walking the streets, panhandling, or – better yet – wearing a McDonald's apron. When the phone rang again within seconds, I snapped it open without looking first.

'What else?' I said, assuming it was Penelope calling back with some forgotten juicy tidbit.

'Hello?' I heard a male voice say. 'Bette?'

Ohmigod, it was Sammy. Sammy! Saaaaaaaammmmmy! I wanted to sing and dance and scream his name to the entire coffee shop.

'Hiiiii,' I breathed, barely able to believe that the call I'd waited nearly four months for – the call I'd *willed* to arrive – was finally happening.

He laughed at my obvious joy. 'It's good to hear your voice.'

'Yours, too,' I said much too quickly. 'How have you been?'

'Good, good. I opened up a place, finally, and—'

'I know, I've been reading all about it. Congratulations! It's a huge success, and I think that's just incredible!' I was dying to know how he'd managed to put it together so quickly, but I wasn't going to risk anything by asking a thousand annoying questions.

'Yeah, thanks. So, look, I'm kind of racing around, but I just wanted to call and—'

Oh. He had the tone of someone who'd moved on, most likely had a new girlfriend who had a fulfilling job helping other people . . . someone who didn't own a pair of tattered, stained sweatpants but who always lounged around the apartment in the cutest silk pajama sets. Someone who—

'. . . and see if you'll have dinner with me tonight?'

I waited to make sure I'd heard him right, but neither of us ended up saying anything. 'Dinner?' I tentatively ventured. 'Tonight?'

'You probably have plans, don't you? I'm sorry to call at the last minute, I just—'

'No, no plans,' I shouted before he could change his mind. No chance of playing it cool, either, but suddenly that didn't seem to matter. I hadn't missed a brunch or a Thursday dinner since I'd quit Kelly & Company, so Will would just have to understand about tonight. 'I can totally have dinner.'

I could hear him smiling through the phone. 'Great. Why don't I swing by your place around seven? We can have a drink in your neighborhood, and then I'd like to bring you by the restaurant. If that sounds okay . . .'

'Okay? That sounds perfect, just perfect,' I gushed. 'Seven? I'll see you then.' And I snapped my phone shut before I could say one word to fuck it up. Fate. It was absolutely, positively, undeniably fate that had inspired Sammy to call on my birthday: a sign that we were, most definitely, destined to be together forever. I was debating whether or not to tell him that I turned twenty-eight that day when it occurred to me that I was going to *see* him that night.

My preparations were frenzied. I called Will from the cab on my way home, begging his forgiveness, but he merely laughed and told me that he'd happily take a rain check if it meant I was finally going out with a boy. I raced into the corner nail place for a quickie manicure and pedicure and then threw in a ten-dollar, ten-minute chair massage to try to relax. Penelope took charge of stylist duties and assembled multiple outfit pieces, including three dresses and an intricately beaded tank top, two pairs of shoes, four bags, and her entire stash of jewelry, which had recently been supplemented by her parents in an attempt to cajole her out of mourning. She dropped them off and left, planning to spend the night with Michael and Megu and wait for an update from me. I tried things on and discarded them, frantically straightened the apartment, danced to Pat Benatar's 'We Belong' with Millington in my arms, and, finally, sat demurely on the couch and waited for Sammy's arrival exactly one hour before he was due.

When Seamus rang my buzzer, I thought I might cease breathing. Sammy arrived at my door a moment later. He had never looked so good. He was wearing some sort of shirt/jacket/no-tie combo that came across as stylish and sophisticated without trying too hard, and I noticed that he'd let his hair grow to that perfect length that wasn't really short or long – Hugh Grant–ish, if I had to explain it. He smelled both soapy and minty when he leaned forward to kiss my cheek, and had I not been death-gripping the door frame, I would've surely collapsed.

'It's really great to see you, Bette,' he said, taking my hand and leading me toward the elevator. I walked effortlessly in my borrowed D&G sandals and felt pretty and feminine in a skirt that skimmed my knees and a summerweight cashmere cardigan that revealed just the right amount of cleavage. It was just like all the Harlequins always said it was: even though it had been months since we'd last seen each other, it felt like not a single day had passed.

'You, too,' I managed, content to just gaze at his profile all night.

He led me to a charming neighborhood wine bar three blocks west, where we settled into a back table and immediately began talking. I was delighted to see that he hadn't really changed at all.

'Tell me how you've been,' he said, sipping from the glass of Syrah he'd expertly ordered. 'What have you been up to?'

'No, no, no way. I'm not the one with the hugely exciting news,' I said. *Well, isn't that the understatement of the century?* I thought. 'I think I've read pretty much every word they've written about you, and it all sounds so fantastic!'

'Yeah, well, I got lucky. Really lucky.' He coughed and looked slightly uncomfortable. 'Bette, I, ah, I've got something to tell you.'

Oh, Christ. There was no possible way that was a good sign, none whatsoever. I chided myself for my premature enthusiasm, for thinking that the fact that Sammy had called – and on my birthday, no less – meant anything more than he was just being friendly and making good on a promise between old friends. It was those goddamn Harlequins – they were the problem. I vowed to quit those miserable things: because they just made it too easy to maintain totally unreasonable expectations. I mean, Dominick or Enrique never said 'I've got something to tell you' before asking the woman of their dreams to marry them. Those were clearly the words of a man about to announce that he was in love – just not with me. I didn't think I could handle even a whiff of bad news.

'Oh, really?' I managed to say, folding my arms across my chest in an unconscious attempt to brace myself for the news. 'What's that?'

Another strange look crossed his face, and then we were interrupted by the waiter placing the check in front of Sammy. 'Sorry to rush you out, guys, but we're closing now for a private party. I'll take this as soon as you're ready.'

I wanted to scream. Hearing that Sammy was in love with a swimsuit model cum Mother Teresa was going to be hard enough – did I really have to *wait* to hear the news? Apparently yes. I waited as Sammy rooted around in his wallet for the exact amount and then waited again while he went to the men's room. More waiting for a cab outside, and then another wait when Sammy and the cabbie discussed the best route to Sevi. We were finally on our way to his restaurant, but there was another wait when Sammy apologized profusely but proceeded to answer his cell phone. He murmured a bit and made some 'uh-huh' noises, and at one point he said yes, but otherwise he was vague, and I knew in the pit of my stomach that he was talking to *her*. When he finally clicked off his phone, I turned to him, stared him right in the eye, and said, 'What did you have to tell me before?'

'I know this is going to sound weird – and I swear I only found out myself a couple days ago – but remember how I told you about those silent investors?'

Hmm. This wasn't sounding like a declaration of love for another woman – positive development, to be sure.

'Yeah. They were looking to back the next hot young chef or something, right? You had to pitch some ideas and menus?'

'Exactly.' He nodded. 'Well, the thing is, I sort of have you to thank for this.'

I looked at him adoringly, waiting for him to tell me that I was his inspiration, his encouragement, his *muse,* but what he said next didn't really have anything to do with me.

'I feel weird being the one to tell you, but they insisted it happen this way. The investors who backed me are Will and Simon.'

'What?' I whipped around to look at him. '*My* Will and Simon?'

He nodded and took my hand. 'You really didn't know, did you? I thought you may have convinced them somehow, but they insisted you had no idea. I only recently found out, too. I hadn't even seen them since they came to brunch at Gramercy Tavern months ago.'

I was so stunned I could barely speak, and yet the only information that seemed to process was what I hadn't heard: so far, Sammy wasn't telling me he was hopelessly, passionately in love with someone else.

'I don't know what to say.'

'Say you're not mad,' he said, leaning closer to me.

'Mad? Why would I be mad? I'm so happy for you! I don't know why Will didn't tell me. I guess I'll get the entire story at brunch on Sunday.'

'Right. He said that, too, actually.'

There wasn't time for me to process this new development, since the cab reached the Lower East Side in record time. As soon as we pulled up I recognized the tiny awning from the pictures in the paper. Just as Sammy slammed the car door, I noticed a well-dressed couple examining the sign posted outside. They turned to us and with great disappointment said, 'Looks like they're closed tonight for some reason,' before turning to find somewhere else to eat.

I looked at him quizzically, but he just smiled. 'I have a surprise for you,' he murmured.

'A private tour?' I asked with such hope in my voice that it was almost embarrassing.

He nodded. 'Yes. I wanted tonight to be extra-special. I closed down so we could be alone. I hope you don't mind that I'll have to be in the kitchen for a few minutes,' he said. 'I've planned a special *Sevi* menu just for tonight.'

'You have? I can't wait. What does *Sevi* mean, by the way? I don't think I've read that anywhere.'

He took my hand and smiled at me before looking at his feet. 'It means *love* in Turkish,' he said.

I thought I might pass out from happiness. Instead I concentrated on putting one foot squarely in front of the other. I followed him into the darkened dining room and tried to adjust my eyes, but a moment later he'd found the lights and I could see everything. Or, rather, everyone.

'Surprise!' came the shouts. There was a cacophonous call of 'Happy birthday,' and I realized I knew every single face that stared back at me.

'Ohmigod' was all I uttered.

The small tables had been pushed together to form a single long one in the middle of the room; all my friends and family had been installed around it and were waving and calling out to me.

'Oh. My. God.'

'Come here, sit down,' Sammy said, taking my hand once again and leading me to the head of the table. I hugged and kissed everyone on the way to my seat and then flopped into my designated chair, at which point Penelope placed a cardboard tiara on my head and said something embarrassing along the lines of *'You're* our heroine tonight.'

'Happy birthday, honey!' my mom said, leaning over to kiss me on the cheek. 'Your father and I wouldn't have missed this for the world.' She smelled faintly of incense and was wearing a beautiful hand-knit poncho that had surely been made from dye-free wool. My father sat next to her, his hair carefully arranged in a neat ponytail, his best pair of Naots proudly on display.

I looked down the table and saw everyone assembled: Penelope and her mom, who was delighted Penelope was in-the-know enough to get them into the new hot place; Michael and Megu, both of whom had specially requested the night off to come celebrate with me; Kelly and Henry, the guy she'd been with at the *Playboy* party; all the book-club girls, each clutching what appeared to be wrapped copies of new paperbacks; and, of course, Simon, who'd swathed himself in what seemed like a surplus of linen, and Will, who was throwing back his namesake martini (I learned later that Sammy had named the house drink The Will) at the foot of the table, directly across from me.

After repeated shouts of 'Speech, speech,' I managed to pull myself out of my seat and say a few awkward words. Almost immediately, a waiter brought out bottles of champagne, and we all toasted my birthday and Sammy's success. And then dinner began in earnest. Heaping platters of food emerged from the kitchen on the shoulders of waiters, all steaming and deliciously aromatic and placed in front of us with great flourish. I watched as Sammy sat across the table, looked up at me, and winked. He began talking to Alex, pointing to her nose piercing and saying something that made her laugh. I watched them for a moment in between bites of a delicious cumin-and-dill-spiced lamb dish, and then let my eyes wander around the table: everyone was chattering happily while they passed the dishes around and refilled one another's champagne glasses. I heard my parents introducing themselves to Kelly while Courtney told Penelope's mom about our book club and Simon told jokes to Michael and Megu.

I was just sitting there, drinking it all in, when Will pulled a chair up next to mine. 'Pretty special night, no?' he asked the moment he sat. 'Were you surprised?'

'Totally surprised! Will, how could you not have told me that you and Simon were the ones behind this whole project? I'm not sure I know how to thank you.'

'You don't have to thank me, darling. We didn't do it for you, or even really for Sammy, although I am quite fond of him. You'd mentioned that he cooked brunch every Sunday at Gramercy Tavern, and it piqued our curiosity. Simon and I paid him a visit there months ago, and I have to say, we were absolutely blown away. The boy is a genius! Not only that, but he must listen when you talk because the entire meal was utter perfection: the Bloody Mary was served exactly how I like it, with an extra dash of Tabasco and two limes. A copy of *The New York Times* was on the table and already open to the Sunday Styles section. And there were no potatoes to be seen. None! I've been brunching at the Essex House for decades now, and they still can't get it quite right. We couldn't stop talking about it, and we decided we'd better snap him up before someone else did. Looks like we were right, doesn't it?'

'You went to brunch at Gramercy Tavern? Just to see Sammy?'

Will folded his hands and raised his eyebrows at me. 'Darling, you were clearly smitten with this boy in a very substantial manner – that much was obvious. Simon and I were curious! We certainly weren't expecting to be so impressed with his skills – that was a bonus. When I asked him that day about his future plans and he began rambling on about something called a "Houston's," I knew we had to step in and save him from himself.'

'Yeah, he'd mentioned in Turkey that he and a few guys from culinary school were thinking about opening something like it on the Upper East Side,' I said.

Will gasped audibly and nodded. 'I know. How dreadful! That boy is not meant for franchise work. I told the lawyer that I'd put up all the money, but Sammy would do all the work. Except for a standing table, I wanted to be consulted *not at all*. Better than the goddamn government getting it, don't you agree? Besides, I was looking for something different to throw myself into; I've decided to retire the column.'

Well, that one shook me. In a night of surprises, this might have been the most shocking of them all. 'You're what? Are you serious? Why now? How many years has it been, a hundred? The entire world reads your column, Will! What'll happen to it?'

He sipped his martini and looked thoughtful. 'So many questions, darling, so many questions. It's not that fascinating a story, really. It's simply time. I don't need New York Scoop to tell me that my column is a relic at this point. I had a great run for many, many years, but it's time to try something new.'

'I can understand that,' I said finally. Somehow I knew it was the right decision. But Will had been writing that column since before I was born, and it was disconcerting to think that it would simply cease to exist.

'However, I'll have you know that I've spoken with my editor – mere child that he is – and have received assurances that there will always be a place for you there, should you choose to pursue it. Now, I don't want to harp on this, Bette, but I think it's something you should consider. You're a wonderful writer, and I don't know why you haven't done anything with it. Just say the word and we can have you in there, first as a researcher and then, hopefully, in a sort of apprentice reporting position.'

'I've actually thought about that, too,' I said, saying what I'd sworn to keep to myself until I'd had a chance to think it through a bit longer. 'I do want to try some writing. . . .'

'Excellent! I was hoping you'd say that. Frankly, I think it's long overdue, but certainly better late than never. I'll call him tonight and . . .'

'No, not like that, Will. You're going to hate this—'

'Oh, dear God, please don't tell me that you want to cover weddings for the Sunday Styles section or some such nonsense. Please.'

'Worse,' I said, more for effect than because I believed it. 'I want to write a romance novel. In fact, I've already got an outline, and I don't think it's half bad.' I braced myself for the verbal barrage, but surprisingly, it never came.

Instead he peered at me as though he were searching my face for some answer and just nodded. 'Maybe it's all these Will martinis, but I think that makes perfect sense, darling.' He leaned in and kissed my cheek.

Romance novels – it was true. Since Turkey and the luxe world Kelly & Company had introduced me to, I'd been imagining a star-crossed pair of characters and the events that would bring them together. One could say I was drawing from experience, or from fantasy, but it felt good either way. And it was the first thing I'd felt good about in a long time. Until tonight.

I was preparing to tell my parents my plans when my cell phone rang. *How odd,* I thought. *Every single person I know is sitting in this room.* I reached into my bag to switch it off, but I couldn't help noticing that it was Elisa calling from her cell phone. Elisa, who I hadn't seen or spoken to since the *Playboy* party, the very same person who, for whatever reason – a malnourished brain, some weird obsession with Philip, or perhaps just for sport – had spoon-fed information about me to Abby for months. I was simply *too* curious. I walked into the kitchen.

'Hello? Elisa?' I said into the phone.

'Bette, are you there? Listen, I've got the greatest news!'

'Really? What's that?' I asked, pleased to hear that I sounded cool and aloof and supremely disinterested, exactly as I intended.

'Well, I remember you had some, uh, some connection to that Bungalow bouncer who opened Sevi, right?'

She was pretending not to remember Sammy's name, as usual, but I was no longer interested in correcting her. 'Yeah, that's right. I'm actually at Sevi right now,' I said.

'You're there? You're at the restaurant now? Ohmigod, that's just too perfect! Listen, I just got word that Lindsay Lohan has a layover in New York for one night on her way from LA to London – you know we're repping Von Dutch now, and she's their new spokeswoman, right? – and guess what? She wants to eat at Sevi tonight! Insisted on it, actually. I'm picking her up from the Mandarin Oriental now. I'm not sure how many she has with her, but it shouldn't be more than a half-dozen. We'll be there in thirty minutes, maybe an hour. Tell your chef friend to go VIP all the way with tonight's menu, okay? Bette, this will be such great press for him!' She was breathless with excitement.

I'd be lying if I said I didn't consider telling Sammy. It *would* be great press – the fastest way to guarantee mentions in the few remaining national magazines that hadn't yet discovered him. But I peeked through the window in the kitchen door and saw Sammy placing a cake in the center of the table. It was a huge, rectangular thing with giant gobs of whipped cream and colored icing, and when I leaned in to get a better look, I saw that the cover of *Tall, Dark, and Cajun* had been airbrushed on in perfect detail. Everyone was laughing and pointing and asking Will where I'd gone.

The split-second window of Lindsay Lohan potential slammed shut and I said, 'Thanks but no thanks, Elisa. He's closed for a private event tonight.'

I hung up before she could protest and rejoined the table. *It wasn't even a lie*, I thought to myself as I looked around. *This just* had *to be the party of the season.*

Acknowledgments

Three people in particular must be thanked for sticking with me on this project:

The only editor worth knowing, Marysue Rucci, who is the master of a hundred elegant and subtle ways of saying 'this sucks.'

David Rosenthal, my publisher, whose Rolodex and dinner parties keep me from ordering in seven nights a week.

Deborah Schneider, my amazing agent. She handles the logistical details of my career so I'm free to write the important literature of our time.

Tremendous thanks also to Hanley Baxter, Aileen Boyle, Gretchen Braun, Britt Carlson, Jane Cha, Deborah Darrock, Nick Dewar, Lynne Drew, Wendy Finerman, Cathy Gleason, Tracey Guest, Maxine Hitchcock, Helen Johnstone, Juan Carlos Maciques, Diana Mackay, Victoria Meyer, Tara Parsons, Carolyn Reidy, Jack Romanos, Charles Salzberg, Vivienne Schuster, Jackie Seow, Peggy Siegal, Shari Smiley, Ludmilla Suvorova, and Kyle White.

And of course, a huge thanks to my parents, Cheryl and Steve, and my sister, Dana. I could have never written such a masterpiece without you.

*** While all of the characters in this book are imaginary, the inspiration for Millington the Yorkshire Terrier is actually Mitzy the Maltese.

The Devil Wears Prada
Lauren Weisberger

When Andrea first sets foot in the plush Manhattan offices of *Runway* she knows nothing. She's never heard of the world's most fashionable magazine, or its feared and fawned-over editor, Miranda Priestly. But she's going to be Miranda's assistant, a job millions of girls would die for.

A year later, she knows altogether too much:

That it's a sacking offence to wear anything lower than a three-inch heel to work. But that there's always a fresh pair of Manolos for you in the accessories cupboard.

That Miranda believes Hermés scarves are disposable, and you must keep a life-time supply on hand at all times.

That eight stone is fat.

That you can charge cars, manicures, anything at all to the *Runway* account, but you must never, ever, leave your desk, or let Miranda's coffee get cold.

Most of all, Andrea knows that Miranda is a monster who makes Cruella de Vil look like a fluffy bunny. But also that this is her big break, and it's going to be worth it in the end. Isn't it?

ISBN: 978 0 00 7156108

Chasing Harry Winston

Lauren Weisberger

Three best friends. Two resolutions. One year to pull it off.

Emmy is newly single. Having always dreamed of wedding plans, she's now buying take-out for one.

Adriana is about to turn thirty. Are her days as a party girl running out?

Leigh has a gorgeous boyfriend and a great job. So why isn't she more excited about her perfect life?

The three best friends make a pact over raspberry mojitos one night – this year everything is going to change. Emmy is going to travel the world, finding a man on every continent for some no-strings fun. Adriana vows she'll secure a five-carat Harry Winston diamond on her fourth finger. And Leigh can't think of what she needs to change – until literary bad boy Jesse Chapman starts to get under her skin.

Let the fun begin.

ISBN: 978 0 00 726860 3

The Love of Her Life

Harriet Evans

Kate Miller is no longer the geeky teenager who preferred curling up with an ancient copy of *Little Women* and pouring over vintage issues of *Vogue* to going out and getting drunk. Now she not only has her dream job – working for a glossy magazine, but a gorgeous fiancée to match.

Then one day, it all falls apart – spectacularly, painfully and forever.

Ever since, Kate has hidden in New York. But when her father becomes ill, she has to come home and face everything she left behind including her friends – Zoe, Francesca and Mac – the friends who are bound with her forever, as a result of one day when life changed for all of them.

Like every woman, Kate often thought she'd never meet the love of her life. But she did – and now she's back, he can't stand to be in the same room as her. What really happened before Kate left London? And can she pick up the pieces and allow herself to love her own life again?

ISBN: 978 0 00 724382 2

My Favourite Wife

Tony Parsons

Bill and Becca Holden and their young daughter Holly leave their north London life for the sexy, gold-rush city of Shanghai – a young family seeking their fortune and an exotic adventure.

But Shanghai proves to be a place of temptation as well as opportunity.

Becca finds not the exotic east she dreamed of but a hustling, brash modern city. How does a modern woman find her place in a medieval country?

Bill, working day and night, finds himself caught up in a mess of his own making as a friendship grows into something more – something that threatens all he holds dear. How can the love triangle ever have a happy ending?

When Becca comes back, it is time for all of them to learn something about the meaning of love and the bonds of family.

'Tony Parsons is the master of the bittersweet love story'
Red

ISBN: 978 0 00 722649 8

SUBSCRIBE TO *RED*
HALF PRICE

TREAT YOURSELF, OR SOMEONE SPECIAL, TO A SUBSCRIPTION TO *RED* FOR JUST £20.40 – SAVING **50%**

GREAT REASONS TO SUBSCRIBE TO *RED*:

- **JUST** £20.40 for 12 issues
- **ONLY** £1.70 a copy (normal price £3.40)
- **EXCLUSIVE** *Red* Subscriber Extras throughout the year
- **FREE** delivery, direct to your door every month
- **PLUS!** Never pay full price again as, after your first 12 issues, your subscription will run at £16.32 every six months, still saving you 20% on the normal price

www.subscribe2.co.uk/red/xa09